Colours of Siena

by

Judith May Evans

The Conrad Press

Colours of Siena

Published by The Conrad Press in the United Kingdom 2023

Tel: +44(0)1227 472 874
www.theconradpress.com
info@theconradpress.com

ISBN 978-1-916966-01-7

Typesetting and Cover Design by: Levellers

The Conrad Press logo was designed by Maria Priestley.

Printed and bound in Great Britain by Clays Ltd, Elcograf S.p.A.

In memory of the very special Karen Murphy, who died 6 January 2023, leaving her great book unfinished.

Colour is a power which directly influences the soul.
Wassily Kandinsky

If you love somebody, let them go, for if they return, they were always yours.
Kahlil Gibran

Colours of Siena

Part One

Red

Siena, 1311

Chapter 1

The day Duccio's painting was to be installed in the Duomo I woke up so excited, though Mamma could ruin even this. If we didn't complete our chores, none of us would be allowed time off, and this was my only chance to see the picture everyone was talking about. Careful not to disturb my sleeping parents, I dressed in my working clothes, tip-toe-ed over the sleeping bodies in the gallery outside our room and raced up the stairs to the top-floor kitchen. I threw open the door and panted to Cook. 'Today I'm going to see the costliest painting in Christendom!'

Cook was as round and soft as the dough she kneaded and stroked my head before pushing me away. 'If you ask me, it's Duccio's pockets that are lined with gold – paid others to do all the work! Now help me set things up. Pastry making by the window, vegetable chopping in the middle and we'll assemble the pies by the oven.' My other job in the Palazzo Salimbeni household was more absorbing, but this morning I was determined to be the best skivvy ever.

I'd almost finished laying everything out, when in poured the maids.

'To work, girls,' Cook shouted over their chat of acrobats and jugglers that were part of the entertainment paid for by the state.

While I waited for the floor to need sweeping, I grabbed scraps of pastry and squeezed them into a ball which I flattened with the palm of my hand. With the sharpened twig I always kept in my pocket, I drew my version of Duccio's Maestà, the Virgin in Majesty – like the Conte presiding over a banquet, but with her head covered in a mantle of her special blue (on the buff-coloured pastry, I could only imagine the blue). I finished with a crescent of a smile and looked for more scraps.

Then Mamma walked in. Though dressed in a linen shift like the rest of us, she held her nose in the air like the Contessa. As she passed, her hand flicked out and swept my pastry sketch onto the floor. I stifled a cry.

'Late as ever, Maria,' Cook said.

Mamma raised an eyebrow and I braced myself for one of her rude quips but she held her tongue and started chopping. I'd have preferred that to sweeping but Cook said nine-year-olds shouldn't use knives.

Brushing around the maids' feet, I removed the worst of the debris as it spilt onto the floor. The smell of onion and garlic softening on the flame was soon joined by that of summer spinach and herbs. Once that too had mellowed, the cheese was added and the pies assembled. Cook pushed them into the roaring oven with the pala, the large, flat shovel that hung above. At last she wiped her hands on the cloth she kept tucked into her skirt, then hoisted her bosom with her folded arms as if to give us a lecture on the festa. I'd had plenty of those in the lessons I shared with Vanni, the Conte's youngest son – for that was my other job. His mother, the Contessa, thought him more likely to study if he had company, and I was the only person in the palazzo near his age.

'Don't stare at me like you expect the rest of the day off!' There was a glint in Cook's eye but was she teasing or not? I'd expected Mamma to spoil my day, but never Cook!

'Now I'll never see it!' I burst into tears. In my lessons with Vanni, I galloped through the tasks we were set. But our one art class had transported me to another world. The balance of shapes, the message without words. But most of all, I was entranced by the colours – the warming red, the dulling brown. Vanni thought the subject so pointless, he threw down his brush, knocking paint over his expensive clothes. One plea to his mother and the lessons were stopped; my one chance of painting ended before it had begun.

'Very well, tesora.' Cook squeezed my shoulder – I was always her little treasure. 'Now you've prepared all the food for later, the Contessa says you can have the day off.'

I wiped my eyes and joined in the cheer, then brushed the last of the leftovers into a corner for the dogs.

'Say a Hail Mary for me – and the Contessa – while you're at it.'

'You'll be lucky,' Mamma muttered.

No! Not today, not now.

'What did you say, Maria?' Cook grabbed my shoulders to stop us both leaving.

'I said we're very lucky.' Mamma looked all innocence.

The other maids smirked.

'I'll ignore that this once, Maria, for Clara's sake, but be aware, I'm tiring of your jibes.' Then she pinched my cheek. 'Go on, enjoy yourself.'

'Hurry up or Babbo will go without us.' I shouted to Mamma as I ran down the stairs. The day would be so much more fun spending it with him.

As soon as I reached our room, I opened the chest and breathed in the smell of cinnamon. Then I found the pink dress Mamma had recently altered for me. Like all our special clothes, they'd once belonged to the nobles; passed on to servants when they went out of fashion. Only when Mamma, too, tired of a dress did she cut it down to my size. By the time she arrived, I'd put it on, and was almost ready to go.

Mamma was in no mood to hurry.

She stepped out of her linen shift and picked out of the chest a fine citrus-yellow silk recently donated by the Contessa. I hovered, waiting for her to tie my sash at the back, but as ever, she was too absorbed in staring at the glass as she arranged her thick, black curls.

'Wey hey, my beauties! Are you ready?' Babbo's head appeared round the door. Dark hair, as straight as Mamma's was curly, poked out from under the red and gold hat of his uniform. Because he was the Contessa's favourite, we were allowed to live in one of the guest rooms, though Mamma claimed it was down to the Conte; that he'd recognised quality in the wooden chest she'd brought as a dowry and wouldn't let her slum it with the rest.

'Babbo!' I ran into his outstretched arms, squealing as he swung me round in the corridor.

He put me down and tied my sash. 'There! You look lovely, Clara.'

Mamma pushed between us and stood to be admired.

'And how is my lovely Maria?' He put his hand around her waist and drew her towards him. 'Looking forward to the fun?'

'Pazzi, you Sienese are, going mad about some panel.' Mamma pushed him away, laughing, today some sunshine between the showers.

'Not just any panel. It's to thank the Madonna for saving Siena from the flea-ridden Florentines.'

'Get that from Vanni Salimbeni, did you?' Babbo roughed my hair.

But Mamma still wasn't ready. I'd never forgive her if we missed the parade.

Babbo sighed. 'Show me how many jacks you can

pick up, Clara.'

I scooped the stones from the windowsill and cast them onto the floor. Up, scoop, catch. First one, then another, until I was clutching eight small stones in my palm.

'That's my girl!' Babbo kissed the top of my head. 'When you get to ten, Babbo will give you a big surprise.'

Bathed in his sunshine made me even more determined, and I was about to give it another go when Mamma kicked the unclaimed stones under the bed.

'I'm ready. Let's go!'

Putting his arm around Mamma's waist, Babbo steered her out the door.

Once outside, I grabbed his spare arm and we joined the crowd hurrying towards the Campo. But when I saw the dark blue livery of the Tolomei guards outside their equally palatial mansion – only a hundred paces down the road – I was scared. 'Let's go the long way round.'

Every noble family had its sworn enemy and the Tolomei was ours. However much the authorities clamped down on fighting in the streets, our rivalry seethed under the surface like gathering pus.

'No need to be afraid today, little kitten. Our Count and theirs have agreed there'll be no trouble.' Babbo patted my arm and began singing our tribal song.

The Tolomei think they're so smart
But cowardice is at their heart.
Only we are brave and free,
The valiant hearted Salimbeni.

6

We'd sung it so often to boost our spirits, I soon felt confident again. Though just in case, I kept my shoulder to the left-hand wall as we approached their main entrance. So many of their servants out today, we were lucky not to bump into them. As usual, Mamma scanned the eyes of all onlookers – even them – to make sure she was the centre of their attention. We were almost past, when a glistening black beard oozed out of the main door and blocked our path.

'Well, if it isn't Guido and his tarts.' He eyed Mamma. 'Too pretty to grace the bed of a Salimbeni. I'll give your wife a taste of Tolomei any time she likes!'

Mamma's spittle landed on his chin.

We could have ignored them, and now she'd made matters ten times worse.

'Warm and wet.' Blackbeard stared at my mother as he wiped it away with the back of his hand.

'Keep your filthy mind off them, or...' Babbo's head shot forward like a tortoise's coming out of its shell.

Sensing danger, the passing hordes scuttled down the side streets and my tummy turned a somersault. I tugged Babbo's arm. 'Don't listen to him!'

'A girl with spirit! Just how I like them.' Blackbeard leant towards me, but I dodged behind Babbo's back before he could grab me.

'Don't you dare ruin my holiday with a fight,' Mamma threatened them both.

'The mother too!' Blackbeard winked at Mamma. 'Don't worry, I can pluck ripe fruit any time I like.'

Then around the corner came the city militia, patrolling the streets to quash any trouble.

Blackbeard's eyes lingered on Mamma, then he disappeared with the other Tolomei inside the heavy palazzo doors.

I was close to tears as we left. 'That horrible man has spoilt our day!'

'Only if you let him.' Babbo smiled and squeezed my hand.

'Then cheer us up!' Mamma snapped.

We walked on in silence then Babbo turned to Mamma with a wink. 'Got any clothes pegs to sell?' And the two of them collapsed into giggles.

I'd heard the story of how they'd first met many times though, given Mamma's fondness for the Contessa's cast offs, I found it hard to imagine her as a country girl.

'Seeing you selling pegs at market that day, I couldn't believe my luck,' Babbo nudged her.

'But we only sold them in threes.' Mamma looked so much prettier when she smiled, though she feared smiling would give her wrinkles.

'Pinched my nose with one.'

'You put another on your lips – that stopped you gabbing – and the last one ...'

They were now laughing so much neither could speak but I knew anyway. Babbo had put the last peg on his codpiece.

'And a month later, Babbo rode out to Monticiano and married you.' I finished the tale.

'And brought me here!' Mamma ran a hand over the smooth fabric of her dress.

The crowd thickened as we approached the Campo,

and we had to fight our way through. But instead of getting annoyed, Babbo gave a big whoop. Mamma and I started whooping too, and soon everyone around us was doing the same. Now I was sure it was going to be a great day.

Suddenly we were at the top of the steps looking down on the scallop-shaped piazza filled with a sea of colour. Above us, bright banners in burgundy and vivid green fluttered on a balcony. In the Campo below, citizens sported their holiday finery. Servants in their households' colourful liveries congregated in the usual places. The Marescotti's yellow and black wasp stripes gathered at the San Marco corner; next to them their Piccolomini allies, in gold-trimmed blue. My spirit soared as I inhaled the colours.

'Over there.' Babbo pointed to our own red-and-golds; opposite the entrance of the new Palazzo dei Signori, from where the Nove, the nine elected governors, ruled our city-state. He led us across the well-trodden earth of the Campo – baked hard as tiles in the dry summer – until we reached familiar faces.

'Where've you been, Guido? You nearly missed it. Word from Castelvecchio says the painting's already left Duccio's.' Francesco, another Salimbeni guard and a lankier version of Babbo, wore his cap at a jaunty angle – to show the girls I'm willing, he always quipped.

'Trust you to grab the best spot.' Babbo clapped him on the back. 'You'll have a good view of the painting from here, Clara.'

'It had better come soon, or I'll collapse in the heat,'

Mamma grumbled. 'And where's the juggling you promised me?'

'That'll be later. Go find some water if you're hot. I'll stay here with Clara – unless you want a drink too, little kitten?' Babbo put his hand under my chin.

I shook my head. Staying with Babbo was better, this and every day.

'I'll go with Maria, you know, to keep her safe,' Francesco winked and Mamma preened at the extra attention she always received from Babbo's best friend.

Then just as they returned, the crowd around the road from Castelvecchio surged forward and my heart leapt.

'Here they come!' Babbo pushed me to the front.

First into the piazza came a procession of the parish priests, chanting psalms and swinging censers.

'They're purifying the air in the painting's path,' Francesco explained. 'Now the monks.'

I recognized the black gowns of the Dominican friars, the greys of the Franciscans and the white of the Cistercians from San Galgano – a shame they all wore colours of sludge. Then the crowd of thousands gasped as white oxen pulled into the Campo the self-same carriage that had taken the Sienese standard into battle against the Florentines. Behind the black and white flag two men supported the sides of a huge wooden panel, glittering with gold front and back. It looked so like butter, I was afraid it'd melt if it didn't get to the Duomo soon.

The carriage passed around the perimeter, people falling to their knees before it, so a giant human wave rippled slowly round the Campo. As the painting approached, we, too knelt, to give thanks to the Madonna, our patron saint and protectress, for victory over the Florentines and half a century of peace.

But as soon as the painting was in front of me, I jumped up. Row upon row of gold-haloed saints and bishops were dressed in cloaks of crimson, lemon, peach, apple, sage, ivy, lavender, forget-me-not, mustard, dandelion, and others I couldn't even name. No wonder this was the most expensive painting ever. Enthroned above them, the Madonna sat, dressed from head to toe in the deepest, truest, most magnificent blue. I longed to plunge my hands into those gentle folds and feel that rare paint squeeze through my fingers. I yearned to know the secret of that so-realistic colour of her skin.

The colourful garb of the two men holding the panel upright was also breath-taking, as much a part of the spectacle as the small paintings that framed the Virgin in Majesty. These must be Duccio's assistants; the people who washed the brushes, ground the ores and mixed the paints. The one nearest to me was frowning; a fair-haired young man dressed in blue and pink. How could he be so miserable when he had the best job in the world? And despite the heat, I felt a shiver down my spine. Impossible though I knew it was, I longed to be him; to spend the rest of my life immersed in the wonderful world of colour the paints conveyed.

'They've all got nice legs.' Mamma's words burst in on my reverie. She smoothed her hands over her yellow dress as if checking she too was attractive. It was sickening how she thought only of herself even in the presence of such majesty.

'The one with the stick is the great Duccio.' Francesco pointed to the man walking behind the carriage, so red-faced he could have been baking pies with Cook. He was helped along by a smiling, ginger-haired companion dressed in orange.

But before Francesco could tell me about the others, trumpets sounded a fanfare. The nine Signori – the governors of our great city state – strode out of the palace and bowed to Duccio. He responded with an elaborate flourish and we all cheered. The cart moved off, making its way to the Duomo and I saw the panel was double-sided. I tried to run after it, to see more, but the thousands of citizens in the Campo were of the same mind. We poured through the narrow exit like sugar into a kitchen funnel, Babbo keeping us close as we jostled our way towards the Duomo, my only aim, to catch another glimpse of that magnificent creation.

All at once, we were next to the black and white striped building Vanni and I had looked at from Palazzo Salimbeni's tower for as long as I could remember. Like an all-seeing eye, it followed us whenever we accompanied Cook to market, and now I was standing in front of it, I saw the Duomo was as imposing as the Palazzo dei Signori. But before I could study the façade, Babbo steered us through the bronze doors, and into the gloom within.

'I can't see a thing.' Mamma complained.

'I've an idea. Come with me.' Babbo took us by the

hand, pushing through the side aisle until we reached the front, where all the nobles sat.

'Sorry, no further.' A city militiaman barred our way.

Babbo bowed towards our mistress. 'The Contessa isn't feeling well and needs her maids on hand.' Tall and some ten years older than my mother, she was in charge while the Conte was away. She saw us and gave us a nod.

'Very well,' the soldier said. 'Wait at the side.'

'Thanks, brother.' Babbo pushed past.

'Not you, just the women.' The soldier stood in his way.

'I'm staying with you.' I clung to Babbo's arm.

'No, kitten. You look after the Contessa and I'll collect you later.' Babbo pinched my cheek then disappeared into the crowd, half the fun of the day leaving with him.

'And you can stop those tears, at once,' Mamma hissed.

I wiped them on my sleeve and looked around. The cathedral was even larger inside than out. Black and white striped marble columns flanked the nave, looking like ladders to heaven. But nothing could match the new altarpiece. Among the hundreds of figures, not one was repeated – different clothes, hairstyles, expressions on their faces, so familiar-looking I felt I'd seen them at market. And so much gold! Halos not just around the head of the Madonna and baby Jesus, but also on everyone else who knelt before the throne. But splendid though that shiny metal was, nothing could beat that deep blue of the Virgin's cloak, made from the lapis lazuli our art tutor told us had travelled all the way from the Hindu Kush. I had no idea where that was, but the name alone was magical.

As the hum of low-voiced gossip gave way to Gregorian chant, I knew this was my chance to see the back and crept to the place that after today only priests would see.

There Duccio had created a series illustrating the life of Christ – as if Jesus had lived in Siena, not Judea! And my eyes nearly popped out when I saw the scene in the Garden of Gethsemane – for Peter's knife had a handle just like Babbo's; the white spots on black indicating it was covered in perforated leather. Then as the priest blessed the bread for mass, I returned to Mamma's side to re-examine the front. Along the top and base were two rows of smaller paintings of the life of the Madonna. My eyes were drawn to the Annunciation, where the Angel Gabriele wore a cloak, the same colour as my dress. But more unusual was his hair, fair as that of the surly young man in the parade.

As soon as the bishop gave the final benediction, Mamma grabbed my hand. 'Let's slip away before the Contessa starts bossing us about.' I wasn't going to spoil my mother's good mood by reminding her that Babbo had told us to look after the mistress.

'Maria, where's that husband of yours?' The familiar voice stopped us.

'Guarding the palazzo.' Mamma made a point of not using the Contessa's title, as if they were equals and only got away with it because Babbo was everyone's

14

favourite.

'Then you'll have to do. Help me through this crowd or I'll faint.' The Contessa rested her arm on Mamma's. 'And pick up my cloak, Clara. The gold embroidery is worth a fortune.'

Mamma wanted me to become the Contessa's maid when I grew up, though Cook said I'd be better suited to her job. But the brocade weighed a ton, and I could hardly lift it.

'Higher, girl, or the crowd will ruin it with their dusty footprints. You, sir, make way for nobility.' The Contessa waved her closed fan, catching the ginger artist who'd helped the old man round the Campo.

He bowed. 'Pietro Lorenzetti, at your service. I worked with Duccio on the Maestà.'

An artist – talking to us! And beside him the fair-haired Angel Gabriele!

'Then you'll be going to the lunch at Palazzo d'Elci. Get me there faster than these useless women.'

But I was doing my best! I stopped short and the Contessa was brought up, like a horse reined in by its rider.

'Clara! You may be good at lessons but you're useless at carrying cloaks.' The Contessa's fan clipped my scalp. 'You carry it, young man. Yes, you, the blond one.'

'Ambrogio Lorenzetti, ma'am; Pietro's younger brother.' He picked up the cloak and lifted it out of the dust.

Brothers? They looked more like father and son. But for taking my job. I gave him one of my blackest looks.

'Have it back, if you're so keen,' he said, offering the train. 'I want to be an artist, not a cloak carrier.'

That made two of us, but we'd both be in trouble if he didn't do a better job. 'Do as the Contessa asks, or you'll get a clip, whoever you are.'

'Then grab my arm or you'll get lost.'

No longer needed by the Contessa, Mamma stepped back and linked with his other arm.

I watched as Pietro took the noble hand in his and brought it to his lips, holding it longer than courtesy demanded. 'What a delightful cloak the Contessa is wearing.'

'You're a man of great taste, Signor Lorenzetti.' Perhaps it was the heat of the day, but the Contessa seemed to be blushing.

'On the contrary,' Pietro said, 'it is the lady who is discerning.'

Ambrogio made as if he were about to vomit in the Contessa's cape. And despite my annoyance with him, I couldn't help laughing.

'If you ever want to set up your own workshop, Signor Lorenzetti, let me know,' the Contessa continued. 'The Salimbeni would be pleased to support a man of your talent.'

'There he goes, charming his way into another assignment.' Ambrogio muttered.

We'd reached Palazzo d'Elci – smaller than our palazzo, but it looked over the Campo, and today its guards were out in force. 'Contessa Salimbeni, welcome.' They bowed.

'And I'm with Duccio – Pietro Lorenzetti, the artist.'

'Please enter.'

'And I'm with him.' Ambrogio leapt forward.

'Sorry, sir. We've only been told of one Lorenzetti guest.'

Pietro led the Contessa through the gates. As they entered the courtyard, she turned. 'Maria! Remind that husband of yours to collect me later.'

'If you will allow me, Contessa, I'd be honoured to escort you home.' Pietro continued to charm.

The gold train swished into palazzo, accompanied by Pietro's burnt umber hose.

'He gets to dine with the nobles, while I'm left to sweat in the sun. I was only allowed in the procession was because Duccio needed Pietro's help.' The archangel turned to walk off.

But Mamma hadn't finished with him.

'Is there somewhere we can go? I'm not going home until I've seen the jugglers.' Mamma tilted her head in the way she often looked at Francesco.

'Somewhere cool?' I pleaded. The noonday sun had stolen all the shade.

'I know just the place.' Ambrogio took Mamma's arm, while she fluttered her eyelids.

I crossed my fingers and made a wish. Please let it be the studio.

Chapter 2

Arm in arm, like three kitchen maids, we walked up the hill towards Castelvecchio.

'If we're spending the afternoon together, you'd better tell me your names.' Ambrogio looked more handsome now he'd lost his frown.

His eyes were for Mamma but I didn't mind, especially if we were going to see where the Maestà was painted.

'Maria, servant to the Contessa.'

That was stretching the truth given she was a kitchen maid, like me.

'And I gather, not her favourite.' His voice turned syrupy.

'She can boil in oil as far as I'm concerned!' Mamma's fleeting frown was replaced by a disarming smile.

'And I'm Clara.' I tugged at his arm. Clara who'd love to be an artist like you. 'Will there be any food where we're going?'

'Ignore her. She was picking at bread dough all morning.' Mamma looked across Ambrogio to give me one of her say-nothing glares.

The crowd thinned out once we'd passed the

Duomo. We walked on until we reached a three-storey house next to a gate through the old city walls. Bricks above the main door were missing.

'Had to get the Maestà through somehow,' Ambrogio said.

What a rough start to the Virgin's journey.

'The others are at the lunch, so we'll have some seclusion.' Ambrogio's mouth was so close to Mamma's neck he was almost kissing it.

Francesco could be cheeky, but this made me sick.

'As long as you take me out of the sun.' Mamma put on her teasing voice.

I'd have said something rude if I weren't so eager to see where the great painter worked. Had everything been put away in its proper place, as Cook insisted in the kitchen, or was it more like the bedroom we'd left, clothes strewn everywhere in our hurry to get to the Campo?

'Welcome to Casa Duccio,' Ambrogio poked his head inside then showed us in, 'where the Maestà was created.'

Though no bigger than our bedroom, it was unlike any room I'd seen. The plastered side walls danced with small sketches and streaks of colour. The wall ahead was blank, but along the floor stretched a multi-coloured strip of paint splashes almost as beautiful as the painting itself. The place smelt strange; of oil or egg or soil, or maybe all three; the only furniture a large table tucked under the stairs to the right. On it rested pots containing that rainbow of colours I'd studied in the Duomo. For letting me in on this amazing sight, I'd love Ambrogio forever.

'What a mess.' Mamma raised her chin and offered Ambrogio the profile someone had once told her looked aristocratic.

'Ambrogio! How dare you bring whores here, today of all days.' A woman whose coarse voice belied her serene face appeared at the top of the stairs. 'I thought you were with Duccio.'

Unusually, Mamma stayed silent, though she was generous with her glare.

'Only members of the Guild were invited. These delicate ladies are Contessa Salimbeni's maids, and need protection from the sun until their mistress is collected.'

Despite the unkempt hair straggling over her shoulders, I recognized that long nose, the fair complexion. 'It's the Maestà,' I whispered.

'Well observed,' Ambrogio said. 'May I present Monna Duccio.'

It wasn't the Maestà's face I wanted to see, but what she'd been wearing. I took a deep breath. 'Would it be possible to see the cloak?'

'Is there no end to this posing?' But she smiled and reappeared, wrapped in a swathe of un-dyed linen.

'That's not blue!' I was wearing richer material myself.

'An artists' trick.' Ambrogio smoothed my frown with his finger. 'Duccio used this to sketch in the folds, then Simone – Simone Martini, if you've heard of him – he coloured them, though grumbled all the time about painting fabric being beneath him.'

20

'It's hot. Any chance of some water?' Mamma pulled his attention back to her.

'And I'm hungry.' Having been up since first light and not yet broken my fast, I had a hole as big as a loaf in my middle.

'Can I get her something?' Ambrogio pleaded.

'You'll be the ruin of us. If it weren't for that brother of yours, you'd be out on your ear.'

'And if Duccio didn't keep me mixing paints, I'd be earning my own living.'

'See what you can find in the kitchen, though Lord knows what's left after the scavenging you all did last night.'

Ambrogio winked at Mamma and indicated for her to follow him upstairs.

'Clara can play with all this painting stuff.' For once Mamma read my mind, though it was unusual for her to be keen on visiting a kitchen.

'I'll keep an eye on her.' Monna Duccio wiped her face with the linen cloak and yawned.

'Here's a brush and some drawing ink.' Ambrogio pulled out a pot of reddish liquid. 'Sketch on the wall like everyone else. Use any space you can find.' He took Mamma's hand and led her upstairs.

I could hardly believe I was being invited to add my scrawl to those of the maestro. Having practised on pastry all week, I knew exactly what to draw. Biting my lower lip in concentration, I drew a shape, not as good as Duccio's, but definitely a woman. Adding a baby was far beyond my skill, so I drew the Virgin Mother with her arms widespread. Oops, too many fingers, and I corrected my mistake like a proper artist. Upstairs, Mamma giggled, she was teasing him, like she did Francesco. A door upstairs was kicked closed, then all was silent apart from Monna D's snoring on the stairs. This was my chance.

Instead of drawing the details of the face, I turned to the paints before I was discovered. I squeezed through my fingers the clods of Raw Siena, Burnt Siena and Raw Umber – the different browns visible in the hills beyond. Then I felt the weight of rocks and marvelled at the blues, purples and pinks riddled through the stones. I moved on to the pouches, light and stuffed with faded flowers which had blossomed again in Duccio's painting. If only I knew how to transform them into the array of mixed paints abandoned on the nearby table.

I found an almost empty pot of ultramarine and picked up a brush – thicker than the one Ambrogio had given me for drawing. A hint of that magical blue – that most expensive of pigments – lurked at the base of the bristles, but to use something so precious on my own meagre drawing would surely be sacrilege. Yet I longed to try it. Checking again that Monna D was asleep, I dipped my finger in the pot of blue, but where to dab it so as not to be discovered? I lifted the hem of my skirt and smeared it on my leg. Against my skin it was spectacular. Only when I was sure it had dried did I turn to the other pots. I yearned to use them all, and who would tell me not to? Taking a clean brush for each one, I streaked colour after colour onto my drawing of the cloak until it was as bright and vibrant

22

as the floor.

On hearing stirrings above, I added rough features to the face, finishing with the smiley mouth I'd put on my pastry. Standing back to admire, I saw that instead of the regal creature I'd hoped to create, my Madonna looked like a bird with multi-coloured feathers, and with a face as red as a turkey. Duccio would not be impressed.

'Here, Clara, I found this apple and a rind of cheese.' Mamma descended the stairs, with her head held high, and Monna D disappeared into the upper regions of the house. Ambrogio came down a few moments later, face as dark as the Madonna's cloak. What had Mamma done now? She put everyone except Babbo in an ill humour.

'Why did you use so many brushes?' He went straight to the paint table and rearranged the pots I'd disturbed. 'You'll have to clean them all before we go.'

I pointed to my picture. 'I ... er ... was trying out the colours.'

He stood in front of it, tilting his head from side to side. 'Hmm. That's audacious.'

It was a new word to me but his frown suggested it meant something bad. I studied and identified its biggest flaw. 'The face, it's too pink.'

'That's because you didn't use terra verde – this green paint – underneath.' He daubed the wall with it, then overlaid it with pink. 'See, more of a flesh tone.'

'Stop going on about that stupid sketch, I want to go.' Mamma picked up a paintbrush, dipped it in a pot and obliterated my colourful cloak.

Worst of all, she'd used the precious blue I'd denied myself.

'You vixen!' Ambrogio seized the brush. 'That's no way to treat a painting, even a child's. If Duccio were here, he'd throw you out.'

'Don't fret, we're leaving anyway. Come, Clara,' Mamma said, with a smug smile. I could have killed her.

'Not until she's cleaned the brushes.' Ambrogio stood between us.

'I'll wait outside.' Mamma stormed out. Though she too had used a brush, wild horses wouldn't get her cleaning on her day off.

'That mother of yours,' Ambrogio said, once the door had closed behind her. 'How do you ever know where you stand with her?'

'I don't. Babbo says she's as changeable as a bee's flight, though he can always put a smile on her face.'

'Then I hope he finds her worth the trouble, for I didn't,' Ambrogio said bitterly. 'Do you know how to clean brushes?'

I shook my head. The tutor cleaned up after my art lesson with Vanni.

'Then let me teach you.' Ambrogio poured oil into two dishes. 'Use this first one to get out most of the colour.' He soaked the brush in the oil, then stroked it against the sloping base of the dish, always towards him. I was mesmerized as the pigments eased out as if by magic. 'Do it several times, until it's clean, then give it a final rinse in some fresh oil. See?'

I nodded.

24

'You do the rest.' He sat on the stairs as I worked my way through the brushes. 'How do you put up with her?'

One encounter and he'd got Mamma's measure.

'Families!' He groaned as he held his head in his hands. 'Pietro would have me mixing paints the rest of my life.'

'I'll mix the paints for you!' How wonderful that would be compared to the palazzo kitchen.

'Very funny. Women can't paint.'

The dream, which in the space of my time in the studio had grown into a huge fluffy cloud, shrunk to the size of a raindrop. I cleaned the brushes through my tears, so slow, Ambrogio had to help. Eventually they filled a large pot, ready to use again.

'But if I'd painted a cloak like that at your age, I'm sure Pietro would have encouraged me.'

Was that praise for my painting? Our tutors saved their rare praise for Vanni, and my only known talent was for Jacks.

'Let's find that mother of yours.' Ambrogio sighed as he steered me out.

'We'd better not have missed the juggling.' Mamma pushed me out of the way to take his arm.

Although Ambrogio was now her reluctant companion, Mamma coaxed him into paying her court for the rest of the afternoon. It made no difference to my enjoyment. I laughed at the antics of the jugglers, and gasped at the tumblers' acrobatics, all paid for by the State. Even Mamma looked happy. The whole city was squashed into the Campo and we put aside our enmities as Malavolti mixed with Tolomei, Salimbeni with Piccolomini. Wine shops did good trade, and when we felt hungry, Mamma cajoled peddlers to give us pieces of pecorino, slices of fruit and the chewy remains of last year's nuts. Then, as shadows lengthened, stalls were cleared away for the dancing to begin.

'You have to join one of the women's circles,' Ambrogio said.

Mamma gave him her hand to kiss, and I watched him disappear into the crowd, sad that my glimpse into the artist's world was over.

Mamma dragged me to the front of the women's rows, giving us the best view of the men dancing past. Outside the Palazzo dei Signori, drummers beat out the rhythm while trumpeters blasted a tune the kitchen girls often hummed. The dance started slowly, and I picked up the steps. 'Step right – left foot across – step right.'

The woman next to me thrust a tambourine into my hand and I rattled its bells. Mamma looked so carefree I almost forgot she was my mother and already twenty-six. Blues mixed with reds, yellows with greens, and the colours of the great houses of Siena blended in a moving replica of Duccio's studio floor.

'Glo-ri-a.' Clap, clap.

If only the celebration would go on forever. This had been the best day of my life: better than any of Vanni's birthday celebrations, because this was shared with the whole city.

'Today, we are sisters,' Mamma said, as we changed direction yet again. 'Let's pick out the handsomest man

26

to take us home. What about that one?' She pointed to a young lad just out of his teens. He blushed at her attention.

'Stop it, Mamma.' Once again, fun had turned to embarrassment. Then I saw Ambrogio's fair head bobbing towards us at the front of the men's circle. I rattled my bells in his direction.

'Don't waste time on him.' Mamma snatched the tambourine and gave it back to the woman next to me. 'He's a nobody.'

If he'd seen us, he was pretending not to have.

Walk, walk, walk, point – I could ignore him too.

Only when he was facing me did he acknowledge me with a quick smile. Immediately the dance took him to my right. When the circles retraced their last move, he was opposite me again. This time he nodded in the direction of Mamma and rolled his eyes to the heavens. I laughed.

The third and last time he faced me, our toes touched as we both kicked out our feet. He smiled at me, not man to girl, but artist to artist, before dancing away.

'Look, who's here.' Mamma pointed towards the approaching men.

'Babbo!' I'd been so busy thinking about my time in the studio, I'd forgotten he was collecting us.

'I guessed my lovely Maria would be at the front,' he said, then pushed between us, into the women's circle. 'Don't you recognise one of your sisters?' he said in a falsetto voice. The woman next to me giggled and offered him her tambourine. Everyone loved Babbo, however outrageous he was.

'Time to go, dearests,' he said in his proper voice. 'The Contessa's made her own arrangements so Francesco and Domenico are waiting for us by the steps.'

A blood red band of light coloured the sky above the palazzi. I searched for the pink and blue of Ambrogio to say goodbye, but the colours merged into a golden glow.

As soon as the music paused between dances, Babbo opened a path for us through the circles and up the steps.

Once out of the Campo, the noise dropped. Shadows of the few people walking home flickered in the light of torches hanging from the palazzo walls. I'd never been out this late, and clutched Babbo's hand. Domenico and Francesco were waiting for us and, full of wine and bravado, Francesco turned up the main street.

'Not through Tolomei territory,' Domenico's voice quivered as he wiped away the sweat sticking his ashen fringe to his brow. Everyone had been dancing this most special of nights.

'Afraid of those wasters, you old fart?' Francesco elbowed him. 'They're all dancing in the Campo!'

Still Babbo hesitated.

'Stop fretting, Guido. It's quicker this way,' Mamma added.

'Pull me up the hill, Babbo?' I pleaded, suddenly dog tired – and afraid of whatever lurked in the shadows.

Babbo led the way, dragging me along after him. Francesco took Mamma's arm and Domenico plodded behind.

The air was sultry. Too tired to talk, I was relieved all was quiet as we approached Palazzo Tolomei.

Then something moved and I screamed.

'Well, if it isn't Guido and his tarts again.' Blackbeard slunk out of the shadows, as slimy as the serpent tempting Eve. He was flanked by two other guards, dark blue like the night.

Mamma threw her head back and flicked under her chin with the backs of her fingers. Go to hell, her gesture indicated. I hid behind Babbo.

'Are you sure the girl's yours, Guido, for someone else was entertaining your wife this afternoon.' Blackbeard leered. The Tolomei had spies everywhere, but then so did the Salimbeni.

'Stop your mouth, you filthy rat or I'll stop it for you.' Babbo let go my hand and lunged, fixing his hands around the Tolomei's throat.

'Mamma mia!' Domenico crossed himself.

But Blackbeard was the bigger, stronger man, and he pulled Babbo's hands away and pinioned him in a bear hug. Babbo struggled but Blackbeard held tight.

Francesco was being held by the other two Tolomei and shouted. 'Let me go, you stinking turds.'

'Leave Babbo alone!' I rushed forward and scratched at Blackbeard's hands.

He kicked my shin and I fell to the ground.

'Dear Lord, she's only a child.' Domenico's voice trembled as he pulled me to my feet and pulled me to him.

'Do something, Mamma,' I screamed. But she

stayed cowering in the doorway opposite.

Then a clink. Babbo's leather-handled knife – like the one I'd seen in the painting at the Duomo – had worked loose from his doublet and clanked on the ground.

'So you came prepared, Guido.' Blackbeard hissed, then brought up his knee.

Babbo doubled up in pain. I wanted to run to him, but Domenico held me fast.

'From now on, it'll be Tolomei servicing your wife. And the little plum? I'll save her for myself.'

'You evil snake!' Babbo lunged at Blackbeard's ear and sank his teeth into the lobe.

Blackbeard yelled, let go and drew a knife from his belt. I opened my mouth to shout Babbo a warning, but the blade had disappeared into his doublet and a patch, the colour of ripe cherries, oozed through the red and gold fabric.

'Dear God!' Domenico covered my eyes.

'Guido, Guido!' Mamma dashed out from her hiding place and knelt at Babbo's side.

'Get up, woman!' Francesco pulled her to her feet as the Tolomei disappeared into their palazzo, like scorpions discovered under wood.

'With me!' Ambrogio appeared from nowhere. His hands were shaking as he grabbed me from Domenico.

'You go too, Maria,' Francesco ordered. 'We'll bring Guido back before the city militia find him. You know both sides get punished when there's been a fight.'

In the Tolomei torchlight, Mamma looked helpless. Ambrogio put his arm around her waist and steered us both towards Palazzo Salimbeni.

'What about Babbo?'

'Hurry home, Clara!' Francesco said as lifted Babbo's by the armpits, while Domenico took his legs.

Ambrogio only spoke when we reached our steps, his voice trembling. 'I followed when you left, thought I should make sure you got home safely.'

I was glad that he had, but Mamma turned on him. 'Leave us alone – and next time you need company, find someone in your own league.'

She bundled me inside the door and as soon as we crossed the threshold, raised her hand. I felt the sting as it whipped across my face. 'Go to our room and stay there.'

If ever I needed her to put her arms around me it was now, and yet she was sending me up on my own, and without a candle. I crawled up the stairs, hoping with every tread that she would call me back. But when I reached the top, she was still there, watching, making sure I did as I was told.

Once inside, I threw open the shutters to let in some air, though it was no cooler outside. I sat on the bed, leg throbbing, eyes burning and cheek smarting. Over the years, Domenico had tended all injuries. He knew which herbs to apply and now he had to save Babbo, though I'd never seen as much red as on his doublet.

I lay down, shivering despite the heat. Yearning for comfort, I curled into a ball and felt a strange roughness on my leg. The Madonna's special paint! I rubbed at it, remembering making my own version of the Maestà's cloak on Duccio's wall. And as I scratched away, my heartbeat slowed and I drifted into a deep blue sleep.

Chapter 3

aking with a fright, I smelt burning. Was the palazzo on fire? The shadow of a witch filled the whole wall facing me, then shrank to life size. I covered my face with my hands, fearing I'd died in the night and had descended into the world of the damned. Then I peered through my fingers to see the outline of a hag, burning off her hair with a candle. 'Whoever you are, show your face.' I turned to face the creature.

The candle stilled. I held my breath as the creature turned to face me.

Madonna preserve me, it was Mamma. But what was she doing? This time she really had gone mad. I watched in horror as she put a comb through a couple of inches of hair and put the candle to the rest. The hair crackled and shrunk, then dropped to the floor in a final flurry of sparks. I grabbed her hand. 'Whatever you're doing, stop!'

'I'll not give those sluts in the kitchen the satisfaction of cutting off my hair, so I'm burning it off myself.' Half laughing, half crying, she pushed me away, and singed off another tress, stamping out the glowing embers with her bare feet.

I stared in disbelief as Mamma's beautiful locks disappeared.

'Now get back to sleep. We've a busy day tomorrow.' She blew out the candle.

But however much I tried to reclaim that ultramarine darkness, I couldn't. My mother was mad - and where was Babbo? He was badly hurt, so why hadn't they brought him here for us to nurse him?

I turned towards Mamma's back – as closed as a cupboard – then to the blackness of the door, willing Babbo to come through.

'For goodness' sake be still.' Mamma put her feet on my hips and with one massive shove, pushed me onto the floor.

I lay there, too terrified to move, waiting to hear the regular breathing that told me she'd fallen asleep. Only then did I creep back into bed, so tired, I drifted into a doze.

I'm running through the streets of Siena, searching. At every turn a saint with a gold halo beckons. But as soon as I run towards them, they disappear. Suddenly I'm in the Duomo. At the end of the nave, bathed in a sunbeam, is the Virgin Mary, stretching out her arms. I run towards her. But her cloak is covered in the white half-moons of the Tolomei. A boot appears from under her cloak, and I wake up, heart pounding.

Putting an arm against my mother's sleeping form, something I'd never do if she were awake, I nuzzled against her warmth and drifted off.

33

When I woke again, I stretched out my hand to feel Babbo's presence but the sheet his side of the bed was cold. I leant over Mamma and opened the shutter a crack to let in some light. Why was I still in my festa dress? Images of knives and blood flashed into mind, a horrid nightmare the morning light failed to wake me from. And still no Babbo. He'd been in fights before, with all the female servants taking turns to look after him, as Mamma claimed she couldn't stand the sight of blood. I shook her awake. She covered her eyes with her arm and turned onto her back. I gasped. Her yellow dress was covered in blood.

'What have you done with Babbo?' I screamed, for I'd seen Francesco and Domenico carry him home.

'You were there. You saw how badly hurt he was. And now he's dead.' Mamma curled into a ball.

'They said they'd look after him.' I pummeled her back.

'Your father loved these curls.' Mamma picked up a couple that had escaped the flame then let them fall back to the floor. In the light of day, she looked like a badly shorn sheep. 'But a widow has to cut them off.'

My body went as cold as the stone slab in Cook's larder, and a high-pitched whine screeched in my ears. 'You're lying,' I screamed, covering them with my hands.

'Don't believe me? I'll show you!' With a tight grip on my arm, Mamma steered me down two flights of stairs to the cool of the cellars. She pushed open a door to one of the cantinas. I recognised the sickly-sweet

34

smell of cured hams hanging from the wooden beams, and the heady aroma of wine maturing in the barrels. But on the table which Cook used to salt meat, lay Babbo's blood-stained body; his face the creamy-pale of pig fat. I closed my eyes, afraid I was going to be sick.

'Now do you believe me?' Mamma said.

Step by dreadful step, I crept towards the body. Yes, it was Babbo's face, and Babbo's blood-stained jacket. I waited for his head to turn with a wink and say, 'hello, little kitten.' And in the silence that would last the rest of my life, I understood that Francesco and Domenico had failed to save him. I knelt on the floor and wept. All the gold on Duccio's painting couldn't make up for the sunshine that had disappeared from my life.

'We're done for, that's the truth. Everyone hates me, and without your father, they'll throw me out.' Mamma sat behind me, on one of the smaller wine barrels.

'They can't. It's our home!' And what would Vanni do, without me to keep him at his studies?

'I've done my best to learn their city ways, but those kitchen girls have always had it in for me. I'll bet they're already making plans.'

'They won't. They can't.' I ran to my mother and put my arms around her waist.

She wrapped hers around my back. 'I hated everything about the small-town I came from. I'd die rather than go back there.'

'I'll look after you, Mamma.'

'What do you know about a woman's needs!' She pushed me away.

I turned to the body on the table, expecting Babbo to

35

give me a reassuring smile, but he just lay there.

'Now back to the room. The women will be coming to help me bathe and dress his body. You can't be here for that.' She pushed me towards the stairs, through servants collecting stock for the factotum's office where all business was conducted. Not even the death of a servant as popular as Babbo got in the way of trade.

For a moment, I thought one of them was Babbo, but it was Francesco. When he saw us, he put down the bale of silk and put his arms around me. I pushed him away. 'You should have saved him.'

'I know, cara. I'm so sorry.' He stroked my hair, then kissed my head. He reached out to Mamma too, but she jerked her arm away.

'How could he have been so stupid? And you! Tah!' Mamma tossed her head back in disgust. 'Useless.'

Francesco looked helpless, arms dangling by his sides. 'I'm sorry, Maria. I've lost my best friend too.'

'Cowards, the lot of you!' Mamma spat out the words. 'The next time I see that Blackbeard, I'll kill him myself. And not care if I go to hell for it.'

'Stay away from him, Maria.' Francesco held Mamma by the shoulders, 'or you'll be hurt too.'

Mamma stood there, staring into Francesco's face. The anger drained away, and a hint of a smile hovered around her lips. Still holding Francesco's gaze, she twirled what remained of her curls around a finger.

'Promise me?' He spoke softly this time, in his teasing voice, and Mamma nodded. He let her go and she marched me back to our room.

Mamma went straight to the mirror and started

preening herself; arranging a scarf to cover her shorn head then pinching her cheeks and biting her lips to add a bit of colour.

'Stay here and find a clean shirt for your father. The Contessa said we don't have to work today.' The door closed behind her.

I stared at the chest but couldn't face seeing the clothes Babbo would never again wear.

For once, I longed to be sweeping floors or filling water jars, instead of sitting in eerie silence. Through the shutter slats, I saw customers coming out of the factotum's office, oblivious to the body lying in the cellar.

I scrabbled under the bed to find my pebbles.

Throw one up in the air and see if you can pick up a stone before you catch it. And when you can pick up ten, Babbo will give you a big surprise.

I closed my eyes and touched the top of my head, the spot where he'd kissed me when I'd reached that milestone. Now I'd never know what ten would have earned me. I gave in to tears.

Over the street's hubbub I heard the town-crier with his daily news. 'Hear ye. Hear ye. Thanks be to God, Duccio's Maestà installed in the Duomo, alleluia, alleluia. Funeral mass for Guido, servant of the Salimbeni household, leaving Palazzo Salimbeni at Vespers.'

If I needed further confirmation Babbo was dead, that was it. The stones were all I had left of him and I had to keep them safe. Searching through the chest, I found a worn leather purse. Kissing each of the stones before putting them in, I tightened the string, and hugged it to my chest. And when someone tapped on the door, I hid it under the mattress. 'Who is it?'

'Vanni. The Contessa's asked me to bring you these cloaks.'

What a relief it was to hear his voice. Yet he sounded so formal, so unlike the Vanni I spent most of my time with. I stuffed our belongings back in the chest, and checked the room was tidy. Now Babbo was no longer there to protect us, I couldn't give the Contessa any excuse to throw us out. When I opened the door, Vanni stood, arms full of black material, his dark hair scraped away from his face.

'These are for you, to wear at the funeral this afternoon. Special long ones.' He hopped from foot to foot, looking everywhere but at me. 'The Contessa offers them with her condolences. The rest of us will wear short ones.'

I wasn't surprised that he referred to his mother as the Contessa. That was normal. But did Babbo's death mean we had to behave like proper master and servant? Just in case, I responded stiffly.

'Thank you.' I took the cloaks from him. 'Please tell the Contessa how grateful we are.' Palazzo protocol dictated we keep the lady in charge happy.

But instead of turning on his heels, he hovered in the doorway. 'I'm sorry, Clara. It's awful to lose your Babbo like that. I'd kill the man who did it, if I could.'

He looked at me at last. 'I miss my father so badly when he's away on business. But this is much worse. At least you've still got your mother.'

38

'I wish she'd been killed and not Babbo!' I found myself in tears again, ashamed at what I'd said, yet relieved to have blurted out what I truly felt.

Vanni closed the door and we sat side by side on the chest. 'In a competition for bad mothers, there wouldn't be much to choose between them, Maria and the Contessa.'

I laughed, despite myself, and wiped my tears on my sleeve. 'She's convinced she's so unpopular, that without Babbo to protect us, the Contessa will want us out.'

'She can't do that. You're family. The Salimbeni will always look after you, especially as Guido died fighting a Tolomei.'

His words were comforting, and I rested my head on his shoulder. 'But you don't know the half of what she does. She's rude to the Contessa, and even worse to Cook, and I'm almost as bad. In the crush outside the Duomo yesterday, I nearly yanked off the Contessa's cloak!'

'She can be very irritating!' Vanni smiled. He was three years older than me, and despite the differences in our status, more brother than friend. Then he cleared his throat. 'Especially as she's asked me to collect your father's things. I'm so sorry. Are they in here?' He rapped the chest we were sitting on.

'Can't you take them later?' My memories of Babbo were disappearing too fast.

'You know what she's like. Nothing wasted, nothing delayed.'

I was tempted to refuse, but that would get Vanni

into trouble. So I slid off the chest, my heart plummeting as Vanni picked out all items of Babbo's.

Through my tears I tried to speak. A tiny voice came out. 'Leave him a clean shirt, please, to be buried in.'

Vanni put down the clothes, found a shirt and laid it out on the bed. Then with his arms full, he stood in the doorway. 'I'm most awfully sorry, Clara.'

He left me and the chest emptier.

At the end of the funeral service, I looked at the handful of earth in my fist and let it trickle through my fingers, losing a little more of Babbo with each lump that fell. The solemnity over, the servants erupted into everyday chatter, but I couldn't join in. The burden of sadness I carried back to the palazzo was almost unbearable.

Inside the Salimbeni hallway, maids helped us out of our long cloaks. Even though it was too warm to be wearing them longer than necessary I was reluctant to give up this last connection with the father I'd loved so much.

'What you need, Maria, is some wine to get your blood flowing again.' Francesco ran a finger along her mother's arm. 'Let's go and steal some!'

'Leave her alone, Francesco!' I stood between the two of them.

But Mamma pushed me away, finding that voice that had persuaded Ambrogio to look after us at the festa. 'Exactly what I could do with. Go upstairs, Clara. I'll see you later.'

I felt numb as I entered our room, knowing all trace of Babbo had already been removed. By the light of fading evening sun, I lifted the mattress and took out my bag of stones.

Up and over, catch one.

Up and over, catch two ...

... Up and over, catch eight.

Over and over, I attempted to catch nine. Eventually I managed it and started work on the final challenge. My hand was so full of stones, I'd catch the tenth stone only to let another one fall out. But I was determined to do it – for Babbo.

Up and over, catch ten!

I'd done it!

I stood up, ready to race and find Babbo to give him the news, but of course he wasn't there. I rested my chin on the sill and stared out of the window. The heavens were so full of stars I hoped one of the twinkles belonged to Babbo. And then, as my eyes adjusted to the dark, one raced across the sky. A shooting star! I spotted another, and another. It was as if Babbo were smiling down at me and orchestrating the universe to applaud my efforts. Lying on the bed, in the hollow worn by his weight, I fell asleep.

It was fully dark when I was woken by low voices and laughter outside. How could someone play a prank on us, the night of Babbo's funeral? But after some fumbling with the latch, Mamma came crashing into the room dragging Francesco after her.

'Get out, Clara, and don't come back until I say so.' Mamma's familiar temper had returned, the voice that had to be obeyed.

I stood outside. But where to go? I'd slept in that room my whole life. As I leant against the door, I heard Mamma's deep-throated laugh and soft words from Francesco I couldn't quite catch.

'It's Babbo's room, it's Babbo's room!' I hammered on the door.

But the two inside ignored me and the laughter and giggles turned to sighs.

Tears streaming down my face, I slid to the ground. As the noise diminished, I wrapped my arm round my head, and lay on the floor outside, my only cover, the warm night air.

Chapter 4

Next morning, I dragged myself up to the kitchen. The terracotta-tiled floor was covered in vegetable peelings, pieces of animal skin had been kicked to one side and Cook was already impatient with the pots. The girls, all watery-eyed, looked away as I entered the kitchen as if I carried some sort of plague, but it was a stone in my

42

heart.

'Glad to have you back,' Cook said. 'There's a day's work to catch up on.'

I fetched the broom then stopped. This was my first day's work without a father.

'We're all missing him, tesora.' Cook stroked my cheek with her garlic smelling fingers.

I wiped my eyes and started brushing, scuttling mice to quieter quarters.

'But where's that mother of yours?' Cook lifted the cast iron pan off the fire.

'She'll have a sore head, after that wine last night,' thin-as-a-broom Teresa said.

'And that's not the only place she'll be sore, if I know Francesco.' Susanna's cackle was worthy of a whore, as was the low cut of her shift.

'That's enough. She's just lost her father, poor lamb.'

If Cook could be kind to me, why couldn't Mamma?

When she eventually arrived, the chatter stopped.

'No need to ask who you're talking about.' Her eyes were underlined by dark shadows. 'And it's none of your business if I needed cheering up.'

The maids said nothing but their eyebrows spoke volumes.

'That's as may be.' Cook slapped a mound of pastry onto the table, 'but it disrespects Guido.'

I needed her too.

'Go to hell the lot of you! I'm taking the water down to the Contessa.' Mamma grabbed the waiting pail and stormed out.

43

'That's my job!' Susanna shouted after her.

'Today she's excused. After that she's in for a thrashing if she gives me more lip.' Cook flattened the pastry with a thump. It would end up a biscuit if she hammered it more.

'Talk of the devil,' Susanna said, as Francesco came in whistling a tune as jaunty as his hat. When Babbo was alive, he'd been my friend too.

'Any of last night's sausage left? I've such a hunger.'

'You've had enough sausage, my boy! Shame on you, the night of the funeral, too.' Cook waved her rolling pin at him. If I were holding it, I'd have whacked him.

'Me?' Francesco pointed at himself, his wide eyes feigning innocence.

'Don't pretend, Francesco, we all know what you've been up to, though we'd no idea you'd such a taste for vinegar,' Teresa said, no stranger to bitterness herself.

'If the gate's open, go in, I say.' He found some salami and bit off the end. 'She was forbidden fruit while Guido was alive, but now's another matter.'

Babbo would be spending time in purgatory and so was I. Looking around for an excuse to get out, I grabbed the pail of slops, and rushed downstairs. I emptied it in the cess pile at the side of the palace, all the while wiping away my tears. Who could I turn to? I looked out to the next hill and saw the Cathedral's dome peek over the rooftops. Only the Maestà.

Dumping the pail inside the entrance hall, I raced down the main street, blinded by tears. When I reached the Campo, I remembered my hand in Babbo's two days before and took the road to the Duomo. The crowds led me to the busy piazza, in front of the grand building. I climbed the steps to the bronze doors, wiped my eyes and paused. I'd imagined slipping unseen among worshippers, but the nave was empty. I was fearful to go in on my own but the glittering painting on the altar beckoned and I tiptoed in.

As I knelt before it, the colours seemed less vibrant, the gold less bright. But the Madonna looked after the whole of Siena, so she'd look after me too. My prayer came out in a rush. 'Babbo's just died, Francesco's sleeping with Mamma and she doesn't want me. What shall I do?'

I dared to look up, but the eyes I needed to watch over me belonged to Monna Duccio.

'Oy, you little urchin.' A fat, tonsured friar appeared from the sacristy.

I looked around, then realized he was talking to me. Dirty after my chores, there was nothing to indicate I worked for the Salimbeni.

'Trying to steal alms? I'll teach you.' He waddled towards me, undoing the belt around his waist. The great bronze doors were a long way off, but a marble pillar was close. I dodged behind it, then ran to the next one, and the next, keeping ahead of the panting friar.

'Someone help me!' he shouted. 'Stop the little cat.'

But I was in luck. By the time he reached the doorway, I was already in the piazza, hiding behind a stall selling religious artifacts. I waited until he went back into the Duomo.

Outside the hospital opposite, men hobbled on

wooden crutches, rags covering their festering wounds. Women nursed sickly children, their free hand outstretched for alms. I was frightened and wanted to go home but had no idea of the way. If only Babbo could tell me.

Downhill.

Showing more bravado than I felt, I took the road down the side of the Duomo. This wasn't the way I'd come, for I found myself outside the Baptistry. However white oxon wouldn't drag me back to that friar. I took another turn downhill and caught a glimpse of the Campo through a gap in the buildings. Thank you, Babbo! I raced up the main street, overjoyed when Palazzo Salimbeni came into view.

'Not so fast, little plum.'

Madonna preserve me, the man with the black beard, the brute who'd killed Babbo, was after me too! Who would protect me now Babbo was gone? Screaming 'the Tolomei will kill me', I ran for my life, covering my ears against the evil man's sordid taunts. Only when the colours around me changed from indigo to scarlet, and I'd reached the top of our steps, did I stop to catch my breath.

Inside the palazzo, the entrance hall was busy as a beehive ready to swarm.

'Francesco! Put your back into that sweeping.' In the centre of activities was the queen bee herself, the Contessa. 'And what stupid person left that bucket for someone to trip over?'

'Sorry, Contessa,' I picked it up and made for the kitchen, glad of the excuse to stay out of Francesco's way.

'Psst, here!' Vanni was hiding in the crook of the wooden staircase, dressed in his smartest outfit, the one embroidered with gold thread.

How glad I was to see my friend. 'What's going on? They're going mad down there.'

'Babbo's back,' he beamed.

I felt the blood draining from my face. Had my visit to the Madonna made my wildest dream come true? 'What do you mean? We buried him yesterday.'

'I'm so sorry, Clara, I meant my Babbo. He sent a rider to tell us his caravan will be here later today.'

If this was the news, of course Vanni was full of it. As the youngest of the Conte's sons. He was too young to travel with his father and desperate for his attention when he returned.

'Lucky you.' I swallowed the lump of disappointment in my throat. 'I must go and face Cook. I ran out without permission and she won't be pleased.'

'I'll come with you. It might save you a telling-off. And maybe I can persuade her to make some of that panettone they brought back from Milan last year.'

Kitchens were always on the top floor, so if a fire broke out, as it occasionally did, it was unlikely to spread to the floors below. In summer, we had the sun bearing down too so we cooked early in the morning. However news of the Conte's arrival had come too late for that and a wave of heat engulfed us as we opened the door. The air was thick with flour as army rations of pasta were being kneaded, flattened and cut into squares. Trickles of sweat ran down the maids' brows and Cook looked as if she had fallen asleep in the noonday sun.

'Where in the name of Christendom have you been, Clara? Losing your father doesn't give you permission to come and go as you please. And Vanni, if you want to keep out of the way of the Contessa,' Cook gave him a knowing look, 'you'll have to help out, gold trim or not. Take Clara to the orto and pick all the green beans you can find.'

Despite the heat, I started shivering. Out there was Blackbeard. 'Please don't ask me to do that.'

'It's better than staying in this heat.' Vanni held out a basket.

'The man who killed Babbo ...' I wrung my apron. ' ... he's after me too.'

The maids stopped and looked at me and, for a few moments, Cook said nothing, then shook her head. 'As if I haven't got enough on my plate without you being so particular, but I suppose you can grind some spices. Fine powder, mind.'

'I'll pick the beans,' Mamma volunteered.

'Anything to get Francesco to take another poke,' Susanna said in a low voice that only Cook failed to hear.

'Go on, then.' Cook wiped her brow on her sleeve.

Mamma looked smug as she took the basket.

I smashed the peppercorns with the pestle.

'Cook,' Vanni hesitated. 'I was wondering if you might make panettone to celebrate the Conte's return?'

'Baking! In this heat! They'll have pecorino and honey to clear their palates and be grateful. Now get out of this kitchen, Vanni Salimbeni. I'll not be responsible for mucking up that doublet of yours.'

'See you later, Vanni,' I whispered, as he slipped out of the kitchen. Thanks to his presence, I'd got away with a mild reprimand.

'They're here! Everyone down to the stables!' Well after he'd returned from the orto with Mamma, Francesco stuck his head around the kitchen door. The long table in the centre was overloaded with food. Huge pots waited to boil the pasta. With the celebratory meal to serve that night, the day was far from over.

'Downstairs at once.' Cook wiped her face and hurried us down the wooden staircase.

'Come on, tortoise, or you'll get us into trouble.' Mamma grabbed my elbow, though she had time to pull out strands of her shorn hair to frame her face. 'And don't you dare make a fuss when Francesco comes again. He's always thought the world of me, and now Guido's gone, he can have me for his own.'

I pulled away and stamped down to the stables.

There, mules were being rubbed down after toiling, laden, up the steep hill to the city. The nobles' mounts were covered in blankets of Salimbeni red and gold. Vanni's head rested against the neck of his father's horse, his eyes closed while he stroked its nose, while the grey-haired noble instructed the factotum on where to store each item. Pride of place would go to the bales of Welsh wool, now woven by Belgian weavers and eagerly awaited by the city's rich dyers. But before we set to work on this task, we were lined up to greet the

Conte. Though I tried to stand as far away from Mamma as possible, Cook moved me next to my mother. When he reached us, he paused.

'My deepest sympathy,' he said, taking Mamma's hand in his. 'Guido was everyone's favourite, and his death is a tragedy.'

I felt a prickling in my eyes, and only stopped myself from crying by staring at the mole on his temple. He was a kind man, as long as Tolomei weren't involved.

'And Clara,' he put his ruby-ringed hand on my shoulder, 'you may have lost a father, but the Salimbeni will always be your family. You'll have more fathers than you could ever want!'

'Thank you, sir,' I managed to say, though my insides were churning. With such kindness from the Conte, why did Mamma need Francesco?

When the ceremonial greetings had ended, I hovered, watching everyone rush round with armfuls of goods, taking them to different parts of the cellar.

'Look,' said Vanni, showing me a sweet-smelling sack, 'raisins from Malaga. Now we can have our panettone!' His cheerfulness roused me into action, and I picked out one of the smaller parcels, some salted sardines from Marseilles.

'What you got there, Clara?' Francesco said as we made our way to the same cantina. 'Smells worse than my dried cod, and whiffy as a whore's arse.'

And I laughed, despite myself, remembering the things he and Babbo were always saying.

'Talking about Maria?' Susanna swayed her hips as she let a box of Toledo blades slip out of her hand. 'Dio

50

mio, what am I supposed to do now?' She made eyes at Francesco.

'I'll pick them up for you.' I ran forward.

'Don't worry, pet, me and Francesco will do this,' said Susanna.

'Who'd be so popular, eh?' Francesco winked.

The next time I passed, struggling with a light but bulky piece of Milanese armour, they were kneeling, heads together and laughing, blades still splayed on the floor. If only Mamma could see Francesco for the false friend he was.

When all was safely stored, and the Conte wanted a rest before dinner, I climbed up to the roof. Even when the tiles were too hot to walk on, this was our favourite place of escape. Our cool spot was in the shadow of the tower, under the wooden seat that ran around the battlements. Vanni was already there. Lying on his stomach and raised on his elbows, he was playing cat's cradle with spun wool stolen from the factotum's stocks.

I wriggled under the bench to face him. 'Honestly, Vanni, I could kill her. First she kicks me out of bed because I'm not Babbo, then she turns me out of our room to sleep with Francesco. Now she wants him to marry her. If only Babbo were still here.' I buried my head in my arms to cover my tears.

'She can't marry him, not so soon.' Vanni prodded me to take the cat's cradle. 'My father will forbid it – unless you want me to put in a word...'

I shook my head as I hooked my fingers round the wool. 'She follows him like a kitten looking for its mother's milk.'

'You could do a lot worse than Francesco for a step-father – in time, I mean. He's almost as popular as your father, more so with the women.' Vanni intertwined his fingers in the wool and took it back.

'Huh! This morning he went with Mamma to the orto, yet this afternoon he was canoodling with Susanna.'

'Look on the bright side. Your mother will have changed her mind by next week. You know those spiders you expect to run along the ground but they make a wild jump instead.'

'I wish she'd jump back to her home in the hills so I never had to see her again.' I scrunched up the wool and threw it at him.

'Don't say that, because you'd have to go with her.' He unravelled the strands. 'Anyway, the Conte will never send you away. He owes it to Guido.'

'Give me the wool. My turn to start.' Talking to Vanni may not have solved anything but it made me feel better. We had only managed a couple more rounds when we heard familiar voices on the stairs.

'Tuck your feet in,' Vanni whispered, as Mamma and Francesco came onto the roof. We rolled onto our sides and flattened ourselves against the wall.

'Uffa, it's hot up here. Let's sit in the shade.' Francesco chose the spot above us on the bench. 'We should have gone down to the orto again.'

'I didn't ask you up here for that.' Mamma sat next to him.

'No?' He used that oily voice again.

We heard the light popping of lips on flesh, and Vanni raised his eyes to the heavens.

'You've always liked me, Francesco,' Mamma purred, 'even when you came for me in Monticiano. If I hadn't promised myself to Guido, I'd have gone with you then. Guido was fun, but you were more exciting.'

I stuffed my fist in my mouth, afraid I might scream.

'I'm a danger to the ladies for sure,' Francesco laughed.

'Now Guido's dead, I'm yours, Francesco.' There was a pause. 'We'll marry as soon as the Conte will allow.'

'Me, marry? That's a laugh. Climb on my lap, you sexy strumpet.'

I pressed against the wall to make sure they didn't find me with their feet.

'Say you'll marry me. You know you want me.' Mamma caressed his ankle with her foot.

Francesco found his sensible voice again. 'Slow down, Maria. What need have I of a wife when women throw themselves at me? Even Cook lets me get away with murder – I don't mean in that way, well not recently.'

'But you've always said I'm the most beautiful woman in the palazzo. You told me again in the Campo last week. Now you can have me for your own.'

'Maria, I can't love you like Guido. He worshipped you, and he was blind to – what shall we call them? – your inconsistencies.'

'Inconsistencies? What rubbish. You'll marry me,

Francesco, and we'll be the most admired couple in the palazzo, just like Guido and I were.'

I needed air but didn't dare move.

'Don't ask this of me, Maria. We'll have some laughs, but I'll not pledge myself to one woman, even one as handsome as you.'

'You toad, lying to me all these years.' Mamma stood up and paced in front of us. If she paid attention to anything but her own thoughts, she'd have seen us.

'Not lying, being playful. Like this.' His voice softened and he tried to pull Mamma to him.

'They hate me. Without Guido, my life will be a misery. Please, Francesco, I need someone to look after me.'

'That's not going to be me.'

For a moment, nobody moved. Vanni and I held our breath.

'Then I'll go to the Tolomei. That Blackbeard will marry me. And while I'm at it, I'll ask him to finish the job and kill you too.'

I went cold, unable to believe what she'd said.

'Don't say that, even in jest,' Francesco jumped up, 'or you'll wish you'd never seen Siena and the Salimbeni.'

'Then marry me! You owe it to Guido.'

'The devil take you, Maria. Seems to me I've already done too much for Guido.' Francesco stormed across the roof and disappeared down the stairs.

Mamma howled like a dog baying at the moon. She ran around the terrace, bouncing from wall to wall. When I poked my head out, she was staring towards the white mooned flag of the Tolomei, fluttering down the street.

'I'd better make sure she's all right,' Vanni whispered. 'In this mood, she might throw herself over the side.'

'I wish she would.' I said, shocked she could contemplate marrying Babbo's murderer, even if only to persuade Francesco.

Vanni edged himself out from under the seat, but Mamma had already disappeared down the stairs. I climbed out of our hiding place and we sat side by side on the bench. He was as white as the Contessa's linen. 'If she's going to the Tolomei, I have to tell the Conte. Do you think she's being serious?'

'She's mad, but not that mad, and as much a Salimbeni as I am.'

'Even so, we should keep an eye on her. You'll have to go with her, whenever she goes out.' Vanni's eyebrows met in the middle as they tended to do when he concentrated.

'But he'll kill me too!'

'I doubt even a Tolomei would stoop that low. And you're the only one she'll trust to go with her, and Domenico. Tell Cook you're worried about losing her.' Vanni sounded like his father when he issued instructions, and I knew I'd have to follow them.

Shutters squeaking on their hinges signalled the end of siesta.

'Time for my lesson with the factotum. Come and keep me company or all his figures will dance before my eyes.' Vanni yawned. The Conte had decided it was time for him to learn about the family business.

I, too, found the man who ran the business boring. But today, discovering the secrets of a successful trading house might keep at bay my fears.

Chapter 5

Through the night, I prayed Mamma would come to her senses. But next morning, she insisted on going to the orto.

'Most days I can't get you to do anything, Maria, and now you're my most willing helper. I don't know what's got into you.' Cook looked up from separating fava beans from their skins.

'Or who!' Teresa said.

'Francesco won't take her.' Susanna smoothed her hands over her full hips. 'He's better things to occupy him.'

I took a deep breath. Though I was terrified of meeting Blackbeard again, I said the words I'd rehearsed all night. 'I'd like to go too. I don't want anything to happen to her.'

'Changing your mind from one day to the next, you're getting too much like her, my girl!' Cook gave me a light clip on the ear. 'Go on, both of you, and be quick about it. Twenty zucchini, Maria, and with the flowers on. Take Domenico to keep you out of harm's way.'

Mamma grabbed the basket, and ran down to the entrance hall, where Domenico was asleep in his favourite chair. 'Cook's orders. Escort me to the orto!'

'We can't be long.' Domenico groaned as he got to his feet. 'The Contessa needs me soon.'

Domenico would be no match for Blackbeard, nor for Mamma when she had that harsh glint in her eyes, but losing my hand in his gave me comfort.

As soon as we were within sight of the orto gate, Mamma stopped. 'You two, save your legs and rest in the shade. I'll be back before you know it.'

Domenico wiped the sweat from his brow. 'I don't know. After what they did to poor Guido, there would be hell to pay if anything happened.'

'You can keep an eye on me from here.' Mamma gave him a sultry smile. 'I'll be back in no time.'

Checking the road to make sure there were no Tolomei, I took her free hand, tethering her to me. 'I'll run back for help if we need it.'

'If you're sure,' Domenico made for a doorway and lowered his frame onto the step. He pulled his hat over his eyes to shield them from the sun. Before we reached the orto, he'd be asleep.

'Twenty zucchini and be quick about it. Twenty zucchini and be quick about it.' Mamma repeated to herself. 'Well, quicker than you think, you old crock.' She cut the largest tubes from the sprawling plants, and I laid them side by side in the basket, all the time keeping my ears open for Tolomei intruders.

'Twenty she wanted and twenty she'll get.' Mamma said, as if in a trance.

Mission nearly accomplished, I carried the basket uphill, smiling to see Domenico asleep ahead of us.

Then as fast as a scorpion shaken out of a shoe, Mamma dodged down the back alley that led to Palazzo Tolomei.

'Come back,' I shouted, torn between protecting her and fear of Blackbeard. Yet to let her go on her own, would be failing Vanni. I followed at a distance and hid round a corner, close enough to catch their words. A small mercy – none of the Tolomei I'd seen on the day of the festa were on duty. Giving the lack of insults, they didn't recognise her as a Salimbeni either.

'Don't gawp!' Mamma tossed her head back. 'Where's that man with the black beard? I need to speak to him.'

'He's not here, especially if one of his whores is looking for him!' The man who spoke had an irritating high-pitched giggle.

'Tell him Maria needs to talk, Guido's Maria. It'll be in his interest.'

'Guido's Maria, eh? We know all about you! Come back this evening. He'll be here.'

I followed her up the hill. How could she think of speaking to the man who'd murdered Babbo?

'Your charges have returned safely.' Mamma nudged Domenico with her foot. If only he'd been with us, she wouldn't have dared speak to them.

'You sound cheerful.' Domenico held on to his stick as we each took an end and pulled him to his feet.

'You can't expect me to mourn Guido forever.'

Days after Babbo's death was hardly forever!

'And be ready to take me down to the orto later. I'll wager a florin I don't have, I'll have to make another trip.'

Not if I could stop her.

As we approached Palazzo Salimbeni, Francesco was barring the door to a man trying to gain entrance. 'Don't let him in,' I shouted. After my outing with Mamma, I feared any outsider.

Mamma pushed past and headed straight for the kitchen.

I would have followed her, but once I shaded my eyes, I saw this was no Blackbeard. His hair was fair – yellow ochre with a tinge of umber. 'Ambrogio!'

'How pleased I am to see you, little artist. A dreadful thing about your father. I lost mine at about your age, too.'

My eyes welled up. I'd been so preoccupied with Mamma's capers, I'd forgotten my own loss.

Ambrogio put his arm around my shoulder. 'I know. My brother tried to fill the gap, but nobody can.'

I longed to tell him about Mamma and the Tolomei, but not in front of Francesco.

'Get them to let me in, can't you?' he whispered, then louder, 'you heard the Contessa say she'd like to sponsor a Lorenzetti?'

So that was the real reason for his visit. However, he had let me paint in Duccio's studio. 'She did say that, when he escorted her from the Duomo to Palazzo d'Elci.'

'Very well, wait in the hall, and you tell her she has a visitor, Clara.' Francesco shoved Ambrogio through the door with more force than courtesy.

I climbed the stairs two at a time and the Contessa agreed to give an audience to the man who had looked after her at the festa. I failed to mention the wrong brother was waiting downstairs.

'She'll see you!' I told Ambrogio, pleased to have accomplished my mission.

'Think she'll sponsor me?' he said, as we climbed the stairs. 'A commission from the Salimbeni would be my making.'

'You'd better have a good reason for not being Pietro, because that's who she's expecting.'

'Wish me luck.' He removed his cap then ran his fingers through that fair hair.

I announced his arrival and showed him in. Curious to learn what happened, I knelt down, and put my ear to the door.

'Caught you!' Vanni made me jump.

'It's Ambrogio Lorenzetti, the artist Mamma and I spent the festa with. Thinks the Contessa would like to give him a commission.'

'Then it'll have to be wearable...' Vanni slid his back down the wall.

'A dress made of tapestry!' I slid down beside him.

'A folded triptych made into a hat!' Vanni laughed, then turned serious. 'I saw you go out with your mother and came to find out what happened.'

How much should I tell him? Only the Conte had the power to stop Mamma doing something silly.

'All was well until she made a detour to Palazzo Tolomei. Blackbeard wasn't there, but she's going to meet him later.'

'That's serious.' Vanni shook his head.

'If only I could stop her but she'll not listen to me.'

Vanni's eyebrows met in the middle again. 'I'm sorry Clara, I'll have to speak to the Conte. Let's hope she's thought better of it by tonight.'

The Contessa's door opened and Ambrogio reappeared face as dark as a Tolomei's.

I led him down the stairs. 'What did she say?' I said by way of comfort.

'That I was a rogue and a charlatan, and the Salimbeni hadn't got rich by giving money to people like me.' He stormed ahead and out into the street.

And even though the Contessa was right, I felt sorry for him, for I, too, would love to spend more time painting.

The factotum's office bordered the main thoroughfare. The wide shutter that looked out on the street was open, though he was closed for business until the evening. A door at the back led to the cellars. Around the room, samples of goods waited to tempt customers into buying the spoils from the Conte's recent travels. Vanni and I sat on the customer side of a large oak desk piled with accounts books, an abacus and worn brass scales. I was so concerned about Mamma, I was in no mood for study, but Vanni hated these lessons so much, he only went if I did too.

Unlike our other tutors, the factotum was patient

and courteous, a well-rehearsed manner he used to convince a stream of loyal customers he had their interests at heart. 'You can start by telling me the first rule of trading.'

Vanni was even more distracted than I was, so I spoke first. 'Try and sell it for double what you paid?'

'That goes without saying. I meant something about the goods.' His pale eyes darted round the shop. 'Especially when they're so recently arrived.'

It was Vanni's turn now, but he was studying one of the newly arrived daggers. I kicked his foot, but he hadn't heard the question.

The factotum sighed. 'If you want to sell that at a good price, create a story around it – say, that one like it was used to kill somebody well known. Nothing like a bit of scandal to get tongues wagging.' One of those pale eyes winked, but mine filled with tears, and I ran out of the shop.

I sat on the ledge that ran along the front of the palazzo until my sobbing eased. Then I pulled out my leather pouch and tipped out the stones. I no longer threw them wildly, as I'd done just after Babbo's death. By casting them within easy reach I could now confidently scoop up all ten.

'The factotum says sorry. He didn't intend to refer to Guido. He's let us off the rest of the lesson.' Vanni sat a few feet away and stretched out his hand. 'Give me a go.'

'Don't lose them.' I dropped them into his palm. 'They're all I've left of Guido.'

He hesitated.

'No, go on.' If I couldn't trust Vanni, who could I trust? But he wasn't concentrating, and despite his larger hands, he never reached ten. After a couple of goes, he handed them back.

The air was hot and sultry. We kicked our heels against the stone, listening to thunder rolling around the hills beyond the city. The clouds were heavy, but not dark enough to give us a healing downpour. Vanni said, 'just the weather for a fight.'

More thunder growled in the distance but, coming closer, was a ruckus in the street.

'Inside!' Vanni grabbed my hand and pulled me up the steps.

At the doorway, I turned to see Mamma being dragged by Teresa and Susanna, Domenico, already the colour of beetroot, a few yards behind.

'What are you doing? Let her go!' I tried in vain to free her from the maids' grip. How had she managed to slip away?

Teresa's hand whipped across Mamma's face. 'You, snake, talking to the Tolomei! Hold her firm, Susanna, while I fetch the Contessa.'

'No. This needs the Conte,' Vanni said. 'It's far more than a domestic matter.'

How could he? In Salimbeni terms, involving his father suggested high treason. Susanna yanked off Mamma's headscarf and tied her hands with it. Yet despite being bound, Mamma held her head high.

The Conte descended the stairs and sat on the chair. Francesco led Mamma to face him.

'Domenico, you accompanied them. Tell me what

happened,' the Conte demanded.

'We were on our way to the orto and she tricked me into resting half way down the hill. Now there's all this trouble and it's my fault.' Domenico wrung his cap in his hands.

'I'll deal with you later. For now, tell me if you saw her speaking to this Tolomei they call Blackbeard?'

'No, sir. I only know she came back with her basket full.' Domenico's voice quivered and he wiped the sweat off his brow with his sleeve.

The Conte turned to his son. 'Vanni, you have some evidence, I believe.'

Judas! My so-called best friend avoided my gaze.

'Clara and I were playing on the roof. We were hiding under the bench when Maria came up with Francesco. She told him that if he didn't marry her she was going to the Tolomei and get Blackbeard to kill him.'

What Vanni said was true, but Mamma said lots she didn't mean.

'He's making it up.' Mamma shouted. 'Francesco and I were alone.'

'I was there too,' I shouted.

'And then this afternoon,' Teresa stepped forward to claim her role as major witness, 'she sneaked off again. But me and Susanna followed her and found her doing a deal with that Blackbeard – that if he married her, she'd help him take down the Salimbeni.'

'God's teeth, Maria,' Francesco shouted. 'How could you even speak to a Tolomei after they killed Guido?'

64

The small crowd of servants muttered variations on treacherous bitch.

'She's a wicked woman, sir, and deserves the worst of punishments.' Susanna was enjoying this, but if Mamma was punished, what would happen to me?

'What have you to say for yourself, Maria?' the Conte asked.

I willed her to get down on her knees and beg forgiveness, but her only response was to land a gobbet of spittle on the Conte's jacket.

'Very well.' The Conte prepared to pass judgement. 'Since your marriage to Guido, we have provided you with a home, even allowed you to live in one of our guest rooms. Yet you repay us by conspiring with our greatest enemy. Such perfidy should be punished by death.'

'No!' I went cold.

The Conte nodded. 'However, such a penalty would fall too heavily on your daughter who has already lost her father. Instead, you will receive six lashes.'

I breathed a sigh of relief. It was a harsh punishment, but a fair one. Maybe now she'd start seeing sense.

The Conte continued. 'For Clara's sake, I wish you were a good servant, Maria. But you are a lazy troublemaker, and your betrayal has squandered your right to a home here. We will escort you and your daughter to your carpenter father at tomorrow's market and he can take you back to your home in the country. After that, you have no further claims on the Salimbeni. Francesco, take her away.'

Me too? I ran after the Conte and dropped to my knees, 'Please sir, I beg you to let me stay.'

'I'm sorry, Clara. You have already lost your father. I cannot separate you from your mother, too.' The Conte put an arm round Vanni, who wouldn't even look at me, and steered him up the stairs. I was used to Mamma letting me down, but never Vanni.

'But I've done nothing,' I shouted after them.

'Nobody who talks to Blackbeard after he's killed her father is innocent,' Teresa snarled.

I knew it was useless to point out that, even though he'd taunted me, I'd never answered back. Instead I clutched the stones in my pocket and dragged my feet up the stairs, back to what I could call for one last night – our room.

Chapter 6

How could he? I threw myself onto the bed, furious with Vanni for his blind allegiance to the Conte, and with Mamma for betraying the Salimbeni. But most of all I was livid with Babbo. If he were still here, none of this would be happening.

I wiped my eyes, then looked around the room. Fingering the wood on the chest, I thought about the grandfather who'd made it. By his handiwork, he was careful. But caring? I could only hope. I lifted the lid and breathed in the smell of cinnamon as I pulled out my clothes: two linen working dresses and the one I'd worn to the festa. I hugged the pink to me, wondering if I'd ever wear it again. Hearing someone at the door, I stuffed everything back.

'In, hussy.' Francesco pushed Mamma before him, a rare harshness in his voice.

I gasped at the stranger she'd become. Her eyes were puffed by tears, snot dangled from her nose and her hair was tangled with straw. Her dress had been ripped to bare her back, which was covered in six red welts. Though the room was warm, her teeth chattered and her body shook. She coiled into a corner, a viper waiting to strike. I shivered, too, afraid of what she'd do next.

'I'll send one of the girls to help.' Francesco pinched my cheek, but I pulled away. 'And pack up your things. You know what the Contessa's like.'

Packing? With Mamma like this?

If she were a kitten, I'd coax her out of the corner with milk.

'Your dress is ruined. Let me get you out of it.'

She crept out of the corner, more panther than domestic cat. Now everyone was her enemy, even me. But I helped her out of her blood-soaked dress, horrified at the criss-cross bands of swollen flesh on her back. Francesco, of all people. Some of the welts oozed blood and needed to be cleaned. I poured the last of our water into the washbowl and dipped in the wool flannel.

67

Bathing the livid skin as gently as I could, I wished she would complain, but she'd gone beyond being Babbo's wife, or Francesco's favourite. Hard though it was seeing her wince at every touch, I found some comfort in this small service. She was still my mother.

The closeness of the moment was broken when Teresa marched in. Behind her Susanna carried a small bowl of vinegar.

'Cook sent us to clean her up.' Teresa sat on the bed and dabbed at the cuts with the sharp smelling liquid. 'See how you like this, bitch.'

Mamma winced and pushed at Teresa, who laughed. 'Think I care about hurting someone whose chosen enemy colours?'

'The Contessa's told us to take all your clothes.' Susanna made for the chest.

'They're ours.' I threw myself on top of the lid to stop her. I should have followed Francesco's advice and already packed them.

'Everything belongs to the Salimbeni – even you until tomorrow. Move away.' Susanna yanked my arm and I fell off. She picked out Mamma's yellow dress. 'This'll suit me nicely. Homespun is all she's good for now.'

Mamma groaned from the depths of her being as the oatmeal-coloured gown landed on the bed. Then Susanna pulled out my festa dress.

'That's mine.'

'Let her keep it,' Teresa softened. 'It's too small for anyone else. And her working clothes. She'll need them in the country.'

'And not much else.' Susanna smirked, her arms full of the beautiful gowns Mamma had worn over the years.

Teresa checked through my things on the corner of the bed, quite a pile compared to Mamma's single dress; the one she'd be wearing. 'Pack them into a bundle and hide it under the bed, just in case someone comes to check we've done our job.' They left the room discussing which garments they'd ask for; gowns only Mamma had the poise to carry off.

While Mamma lay dozing, I hugged my pink dress. I'd never again own anything so grand. Then I smoothed my hand over the wall, wishing I could take with me every stone. The room had been my life.

'Take my woollen cloak behind the door. They didn't see that.' Mamma's voice was as flat as a well-used mattress. 'You'll need it when it gets cold in the mountains. What's left in the chest?'

'A few old rags.' And some broken bits of Cook's cinnamon. I'd miss her too.

Mamma sighed and closed her eyes.

I tied my belongings into a bundle and put them by the door. No vestige of the red and gold that had been so much a part of our lives. I'd kept out the pink dress, for whatever anyone said, I was going to wear it on my last day.

'Into every corner with that broom this morning, Clara.' Cook wiped her forehead, then her eyes, with her sleeve. 'Now the Conte's back, we must be early to market to get the best vegetables. Teresa, Susanna,

69

fetch the baskets. I'll see you in the entrance hall.'

The maids disappeared as fast as cockroaches discovered by candlelight.

'Look at you, so pretty in that dress.' Cook drew me to her in a squashy hug. 'I'm going to miss you, petal.'

'I'll miss you, too.' She smelt of the sauce just prepared, something else I wished I could take with me.

'Now, where's that slate?' She wiped her eyes. 'I told them I needed you to read your list of squiggles. Francesco will bring your mother down later.'

'I won't be coming back?' I took a last look around the kitchen. 'But I haven't said goodbye to Vanni.' Even if he had betrayed me, I needed to say goodbye.

'The Conte will be keeping him out of your way, thinks you're a bad influence. Come on, little lamb. Hold the slate for me.' Cook rested her hand on my shoulder and edged me out of the kitchen.

But Vanni was outside the kitchen door, hiding in the corner. 'Just a moment, please, Cook.'

'You'll get me into trouble, Vanni Salimbeni.' Cook put on her stern face. 'Don't keep her any longer than it takes my poor legs to get to the front door. I'll not lose bargains at market because of you.' She started puffing her way down the stairs.

'I'm so sorry, Clara. I never dreamt he'd make you leave too.'

'Why did you tell him she wanted the Tolomei to kill Francesco? That's what made the Conte expel us.'

'I had to, for what if she persuaded the devils to do it?' Vanni sounded like his father. He even looked taller.

'Now I'll never see you again.' I couldn't stop

myself crying. First Babbo, now everyone I loved was being taken away.

'Oh, but you will. As soon as I'm allowed to travel with the Conte, we'll come and see you in Monticiano.'

If only that were true.

'Take this.' He pulled the ring off his finger and held it out to me. No mistaking the Salimbeni insignia: three small rubies cut into diamond shapes, set in a band of gold. 'Don't show it to anyone, especially not your mother.'

'But you can't, it's your family ring! The Conte will have us both whipped.'

'If they find it, which they won't, I'll take the blame.' Vanni pressed it in my hand. 'I want you to have something to remember us by. And it will guarantee you entry into Siena when you come back; so when you need the Salimbeni's help the most, I'll be there!' He looked as though he had come up with a great trick.

'I don't know what to say.' My voice was thick with sadness.

'Wrap it in this.' Vanni pulled out from his jerkin, a fine piece of red and gold cloth. With it I wrapped the ring, put it with my stones and buried the pouch deep in my bodice.

'Let's race down to Cook,' Vanni smiled. For one last time, we stood side by side at the top of the stairs and Vanni said, 'go'. But when I panted into the entrance hall, I was on my own.

'Here she is.' Cook squeezed my shoulder. I'd miss that smell of the day's cooking.

71

Teresa and Susanna linked arms, swinging baskets by their sides. I turned back for one last glimpse of the palazzo and we set off. At the bottom of the hill, we joined the crowd pouring into the Campo, ants going after spilt sugar.

The myriad colours on the stalls below reminded me of what I'd be missing. Green zucchini with their golden flowers were piled next to pink and white borlotti pods. Sacks of dried lentils offered winter stocks of brown, olive and orange-coloured beans. Cages of red cocks-combed birds with bronze plumage were on sale next to pens of squealing rose piglets. Dairymen showed off their creamy pecorino, their carts stacked high with cheese drums cased in lemon, ochre or deep green vine leaves. Between the stalls, customers pushed and shoved to gain vendors' attention, arms waving to argue a good price. In the far corner, in the dry goods section where my grandfather would be, men waved sheets of woven cloth, pelts of sheepskin and skeins of spun wool at passing customers. They hammered straps on sandals, sawed wood to order and held fiery rods in braziers ready to solder repairs. The sights, the smell, the hubbub – I'd miss them all.

'Oh look, cannellini, first of the season. Let's get some before they all go.' Cook led us down the steps, into the thick of the crowd. I read from the slate the items Cook needed and put to the back of my mind this was my last market. As the morning wore on, the crowd increased, and we had to push through it to buy the last item on the list.

'That man had better not buy all the eggs,' Cook said. 'He could feed two palazzi with the number he's got there.'

Fair hair. The only artist I could call a friend.

'Put it on Duccio's account. He'll pay you later.' He lifted the basket brim full of eggs.

The stallholder shook his head. 'Tell that old skinflint, I'd like the reckoning in this world, not the next.'

'Don't worry. I've left some for you.' He nodded at Cook and walked off.

'Ambrogio!' I called after him.

He shaded his eyes with his spare hand, then, when he recognised me, beckoned me to a bench outside one of the Campo's shops. I had nothing to lose, and Cook could easily see where I was.

'I'm sorry for being so rude after seeing the Contessa.' Ambrogio placed his basket on the ground with care. 'I was convinced my future would be secured if I could present my case to her.'

I kicked at the loose stones. 'Don't worry, worse has happened since. The Salimbeni have thrown us out.'

'They can't. Your father's just been murdered!'

Then Ambrogio's eyes filled with tears. 'Ever since my father died, I've had to rely on whatever scraps Pietro throws me. But to lose the Salimbeni, that's much worse. What'll you do? Simone Martini's asked me to help him paint another Maestà for the Duomo. If you were a boy, I'd recommend you take my place mixing Duccio's paints.'

'Thanks, but I couldn't anyway. Once Cook's

finished shopping, I'm being sent to Monticiano, wherever that is.'

'Is this something to do with that mother of yours?'

The story of Mamma throwing herself at Blackbeard, spilled out of me like boiling water from an overfilled pot.

'Then I thank my stars she rebuffed me the day of the festa, or I dare say I'd be involved in this. She's a handful, isn't she?'

He took a piece of charcoal from his pocket and an egg from the basket. With a few deft strokes, he drew a face front and back. 'This is your sad face now, and this is the happy one you'll have once you've settled in your new home.'

I turned the egg in my hands. 'I'll remember it when I'm missing Siena.' I handed back the egg. It deserved to be used for mixing pigments not cheering me.

'Keep it, so you remember to smile. You don't want to become bitter like me.' Ambrogio stood up and lifted his basket. 'Tell you what, if I ever make some money, I'll come and see you in Monticiano.'

I so wanted to believe him, for I knew that in reality, like Vanni, he'd never come. The egg's surface was as smooth as Babbo's stones and I placed it in my purse alongside Vanni's ring.

'Clara!' Cook called me over. 'Francesco's here with your mother. Time to go. No more dilly-dallying.' Cook patted my shoulder and left. A soft-boiled egg, hard on the outside, runny in the middle.

'Where's your father's stall?' Francesco asked.

Mamma shrugged. 'Haven't seen him all the time

74

I've been in Siena.' She swung my bundle of clothes with one arm, while Francesco held the other in a tight grip.

'For your sake, I hope he's here, or you'll be on the street tonight. You're nothing to the Salimbeni now.' Francesco steered us through the sickly-sweet smelling meat stalls to the carpentry and ironmongery beyond. 'Is that him?'

Sitting among a collection of wooden furniture at the far end of the market, the man had hair as curly as Mamma's, though his was grey. The chest for sale was almost identical to the one at the end of our bed – what had been our bed.

'Greetings, Niccolò. We met at Guido and Maria's wedding.' Francesco held Mamma still with her arm behind her back. 'And this is your granddaughter, Clara.'

'You've ignored me for ten years. What do you want with me now?' Niccolò scowled at Mamma but stood in the presence of a Salimbeni uniform.

'I'm afraid Guido was killed in a fight, and for reasons Maria will explain, the Salimbeni have thrown them out. It's you or the street for them. These are their things.' Francesco threw my bundle on the cart.

'You can't get rid of them like that.' Niccolò shouted but Francesco had already disappeared.

'What's this about?' he growled to Mamma, so unlike the greeting I'd have been sure of from my Babbo.

I crept into the shade, to study him without being seen. Was he as fierce as he looked?

'The ungrateful pigs.' Mamma sat on a stool for sale.

'Because Guido's dead? That's impossible. When you married, they took you on as property.' The lines on Niccolò's forehead deepened with his frown.

If Mamma wasn't going to tell him what had happened, I'd do so myself. On second thoughts, I'd keep my mouth shut in case he left us to survive on the streets. Yesterday, the idea was unthinkable. Today I feared it.

'The vengeful scum! I hope I never see them again.' Mamma spat out her venom.

'They must have given you money. Nothing to them, but for us, two extra to feed won't be easy.'

A group of Tolomei approached the nearby water pump. One was Blackbeard and I shuddered. Mamma jumped up. 'Maybe you won't have to.'

No way would I follow her. Hiding behind the cart, I watched her run into the arms of that evil man. He pulled her to him.

I bit my fingers in disgust.

Under the guise of whispering something, Blackbeard took a not-so-gentle bite of her ear. They exchanged a few words and she returned, smiling.

'Why are you talking to him, Mamma? He's a snake.'

'Nonsense. Come with me, Clara.'

'Never! They killed Babbo!'

'You stupid girl, we've crossed sides. We're Tolomei now.' Her eyes gleamed with triumph. 'Those maids think they've punished me but wait till they see the dresses I'll have now.'

'I'd rather die than live with them.'

'Please yourself.' Mamma paused only a moment, then ran to her new family with a lightness of step that had eluded her for days.

'You can't,' I shouted after her. But she didn't even turn, and I watched her walk off on Blackbeard's arm.

'Porca Madonna!' Niccolò sunk his head in his hands. 'Who'll look after you now?'

I was asking myself the same question. Yet a stampede of horses wouldn't persuade me to go with Mamma.

He stared at me for what seemed ages, then gave the grandfather of all sighs. 'Family is family. You're coming to Monticiano. Don't you have anything else to wear? With you dressed like that, we're asking to be robbed.'

'Only my working clothes.'

'Put them on.' Niccolò bit into a pumpkin seed and spat out the husk.

'But where do I change? They won't let me back into the palazzo.'

'Nobody will see you under the cart.' He indicated behind us with a slight nod. 'A bit of dirt won't hurt.'

I crawled between the wheels and found a spot clear of horse dung. Even so it smelt like a latrine.

'That's better,' Niccolò said when I came out. 'Want some of these?' I felt his rough hands as I took a fistful of seeds, a poor lunch compared to whatever the Salimbeni would be eating.

Noon approached, and I was melting. By way of

distraction, I studied the customers. First they walked past pretending to be uninterested. Then they came back and fingered an item, but with a face full of disdain. 'Chestnut,' Niccolò would grunt, 'top quality.' If they still hovered, he would tell them of the hours involved in the making. He could do with one or two of the factotum's stories if he wanted to sell more. It was the quality of his workmanship, alone, which gave him his few sales.

'How much longer?' I should be having my afternoon's lesson with Vanni.

When the sun dropped in the sky Niccolò began packing up. 'Don't look so scared. It's Monticiano, not the moon, we're going to.' It might as well have been the moon. In fact, the moon would have been preferable. I'd seen the moon.

Just when nothing could be worse, I saw Ambrogio's fair hair coming towards our stall. I waved at the man I now thought was a friend, but he passed without a glance. Without my pink dress I'd become invisible.

While Niccolò harnessed the horse to the cart, I looked around. Would I ever again see the Campo, the Duomo, the towers of the nobles' palazzi? Beyond the walls were vegetable plots, like the Salimbeni's, which gave way to purple hills, devoid of any sign of life.

'Jump up!' he said, more resigned than angry. 'We've a long journey ahead.'

It took an age to leave the confines of the city. Just outside the gate, we joined other traders making the journey south. Niccolò hunched over the reins and stared at the road. I tried to cheer myself up with the funny face of the egg but what was there to be happy about? Twisting round I saw the towers grow smaller until we turned a final corner. The egg rolled out of my hand and smashed - bright yellow and shiny on the road. Then that, too, disappeared.

Part Two

Brown

Monticiano, 1320

Chapter 7

ate snow on the hill beyond the town had melted, though the trees were still bare. Most people of Monticiano could name them, but even after nine years of country living, I was unable to tell my oak from my acacia. Yet I sensed the sap rising – the winter's bitter wind had lost its edge – and I was furious with myself for allowing another year to pass in this borgo of boredom. Wearing my favourite frown, I turned the mattresses, swept the kitchen and got my cousins up and dressed. Then I grabbed the bucket to fetch water, my daily escape from Aunt Orsola's critical eye.

She'd been so welcoming when I arrived, mourning my father and the city I'd lost. With Stefano only two, and Laura born six months later, she'd been glad of my help and I threw myself into looking after the little ones. But everything changed when I grew into womanhood. Orsola saw in my emerging looks, the potential to advance her position in society. Her mission became – my Uncle Bruno's too – to marry me into one of Monticiano's better families. However mine was to find a way of returning to the city of colours and home of art embedded in my soul.

Standing at the top of the steps that led from their house to the piazza, I took a deep breath. I'd wriggled out of marrying sons of butcher, baker and blacksmith and, at nineteen, my time was running out. But if Mamma could find a husband at Siena's monthly market, surely I could too. Except my aunt and uncle refused to let me go. Only connections in Monticiano were useful to them.

To my right, widows chatted on their way into church but I turned left towards the town hall. Pushing through groups of women carrying empty baskets to the shops, I walked down Via di Mezzo – Half Street, the smell of food coming through the part-open shutters above. At the crossroad of Incrociata, I turned right and, a few yards on, reached the Piazzetta where Ugolina lived. Though two years younger, she was my best friend because neither of us took life in Monticiano seriously. Yes, she was after a husband, but not with the fervour of the rest. Bold and brassy, Orsola called her, which described both her manner and vivid red hair. We both suffered from an exuberance of curls, for with puberty mine had become like Mamma's. My grandfather, Niccolò, said it was the Monticiano air, but

I sensed her invisible influence. She may have left me for the Tolomei but she'd not finished with me yet.

'Before we go down to the fonte, let's take a turn to the butchers'. I've taken a shine to Macellino and want him to notice me.'

Could anyone go unnoticed in a place this size?

'You devil, Ugo, but what do you see in him? His fingers are as fat as his sausages, and his eyes like the pigs they come from.' Not to mention a horizon that went no further than the town wall. I yearned for someone, anyone, to take me back to the city, and with a family business to step into, that would not be Macellino.

'Don't be horrid.' Uglonina put on her "I'm going to cry" face, then chuckled. 'Well, maybe his eyes are a bit on the small side. But have you seen his muscles?' She dug me in the ribs.

'As long as you hide me as we pass our place.' I left my bucket outside my friend's.

'And don't you dare say anything to Mamma. She'll be so keen on free meat, she'll have me married before I'm sure I like him.'

That I doubted. Ugolina might be short, but she was no pushover.

'How do I look?' Her face was even pinker than its usual rosy glow.

She bit her lips to redden them and I arranged her curls around her face. We linked arms for the final steps to the butchers'. I had a sudden picture of Teresa and Susanna walking arm in arm to market on my last day in Siena. Strange, I hadn't thought of those two hussies in years.

'Has he seen me?' Ugolina looked everywhere but at Macellino, and he looked everywhere but at me, for he'd been sweet on me once.

'Maybe. Let's join the queue.' I said, as we hovered beyond the cutting table separating customers from the meat.

'Look after these pretty girls, Macellino.' The butcher winked at his son as they lifted down a large side of mutton and dumped it on the table at the back.

'You're right about those muscles!' I whispered, though they'd not swayed me.

'Shhh!' Ugolina blushed.

Macellino winked at her from behind the carcass. 'Can I tempt you to a sausage?' He pulled out a string and stroked the last link with his thumb.

Ugolina yanked my arm and we rushed out.

'He's yours if you want him,' I said.

'Bit of a devil though! Do you think he's serious, or just looking for a romp?'

'You'll know if he picks you for the walk to Camerata. But I'd say I'm looking at the future Monna Macellino!'

The annual walk to the Camerata hermitage took place on Easter Tuesday. Although ostensibly a pilgrimage, it was famed as the opportunity for the youth of Monticiano to find their future partner. Indeed, the last three years I'd partnered the most sought-after boys in town, only to discover their credentials were no substitute for narrow minds. None of them knew about art, so I couldn't find out whether

83

Ambrogio had made his name as an artist. They relished the predictability of Monticiano life which was smothering me, and two hours in their company served only to confirm their uselessness.

Ugolina rolled her eyes and groaned. 'Did you see him stroke that sausage?'

'Stop it, Ugolina, or I'll have to dip you in the spring to cool down.'

She shrieked and ran out of my grasp as I chased her to the Piazzetta. We picked up our pails and went out the Maremma gate. The other side of the valley was the main road South, but we turned right, following the track as far as the mountain spring that supplied water to the town.

'And who have you got your eyes on?' Ugolina teased.

'No-one.' The good looks I'd inherited from Mamma assured me I'd already sampled the best of the bunch. I needed time to work out how to get to the Siena market. 'I'll walk with Stefano.' At twelve years old, he was the closest to me in age, and my favourite because, although quiet, he was honest and sincere.

'Walking with your cousin is giving up. They'll call you the family spinster.'

'Let them! Camerata's a horse fair, and I don't want to be picked for my sleek haunches and shiny fetlocks.'

We avoided the icy patches left by the overnight frost and stepped over streams of melted snow trickling to the rivulet below. The air was fresh but not biting and we felt the thin warmth of sun on our faces.

'You can't spend the rest of your life single. Think of

84

the fun we'd have if we both had suitors – swopping notes, arranging secret meetings ... I bet Macellino doesn't kiss like a pig.'

I made snorting noises and stuck my nose into Ugolina's neck as if searching for truffles, and we burst into giggles.

'I'm serious, Clara. If you don't marry soon, there'll be no one left worth having.'

'There's no-one worth having now.' First to reach the spring, I held my hand in the water pouring out of the rock until my fingers throbbed – a dull ache, like most of my life here. I shook my hands and filled my bucket.

'Do you really want to be a burden?' Ugolina took her turn at the spring. 'Having your own home will be so much better than living under Orsola's feet. Why do you have to be so fussy?'

'I know you love this town, Ugo, but I miss the city.' I placed my pail on my shoulder and thought of Siena's colourful banners and uniforms as we walked up in silence. Weeds sprouted green in the stone walls. Within the month, the path would be alive with dandelions and daisies, and the trees covered in pink and white blossom.

A shutter creaked open, slowly, as if trying not to make a noise. I looked up and a head peered over the ledge. Swarthy chin. A mop of hair, black and straight like Babbo's. Dark eyes stared out from a face paler than a church candle. His sadness was spellbinding and I felt for him.

He raised a hand to shade his eyes, even though it

was only the watery light of a winter morning.

'Salve, Timoteo,' Ugolina greeted him. She knew everyone. 'How's the leg?'

As we put down our buckets, she whispered, 'he's the one who had an accident in the Massa mines.'

Although not as big as Siena, I knew Massa Marittima had a Duomo, so it must be substantial.

'You've grown, Ugolina! You were a babbling tot when I left.' His eyes turned to me.

'You remember Niccolò, the carpenter? Clara's his granddaughter. Born in Siena, but she's lived here for years.'

He studied my face without recognition, and I was sure I'd have remembered him. In unison, we shook our heads. I laughed and he smiled.

'I've been away over ten.' Timoteo looked at me, then looked some more.

'How did it happen, the accident?' He'd lived in a town. Could he be the one to take me to a better place?

'A rush of water, a pit prop collapsed and my leg was crushed. I'd be dead if the other men hadn't scratched away the rubble to free me.'

'Sounds terrifying.' I imagined the blacker-than-carbon darkness, the pain, and the panic he'd have felt, trapped like that.

'Sometimes I think I'd be better off dead than crippled like this.'

Crippled was no good for me, if he'd be stuck in Monticiano for the rest of his life. But maybe he just needed help to walk again. 'I'll ask my grandfather to make you a crutch.'

Timoteo reddened.

'As a gift. I'm not trying to sell you one.'

'Thank you, but we don't need your charity.' His head disappeared below the ledge.

'Hmm.' Ugolina replaced her water bucket on her shoulder and we began the final climb. 'From what I've heard, they need it. His mother, Dorotea, has to beg for food.'

'I wish I hadn't embarrassed him. I only wanted to help.'

'Oooh, is that you smitten?' Ugolina nudged me with her hip once we were through the gate.

'No, but definitely curious.' He was a good-looking man, mid-twenties I guessed. And though Massa wasn't Siena, if it had a Duomo, it'd have art.

'Well, stop there, because in case you hadn't noticed, he can't walk or work. You'll have no dowry from Bruno and Orsola, so a life with him would be very hard. You can do so much better.'

Not if his foot healed and we could go to Massa. When we reached Incrociata, I left Ugolina and continued up the main street. Usually by now my shoulder was hurting but today the bucket could have been filled with air.

My curiosity in Timoteo continued to simmer as I imagined a life in Massa. Other boys – with their brown hair, brown eyes, brown clothes – merged into the town's background of bare brown trees and mud. I looked up each time I went to fetch water and prayed for him to reappear, but his shutters remained closed.

As Camerata approached I was desperate, and in the disarray of our return from the town's annual Easter Monday picnic at the abbey of San Galgano, I ran home ahead of the crowd.

'Timoteo!' I shouted from the path that led down to the spring. 'I know you're there. Speak to me, please.'

Why wouldn't he answer? I threw stones at his window. A heavier one landed with a thwack and I feared I'd split the wood.

'Damaging what little we have?' Timoteo's head appeared at last.

'I know you're avoiding me, but I'm sorry I offended you.'

'Apology accepted. Is that all?'

What had I to lose? I took a deep breath. 'Are you coming to Camerata tomorrow? I'm looking for a partner.'

'Walk to Camerata? Are you mad?' His laugh was bitter. 'I struggle to reach the kitchen.'

My eyes welled up, sorry for him but mainly for myself. He was my last hope.

On the day itself, I writhed and groaned as soon as I heard the others stirring. Apart from my grandfather, we slept in one room: Orsola and Bruno in the matrimonial bed, Stefano, Laura and I on a hay mattress on the floor. 'I can't get up. Must have eaten something rotten.'

'She's bluffing.' Bruno gave me a wink. 'I'll get the wine from the cantina.'

'Oh, but you must come.' Laura hugged my arm,

more sibling than cousin.

'You can forget those games, my girl,' Orsola sat on the side of her bed and glared, 'unless you want to live off water for the rest of the week.'

I cupped my hand over Stefano's ear. 'I'll come if you'll be my partner.'

He nodded, pleased to be part of my conspiracy.

I put on my dirtiest dress, so no Monticiano boy would choose me, then dressed the children. Bundling sausages and bread into a cloth for Stefano to carry, I wiped my greasy hands on my dress.

Orsola caught my hand. 'Anyone would think you were brought up in a hovel not a palazzo. 'Everyone else will be at their prettiest, while you look like a skivvy.'

Niccolò was sitting on the settle that doubled as his bed. Although sixty that year, he was fit and agile, and clutched a seasoned staff ready for the walk. 'Don't shame us, Clara,' his voice more sad than angry.

Orsola bundled me into the bedroom and handed me a clean dress of her own. Too short and too wide, it would still suit my purpose. Though I often went bare headed, I stuffed what I could of my curls under a cap of sun-bleached linen.

'Now hurry, before the best boys have picked their partners.' Orsola pushed me out the door.

Clutching Stefano's arm, I ignored all invitations.

'What do you think you're doing?' Orsola caught on as we reached Sodo. That patch of rough land between town gate and monastery was today filled with people in festive mood. 'One of them must be good enough to walk with!'

'Bruno, you old soak!' The butcher slapped my uncle on the back and steered him towards the cluster of men by the gate. Around us, mothers thrust daughters towards the town's most eligible bachelors and steered them away from boys with crossed eyes, bent legs, or no money. I looked in vain for Timoteo, in case an overnight miracle had healed his leg, and waved to Ugolina, delighted to see she'd linked arms with Macellino.

But before Orsola could separate me from Stefano, the monastery doors opened. Out came the monks, led by Brother Iacopo carrying the banner. Bringing up the rear was Prior Benedetto, diminutive in stature and dressed in black from biretta to boots. The crowd silenced, and the Prior led us in prayer. Spinsters moved to the front, to lead the psalm singing. With Stefano and Laura either side, I joined the women and children next in line and we set off. Behind us were the young couples, awkwardly linking arms as they made their way down the steep path to the river. We helped each other ford the Gonna, then, as we began climbing to the hermitage, Stefano ran off to join the boys his age.

'I wish the poppies were out,' Laura said. 'They're my favourite.'

'Next month, maybe. Red's my favourite colour, too. It was all around us in Palazzo Salimbeni.' A man dressed in red, now he would be a fine suitor! 'And in another area, they wore caterpillar green.'

'Caterpillar green?' Laura wrinkled up her nose

and giggled.

'And others wore snail yellow, and unicorn orange!'

'Unicorns aren't orange!' Laura said.

'They are in Siena,' I smiled.

Despite the coldness of the day, we were perspiring by the time we reached the small clearing in the middle of which stood the hermitage. The small chapel was already packed and we joined the crowd outside.

When Laura's bottom lip stuck out because she couldn't see, I remembered Babbo taking me to the front, in the Duomo. I pushed forward to find a space at the side of the altar. From there we had a good view of the brothers, their hooded heads bowed in prayer, then raised to say the words of the liturgy. One of them was staring at me. He looked familiar, though I'd not seen him at Monticiano's monastery.

Once mass was over, the ground around the hermitage transformed, from open-air church to a human ants' nest. Men searched for kindling, staggering back with armfuls which they used to build fires. Families staked claims to large stones, fallen branches, old stumps: anywhere offering a good place to sit. Food was unwrapped and flagons of wine appeared from inside tunics and folds in frocks. Someone slipped into the church and lit tinder from a candle. Soon all the fires were alight and the clearing was wreathed in wood smoke.

While everyone was busy cooking sausages, I wandered back to the church. After the brightness outside, my eyes found it hard to adjust but gradually I made out the candles on the simple wooden altar at the front.

'Clara?' The deep voice of the staring monk made me jump. 'Don't you recognise me? It's Vanni.'

This man was so much taller, his jaw wider and his dark brows thicker. Only when he stepped into the light cast through the doorway, did I recognise my old playmate.

I ran towards him. His arms wrapped around me, and I felt his stubble against my cheek. His habit smelt of incense, reminding me of the spice that used to impregnate our clothes. Then I pulled back and wiped my eyes on my sleeve. 'It's wonderful to see you, but I can hardly believe it's you. How did you recognise me after all this time?'

'The curls confused me until I remembered your mother's.' Vanni's eyes glistened as he took my hands in his.

'But you! A monk!'

'Masquerading as one. I'm in hiding after a fight with a Tolomei. You remember how lethal our disputes can be.'

'Did you kill Blackbeard?' I pulled my hands away and shivered as I pictured Babbo's jacket stained with blood.

'No, I took the arm off one of their sons; my attempt to avenge your father's death. But they let it be known they were going to kill me in revenge. And they'd probably have succeeded. I'm in hiding until things have cooled off.'

'What a relief you weren't killed for you were never much of a fighter.'

'Neither was Guido,' Vanni said, 'yet he died for the Salimbeni.'

'Don't remind me.' My last days in Siena still brought me to tears. 'But tell me, how is Cook, and Francesco, and the kitchen girls ...'

'Thriving, as far as I know. I miss them all, even the Contessa! But I'm afraid to go back until it's safe for me.'

We crouched at the side of the chapel, reminding me of our times on the palazzo roof.

'I'm not allowed to leave here, but when they told me the Monticianese come every Easter Tuesday, I hoped you'd be among them.'

'Have you heard anything of my mother?' though I wasn't sure I wanted to know.

'The kitchen maids see her at market from time to time, often with a black eye or a bruise. But as far as I'm concerned, she cut herself off when she went to the Tolomei.' Vanni carried on, blind to the fact I'd been cut off too. 'The Nove are still in power: increasing taxes, introducing new sumptuary laws every year to keep up with the new fashions people invent to get round them. You remember the sort of thing: width of sleeve, length of coat, who's entitled to wear fur, and such like.'

'Nothing changes here. All the women dress like this.' I stood up and pulled out the fabric so it looked like a large sail.

'You could at least wear something that fits!' Vanni laughed as he stood up too. We leant side by side against the wall.

'This trip to Camerata is the annual opportunity for

match-making, and I was trying to avoid being picked.'

'Not married, then?'

'I've had admirers.' I didn't want Vanni to think I was a lost cause.

'I can imagine.'

'All the young men here are too dull, too brown.'

'Like me!' Vanni pointed to his habit and laughed.

'To be honest, I was hoping to find someone to take me back to Siena.'

'As you can see, I'm in no position to offer you salvation.' Vanni tugged at his hood and smiled. 'Not that a noble can marry a pleb.'

'I'd clean out slops and never complain, if it would get me back to the city.' The more I talked, the more determined I was to find a way back.

'That I don't believe – about not complaining.' Vanni nudged me in the ribs and we laughed. 'I'm so happy to see you at last. I was worried for you, and deeply sorry about my part in you leaving.' He took my hands. As we faced each other, we took in the changes the last nine years had wrought.

'Now I'm afraid I must ask you to leave. I need to lock up.'

'Before you go, let's see your tonsure!' I teased.

Vanni turned slowly. The shaved circle at the back of his scalp was grey and stubbled, not pink and shiny like that of older monks.

'Very funny, Vanni.'

'Now you know where I'm hiding, come and see me again!' He turned the key, and I watched him disappear into the monks' living area behind the chapel.

'Sausages are ready!' Laura dragged me back to the family. 'Who's that man you were talking to?'

'What man?' Orsola was all ears.

'My best friend from the old days, Miss not-much-gets-past-you!' I pinched Laura's cheek. 'He was like a brother to me, but he's a monk now.'

'Might have guessed it'd be no-one with marriage prospects.'

Soon even the poorest had food in their hand. Wine passed from neighbour to neighbour and good humour prevailed. Camerata was in the Monticianese blood, a fixed point in their universe – like harvest time and Christmas – a universe in which I never wanted to fit.

'Look at Ugolina.' Orsola spat crumbs. 'That boy should have been yours.'

'If he was like a brother, were you always quarrelling – like me and Laura?' Stefano had a knack of deflecting his mother.

'Not really. We played a lot of games, jacks mainly. And cat's cradle, and races down the stairs.' I closed my eyes, to squeeze out the tears.

The way back was easier. Laura and I swung our arms, singing local songs. But all the time I was thinking of Siena, and how to persuade Niccolò to take me to market. And I prayed to the Virgin Mother to find me a suitor when I got there.

Chapter 8

The night before market, I hardly slept. My plan had to succeed or I'd spend the rest of my life in Monticiano. As soon as cracks of grey appeared through the shutters, I sat up, careful not to wake Laura and Stefano sleeping next to me. Bruno snored in the main bed but Niccolò would soon be rapping on the door to wake him. Heart pounding, I dressed and waited on the tiny square of tiles that made up our hallway.

'Bruno's ill, and Orsola told me to take his place,' I whispered as soon as my grandfather appeared from the kitchen where he slept.

'Lazy sot. He'll be the ruin of us.'

Sick with fear of my ruse being discovered, I followed him to the stable where our cart waited, Bruno and Stefano having loaded it the previous afternoon.

Niccolò shook his head. 'Who's going to help me unload this lot at market?'

'I carry water from the spring every day. Lifting furniture's nothing compared to that.' Through the night, I'd rehearsed my arguments.

Niccolò nodded, and I helped him harness the horse

to the cart. 'Now fetch your cloak. It'll be cold until the sun comes up.'

I'd have shivered all the way to Siena to avoid going back inside, but that would have given the game away. Instead I crept back to the bedroom and removed my cloak from the nail behind the door.

My heart skipped a beat when Stefano raised his head from the pillow. 'Are you leaving us?'

'Back in a couple of days.' I squeezed his foot, and he turned back to sleep.

Outside, the cart was ready and I climbed up next to my grandfather.

'And no chatting. I have enough of that with Orsola.'

I pulled the hood over my face, hoping to pass for a sleepy Bruno in the grey morning light. Outside the gates, half a dozen carts were gathered in Sodo. The assembled horses pawed at the ground, breathing out small clouds of mist. Fat Mario entertained everyone with lewd jokes, reminding me of life in the Salimbeni kitchen. Oh, for the chance to see them again. The first cart trundled towards the main road and I could hardly contain my excitement. I was on my way!

Then a monk stepped out of the shadows – Brother Iacopo from the monastery. 'Squeeze me in, Niccolò. I'm a quiet companion.'

I slumped further into my cloak, willing myself invisible.

'Jump up, Brother.'

I shifted to the middle, but kept my head bowed. Iacopo put his sandal on a spoke of the wooden wheel and heaved himself onto the bench. Niccolò shook the reins and the cart creaked into motion.

As crack of dawn became day, we bumped down twisting roads towards the plain of Feccia. As sun dried out the overnight rain, we found ourselves in an eerie, thick mist: disembodied heads of men at work moved around in a sea of cloud. As the mist cleared, I saw what they were doing: one guided a horse, another steered the plough, while a third cast out seeds from a bag slung across his chest.

'And what takes you to Siena, brother, if you can speak of the matter?' Niccolò asked, now the steep bends no longer required his concentration.

'The prior wishes to honour his predecessor with a work of art.'

Art? This was the first time I'd heard the word since leaving Siena.

'A good man was Antonio Patrizi, and much loved.' Niccolò said.

When I'd first arrived, most of the townspeople attended services at the monastery to listen to him preach.

'His miraculous body is as fresh as the day he was buried, and with his healing miracles, too, we hope he'll be canonized. In anticipation of that blessed day, the abbot wants his resting place to be as worthy of a saint as San Galgano's abbey.'

Niccolò gave a short whistle. 'Imagine us, with a church as grand as theirs!'

'Ours is small, but we can outdo them in visual grandeur. My commission is to find the best artist in

Tuscany to create something impressive. Duccio would have been ideal, but of course he's dead.'

My eyes watered. I didn't know the man but I'd been in his house, used his paints and seeing his painting had changed my life.

'An onerous task he's trusting you with, Brother Iacopo.'

'Though excellent at managing our financial affairs, the prior knows nothing about art. I'm no expert either, but it was seeing Giotto's magnificent ceiling in a Padua chapel that convinced me to dedicate my life to the church.'

'Have you seen Duccio's Maestà?' I threw off my hood. 'It was installed in the Duomo just before I left!'

He turned to me, open-mouthed, then cleared his throat. 'I thought I was sitting next to Bruno, though it did concern me how thin he'd become.'

'One of his thick heads.' Niccolò said.

Iacopo frowned. 'The city's no place for a girl.'

If that was his view, I was glad we'd travelled too far for me to be sent back.

'Siena holds no fears for her. She was born and bred there.'

All that would make me panic was the blue and white livery of the Tolomei, especially if the person wearing it had a black beard.

For the rest of the long day, I looked forward to being surrounded by the noise of strangers, being buffeted by crowds, and rediscovering the pungent smell of the streets. But we stopped so many times to water the horses, I despaired of ever getting there. If we didn't arrive by nightfall, they'd not let us in.

As the sun dropped low in the sky, the spring air grew cold as a mountain spring, and we turned a corner. There, perched on the hill ahead, stood my beloved city. Bathed in the glorious pink end-of-day light, those towers of marble, stone and brick were even more beautiful than I remembered. The road was flanked by a swathe of flowers in bloom, yellow dandelions – those I could name – others in various shades of purple and magenta, and the odd solitary poppy. The colourful display was welcoming me home.

Iacopo looked equally moved. 'I pray I can find someone as good as the great master, for our beloved Antonio deserves nothing less. I'm to seek counsel of the abbot at our mother monastery, Sant'Agostino for he's commissioned many works of art.'

I held back from mentioning Ambrogio.

'But I'm determined to consider Pietro Lorenzetti. I hear he's recently decorated the lower church in Assisi and it takes a great painter to stand alongside Giotto.'

'Whoever you choose, I'm sure you'll do Monticiano proud,' Niccolò said as we joined the line of carts queuing outside the gate. San Domenico towered over us on our left, the Duomo on the right. 'Once we're inside, I'll head straight for the Campo. You can make your way to the monastery from there.'

We reached the front of the queue and Niccolò paid a deposit on what taxes might be due on goods sold at market. The guard slapped the horse's flank and we trundled through the stone arch and into the district dominated by dyeing works.

I held my nose, the smell a cross between abattoir and latrine, but a small price to pay for being back in the city of my birth.

We made our way up the narrow streets – I'd never realised how dark they were compared to open roads! From several houses hung green banners, showing this was the territory of the Goose, and I longed to see the red and gold flying from my former home. Who was sweeping the kitchen floor now, and how was Cook? Workmen pushed in front of the cart.

Niccolò shook his head as the cart came to a halt. We're almost at the Campo, but it could take ages to get there. You're better off walking, Brother.'

'Then perhaps I have time to visit the Duomo. I'd like to remind myself of Duccio's genius.' Iacopo said.

'Turn right at the junction and then take a right, but not immediately.' I was trying to remember the route we'd taken on the day of the festa.

Iacopo looked flustered. 'After years of cloistered life, I confess to being somewhat trepidatious. These streets look designed to mislead. Yet Clara seems to know the way. Would you consider allowing her to guide me?'

This was my chance to see the great painting again. More than that, I could say hello to my friends at Palazzo Salimbeni, and still be in the Campo before dark.

'If it were anyone else, I'd say no, but I trust you, Brother to bring her back to the Campo. Anyone will tell you how to get there.'

I jumped down and led Brother Iacopo up past

Palazzo d'Elci, turning right where we'd gone with Babbo and once in the piazza, the black and white stripes of the Duomo greeted me like old friends. Iacopo climbed the steps then stopped short inside the doors. Though the Maestà's golden glow radiated from the end of the nave, my eyes followed his. He was staring at the stained glass in the East window. 'What a master! If only he were alive today.'

From the quantities of ultramarine, I realised Duccio had created this too; nine deep blue and gold windows depicting scenes of the Virgin's life.

'This is my answer. Paintings can be moved, hidden away, transferred to side chapels – I've seen monastery cupboards full of Byzantine icons – but who would move a window? Would you grant me some minutes to pray, Clara, for I have missed all my offices today.' It was a statement more than a question. We walked to the altar and I knelt beside him.

'Dearest Virgin Mother,' he prayed, 'guide me to the right choice for our humble church and to the man who will enable us to accomplish that great work.'

'Amen,' I said as I remembered the joy of painting in Duccio's studio. But the face of the Madonna belonged to Monna Duccio, and her voice told me to hurry to the palazzo.

Festina Lente, hasten slowly, I remembered from our Latin lessons. While Iacopo continued to pray, I sauntered towards the back of the church, pausing at the door. The sin had not been committed until I crossed the threshold. But ever since I'd bumped into Vanni at Camerata, I longed to see my old home, to be welcomed by my true kin. Taking one final look at the praying monk, I ran down the steps. I'd have time if I hurried.

Merchants were packing up their stalls, so I slipped past without remark. A deeply-buried memory led me to retrace my former steps past the baptistry, then trusted instinct to guide me to Palazzo Salimbeni, via side roads to avoid the Tolomei. Even so, I hid in a doorway whenever I spotted enemy livery.

By the time I reached the palace, it was almost dark. If they let me stay the night, I could still be back in the Campo in time to help Niccolò set up the stall. Surrounded on three sides by grey stone walls, the main door faced me, as did the stone bench on which Vanni and I had played our last game of jacks. What would my life have been if I'd never left? One way to find out. I approached the door and was overjoyed to see Francesco on duty. A few lines on the forehead, emerging crows' feet around the eyes, a little sagging around the jaw, but otherwise he was still my father's best friend. I climbed the steps.

'And what business has a pretty, young lady with the Salimbeni? If you're looking to shelter in a handsome man's arms, you've come to the right place.' Francesco smiled the smile that had worked magic on so many.

'Don't be daft, Francesco, it's me, Clara. I've missed you all so much.' If he'd not been such a flirt, I'd have flung my arms around him.

His smile turned to frown.

'You must remember me? Guido's daughter? Let me in – just a quick hello to those who knew me.'

'Not a chance! You're a Tolomei now! Things were bad between us when your Babbo was killed, but since Vanni took an arm off their son, they're ten times worse.'

'But I've not seen or spoken to Mamma since I left. I'm not like her, Francesco, I'll always be true to the Salimbeni.'

'I'm sorry, Clara, but blood is blood. Someone here could kill you in revenge for their latest transgression.'

'I saw Vanni in the hermitage, and he was so kind.'

'Huh! It's thanks to him, we're in fear for our lives on the streets.'

'Then I'll run back to my grandfather in the Campo.'

'And that's another thing that's changed – the strictness of the curfew. Unless you want to get arrested, you've left it too late. The only place for you is Palazzo Tolomei.'

'No, not there!' I tried to run off, but he already had me by the arm. I tried to tug myself free. 'Can't you pretend you never saw me?'

When he refused to loose his grip, I wriggled and screamed, but that only made him hold tighter. 'Please, Francesco, I'm a Salimbeni.'

'Here's your home now.' He pushed me through the doors of the enemy palace. 'She's yours - Maria's daughter.' He ran up the street before the sentries could react.

One of the Tolomei servants held me by the arm. 'She's got her mother's hair, and her looks. Let's hope she's got a better temper.'

I sucked up all the saliva I could muster and spat in his face.

'Maria's daughter all right!' They all laughed as I was steered into the large entrance hall of Palazzo Tolomei.

I was terrified – and how would I avoid the dreaded Blackbeard? I had never been able to rely on my mother, so why would she help me now?

Chapter 9

Home, Francesco called it, yet the place was as hateful as hell itself. Dark blue tapestries in the entrance hall added to the coldness. Behind me two massive bolts, the width of tree trunks, shot across the main door and sealed my fate. Abandoning the struggle with my captor, I closed my eyes, ashamed at my foolishness. My poor grandfather – what heartache I'd be causing him. Tears ran down my face. I had to find a way to break free.

'Please, let me see my mother. It's been ten years.' Let them think the tears were for her. Yet she was my only hope.

The senior guard nodded, and the other set off up the stairs. Even a Tolomei could be moved by a young girl's plight.

Upstairs, the rattle of plates suggested the household was having their evening meal, but I wasn't hungry. Fear of Blackbeard made me feel sick. I could only pray for dark corners in which to hide until morning, when the doors would be open again.

With head bowed like an old woman, a servant in linen shirt and dark blue shift limped towards me. Was she to take me to Mamma? But as she came closer, I recognized the dark curls, which had fought and won against the flax cap. What had happened to the woman I'd last seen at market, skipping off to marry my father's murderer?

She raised her head, her face puffy, all expression knocked out of her.

Any last hope of loving arms wrapped around me was swiftly quashed.

'Mamma, it's Clara, your daughter. Did he do this to you?' I reached for her face, and a look I remembered only too well turned on me. Pure venom.

'The little plum! He said you'd be back! If you take him from me, I'll kill you!' She tried to scratch my face, but I held her fists. 'For he'll kill me to marry you.'

I felt sick at the thought. 'I don't want him, Mamma. In fact I don't want to be here at all. Why don't you hide me so he can't find me.' No point in telling her about why I was in the city, or my problems with the Salimbeni. 'And then you can get me out first thing in the morning.'

'Fetch Blackbeard,' the guard in charge ordered his sidekick.

'Mamma, there's not much time,' I whispered.

Maria closed her eyes and groaned, then limped up the wide stairs to the first floor. Was I supposed to follow? With Blackbeard on his way, I took the stairs in pairs, following her past the dining room, and down one of the wings.

'The Signora's room.' Maria entered a bedchamber decorated with more blue. Curtains, embroidered with the half-moons of the Tolomei insignia, surrounded the bed. Against the wall was a large chest – not as well-carved as the one Niccolò had given the Salimbeni-etched with the same moon shapes as the curtains.

'You can sit on the bed, if you tidy it after.' Maria ran her hands over the blue and gold quilt, then moved to the table of unguents and stuck her fingers in one of the pots. Smoothing a large dollop of cream over her face, she turned from side to side to admire the results in the glass. 'The old bag won't notice. Mean, these Tolomei.'

'You chose them,' I said.

'Nothing of the sort. He chose me.' Maria opened the lid of the chest and picked out a dress. 'How can someone her age think of wearing orange? It needs someone young to carry it off.' She held the dress against her and whirled around the room. 'I could show her, not that we're ever allowed out of these slips.'

I thought back to our trunk filled with the Contessa's cast-offs, but this Maria would be turning no heads. Yet it was some comfort to glimpse her enduring vanity. At least he hadn't knocked that out of her.

Mamma dropped the dress on the floor and I put it

back in the chest, then stood beside her at the mirror.

'Look how beautiful I am!' However, it was the image of my face she stroked on the glass. Her own smile revealed ugly gaps in her teeth. She looked between the two images then turned to face me. 'Who you are again?'

'I'm the daughter you sent back to Monticiano.' This boded ill. How could she help me escape if she'd lost her memory? 'And you're going to hide me from Blackbeard until first light.'

'He has eyes everywhere.' Though the tapestries were flat against the walls, Maria peered behind them. 'The Signora's maid lets me come here to be safe. The Signor is the only man allowed in.'

That would only save me from Blackbeard if I was undiscovered. 'What about the chest?'

She pulled out a couple of dresses. I climbed in and she covered me with them. Though stuffy with the lid closed, among the smell of worn garments was one of cinnamon, and I relaxed. I raised the lid with my foot to create an air hole. As long as nobody searched the chest, I'd be safe.

'I'd better use the chamber pot before you shut me in.' I climbed out and relieved myself.

'I always have a pee while I'm here,' Maria added to the pot, then threw the contents out the window.

'Thank you, Mamma. Come and find me in the morning as soon as you can.' I tried to hug her, but she stiffened.

'I'm the only one the Signora's maid lets sleep here.' Mamma smiled.

As I climbed back into the chest, I praised the heavens for her brief moments of lucidity, yet sad for what she'd become: a mattress with the stuffing crushed flat.

Through the night I listened to the Signora's loud snores, and in the morning, her peremptory demands. By the time the maid released me from the chest, the sun was high in the sky and I was ready to wet myself. She allowed me to use the pot, then I sped downstairs, all the time keeping a look out.

'Thank you for your hospitality,' I said, pushing through the servants on the main door.

'Blackbeard's orders, you're not allowed out.' They blocked my exit.

Now what to do? My mother was my only hope. 'Where's Maria? I'll go and help her.'

'Kitchen, as always.'

I ran up the main stairs and kept climbing, the smells of garlic and rosemary growing stronger at every step. But when I reached it, the kitchen was empty apart from Mamma – sweeping the floor, my old job.

'Why are you still here?' she grabbed a knife.

'They won't let me leave. Blackbeard's orders.' How could I persuade her to help, while she was holding a knife? 'Is there a back way out? Stables?'

Maria put her hand to her head, more confused than ever.

I was on the point of trying to find them myself when she tucked the knife into her bodice and led me down the back staircase. As the air began to smell of horse manure, I knew this had been no wild goose

chase through my mother's mind. A whinny confirmed
we were outside the stable. Maria put her ear to the
door, then stood rigid, face drained of blood. She let out
the whimpers of an injured puppy.

'What's wrong?'

The door creaked open and Blackbeard stood before
us. Face more flaccid than before, his eyes were steely,
his smile terrifying.

'My husband, my love.' Maria wound her arms
around his neck and tried to kiss him, but he grabbed
her wrists and threw her against the door. I started up
the stairs, but he grabbed my ankle.

'Come quietly, if you don't want me to break your
foot.'

In the stable, I looked for an escape but the doors to
the street were bolted. Cowering on the ground, arms
wrapped round her head, Maria was no help. And the
horses pawed their resentment at our intrusion.

'Worth the wait, little plum!' Blackbeard grabbed
my arm and thrust me against the wall, himself against
me. 'Maria was the bait and at last, I've bagged the
prize.'

I screamed and scratched and kicked, but he took
my chin in his hand as if my head were a peach, forcing
my mouth to face his. His beard was damp, his breath
stale and his lips closed on mine.

Now Maria was at him, fingernails scratching both
his face and mine. Holding my throat with one hand, he
cuffed Maria, sending her sprawling. He toppled me
onto the hay and was on top of me. Grabbing me by the
hair, he yanked back my head. I screamed and clawed

and felt cool air on my legs as with his other hand, he lifted my skirt. My heartbeat thundered in my ears and I closed my eyes, trying to transport my thoughts somewhere safe: the clothes chest, with the children in Monticiano, hiding under the Palazzo bench with Vanni Salimbeni.

Suddenly Blackbeard howled and I saw a flash of steel. He rolled off me clutching his arm and Maria stood over him, the bloody kitchen knife trembling in her hand.

'You bitch!' He stared at the blood seeping through his fingers.

I scrambled to my feet, in fear of my life. He reached towards me, then fell back on the straw.

'I'll look after you, caro.' Maria knelt beside Blackbeard and tried to staunch the blood with her apron.

Her body blocked Blackbeard's view of the stable door and I tried to shift the bolts. "Help me, Babbo", I prayed, "don't let him take me too." I gave the bolts all I had. They shot open and I heaved the door ajar.

'God's nails, woman, stop her!' Blackbeard said, though his voice was weak.

My teeth chattered as I raced down the street, tears streaming down my face. All I wanted was for my grandfather's cart to return me safe to Monticiano.

But how was I to explain my absence? If I mentioned I had a right to stay in Palazzo Tolomei, he'd send me back there. I tried to think straight, but in every corner of my mind was the sight, the smell and the weight of that monster. Wiping my eyes on my sleeve, I entered the Campo. But instead of the seething mass of humanity I'd expected, only the local merchants remained. Beggars scoured the ground, claiming bruised fruits, damaged vegetables, discarded sacks and broken baskets. I ran to a costermonger packing up the remains of his wares.

'Where's everyone gone?'

The man shrugged. 'The out-of-towners leave early this time of year, to get home before nightfall.'

'Niccolò, the carpenter from Monticiano, is my grandfather. Was he looking for me?'

'Not that I know. The carts going south left a good hour ago. They'll be beyond the city walls by now.' The man heaved his last basket of vegetables onto the cart. I must have looked needy for he threw me a wrinkled apple. 'And don't try to follow them – too dangerous on your own.'

'What shall I do?' How stupid I'd been to run off. The two pallazzi I might have called home offered no welcome. I watched as a breeze caught up some of the market's detritus and swirled it round in a pointless dance.

'You must know someone in the city.' The man pulled out a rope and began tying down his baskets. 'Or if you can convince Santa Maria della Scala you're a pilgrim, they'll put you up for a couple of nights.'

A couple of nights? It would be a month before my grandfather came again. If only I could go back to the moment before I'd left Brother Iacopo. Blinking away my tears, I wondered if he might help. 'I came here with a monk. He was on his way to see the prior of

Sant'Agostino.'

'Then ask the abbey for help.' He pointed to the road on the left of the city hall.

'Thank you.' I needed a moment on my own in the Campo, before setting off. Blackbeard had made me feel dirty, body and soul. I rinsed my face in the communal fountain, then sat on the wall that surrounded it, hugging my knees to my chest. Through my tears, I watched a handful of last-minute shoppers pick up bargains from the few remaining stallholders. An argument had broken out at the egg stall. Despite my misery, I wiped my eyes, remembering Ambrogio buying eggs on my last day. The buyer even looked like an older version of him; more assured, or maybe more arrogant. So many eggs being bought, he must be an artist. I stood for a better look. His hair was fair and I ran to him.

'Ambrogio!'

'I'm sorry, do I know you?' He looked me up and down, his gaze, playful and admiring. 'Even if I don't, I'd like to.'

'Don't you remember me?' To be my saviour, he had to recall our earlier meeting. 'The day the Maestà was taken to the Duomo, you took my mother and me to Duccio's house and I drew on the wall.' I hesitated to mention how he'd praised the colours in my cloak.

'And your father murdered. I'll never forget seeing that.' Ambrogio shuddered.

I'd buried the memory but now, flashing before my eyes was Babbo's bloody jacket, his sagging body. Blackbeard's on top of me.

'What's happened? You look as though you've been in a fight.'

I looked down and saw my dress was smudged with horse manure. Trying to control my trembling, I told him of my escape from the Tolomei, though not of Blackbeard's attempted violation. 'Can I stay with you? I can clean, mend clothes, look after your children – anything, until my grandfather comes back to the market next month.' And clean up my dress.

'Sorry, I can't. I'm still sponging off my brother and he won't allow it.'

'Would you at least try? My only alternative is to sleep on the streets.' Or a guest room in the monastery, but an artist's house would be so much better. 'I'd be happy to mix your paints.'

'I suppose I could ask him.'

We walked fast across the Campo, then up the main road and I remembered trying to keep up with him and Mamma, as they flirted their way to Duccio's house.

'Still in your brother's bad books, then.'

We turned off the main road at the Duomo.

'Now it's more about artistic differences. He wants me to follow in the "proud Sienese tradition", which I want to break free of. He was going to pay for me to study in Florence, until the Perugians claimed ownership of the Basilica and he lost his commission. Now he's broke and I'm going nowhere.'

We stood outside a dwelling in Castelvecchio with a stables and three storeys above.

'Pietro's wife's the wealthy one. Her brother's the city treasurer. And before you ask, I'm in her bad

114

books too.' Ambrogio opened the door. Unlike Palazzo Tolomei, the darkness inside enveloped me like the Madonna's cloak.

Chapter 10

A wild boar is attacking me, flattening me, its stinking breath in my face.
I wake, heart pounding and check for Laura's warmth beside me but I'm alone on a makeshift bed.

Then my real nightmare came back, and he was there, pushing me down. Would I have to live with this fear for the rest of my life? Light came through the shutters to reveal old chairs and planks propped up on bricks. On them were set out the bags of powders and clumps of earth of different hues I'd explored the previous evening. Safe in Pietro's studio, my breathing relaxed.

I used the buckets they'd left me, to relieve and wash myself, slipped on my clothes and opened the shutter. Above the tiled rooftops, palazzo towers competed in height and flew their colours. Below, a few early risers walked the streets. A church bell chimed the hour, closely followed by others in higher and lower notes. Oh, how I'd missed this music of my city.

Inside, the terracotta floor bore witness to the

artists' work. Around my feet were the fragments of leather, remnants of wood-panels and scraps of parchment that Ambrogio had kicked aside to make space for me to sleep. Though a far cry from the prestige of working on frescos in Assisi's Basilica, Pietro's brother-in-law, the state treasurer, had commissioned him to paint the cover of the next annual accounts book. Two easels stood near the windows, and on each rested an oblong of stiff leather, cut to the size of a ledger. While Pietro would do a traditional front cover, Ambrogio would produce an alternative, and the treasurer would select the one he preferred. I longed to see them both at work.

A tap on the door and Ambrogio entered. 'My room's below and I heard a scream. Is everything all right?'

'I had a nightmare – about the Tolomei.' I closed my eyes to blot it out.

'I'm sorry.' He touched my cheek and the warmth of his breath blew away the terror of my encounter with Blackbeard.

'Ready for work?' he said.

'Does Giovanna need me already?' I didn't want to leave – Ambrogio and the studio – but I was staying on condition I helped Pietro's wife around the house.

'Not yet. And until she does, I'm going to teach you to mix paints.'

Ever since that afternoon at Duccio's, I'd longed to make my own colours.

I tidied away my makeshift bed, while he examined the pots. 'Any preference to start with?'

'That green you used under the Madonna's face.' Ever since he'd shared it with me, I'd nursed that artist's secret.

'Good choice, it's one of the easier ones to prepare.' Ambrogio dipped his hand into a wicker basket and held out an egg, his eyes smiling and locked on mine. 'Can you separate these? We need to make a tempera.'

'Of course.' I could do anything under that powerful gaze. Also I remembered the number of yolks Cook used to make one of her puddings.

He held out two beakers while I cracked the egg on a rim, then shifted the yolk from one half of the shell to the other until the white was in one beaker, yolk in the other. He put the white to one side.

'Now we break the membrane and add oil.' He poured some onto the egg, then handed me a stick.

I stirred the yolk until it was fully blended, then felt the warmth of his hand through my linen shift as he steered me towards the pots. This was everything I'd wished of my escape to the city.

'Take a dollop of verde, that green, then add the tempera until it's like cream; thick enough not to drip, thin enough for good coverage.'

I began mixing.

'Not so ladylike!' He covered my hand in his and we laughed as he forced me to stir with more vigour. This was so much more exciting a way to start the day than fetching water from Monticiano's spring.

After the verde, we went on to the ochres – yellow and red. If only I could paint something with these colours too!

'Have a go!' Ambrogio picked up a wood offcut from the floor and handed me a brush.

I used all that green to paint a leafy glen, the ochres depicting an ominous beast about to pounce on an innocent rabbit.

'I might have known it wouldn't take you long to get up to your old tricks!' Pietro entered the studio in a paint-spattered tunic.

'She's keen to learn,' Ambrogio said.

'Be wary, Clara. My brother can be very persuasive when he wants something.' Below the red eyebrows, Pietro's eyes expressed an avuncular concern.

'But I love colours. I've always wanted to know how to mix them.' Yet I was heady with Ambrogio too, the feeling so much stronger than for Timoteo.

Pietro picked up my mixes. 'How many eggs have you wasted? You know we're hard up.'

I edged towards the door, not wanting to be caught in their row, but I wasn't going to leave unless I had to.

Once Pietro moved to the easel he forgot me. 'I'm going to show the treasurer counting his money.'

'Following convention, as usual. I shall be more imaginative. Maybe the feeding of the five thousand? That's a good reason to pay taxes - so the city buys in enough grain to feed us.'

'Play around if you must, Ambrogio. Just don't waste more eggs.'

Ambrogio reddened and I felt his hurt.

He shook his head and sat down with his slate and chalk.

'Clara!' Giovanna shouted.

I ran down the stairs and spent the rest of the day helping the mistress of the house. Delightful though the children were, most of my thoughts were of the studio, which already felt more my home than Monticiano. If only I could find a way to stay, preferably for the rest of my life. Finally, as the light faded, I was released from my duties and I tiptoed into the studio. The brothers were deep in discussions of each other's work.

Pietro spotted me. 'Come, enough for today, brother, let's eat.' On the way out, he picked up my painting attempt. 'Is this yours?'

'I'm sorry, I was trying out the colours I'd mixed.'

'A red ochre boar and yellow ochre rabbit!' Pietro laughed. 'But it has something – I can feel the menace. Not bad for someone who's never held a paintbrush.'

I glowed under the praise from such a renowned artist. 'Then allow me to mix your paints. I'd help Giovanna after, of course.'

Pietro looked dubious. 'If the Guild finds I've used a woman, I'll be thrown out.'

'Well, I won't tell them!' Ambrogio winked at me.

Pietro shook his head and left. Who cared if his approval was reluctant, I was going to do a real artist's job.

Ambrogio held me in a steadfast gaze and I blushed.

'Shall I wash out the brushes? You showed me how to do that at Duccio's.'

'If only you could be our assistant.' He stroked my cheek and my body tingled.

'Ambrogio!' Pietro shouted from downstairs. 'We're waiting to eat and I'm starving.'

'I'll help you clean those later.' Ambrogio dropped them in a beaker of oil.

I followed him down the stairs to join the rest of the household, my emotions in turmoil. Throughout the meal, Pietro's children climbed over him, while he pacified the youngest by letting it suck on his little finger. When everyone had had their fill, I cleared away, taking the dirty platters into the corridor to wash them in the waiting bucket.

There was a knock at the main door and Ambrogio went to open it.

'The abode of Signor Lorenzetti?' a man asked. I knew his voice at once.

'At your service,' Ambrogio said.

'I come from the Augustinian monastery in Monticiano and would like to discuss with you a commission.'

If Brother Iacopo had been knocking at Palazzo Tolomei, I would have been overjoyed. But with the chance to work with artists now on offer? I bent over my task to keep my face hidden.

'Step inside. What did you have in mind?' Ambrogio's voice was all charm. Then he called to his brother. 'A monk from Monticiano has a commission for me, Pietro!'

'You are not Pietro Lorenzetti?'

'No, I'm his brother, Ambrogio.'

'My deepest apologies,' Iacopo said. 'It was Signor Pietro I came to see. Could I speak to him?'

'He's too busy. Come back in a few days.' Ambrogio ushered out the monk.

I was saved.

'Why did you do that?' Pietro handed the baby to Giovanna.

'To remind you how unhelpful I can be, if you keep holding me back.'

'But we're desperate for work. Run after him and tell him I'll see him!'

'You're desperate for work. I want to go to Florence, which you said you'd pay for. I've learnt as much as I can from you!' Ambrogio stood a couple of inches taller than his brother.

'How do you expect me to do that when the income from this book cover is hardly enough to put food on our table?' Pietro faced him.

I returned with the clean platters and for the first time noticed the brothers' likeness: the shape of their shoulders, the thinness of their legs, the way they stood.

'For the love of the Madonna, stop treating me like your apprentice!' Ambrogio turned away, and I felt his frustration. How I wanted to put my arms around him. When our eyes met, I willed him strength. He took a deep breath. 'I can't spend my life in your shadow, Pietro. If you believe in me as an artist, you should help me become a good one. Persuade the monk that I can do the job in Monticiano...'

Ambrogio working in Monticiano? I'd be at monastery services every day.

'I can't believe you'd take my work, to satisfy your ambition.' Pietro slumped into his chair. 'What about my children?'

'I can't afford to have children!'

Ambrogio wanted children? Could he be the husband I'd come in search of?

'I can't waste my life sacrificing my ambition for yours. I can be a great artist too, and this commission is exactly what I need to prove it. If you must, tell them you're taking the lead but please let me show you and the world what I can do.'

'Don't be ridiculous, Ambrogio. You can't run before you can walk.'

'Then let me learn to walk – if you get this assignment, pay for me to study in Florence. Either way, give me your decision before the monk returns or, I promise you, neither of us will go to Monticiano.' Ambrogio indicated for me to follow him up the stairs.

'I'm not usually this difficult, but I've learnt that Pietro only sees sense when it affects his family and that means hitting him in the purse.' Ambrogio paused outside his room. I'd have carried on up the stairs but he took my hand and led me inside. I should have said a coy goodnight and returned to the studio but I followed him in. As soon as I was inside, I pulled my hand away and leant against the door. 'I'm so grateful to you, Ambrogio, for showing me how to mix paints. More than that, by letting me stay, you saved me from a fate worse than death with the Tolomei.'

With tears pouring down my cheeks, I told him about Blackbeard's attempted violation. He stood before me, holding my hands, and when I'd finished, he pulled me to him. My beating heart slowed as I rested my head on his chest.

Ambrogio was all tenderness. He raised my chin

and kissed my lips. Then he moved his hand to feel my breast. Unlike Blackbeard's touch, this was welcome, yet I recognized the danger.

'I won't be someone you use and throw away, like paints. If I'm to be yours, promise me it's forever.' I'd seen enough of Francesco and his flirtations to know how this could end. I needed someone faithful, as Babbo had been to Mamma.

Ambrogio kissed my wet cheeks. 'Can't you see how much you mean to me? You've got under my skin like this ochre.' He showed me his yellowed nails.

I longed to succumb to his charms but I'd need more commitment than that.

He sensed my hesitation and put my hand to his lips. Then he kissed the ring finger. 'Be mine forever.'

As I melted into his arms, my tears were of joy. His lips, gentle and loving, covered my face with kisses, as if mapping its contours onto his memory. My legs pressed against the bed and, as Ambrogio's hands explored my body more, I was frightened and excited in equal measure.

'Shall we lie down, carissima?' he said gently.

I lay back on his covers and watched him remove his jacket and shirt before lying at my side. He caressed my breasts through the thin fabric of my dress and I thrilled as he ran his hand along my leg.

I smoothed my hand over his chest – skin smooth compared to the hands roughened by mixing paints.

Softly, and carefully he undressed me, kissing each naked spot as it was released from the clothing. He ran over my skin with his fingertips and soon I was

writing in pleasure. My guts were tingling, and I was
overwhelmed by desire for this beautiful man who
wanted me for his own. He continued his caressing,
until waves of pleasure engulfed me and I was
transported to another world. I clung to him, wanting
him closer than I thought it possible for two people to
be, and he entered me, thrusting until he too groaned
with pleasure. Together we tasted the food of the Gods.
I was floating on air, but Ambrogio collapsed beside me,
asleep in a trice. I snuggled closer to this marvel of a
man, imagining our wondrous life together. Ambrogio
roused himself enough to wrap an arm around me and
I fell asleep in his embrace; a long, deep, satisfying
sleep, the best since returning to the city.

I woke up alone, still glowing with happiness.
Relishing my nakedness, I ran my hands along my body
but it felt no different. But when I opened the shutters,
I was surprised to find the street already busy. I dressed
at once and raced upstairs to the studio. The brothers
stopped talking as I entered.

'Giovanna's waiting for you.' Pietro frowned not at
me, but at Ambrogio. My bedding was neatly rolled in
the corner, so no doubts where I'd spent the night.

'I've already mixed the paints.' Ambrogio's face had
a hangdog expression. 'But if you're up early tomorrow,
I'll give you another lesson.'

I hurried to help with the children.

Over the next few days, Ambrogio taught me the
basic colours, and how to blend them – into pinks,
purples, browns and oranges – after which I helped
Giovanna. After dark I was again under Ambrogio's

tutelage, discovering delights I'd never known existed. And we talked into the night, about art and artists; even 'the old man', Duccio.

'He was a great draughtsman, and composer of pictures. Taught us to capture the everyday, even when depicting the sublime.'

'I remember there was a dagger in one of the pictures, just like my father's.' I told him about Babbo taking me to the front of the Duomo so we had a good view of proceedings, and me creeping round the back to get a better look.

'I can see, when you know what you want, you get it!' He kissed my forehead. 'Now let's get some sleep.'

I relished our time together so much, I failed to pursue details about our marriage. He'd given his word and I trusted him. When he came to Monticiano to do the commission – for I was sure he'd persuade Pietro to give it to him – he'd ask Niccolò for my hand. Then I'd follow in my mother's footsteps: wedding in Monticiano followed by life in Siena, my future life smelling of linseed and eggs.

Two weeks later, while Ambrogio and I were mixing colours, a job in which I was becoming proficient, I heard a visitor below. Iacopo had returned.

'You mix the rest. I have to join them.'

'Brother Iacopo likes Giotto. Maybe you can use that to get the assignment.'

'Art should move forward not backwards to that old crock,' he said as he disappeared downstairs.

Though happy he trusted me to work on my own, once I'd prepared a couple of colours, I crept downstairs. I faced the shaven tonsure of Iacopo talking to Pietro, who beckoned me to join them.

Iacopo turned in his chair. 'The Lord be praised, Clara. You're safe!'

'Forgive me, Brother Iacopo, I didn't plan to run away.' I knelt before him, and he placed his hand on my head.

'That you are safe is comfort enough.'

'My brother found her in the Campo after the out-of-towners had left. They knew each other from when she lived in the city. I agreed she could stay and help my wife until the next market. She's been a great help.'

'On behalf of her family, I thank you for your generosity, Signor Pietro. But now our business is complete, I can take her back to her family.'

That wouldn't suit me at all.

'Can't I stay until my grandfather comes to collect me?' It was only another week, but that would be better than nothing. 'I've been learning so much about mixing paints in the studio.'

'What nonsense she talks,' said Pietro. 'To think I'd use a girl for that. We appreciate your help around the house, Clara, but now you must return home.'

Why was Ambrogio letting me go when we were betrothed? But he kept his back to me. Was he banishing me without a word? The room started spinning. Fearing I would faint, I grabbed the back of a chair.

'Please assure me you have looked after her.' Iacopo frowned. 'Any hint of scandal, and I'll find someone else for the commission.'

Scandal? Ambrogio had promised me a life together.

'Never fear, my wife and I have cared for her as if she were our own.' Pietro said. Ambrogio turned to the monk and looked outraged.

I looked between the two of them, unable to believe what was unfolding. Yet, even in my hazy state, I knew it would be foolish to admit my fall from grace.

'Your word is enough, Signor Lorenzetti. Come, Clara, your grandfather will be happy to have you back. I need to tell Sant'Agostino I'm leaving at once. I'll return shortly.' Iacopo left.

'Fetch your things,' Pietro said.

I dragged my feet up to the studio. Taking Ambrogio's brush, I dipped it into the Raw Siena and added a few strokes to his work. Something of me was going to stay in the city.

'Clara, I'm so sorry.' Ambrogio stood at the studio door while I found my cloak. 'Pietro was never going to let me take this work from him. And he gave me an ultimatum, you or Florence.'

'Florence! But what about our marriage?'

'I told you this is what I've been after for months.'

'You also pledged yourself to me and I believed you.'

'Clara, I will see you again. Don't ask me how or when, but I'll find you, I promise.' He put his arms around me and tried to kiss me, but I turned away.

With the taste of betrayal bitter in my mouth, and the smell of tempera in my nostrils, when I heard Iacopo return, I went downstairs.

Pietro put his arm round Iacopo's shoulders and ushered him to the door. 'I'll be in Monticiano as soon

127

as I've finished my current assignment, a matter of weeks.'

I took one last tearful glance at Ambrogio as I followed Iacopo into the street. Around us, people went about their regular morning business, their colours draining away in the blur of my grief. At the city gate, we found a merchant going most of the way to Monticiano. I cried in silence, as each roll of the cartwheel took me further from my dreams.

Chapter 11

On the journey back my mind dwelt on the deliciousness of our bodies intertwined, seeing his head on the pillow when I woke, his good-morning kiss. Marriage to him would realise all my dreams – a husband who loved me, a return to the city and the chance to paint. I refused to believe he'd give up that in favour of studying in Florence. I knew he still wanted me, or he'd never have promised to see me again. I was determined that when he came to Monticiano, I'd make him to take me away with him. I was already nineteen and could hardly be expected to wait for him to marry me on his return.

Close to nightfall and several changes of cart later, we reached Monticiano. Iacopo must have been afraid

I'd run away again for he escorted me home. The workshop door was still open and he went in. I hovered outside, reluctant to return to this colourless world.

'Did you find her?'

'See for yourself.' Iacopo stood aside.

'Clara! I thought you'd left us.' My grandfather came out and put his arms round me, swaying me from side to side. This was the comfort I'd needed after Blackbeard's assault.

'Now I've delivered my charge, I'll to the monastery,' Iacopo said.

'But where did you find her?' Niccolò's gruff voice returned.

'Clara can tell you, for I have much to discuss with the Prior.' I watched him make his way across the piazza and through the arch that led out of the old town, then joined my grandfather in the workshop.

'No lies, cara. You tricked me into taking you to market, then ran off. By rights you deserve a beating.'

'I'm so sorry, Nonno. I thought I'd time to see my friends at the palazzo and still be back with you by nightfall. But the Salimbeni refused to let me in and took me to the Tolomei. They tried to keep me prisoner and if Mamma hadn't helped me escape, I'd still be there.' I didn't dare tell him what had happened with Blackbeard, or he'd never let me out of his sight.

'Madonna mia, I knew the city was evil.' He shook his head, then wagged his finger at me. 'You'd better not be making this up.'

'I wish I were.' I stared at the shavings on the floor, a thick curly carpet which kept the place warm in winter.

'Then why didn't you come to find me at market?'

'You'd already gone.'

'How was I to know you were in trouble? I thought you wanted out of our lives for good.' He pinched the corner of his eyes to staunch the tears.

I felt guilty at having hurt him, but I had to prepare him for what was to come.

'Thank goodness I bumped into the man who looked after us the day Babbo was killed – the artist, Ambrogio Lorenzetti.' Saying his name was hard, I missed him so much. 'His brother let me stay with them and I looked after his children.'

'You didn't think of going to Iacopo for help? Now I'm beholden to these strangers.'

'I'm sure they expect nothing, for I worked hard.' Nothing like the drudgery of working for Orsola.

'You'd better be right, for I don't like making enemies. You never know when they might turn up as customers. Now go upstairs and see your cousins. They've been as crotchety as wasps since you've been missing.' He ran his hand over the piece of wood he'd been working on. 'A crutch for Timoteo. He'll be glad you're back.'

Poor Timoteo! Before Siena, he'd been my only hope.

'Hobbled in asking after you, and took to watching me work, sighing at every mention of your name.' Niccolò winked. 'Nice looking lad; but he'll not be returning to the mines with that foot. A decent crutch, now, and he can get around.'

But Timoteo was of no interest now. My cousins were a different matter.

'Stefano! Laura!' I called up the steps. 'Where are you hiding?'

Their smiling faces greeted me at the door, then they competed to give me the tightest hug.

'Where were you? You said you'd be back straight after market.' It was hard to mar Stefano's good-looking features, but he looked really hurt.

'I tried to, but I'd not seen my mother for years and her people insisted I stay with them. Now tell me what you've been up to while I've been away.'

Laura clutched my arm and leant her head against it, then dragged me to the kitchen.

Orsola's welcome was a sniff and Bruno saluted me with a goblet of wine. Only after I'd cleaned up after dinner, and the children had gone to bed, did they return to my time in Siena.

'Might have guessed you'd cause trouble.' Orsola said. 'You know Bruno's a heavy sleeper and needed rousing. And if anyone takes his place, it should be Stefano.'

'I was homesick.'

'Ten years with us and now you decide you're homesick?' Orsola's face went beetroot. 'You ungrateful wretch.'

'I saw my mother while I was there. You wouldn't recognize her, lost all her teeth one side of her mouth.'

'Too many sweetmeats at the rich man's table!' Bruno sneered. 'Can't expect me to have sympathy for that.'

'I think her husband beats her.'

'Time someone's knocked sense into her!' Bruno reached for more wine, but Orsola removed the flagon.

'He's a brute.' I gave an involuntary shudder, 'and has knocked out of her what sense she once had.'

'Bad at choosing husbands, for sure.' Bruno ploughed on. 'I mean, why marry a Salimbeni, when there were perfectly good men here.'

'Don't speak of my father like that!' I got to my feet. 'We'd still be living in the palazzo if he hadn't died protecting us.'

'But he did die, didn't he, and we took you in!' Orsola said.

'Now, that's enough,' Niccolò said. 'You must be tired, Clara.'

I gave my grandfather a grateful hug and left the room. Sleep had not been a priority during my nights with Ambrogio. In bed with the children, I snuggled up to Laura. She turned and put her arm over my chest. Wishing it were Ambrogio's, I drifted into sleep.

The following morning, I sat on the chest at the foot of Orsola's bed and pulled wool from the hemp sack at my knee. In the chill spring air – noticeably cooler than in the city – we both wore mittens. The annual task of preparing enough thread for our clothing needs was usually one of my favourites, principally because concentration forced Orsola into a companionable silence. But today, as I placed a handful of shorn wool between my carding boards, my head was filled with thoughts of Ambrogio. I mused on the letters carved on the bedstead; N and M - Niccolò and Maria, the grandmother after whom my mother had been named. Soon my C would be entwined with Ambrogio's A – for as soon as he'd claimed my hand, I'd ask Niccolò to make us a matrimonial bed.

Orsola used her right hand to pull the rough wool strands from my carding into a long fibrous thread, then wound it onto the spindle with her left. I was glad that today she'd claimed this more demanding task, for my head was full of Ambrogio. Banging the carding boards together too hard, the fibre fell into my lap in short tufts.

'Useless girl! Carry on like that and we'll have nothing to wear next winter.'

Three paces by four the room measured, yet I felt the walls coming in on me. Stuffing my fists in my lap to avoid the temptation to throttle my aunt, I gave her an elaborate curtsy. 'Excuse me, I need some air.'

'Curtsy indeed, you little minx. Who needs a girl who can curtsy?'

I grabbed the pitcher from the kitchen and set off for the fonte. Weeds extended their tentacles out of the crevices in the walls. Tufts of grass sprouted either side the once muddy paths. In my absence, a profusion of white, yellow and purple flowers had burst across the fallow fields. From across the valley came the light bleating of new-born lambs. I yearned to share these sights with Ambrogio – to see them through his eyes – but how long would he make me wait? By the time I carried the water back up the hill, I determined that once he showed up, I'd force him to take me back with him. Smiling at the prospect, I looked up to see Timoteo waving at me from his window. By the time I reached Incrociata he was waiting for me, armpit propped on a plank, its end buffered by an old rag.

'You're back, then?' He grinned and started limping alongside me. 'Niccolò was very worried.'

'Not so worried that he did anything to find me.' Why did the boy have to cling to me like goose grass. Ambrogio would never follow me around.

'He's caring enough to make me a proper crutch. I'm coming to see if it's ready.'

He looked so cheerful, so hopeful, I was ashamed of my rudeness, but he wasn't Ambrogio. And Ambrogio was coming here to see me again.

I couldn't have Timoteo getting any ideas, so from then on I made sure I was with Ugolina whenever I passed his window. Finding a way of being with Ambrogio was going to be a challenge but, even if it was a secret, we were still betrothed.

A month later, Stefano ran into the house. 'Quick, down to Sodo! He's arrived.'

'What are you talking about?' Orsola shook her head.

'The artist, Lorenzetti, he's at the monastery.' Stefano ran out again.

I thought only of Ambrogio and was alert in every sinew knowing this was the excuse for him to come as promised! Maybe Pietro had changed his mind and they'd be working at the monastery together. Pietro could even have been offered something better, and given Ambrogio this assignment. Even if it meant me staying in Monticiano until the job was complete, I was excited to see him again and my mind raced. As soon as he was here, we could get married– what did it matter where we lived as long as our future together was assured. And maybe the monastery would let me mix his paints until the time came for us to leave – together forever.

'I suppose we'd better see what this fuss is about.' Orsola wiped her nose on her sleeve.

'Hold my hand, Laura.' I was first to the door. 'You've a treat in store. The clothes these artists wear are so colourful.'

'Stop filling her head with stupidity.' Orsola wrapped herself in her shawl and we set off in the afternoon sun.

A crowd had already gathered outside the monastery, curious to see the man entrusted to create a monument to our beloved Antonio Patrizi.

'They say it's being paid for by a man from Scalvaia who left all his money to the monastery!' As usual, Ugolina's mother was the source of all gossip. 'Nothing for his widow and children. What sins he must have committed!'

'Did you see the artist when he arrived?' Hair colour was all I needed.

'Fine black stallion. And that was just his horse!' the woman cackled, and the others joined in once they'd checked none of the men were listening. I'd learn nothing more until the man himself appeared.

While we waited, Ugolina's mother announced her

daughter's marriage to Macellino later in the year.

'By the size of the sausage in his trousers, he couldn't wait long,' Ugolina whispered. For her, marriage was a game, a lark, whereas marrying Ambrogio felt more like life or death.

I kept my eyes on the monastery doors. Eventually they creaked open. First out was Brother Iacopo; clasped hands, black habit, bowed head. Behind him came Prior Benedetto, stretching himself as tall as his torso allowed but still only reaching Iacopo's shoulder. Finally, the artist. The crowd raised a cheer for the man who was dressed to impress: red velvet cloak with gold satin lining, striped leggings, and soft leather shoes that wouldn't last a week on Monticiano's stony tracks. He stood at the top of the monastery steps and acknowledged the crowd's acclaim. But I wasn't cheering. For underneath his velvet cap was the red hair of Pietro.

I longed to run home, hurl myself on the bed and sob. Instead I found my feet glued to the well-trodden soil, listening to a long-winded speech by the prior. The artist would design a glass window to outdo that of the abbey in San Galgano; and everyone in Monticiano was to empty their coffers to pay for it. Pietro said he was honoured to be selected for such a prestigious assignment (and maybe it was, compared to the accounts' book cover) and promised to produce a work worthy of Monticiano's saint. As soon as Pietro and the monks went inside, I led the children home.

'I'll not have it!' Orsola said as soon as she got back. 'Your friend, Ugolina, whose only attraction is her

136

ginger hair, has found a man, and a decent one at that. But for my scrounger of a niece? Not even a nibble of interest.'

Stefano and Laura slipped off their chairs and disappeared into the bedroom.

'We'll not put up with your high and mighty ways any longer.' She prodded my shoulder. 'I've asked you to find a husband, told you to find a husband, and you won't even partner anyone to Camerata! You do nothing to get yourself off our hands except humiliate me. I've had enough. If you're not married by year end, you're on the streets, understand?'

I pushed past my aunt, out of the door and sat on the top step, my head spinning. I didn't give a fig about Ugolina marrying the butcher. But I wouldn't be forced into marriage in Monticiano while I waited for Ambrogio.

Next morning, I woke to the bell – one deep note – calling the devoted to prayer. I dressed and left, ignoring the open doors of the town church to my right. Like its surroundings in Sodo, the monastery was a muted blend of brown and grey. Even inside, the decoration consisted only of a simple wooden cross on a marble altar. I dipped my hand into the holy water and crossed myself. Besides the monks, Pietro and I were the only worshippers and I went to speak to him after the monks had filed out.

'I'm glad Brother Iacopo got you home safely.'

'I came to thank you for your kindness. But my grandfather thinks I imposed on you and is keen not to be in your debt.'

'But we are in yours, Clara. After I lost the job in Assisi, we had to cut back on servants, so Giovanna was grateful for your help. And Ambrogio was very happy to have someone else mixing paints.' Pietro stared at the two tall narrow windows. 'The Prior has got it into his head we should have a round window, like San Galgano. So wrong here, but he's insistent. If only Ambrogio were here to help argue my case.'

This was my opening. 'Are you expecting him?'

'No. But once they give me my first payment, I'm sending him to Florence. Only when he finds his own style will we know if he's any good.'

'But he promised himself to me!' I couldn't hold Orsola off forever.

'Whatever he said, you were mistaken. You weren't the first, and you won't be the last.' Pietro put his arm around my shoulders and gave them a squeeze. 'Forget him, Clara.'

But I was more to Ambrogio than that! He'd been present at the best and worst moments of my life. Why would he break his promise to marry me?'

Remembering my time in his studio, Pietro began talking through his ideas for the design as if I were his brother. And upset though I was about his comments about Ambrogio, I felt privileged to be included in his thoughts on the assignment.

'And I shall need a sturdy scaffold to undertake this work. Do you know of a good carpenter?'

'My grandfather, Niccolò, is well-regarded. His workshop is near the town church. You can see the bell tower from here. I can take you there now.'

'Thank you, but no. I must commit my ideas to parchment at once; first a sketch, then detailed drawings for the glassmakers in Murano.'

I turned to go.

'Get that rapscallion brother of mine out of your mind. It'll be years before he can afford a wife, and when he does, he'll need a wealthy one. And anyway, a bright girl like you should have no trouble finding a husband.'

But I didn't want any husband, I wanted Ambrogio. He'd promised to come and when he did, I'd be ready.

So, for the next few days Ugolina walked with me out of town. Together we sat looking out over the Siena road, but all in vain. And when Ugolina complained I was taking her away from Macellino, I went on my own.

Every morning before I donned my dress, I paused to smooth my hands over my body in eager anticipation of what I hoped was to come. Each afternoon, while the family took its siesta, I ran past the monastery and on down the hill, past the farm on the right where the goats greeted me with their baying; on past fields where men were planting sunflowers. At the track that led through the woods to San Galgano, I waited, only to return home disappointed.

After days of despondency, my eyes fixed on a speck in the distance. A lone rider. Could it be him at last? I looked for somewhere to hide, to savour his approach in secret. The fields were planted, but the corn, which could have offered me sanctuary when grown, had yet to break through. I crouched among the grasses of the hedgerow.

The closer he came, the surer I was. Though his hat covered his hair, the physique – the body I'd grown to know so well – was his. He was wearing a blue cloak threaded with gold, which gleamed in the afternoon sunlight. Then, when I saw his golden hair, I ran to greet him.

'Clara! What are you doing?' He swerved the horse to avoid running into me. 'We could both have been killed.'

'I knew you'd come! I so wanted to see you and it'll be impossible once you're closeted with the monks.'

'Was there some urgent reason you needed to speak?'

Why was he so wary? In the last month I'd yearned for him every waking moment and had no intention of holding back. 'I'd die if I didn't see you again.'

'Then this is a mighty welcome!' Ambrogio dismounted, checked to see if anyone was watching, then kissed me.

I felt a pounding through every part of my body, as if I had a horse race running through my veins.

'Let's get off the road,' Ambrogio said, now smiling, 'away from prying eyes.'

I wanted that too. 'If we walk up this track, you can see the round window at the abbey of San Galgano. Pietro needs your help to argue against having the same in Monticiano.'

'Good idea.' He kissed my neck and my whole body tingled. After leading the horse into the shade, he tethered it to a sapling surrounded by grass. 'He'll be

140

glad of the rest. I can see it's a steep climb ahead.'

Our hands clasped as we walked, binding me closer to him. The hills in Monticiano were steeper than those in Siena and he was soon out of breath. Around us pines changed to oaks – or were they chestnut? – their foliage fighting for sunshine above. Shrubs and dry leaves covered the ground. When we reached the ridge, the abbey was before us. The massive stone structure lay on a stretch of flat land surrounded by hills. Overlooking it was the hermitage of Monte Siepe, and in between, a mill lay idle.

'Magnificent.' Ambrogio stood behind me, his arms around my waist. 'So well-proportioned. If I were designing an abbey, I'd like to think I'd build one as beautiful. Is the monastery at Monticiano as grand?'

'They'd like it to be, but it's just a small church.' I turned to face him, smelling the cinnamon on his clothes. His lips covered mine, and I felt as safe from Blackbeard as I'd been within the Salimbeni's protective walls.

'What say we give our legs a rest?' He took off his jacket and threw it, lining side down, on the grass. He helped me down then lay close beside me.

'How I've missed you, Ambrogio. I've dreamt of you every night.'

'And I you. My bed is empty without you.' He removed my shawl, ran his fingers over my arms, kissed my breast, then he was on top of me.

'I love you with all my heart.' Was there anything more I could say to confirm he was the one?

He pulled back for a moment. 'I'm truly honoured.'

141

Why didn't he use the word love? But soon I was carried away by his caresses and riding the waves of oblivion. Only then did he enter me and satisfy himself. He lay back beside me and smiled. 'I know it's blasphemous, but from now on, whenever anyone mentions San Galgano, I'll picture us here.'

I lay beside him, listening to the birds' evening chorus. Eventually he raised himself on one elbow. 'We'd better get moving while I have energy for the last bit of the journey. If I fall asleep, I'll be here all night!'

'When shall I see you again?' I said as we walked back to his tethered horse. It would be difficult to meet, but there must be a way.

'Pietro will want to discuss what he's up to, and after that I'll come and find you. Your grandfather's the carpenter, isn't he?'

I clung to his arm. He was going to ask Nonno for my hand! Life with Ambrogio was wonderful, without him unbearable.

'If Pietro gives you the money to go to Florence, I'm coming with you, even if there's no time to marry first.'

'That's a lovely idea,' Ambrogio tucked one of my curls behind my ear, then cleared his throat. 'But I need the freedom to find who I am as an artist and I must do that without encumbrance.'

Encumbrance! The word took the ground from under me.

'But I'll cost you nothing. I'll keep house for you, help in the studio, whatever you need. I'd starve by your side rather than drown in this sea of beige.'

'For goodness' sake, be realistic, Clara. I'm a poor

artist, and you're a poor servant girl. Together we'll be paupers. All we have is these last moments together.' He tried to hug me but I pulled away.

'I thought I meant something to you but Pietro was right. I'm like all your others. I wish I'd never met you.' Bitter-sweet tears spilt down my cheeks.

'I'm sorry, Clara. I wish it could be different.'

'I could wait for you?' Now I was clutching at straws, to keep myself in his life.

'No, it'll take years for me to be admitted to the guild. For only then will Pietro accept me as his equal.'

We'd reached his horse and he put his arms around me. 'You deserve to be happy, Clara. Forget me and find a better man.'

Better? There was no better man for me. My sobs were uncontrollable.

'Come now, I'll be consigned to your past in no time at all.'

But he was everything I wanted.

'Now, jump up beside me, and I'll take you up this hill.' He leapt into the saddle and lifted me in front of him. His arms encircled my waist to hold the reins and I felt his breath on my cheek, enjoying his presence for as long as I could. Under the double weight, the horse plodded slowly and all too soon the grey walls of the town came into view.

'I should let you go the rest of the way alone or tongues will wag.' He lifted me down and kissed my tears. 'I'm sure we'll see each other again. Our paths have a way of crossing!'

As I walked across Sodo in the fading light, I

inhaled the lingering smell of Ambrogio on my skin. I longed to hang on to it, but it was too revealing. I cleaned my face with my scarf, leaving a stale sweetness that would not be remarked upon. Before turning up Via del Portico, I checked my dress for grass stains. When I reached the house, I took a deep breath.

'And where do you think you've been?' Orsola wiped the table with vigour. I'd been out much longer today.

'I wasn't feeling well. I had to get some fresh air, sorry.'

'Sorry? Every afternoon this week you've sneaked out leaving me to prepare the food, and all you have to say is sorry?' Orsola looked everywhere other than at me.

'You are right to be angry, Aunt, but what more can I say?' I was too tired to fight back. 'I accept whatever punishment you choose, but I'd ask you to save it for tomorrow. I shall faint if I don't lie down.' I wanted to hang onto the last vestiges of the afternoon before Orsola obliterated them.

'Let her go, Orsola. She's flushed. Maybe she has a fever.' Bruno wandered over to the corner where the wine flagon was stored.

I slipped into the bedroom, being sure to close the door behind me.

I threw myself down on the bed, pressing my mouth deep into the pillow. 'Ambrogio!' I sobbed. Lying on my back, I remembered his weight on top of me, the warmth of his lips, the gentle whisper of his breath against my cheeks. We were meant to be together! I got up and opened the shutter. The sun had disappeared over the town gate opposite and the sky above blazed red. He'd said his goodbyes. But did I have to accept them? If I could find my way back to Siena, surely I could find my way back to Ambrogio?

The door of the bedroom creaked open. But instead of one of the children, it was Orsola. 'With all this acting up of yours, I thought I should ask if everything's all right with your monthly bleed.' She sounded embarrassed.

'Why shouldn't it be?' I turned away and looked at the sunset.

'Just needed to be sure,' Orsola said, and left.

But my heart beat fast. I'd been so preoccupied with Ambrogio's return, I'd not counted the days. But I knew without doing so I was already late. Then, as I remembered how irregular I could be when upset – and that incident with Blackbeard had been terrifying – I told myself not to be hasty. My heart slowed a little.

Yet the suspicion remained.

What if I were carrying Ambrogio's child? I knew he was sad to leave me. Surely a child would bring him back? He might live for his art, but he had some decency. A few more days and I'd know and would go straight to the monastery. Imagining his excitement at the news gave me enough peace of mind to drift into an unsettled sleep. A baby would change everything.

Chapter 12

The moon waxed and waned, and still my maiden's friend didn't appear. If only I could confide in Ugolina, but she'd tell her mother who'd see it as her duty to pass on the news to the whole town.

I walked to the monastery, hoping to see Ambrogio – for I felt so alone – but only Pietro's horse was tethered outside. I stroked its mane and wondered what to do. What sympathy could I expect from the brother who'd warned me off from the start? As I leant against the horse's neck, a picture of Vanni tending his father's mount came to mind. Praying he was still at Camerata, I determined to visit the hermitage the following morning.

That night, I closed my ears to Orsola's rumblings, my nose to Bruno's farts, and allowed myself to drift in and out of a light sleep. At every semi-waking I checked the shutters. Then, at first light, I crept through the bedroom, as silent as the creatures infesting our mattresses. In the early hours, I swept floors, put away candles and cleared out the ashes from the wood-burning fire. Though warm in the day, June was still cold at night.

Anxious and queasy, I set off. I should have been fetching water, but given my disobedience of late, what was one further sin. As I passed through the Porta, Timoteo's shutters were closed. The mist had cleared by the time I reached the turning to the hermitage, though my mind was still cloudy. Already the grass had dried yellow, the fields turned to gold. As rivulets of sweat ran down my spine, I was glad I'd set off early.

When I reached Camerata, the chapel was open and I tiptoed in. A monk was prising wax drips off the candles and saving them in an earthenware pot. Only when he'd finished trimming the wicks did he turn and I saw, for sure, it was Vanni.

'Clara!' In this semi-outdoor life, his face had become tanned and it suited him.

'I'm so happy to see you, Vanni. But are you well? You look thinner.'

'Too much fresh air and exercise and none of Cook's panettone!' he laughed. 'I'm glad you came because they're moving me to another monastery next week, and I was wondering how to let you know. It's closer to the city, so my family can visit. Only so much of this country life I can take!'

He was leaving? 'Then I'm glad I found you in time. I need to discuss something personal, and you're the only one I can trust.'

'That sounds ominous. What have you been up to?' Vanni's frown reminded me of the Conte. 'Shall we sit outside. The rest have gone wood-gathering.'

A fallen trunk at the edge of the clearing offered a seat in the shade. Around us lizards rustled in the undergrowth. Birds hopped from branch to branch in the trees. I took a deep breath. 'I'm with child.'

'You're married? I knew it would happen someday. So who is he?' He patted my knee.

I shook my head. Telling Vanni was harder than I'd anticipated. Eventually I squeezed out the words. 'I'm not married.'

His mood changed at once. He stood up and walked around the clearing, the furrows on his brow deepening. Eventually he turned. 'You could have had the best husband in town. Instead ... you're as bad as your mother!'

'That's not fair.' How could he compare me to her! 'He promised to marry me, but now his situation has changed.' No point mentioning Florence. In Vanni's world, an artistic mission was no excuse.

'Unlike you to be duped.'

'Please don't be harsh, Vanni. I've no-one else to turn to.'

He sat next to me, shaking his head, while I talked through my tears - how I'd returned to Siena and what happened with the Tolomei.

'If I ever get back there, I swear I'll kill that Blackbeard.'

'Don't you dare. He's already taken my father, and my mother's sanity. I'd die if he took you too.'

He punched his fist into his palm, then took a couple of deep breaths. 'If the child's not Blackbeard's, whose is it?'

So I told him how I'd found Ambrogio after my grandfather left.

'That chancer! Remember him trying to prise money out of the Contessa? Bet he couldn't believe his luck discovering a damsel in distress. He's used you and deserves to be punished.'

'What's got into you? You're supposed to be a man of God, but you want to run a sword into everyone!'

'So he took you back to his brother's …'

'And behaved honourably, teaching me to be an artist. I only gave myself to him when he promised we'd be together forever.' The memory of what I was losing brought me to the brink of tears again.

'Was that before he got you into bed, or after?'

'Why do you think the worst of him?' I would have stayed at home if I'd known Vanni would be so mean.

'Think hard.' He persisted.

'Before.' Yet he'd promised. If only I could remember his exact words. All I knew was that they were enough at the time.

'Then he's the rogue I thought he was.' He was as relentless as the Conte on a bad day. 'How could you throw yourself away like that? Are all the women in your family are destined to be swept off their feet by a scoundrel.'

'How dare you compare Ambrogio with Blackbeard!'

'Then where is he, this love of yours?'

I sobbed, unable to hold back any longer. 'He's studying art in Florence and has no money to keep me.'

'And you thought he'd give up that life for you and your baby!'

'But he promised.' The words came out as a whine.

Vanni's sustained attack on Ambrogio was giving me doubts.

'Your only hope is to make him take some responsibility. Ask him for money.'

'I've already told you, he has none. He relies on Pietro for everything.'

'Then write to Pietro. I bet he spends half his life bailing out his brother.'

'I don't need to write. He's working in Monticiano.' I wiped my eyes with the heel of my hand.

'Then there's your answer.' Vanni stayed silent for some moments, then took my hand. 'I'm sorry, I didn't mean to upset you. I'm so angry with that apology for a man I'm forgetting your predicament. Is there somewhere you could stay until the baby comes? Then you could hand it over to the ospedale in Siena.'

'Never! I'm keeping the baby, with or without Ambrogio.'

'Then find someone to marry you before your predicament shows. You're beginning to plump up already.'

'Not while I have hopes of marrying Ambrogio.'

'That donkey doesn't deserve to be your husband but give him another chance if you must. But then you must come to your senses. What you need is an admirer who loves you so much they'll forgive you your sins. Think, Clara, who could that be?'

I'd teased Timoteo, spurned him even, but now he was my only hope. 'I'll die, stuck in Monticiano for the rest of my life.'

'I'd like to be in Siena too, but we can't always have

150

what we want.' Vanni's eyes were sad as he squeezed my hand. 'You have to do what's best for the child. Think how much better a mother you'll be than either of ours was.'

'I'd have to work hard to be worse.' I shook my head and laughed.

'Now, go.' There was a smile at the corner of his mouth, though his brown eyes were serious. 'The monks shouldn't find us together.'

'That's funny. Ambrogio said something similar when we parted.'

'But he had more to hide. Farewell, Clara.' He gave me a hug and I rested my head on the wool of his habit. Would this be the last time I'd see my friend? 'Now, find a way out of this web you've woven for yourself. Next time in Siena, eh?'

'Next time in Siena!' I echoed, with little hope.

As I scrambled down the bank of the stream on my way back to Monticiano, I slipped. This was another answer: to enter eternal darkness in the water below. Shin deep in the cold stream, I imagined weighing myself down with stones. Oblivion was tempting, an easy end to all my troubles. However, Vanni had helped me see what I had to do. Clutching my swelling belly, I crossed the babbling water and climbed the opposite bank.

When I reached the outskirts of the town, I took the well-trodden path to the fonte. The early morning activity was over and I cupped my hand in the spring. Its coldness was comforting – one feature of my life that hadn't changed. I sat on the stones around the pool and examined my reflection, seeing myself as Ambrogio would have seen me. The fullness of my lips had the effect of giving me a permanent, though not unattractive, pout. He'd have noticed the straightness of my nose, more elegant than Orsola's pudgy one. My eyebrows were thick and framed my eyes in a satisfactory manner. I pulled my hair away from my face to allow cool air to my neck, and to look sensible, for now I was going to be a mother. Vanni might think Ambrogio a scoundrel, but I'd always love him – for the colour he'd brought to my life. I dipped my hand in the water and the image disappeared.

I dragged myself up the track to the town, so preoccupied I didn't register Timoteo's eyes on me. But by the time I reached Incrociata he was waiting, blushing, awkward. Eventually he found his tongue. 'Buona sera, Clara.'

Past midday already. 'How's the new crutch?'

'I was wondering' Timoteo's dark eyes courted mine, 'if we could sit and talk on the church steps this evening?'

After my talk with Vanni, I knew I should agree, but my head was still a jumble. And I wasn't yet ready to give up my dreams. 'I'm sorry, Timoteo.'

He closed his eyes as if his world had fallen apart. 'I knew you wouldn't be interested someone with a leg as mangled as mine.'

'It's not that. Just not this afternoon.' Before I committed myself to Timoteo, I had to tell Ambrogio of my state, and that meant speaking to Pietro. 'Though beware. I'm sure to disappoint when you know more about me.'

'Then give me the chance to find out.' Timoteo's smile returned, reminding me of his former appeal. How unfair to encourage him when my heart had already been claimed.

'I'll let you know.' I felt his eyes following me up Via di Mezzo, wishing they belonged to Ambrogio.

As I came within sight of the piazza, I saw Pietro enter the workshop. This was my chance. But I had to speak to him in private. I sat on the church steps, waiting for him to emerge.

'When you've worked out the cost, come to the monastery, so I can advise the prior.' Pietro said, then closed the door after him. I ran to catch him before he disappeared through the gate.

'Clara! I trust all is well?' Pietro acknowledged me with a bow. 'My brother was here for a short while, but you missed him.'

I blushed, as I recalled our meeting in the woods. 'It's of your brother I wish to speak. Or rather, his child,'

'Not again!' Pietro hit his forehead with his hand. 'Follow me outside the town, where we can speak in private.'

He walked ahead. Once beyond the outer gates he turned and threw his hat onto the rough ground of Sodo. 'Christ's nails, I knew this would happen! Didn't I warn you? You went into this liaison with your eyes open, so don't ask for pity. If I paid for every slut he's got with child, I'd be ruined.'

'That's not fair. You know he took advantage of my predicament. He promised to marry me, and that's what I expect.'

'Well, he can't. You think he'll settle for a place in your grandfather's workshop building scaffolding all his life? Though I'd never admit it to him, he could become a great artist, and I'll not let you stop him.'

'But I love him.' My eyes prickled with approaching tears.

'That's not enough. To be a successful artist, he needs money and the only way he'll get it is to marry someone with connections,' Pietro picked up his hat and dusted it against his thigh. 'Can't you see, he'd despise you if you stopped him fulfilling his dreams? Why do you think I paid for him to study astrology at Siena University? Why am I now paying for him to go to Florence? Because he'd never forgive me if I didn't. And if you do love him – which I doubt after an acquaintance of only a week – you'll give him up.'

I covered my face with my hands. Although I could hardly call playing with paints a work of art, by doing it, I'd seen how satisfying it was creating one's own work. Dimly, I perceived the sacrifice it would be for someone with real talent to give that up. But I was with child.

'I belong to Ambrogio.' His name caught in my throat. 'And he gave me to believe he felt the same. Once he knows the circumstances, I'm sure he'll make good his promise marry me.'

'Then I'll make sure he never finds out.'

'But I can't stay the rest of my life in Monticiano. It's not my home, and never will be.'

154

'So, Ambrogio was your ploy to escape!'

I resented the accusation. Ploys belonged to my mother, not me. 'He's far more to me than that. He was with me the night my father died. He was the last person I saw when leaving Siena. He found me when I was fleeing the Tolomei. He was destined to be part of my life and I gave him everything.' What more could I say to convince Pietro?

'Then he has done you a great disservice by disposing of your virtue so lightly. My advice is to find someone in the town and convince him the child is his.'

Marry someone else? 'But Ambrogio's the only man I've known.'

'Well, I'm sorry, I can do nothing for you.' Pietro walked off.

How could he abandon me! He knew what had been going on, and did nothing to stop it, even lied to Iacopo. I called after him. 'Then I shall tell the Prior how your family have treated me.'

'He won't believe you.' Nonetheless, Pietro walked back.

'You forget it was Brother Iacopo who found me at your house. You swore to him you'd looked after me "as if I were your daughter". It'll be the end of your assignment when the Prior learns what you let happen under your roof, and how you lied to his envoy.'

'No need to be hasty. I'm sure we can settle this amicably. How much?'

Did he think I'd sell my life with Ambrogio for thirty pieces of silver? Yet Vanni's words reverberated in my head. What would it take for Timoteo to accept me when he knew the worst? 'I'll need a dowry to persuade someone to marry me – someone who has no money of their own, and no means of supporting either himself or me. If we're going to have a life together, we need help.'

'Who is this man? I'll come and agree the sum with your grandfather this evening.'

I closed my eyes. To give him Timoteo's name would be to give all my dreams – of love, of returning to the city – saying goodbye to colour to be with a man I hardly knew.

'Don't tarry, for people will soon work out from your girth what's happening.'

I had no choice. I spoke the word that would clinch my fate. 'Timoteo.'

A few months earlier he'd been my harbinger of spring. How quickly his appeal had been eclipsed by the man I'd touched toes with at the fiesta a decade earlier. Now this former miner was my only hope of propriety; a propriety I'd have sacrificed only too willingly for a life with Ambrogio.

'Tell your grandfather I have some further business to discuss with him and will come this evening. Arrivederla, Signorina.' We'd been on friendly terms in Siena, but now he addressed me formally. As the monastery door thudded behind him, I wrapped my arms around my stomach as if it were Ambrogio himself. Whatever happened, he would live on in our child; a piece of Siena I would forever nurture and love.

As I walked up Via del Portico, I acknowledged Ugolina's fiancé at the butchers'. My friend was marrying the man she loved, while I would be spending the rest of my life with someone I hardly cared for, that was if he even agreed.

That evening Pietro called at the house. 'It's Signor Lorenzetti,' I said, letting him in. Although not a tall man, his bright clothes made him seem too large for our kitchen.

Niccolò wiped his hands on his apron and extended one to the artist. 'You are welcome, signor. Have you changed your requirements for the scaffolding?'

I hadn't been able to bring myself to tell him to expect the artist.

'No, no, another matter. May we talk in your workshop?'

'Certainly, Signor Pietro.'

'I'd like Clara to join us.'

'What's she been up to now!' Orsola rattled the pots on their shelves, while Bruno raised his eyes to the ceiling. However, Niccolò fetched the keys and led our guest down the front steps.

'Niccolò, my esteemed man, I don't know how to put this delicately, so I'll just out with it.' Pietro began as soon as the door was closed. 'My brother, Ambrogio, and your granddaughter have had a liaison. And Clara is carrying his child.'

'No!' Niccolò shouted and overturned a workbench. Tools clattered to the floor. His livid eyes turned on me, then back to Pietro. 'Then he must marry her.'

'That won't be possible. He needs money and Clara

157

has no useful connections.'

'Useful connections!' Niccolò spat on the floor. 'We are respectable people yet you speak of her as a handicap when she could have made a fine match. Instead, your brother has ruined her, and is too much of a coward to speak to me himself!'

I'd never seen my grandfather so angry, in no way cowed by Pietro's fame.

'I'm sorry, Niccolò, I'm a man of pictures. I should have chosen my words with more care. Whether he's here or not, the nub of it is, Ambrogio won't marry her.'

The finality of his words cut deep, like the blade that had killed Babbo.

'However, to ease matters, I am willing to provide a dowry to enable her to make a respectable marriage – to a man called Timoteo.'

'The cripple! What makes you think she'll accept him when she's rejected everyone else?'

'Because that's who she suggested.' He looked to me to confirm and I nodded. 'This money is all I have with me. Please accept it on Ambrogio's behalf.'

Niccolò opened the leather purse and poured into his hand more gold florins than I had held in my life.

'I suggest you act quickly.' Pietro glanced at my belly. 'Buona notte.'

I looked at the ground, expecting Niccolò to pour his wrath on me. For once a beating was justified. Yet when I looked up, his eyes were red; full of hurt and disappointment. 'I wanted the best for you, Clara.'

Kneeling before him, I hugged his knees. 'I'm sorry, Nonno. You've been so good to me, and I've repaid your kindness by bringing you shame.'

His firm hand pulled me to my feet and pushed me out of the workshop. After locking up, he followed me up the steps to the kitchen. 'Go to bed, children. We've something to discuss.'

With only mild protests, for they heard the firmness in their grandfather's voice, Stefano and Laura disappeared.

'Orsola,' Niccolò said. 'How friendly are you with Timoteo's mother?'

'She's always at the fonte doing other people's washing. That's how she makes money now her son can no longer provide for her.'

'Go now and speak to her about Clara marrying her son.' Niccolò sat on the bench, holding the inner corners of his eyes to stop the tears.

'Why should I stoop so low?' Orsola folded her arms and settled herself more comfortably in her chair, making clear she was not intending to budge. 'Timoteo should be doing the asking, though it's laughable she'd accept someone like him.'

'She is with child, and it's not Timoteo's. Here's the dowry to persuade him to marry her.' Niccolò put Pietro's purse on the table. Bruno took it at once and counted the coins. I felt like a lame horse being sold off at market.

'I knew it,' Orsola shouted. 'After all we've done for her, she repays us with a bastard. She's a trollop just like her mother.'

'That's right, tell the whole town.' I said, just loud enough to be heard.

'I'm not lifting a finger for the little slut.' A gob of Orsola's spittle landed on my cheek.

'Every day you tell me how much you want to get rid of me, yet when you get your chance, you won't take it.'

'Go now, Orsola, and see what you can agree with Dorotea. If there's any money left over, it can go towards Laura's dowry.' Niccolò broke the impasse.

'If I arrange this for you, you little harlot,' Orsola pulled my ear, 'you can be grateful to me for the rest of your life.' She grabbed her woollen shawl and left.

I cleared away the dishes and made some pretence of occupying myself with chores. Niccolò sat with his head in his hands, and Bruno nursed his drink. Then, impatient to know if my fate had been decided, I went after Orsola.

The evening was humid. Around the piazza, women were sitting on their front steps, chatting to neighbours. I walked down Via di Mezzo and through the Porta, to sit on the wall outside the gate. Looking out over the valley, I knew all hope of leaving Monticiano was lost once Orsola accomplished her mission. I bit one of my nails, relishing the pain as I exposed some of the soft skin below.

Through the half-open shutters I heard female voices. Was Orsola putting my case well? Would she mention the child? I ripped off another fingernail. Then the voices ceased. I heard footsteps and ran to catch up with my aunt.

'You'd better be grateful to me, you hussy. The pheasant isn't in the bag, but he's drawing into the trap.

With that foot of his, he's as low on the list of eligible men as they get. Yet even he's not sure he'll stoop to marrying you.'

'Now he knows about the child, he'll never want me.' Yet he was my only hope.

'Believe me,' Orsola dug her nails into my arm, 'I long for you out of my house, but now we have to wait.'

Chapter 13

Friday was market day in Monticiano. The man who repaired crossbows was in his usual place inside the main gate. A crowd of men had gathered, watching him replace and tighten strings. Next to him a stall sold arrows in a range of weights suitable for catching bird to boar. Beyond them carts lined the piazza selling sacks, harnesses, belts, nails, rope, chains, hats of cloth and hats with trims, and furniture. Ugolina was busy with arrangements for her forthcoming marriage. So I trailed after Orsola, carrying a basket of green beans and another of fava to dry for the winter. For how much longer could I hold my head up here?

A woman half Orsola's girth approached. 'About the matter we discussed,' Dorotea muttered. 'Timoteo would like to talk with Clara. He's waiting, at the

Porta.'

What would he say? I doubted I could take more scorn.

'Stefano! Where's that boy when I need him?' Orsola shouted. 'Here, Laura, you take one basket, I'll hold the other.'

The sun was high, but Timoteo had found a patch of shade. He was sitting on the wall with his legs stretched out, his mangled foot healed into a mess like part-kneaded dough. His other calf was also scarred.

'Sit down,' he said, putting feet back in sandals.

I took off my headscarf and wiped the perspiration running down my temples.

'I know about the child.' He looked angry. It crossed my mind that if we were married, he might hit me. 'I don't want to know how it happened, or who the father is.'

'It's the artist, Ambrogio Lorenzetti.' I wanted no secrets if we were to spend our lives together.

'It doesn't matter who he is, or what he does.' He looked out over the valley, but when he turned back, his eyes were wet, 'only if you have feelings for me.'

My mind raced as I struggled to recall what I'd felt before Ambrogio. 'You arrived, this mystery miner from Massa and I was intrigued. When you called from your window, I thought you were the most attractive man in town. I wanted to get to know you, but before I did,' I looked in despair at my expanding body, 'this happened.'

'So you don't love me?' He looked crestfallen.

I closed my eyes, trying to put out of mind

162

Ambrogio's fair hair and impish grin, his colourful clothes. A few tears spilt as I turned to head-to-toe-in-brown Timoteo. 'I could, in time.' I hated how my words hurt him, yet I dared to take his hand. 'I deserve nothing but if you take me on, I'll be grateful to my dying day.'

'I was in love with you from the first moment I saw you.' Timoteo gazed towards the fonte as if recalling me walk past. 'You were beautiful and aloof, a princess, and I was your vassal to command. Even though you were beyond my reach, I had hopes. Then yesterday my mother gives me news beyond my wildest dreams; Clara wants to marry me! I'm in heaven. Then she tells me you are carrying another man's child.' Emotions blew across Timoteo's face like clouds on a windy day. He hit the stone with his fist.

'I deserve all your reproaches.'

In the long silence between us, the cicadas in the surrounding fields began their whistling chorus. I looked out to the Maremma road, one last vain hope that Ambrogio would appear, but all was brown, brown and more brown.

'I will marry you, as long as you agree to my conditions.'

How odd to discuss marriage, without any prior kiss.

'First, as that man's from Siena, you must promise never to go back.'

'Not ever? What if I have good reason?' He couldn't have asked more of me. How could I sacrifice the hope that had kept me going the last decade? Yet what choice

163

did I have? I was a boar cornered by hunters with no chance of escape.

'Even if there is, you must never ask.'

'What are the other conditions?' How much more joy I'd have had discussing marriage to Ambrogio.

'Promise this first, or it's all off.' Timoteo looked sterner than I could have imagined.

I swallowed hard, nodding to the end of all my dreams. Please God, let his other conditions be easier.

'Secondly, you must get your grandfather take me on in the workshop.'

'Orsola will object. I'm already the cuckoo in her nest. And Niccolò's promised the workshop to Bruno when he dies.'

'I'm not asking for ownership, only to earn enough money for us to live. They should see it as the price for preserving the family's reputation.'

'I'll ask.' I guessed Orsola had hung on to most of Pietro's purse.

'And finally, you must bear me children. I don't want our only child to be that of another man.' Timoteo was no longer the boy in the window. We'd both grown up in the last few days.

Somewhere out of sight, a shutter opened, but my hoped-for life was closing.

'Is it agreed?' Timoteo covered my hand and I felt the calluses gained swinging picks in the Massa mines.

'Be a good husband to me, Timoteo, and I'll do my best to be a good wife.'

'You won't need to worry about keeping house. My mother will continue to do that.' He gave my hand a

164

squeeze.

I sighed, realizing I'd be a servant in my new home, though hopefully Dorotea would be an easier mistress than Orsola.

'Talk to your grandfather. When he agrees, I'll speak to the priest.'

Ambrogio, Ambrogio, what have you done? If I didn't love him so much, I'd be angry with him for leaving me with child and forcing me into this.

Within the week, Timoteo and I were married: a quiet affair attended only by Niccolò and Dorotea. Not even Bruno and Orsola graced us with their presence. I wore my everyday homespun. With all the last-minute chores Orsola insisted on, I'd had no time to sew on ribbons or collect flowers for my hair. After the ceremony we walked to my new home and ate a wedding breakfast of bread and cheese washed down with water. It wasn't the celebration I'd imagined. All that was special about the meal was that Dorotea had collected the water.

The only good part of my new life was that I'd never again face Blackbeard.

Ferragosto came and went, Ugolina married her butcher boy, summer became autumn and Christmas approached. On the last Sunday before Advent, the monastery bells called us to a special mass. My expanded belly now prevented me sleeping well, but no discomfort was going to make me miss the celebration of Pietro's windows. But what made me take extra care with my appearance was the hope, buried in some

165

unswept corner of my heart, that Ambrogio would come to share in his brother's triumph. I'd made no promise to Timoteo not to speak to him if Siena came here.

'Let's set off in plenty of time. It isn't every day Monticiano gets stained glass windows like the Duomo in...' I caught myself in time, now avoiding all references to the city. 'Take my arm, Timoteo.' I wrapped a shawl around to disguise my belly. No need for its size to be more of a source of gossip than it already was.

The townspeople had gathered in Sodo, enjoying some December sunshine. Standing out against this brown palette, Pietro Lorenzetti – the man who had stood between me and the life of my dreams – waited at the top of the monastery steps. He was dressed in a green brocade outfit trimmed with orange. Below a band of musicians from nearby Torniella played their five-tune repertoire. But my eyes were on the Siena road, anticipating the arrival of someone on a grey stallion.

Monks from local Augustinian monasteries had arrived the day before and flanked the doors. Of the two guests of honour, first to arrive was San Galgano's abbot; a man approaching his dotage, who had once been in charge of works in Siena's Duomo. I could keep Siena from my lips but not my mind.

No Ambrogio.

Finally the town overlord arrived, having undertaken the short journey from his palazzo, a few doors from our workshop, on horseback. Prior

Benedetto greeted him with a bow and we processed inside. Turning to check the Siena road one last time, I helped Timoteo up the steps. He'd always have a limp, but with luck would soon be walking without a crutch. An old man gave up his seat on one of the side benches. But despite my expanded girth, I stood, wanting to take in my fill of the art.

The two tall columns of glass were everything I expected of a Sienese master: pinks, reds, greens and golds plus lots of the deep blue I loved; sharp modern images, each depicting an extract from the life of Christ. I worked my way through depictions of the nativity, crucifixion and resurrection. Though I despised the way Pietro had separated me from his brother, I admired how movingly he'd captured Christ at the moment of death: the muscles of a man in his prime, excruciating pain on his face, body sagging as all life departed. Yet the effect was uplifting rather than sad. With so many emotions portrayed in so few brushstrokes, he must now rival the great Duccio.

I laid my hands across my belly, and the baby moved beneath my touch. A month or more and I would be a mother. I looked at the stained glass and tried to imagine the life of Ambrogio's child – for that's what it would always be to me.

At the end of the service, a clear passage formed to allow the overlord to leave.

'Let's wait for the crowds to clear,' I said, sitting beside my husband, now the seat next to him had been vacated. Despite everything, I'd found myself a good man.

Bruno and Orsola ignored us as they passed, but the ever-affectionate Laura came to give me a hug. 'I miss you, Clara and so does Stefano.'

'Come and see the baby when it arrives.' I gave her hand a squeeze.

Before the altar, a small group had gathered around Pietro. If only one of them were Ambrogio, but Pietro's was the only brocade in church now the overlord had left.

'So kind of you to share in our celebration.' Benedetto led the abbot down the nave. 'I wanted a round window as you have in San Galgano but was told it would be vulgar.'

The abbot's reply was lost in the hubbub.

'Let's go.' Timoteo tried to pull himself up.

'Let me help you.' Niccolò offered his arm to my husband.

'Niccolò, so glad to see you.' Pietro strode towards us. 'These windows are as much your triumph as mine. None of it would have been possible without the scaffolding, sturdy and strong like the man who put it up.' He put his arm round my grandfather's shoulders, then looked at me. 'I'd have liked my brother to see this, but he's far too busy in Florence. Doesn't give the rest of us a thought.'

His tone was one of triumph, and I was the vanquished, my last chance of escape gone. From now on, Monticiano was my prison. Not trusting myself to speak, I put one arm through Timoteo's and steered him out the door. With the other I hugged my belly.

'The Lord be with you all.' Benedetto waved a

blessing in our direction as he made for the door of the church.

'Amen,' we all said. So be it.

blessing in one direction as he made for the door of the church.

'Anna,' my aunt said, 'where is ...'

Part Three

Gold

Monticiano, 1338

Chapter 14

I checked Casa Grande's kitchen. All day I'd been scrubbing pans, cleaning floors and polishing coppers after the lavish dinner the previous evening. Now cooking pots were simmering on the fire and there was ample wood to feed the flames. Once my children were old enough to leave with my mother-in-law, I had worked in the country home of Monticiano's overlord whenever he visited. I loved picking up snippets of Sienese life from the family and their guests – fashions in food and clothing, and the latest battles between Tolomei and Salimbeni. But tonight I had more to enjoy at home.

'Can I go now?' I asked. 'It's Gabriele's birthday and the girls are making him a cake.'

'Be off then.' The housekeeper was a stiff knee-ed

version of Cook, grateful for me undertaking jobs involving stairs. She unlocked a small wooden chest and took out two coins. With Timoteo's modest income from the workshop and three children to feed, on top of Dorotea and ourselves, this extra was needed.

The box locked with a click and the keys jangled at the housekeeper's waist. She handed over the money. 'Watch your step out there on that snow – and enjoy the evening with that lovely lad of yours.'

Turning my back on the luxurious fire, I climbed down the stone steps. At thirty-six I could no longer race Vanni Salimbeni down two flights. Only that morning I'd noted with horror a V emerging between my eyebrows. An icy blast greeted me at the door. The fresh snow snapped under my feet like velvet pile accidentally trodden on. I wanted to enjoy every moment with my golden boy, so instead of rushing home to rest my feet and ease my back, I turned towards the workshop.

I'd fought against Gabriele moving in with Orsola, but once Laura reached puberty, it made sense for her to sleep with my girls and for him to share the bed of my youth with Stefano. Laura had since married and moved away, but the arrangement continued and time with my boy was all too limited. I reached the workshop and opened the door. Gabriele looked up and smiled, his fair hair catching the last of the light.

'Happy birthday, carissimo!' I kissed the top of his head – a miracle in a town where everyone else was dark.

'Don't fuss, Mamma!' Gabriele carried on working.

171

Over the years he'd asked why his hair was different, and we'd told him it came from the 'Siena side of the family' – neither lie nor full truth.

'Niccolò no better?' I said, noticing my grandfather's empty seat.

'Coughing all day,' Timoteo pointed to the rooms above, then tested the balance of a chair, no doubt one of Stefano's he was making good.

Bruno and his son had already given up for the day, so I sat at their bench and watched my son work: forehead puckered in concentration as he ran a plane over the wood's surface. With each step towards manhood, he looked more like the young man I'd met the day of Duccio's festa. Would he turn out to have his talent too?

Ambrogio's appearance in my thoughts came as a shock. Over the eighteen years since his departure, my hurt at him leaving me had dissipated. His image in my mind had blurred; my intense love for him now invested in his son.

Gabriele showed me the finished article. 'Look, I'm doing all Niccolò's work though I'm the most junior. Bruno should have taken it over, but he says he's touting for business round the town.'

'Round the hostelries, more like.' Timoteo had little patience for the man supposedly in charge in Niccolò's absence.

'I'm done, can we go?' Gabriele took down the cloak from the nail and handed it to the man he knew as father. 'Wrap up, Babbo'

'Your sisters have been baking all day.' I held his

hand, happy he still allowed me this indulgence.

Within minutes we entered the cosy warmth of Dorotea's kitchen.

'Gabriele!' My younger daughter, nine-year-old Viola, gave a precocious toss to her curly tresses, and ran towards her brother. 'I've made you an apple and chestnut torta.'

She was attempting to decorate a cake with swivels of the skin.

'Who did you say made the torta, Viola?' Gawky, and five years older than her sister, Rosa was Dorotea's second-in-command, alike in their deep love of tidiness and all things religious. Wiping her hands on her apron, Rosa kissed Gabriele lightly on the cheek. 'Seventeen, eh? A few more years and we'll have to start treating you with respect!'

'Nice to see you too, Rosa!' Gabriele gave his sister a playful punch on the shoulder. Closer in age and in sharpness of wit, my two older children shared a bond of banter that left Viola struggling.

'Are you trying to make the shape of a G, Viola?' I'd spent years trying to teach her letters.

'Icy out there tonight.' After removing the wooden pattens tied over his shoes, Timoteo limped to his chair at the head of the table.

'Everyone sit down,' Rosa placed the bread in the middle, while Dorotea transported a steaming pot of rabbit stew to the end opposite her son. She was still second-in-command of the household.

'Your day, Gabriele, you say Grace for us.' Timoteo looked proudly on the boy he loved as his own. I couldn't have asked more of him.

Gabriele put his hands together and bowed his head. 'Thank you, God, for the delicious food Nonna's cooked for us, and for the love of my family, and forgive Rosa for being exceptionally annoying most of the time. Ow! Amen.'

'Enough of that.' Timoteo poured everyone wine, weak after several pressings.

'Pass this bowl to your father, Rosa. Even if it's your birthday, Gabriele, those who bring in the money are served first.' Dorotea had been boiling bones all day to make the rich stock.

'Not my fault I don't bring in money. I work harder than Bruno, and what Stefano does is a joke. If you didn't spend all your time putting it right, Babbo, his work would contribute nothing.'

'You have to learn your trade, caro.' I said, passing around the plates.

'And you'll become a journeyman as soon as you're twenty-one,' Timoteo said.

'Four more years! I bet they make Stefano a master craftsman before then, which would be a travesty.'

'What big words your mother's taught you.' Dorotea filled another plate.

'It's not fair! Niccolò says there's nothing more he can teach me. If I can't be paid, I'm better off taking my chance in the city.'

I went cold. 'You can't do that.' Without him in my life, I'd never drag myself out of bed.

'Bruno says someone with my skills could make a

good living there.'

'The dirty weasel.' I knew how my uncle's mind worked, or rather his wife's. They wanted Gabriele out of the way, to be sure the business passed to Stefano.

'Be humble, Gabriele, for the meek shall inherit the earth.' Dorotea said. 'Now eat up, before it gets cold.'

We tucked into our food, the only sounds, slurps and satisfied grunts. But as soon as Rosa removed the platters, I tackled my husband. 'Timoteo, you must speak to Bruno about paying him.'

'He'll not listen to me. Anyway, four years will pass faster than you can say Antonio Patrizi.'

'I hoped you'd be on my side.' Gabriele stood to leave.

'Wait!' I grabbed my son by the arm. 'Babbo and I will speak to Niccolò, won't we? But only on condition that if he says no, that's the end of it.'

'Tomorrow?'

'If he's well enough.'

Gabriele resumed his seat. 'And you can ask him to make me second-in-command. I'm fed up of taking daft instructions from Bruno.'

'That's going too far. Think I'd work for my seventeen-year-old son?' Timoteo gave him a gentle clip to the head.

'But as for being paid, we'll fight as hard as we have to.' I'd do everything in my power to stop him leaving.

'Thank you, Mamma. Now where's that cake, Viola? Is it as delicious as it looks? And what's that letter on the top? Not a G, is it?'

'Definitely not a G,' Rosa muttered under her

breath, but Viola radiated happiness as everyone praised 'her' cake.

The following morning, we picked our way through the slush to the carpentry. But instead going into the workshop, Timoteo and I climbed the steps to the dwelling above. Orsola opened the door, barring the entrance. Even though I was twenty years married, she still regarded me as a fallen woman who'd soiled her respectability.

'How are you, Nonno?' I shouted through to the kitchen where he was sitting in front of the fire.

'All the better for a visit from you. Come in, cara. Goodness, your hem's soaked. Come and dry out.'

I kissed his cheek, skin wrinkled like a walnut, then sat next to him. 'Timoteo says he can hear you hacking away. Is it easing?'

'Much better,' though his words prompted a coughing fit.

'Not that you've been any help nursing him.' Orsola folded her arms across her large bosom and glared across the table. Timoteo hovered near the door, ready to make his escape.

'They're missing you.' I took my grandfather's hand, feeling the blue veins that ran rivulets along its back.

Timoteo cleared his throat. 'Gabriele's doing an excellent job in your place.'

'He's a fast learner, but I shouldn't be leaving him to it.' Niccolò rubbed his chest, as if that would make it better.

'You'll go back when I say so and not before,' Orsola sniffed.

'Orsola, Orsola!' Bruno called up from the street.

If we weren't there, Orsola would probably have opened the window to reply. Instead, she took her shawl from its hook and went outside.

'We need to ask you something.' I spoke quickly, for there was no time for Timoteo to find his words. 'You know what a good worker Gabriele is, and he knows it, too. He's tired of being the only one not paid. Can't he finish his apprenticeship and be made a journeyman.? Unless we do something for him, he'll seek his fortune elsewhere.'

'He can't do that. I know he's only a lad, but I rely on him, perhaps more than I should.' Niccolò ran his fingers through the white waves of his hair. 'But the business is not what it was. I'm not sure we can support another paid hand.'

'I told you it was no use, Clara.' Timoteo turned to go.

Through the wooden shutters I heard Orsola winding up her conversation with Bruno.

'But can it survive without him? He's worth more than Stefano and Bruno put together.' Since marrying Timoteo, I'd lost most of the fight in me, but this one I wouldn't give up.

Timoteo looked as though he was going to add his name, too, but I glared at him to stay quiet. Orsola would have him out of the workshop before the air had left his mouth. As it was, we were all quiet when she bustled back.

'I smell a rat. What have you been hatching behind my back?'

'We were talking about the future of the workshop.' I squeezed Niccolò's hand, encouraging him to speak up.

He cleared his throat. 'We must find the money to pay Gabriele. It's only fair he becomes a journeyman.'

'You scheming hussy, pretending to be concerned for your grandfather's health.' Orsola advanced on me, but I stood my ground. I was no longer her property.

'Bruno will never agree. And don't you forget, if the business collapses, your family's ruined too. Now get out, both of you.'

'Help me up, Timoteo.' Niccolò walked us to the top of the steps. 'Don't worry, Clara. I'll speak to Bruno.'

I put my arms around his neck. Even if Gabriele left when he was older, he'd be with us a few more years.

'Hang on, what's going on down there?' Niccolò shaded his eyes against the snow's glare.

I followed his eyes to the piazza. A small crowd had gathered outside the workshop and the rest of the square was unusually full for a cold day. A man came out, wearing a burgundy, fur-lined cloak and a hat in the fashion I'd seen the overlord wearing: sculpted to cover all his hair.

I shivered, fearing a friend of the Tolomei was bringing news of my mother and it could only be bad. But why a gentleman not a servant? Or was it Vanni, come to tell me he was no longer a monk. But this man was the wrong shape: slim legs, broad shoulders.

My gut lurched.

Ambrogio.

I closed my eyes, for I was back in his embrace, breathing faster as I felt the softness of his skin against mine. Except to give in to desire, would lose me everything. I checked to see whether Timoteo had noticed my flush, but he was negotiating the slippery steps and the burgundy cloak had already disappeared down the main street.

Why had he come, and why now? Seventeen years ago, I'd have dropped everything to be with him. If he was coming to claim me now, he was far too late, but what if he claimed our son? Heart pounding, I followed Timoteo into the workshop. Bruno gave me a sly wink and Stefano looked away. Gabriele looked at me eagerly, only interested in the result of our conversation.

I put the visitor out of mind. 'Niccolò says they'll pay you as a journeyman if Bruno agrees. Can't have you leaving the workshop in the lurch.'

'Well done, Gab,' Stefano hugged his nephew-cum-brother. 'You deserve it more than me.' Unlike his parents, Stefano bore our family no grudge.

'Four, five carpenters, what does it matter. For while you two have been upstairs hatching that deal, we've trapped a fine cockatoo with gold in his pocket.' Bruno rubbed his palm with his finger as if it were full of florins. 'And, Clara, you'll never guess who it was.'

Bruno eyed Timoteo. 'The artist, Ambrogio Lorenzetti, no less. Said he wants the carpenter who built the scaffolding at the monastery for his brother's work. Seems he has a commission from the Salimbeni, to paint the Monte Siepe chapel at San Galgano.'

My head was reeling, both relieved and disappointed his visit was nothing to do with me. He must be a recognised artist too, so something good had come from his abandoning me for Florence. But with a significant assignment to complete – from the Salimbeni, no less - he'd be around for months. He'd ruined my life before. Would he find a way to do so again?

'We don't do scaffolding.' Timoteo was trembling.

'Told you Timoteo wouldn't like it, didn't I, Gabriele!' Bruno winked again.

'We can't let the job go. It'll cover my wages for at least a year.' Gabriele was already a sounder businessman than Bruno would ever be.

I scrutinised my son's face again. No, he'd no idea about his connection to the artist. But for how long could we keep it from him?

'Niccolò can tell us what to do - we'll wrap him up for the journey - and the rest of us will do the hard work.' Stefano sounded excited. 'Lorenzetti will be putting his life in our hands while he works, so we must make sure the platform's sturdy.'

'Better not let you at the construction, eh Timoteo?' Bruno needled again.

'I need some fresh air.' Timoteo pulled me out of the workshop. We stood in the middle of the icy piazza, away from prying ears.

'Did you know about this? Have you been planning it behind my back?' His breath came out like dragon-fire in the cold air.

'Of course, I haven't. I'm as shocked as you.'

180

'Then why does he want us? The carpenters in Chiusdino are closer.'

'I've no idea, but it can't be on account of Gabriele. Pietro would never have told him.'

'Then he's come to see you.'

He had promised to come back, but why now? And why were the Salimbeni involved? Had Ambrogio prised a commission from the Signora at last?

'Timoteo, I'm as upset about him being here as you are. He ruined my life once and I won't let him sweep away the life we built together as if it were a fall of snow.' It had taken me long enough to come to terms with country living.

'The Devil take him!' Timoteo stamped his bad foot.

I had to be optimistic, for Timoteo's sake. 'Go back to the workshop and look pleased about Gabriele becoming a journeyman, or he'll sense something's up.'

'I'm off to toast our new customer. Want to join me, Timoteo?' Bruno was making for the tavern.

Timoteo scowled. 'I see no cause for celebration.'

'Cornuto, cornuto!' Bruno sneered, the index and fourth finger on his right-hand waving in the horned sign of a cuckold.

I could have punched him. Instead, I held on to Timoteo, guessing he'd like to do the same.

'You thought you could get away with it, Miss High and Mighty. Let's see how long it takes people to work it out, now another Goldenhead's in town.' Bruno chuckled. 'Ignore my advice, as you always do, but I say you should tell the lad before he hears it from someone else.'

'Then make sure it's not you.' I called after him.

Bruno winked again, hinting how much he'd relish spreading such a tasty morsel of gossip.

Bruno's comment made me feel sick to the gills. One way or another my secret was going to come out, and the person most hurt would be Gabriele.

'If Gabriele sees they have the same colour hair, he'll guess there's a connection. Others will too. We must tell him before anyone else.'

'Never. He's not taking away my son.'

'And he won't, because you're the best father Gabriele could ever have wished for. He'll be devastated to discover you're not connected by blood, so before anyone else tells him, we must.'

'Not yet.' Timoteo limped back to the workshop. He was lucky to have his work to absorb him.

I pulled my shawl around me and walked home. But before I could face the girls, I sat on the wall beyond the Porta and thought back to the last time I'd seen Ambrogio. How happy he'd been to enjoy me in the woods, happier still to leave me for Florence. And the security I now enjoyed was down to Pietro's generosity, not his. More than that, it was because of Ambrogio, and only Ambrogio, that I was stuck in this town for the rest of my life. I looked out over the valley.

I'd only glimpsed Ambrogio and already he was upsetting my life. But if Orsola had taught me anything, it was to fight for one's firstborn. Yes, they'd have to meet, but Gabriele was mine and no former lover was going to take him away.

Chapter 15

now became rain, slush became puddles and while I went foraging for tinder to supplement our dwindling supplies, I worried. What if Ambrogio returned to the workshop and asked about Gabriele's fair hair? We had so little time if we wanted our son to learn of his origin from us.

I climbed up the track I'd once ridden down with Ambrogio, not for remembrance but in the hope of finding some overlooked cones under the pine trees. Once dried out, they were excellent for lighting fires.

No, Ambrogio would be too preoccupied with work to visit Monticiano. The danger would be Bruno, unable to contain himself after too much wine.

And whenever Gabriele found out, he would be hurt beyond measure, but especially if he learnt by chance. I paused in my gathering, feeling his pain. We had to spare him that. I stared at my basket. The handful of cones I'd gleaned were hardly worth the effort, but they'd dry out faster than twigs. And however hard us telling Gabriele would be, it was better than him finding out some other way.

But whenever I tried to discuss the matter with Timoteo, he refused. He'd long buried the reason for

183

me being forced into marriage. Me raising it now seemed like at best ingratitude, at worst, betrayal. Over the years, I'd found his intransigence calming, a solid rock on which to lean. But with our relationship with Gabriele at stake, I had to convince him.

Two weeks later the skies turned blue and the road to San Galgano was firm enough to bear a cartwheel. Niccolò's cough had reduced to a tickle, and he pronounced himself fitter than a man half his age. Though still holding Ambrogio responsible for my near ruin, he agreed the job was too lucrative to lose and would supervise the measuring of the chapel. Bruno, as the man in charge of the workshop, would have to go to negotiate terms, and it caused no comment that he chose Stefano to provide the younger limbs to climb the ladder. Gabriele would remain out of Ambrogio's sight. But there was room in the back of the cart for Timoteo and me. Now all I had to do was persuade my husband to come.

On the morning of the visit, I lay awake in the early dark. Rosa was already helping in the kitchen, while Viola slept fast in the next bed. Timoteo dozed, waiting for Dorotea to tempt him out of bed with his usual winter drink of hot water. I snuggled into his night warmth, and he turned to rest his arm in the crook of my waist.

'Let's go to San Galgano together. This is our best chance to tell Ambrogio about Gabriele.'

Timoteo rolled onto his back. 'But I stopped Gabriele going to San Galgano, so neither of them would find out.'

184

I ran my hand over his smooth-haired chest. 'You heard Bruno. He's bursting to let it slip. Don't let Gabriele find out by accident.'

'We're not going, and that's that.' Timoteo sat up and pulled on his clothes.

For once, I couldn't go along with his decision. 'Then I'll go on my own.'

'Don't make me more jealous than I already am of that man, for providing you with the son I failed to.'

'Timoteo, it's not your fault the baby died. And haven't I kept all my promises? Borne you two children? Never mentioned Siena, let alone asked to go there? You're my loving, caring husband, and a more decent man than Ambrogio will ever be.'

'I'm sorry, but his arrival has upset me.'

'I don't want him here either,' I took his hand. 'But he is, and we must tell him about his son before we tell Gabriele.'

'I'm Gabriele's father, and I won't let that cockscomb steal him away.'

I watched my husband pulling on the thick socks I'd knitted for him the previous winter. 'You'll always be his Babbo. Remember standing with him, knee-deep in water, teaching him how to spear fish? Ambrogio can never take that from you. And Gabriele will never forgive us if finds out from someone else he's the son of a famous artist.'

'And not of a lame miner who spends his life fixing Stefano's chairs.'

'I didn't mean it like that.' I donned a dress, unchanged in size despite some thickening of my waist after three children. 'And you know Gabriele as well as I do. Once he finds out, he'll rush over to see who this man is. That's why we have to tell him first. If you won't come, I'll have to do it on my own.'

'Your drink's ready!' Dorotea called from the kitchen.

Timoteo stood up and shook his head. I was running out of time.

'Do you think I'll run off with him? My life is here now. But if you must, ask Bruno and Stefano to guard me, though you can be sure Niccolò won't let me out of his sight.'

'I won't demean myself by asking them to be your gaolers.'

'Then let me tell Ambrogio, before we speak to Gabriele. I must have your agreement.'

There were tears in his eyes when he took my hands in his. 'Can I trust you?'

'I pledged myself to you in the sight of God, and nothing will make me break that.' I would never break my vows. And yet I longed to see Ambrogio again, for as well as my former lover, he was my only connection with art.

Timoteo pulled me to him in an all-enveloping hug. 'Then go, and when you get back, we'll tell Gabriele.'

'My dear husband, blessed is the day you took me on.'

Huddled in the back of the cart, the confidence I'd displayed talking to Timoteo, evaporated. How would Ambrogio take the news he'd had a son by me? When

186

I'd last seen Ambrogio, he'd been desperate to prove himself. But now he was important enough to have been given an assignment by the Salimbeni. Would he even remember me? At the time, I'd thought I was important to him, but he'd never visited again.

Now I was approaching forty; country living had darkened my complexion and coarsened my hands. Everyday worries had puckered my brow, whereas success might have made Ambrogio pompous, unwilling to give the time of day to a poor county woman. I hugged my knees as we wound down the Siena road.

'Looking forward to seeing lover boy?' Bruno shouted from the bench at the front where the three men sat.

'Wash your mouth out! Remember you're talking of Gabriele's father, and our valued customer,' Niccolò said.

'Gee up, my beauty.' Stefano shook the reins, so much happier with horses than wood.

'Got to hand it to you, niece, getting that husband of yours to let you come on your own. The pretty peacock still tempts you?'

'What! Three grown men can't look after my virtue, even in a house of God?'

'If Babbo's upsetting you, cousin, I'll make him walk the rest of the way,' Stefano said, making Bruno shut up.

Halfway across the plane at the bottom of the hill, we turned left to the abbey. In summer we'd have been faster on foot, but none of us wanted to cross an icy river in flood. Soon the abbey came into view, rising above the fallow fields beyond. However, as we drove into the complex of granaries, mills and workshops – a small town in its own right – my insides turned to marrow jelly at the prospect of telling the artist he was the father of my child.

When we reached the chapel of Monte Siepe, Bruno jumped down and clapped his hands to warm them. 'Let's be seeing what the gander wants.'

The three men entered the chapel built around the stone in which Galgano had embedded his sword after renouncing his violent life as a knight, leaving me alone in the porch. Along one side was a stone bench, opposite which was a small room where pilgrims could buy mementoes.

'I'm with the carpenters.' I told the monk who presided over the sale of crosses and minor relics. He paused in his work – inscribing biblical texts on small pieces of parchment – and nodded. I sat on the grey slab and looking out on the town of Chiusdino, glad Timoteo had stayed at home. I had mixed feelings about seeing Ambrogio again, and if I was to broker a civilised encounter with the son he'd never known, I had to speak to him alone.

The men got down to work and I was as cold as the stone on which I sat, by the time Ambrogio appeared. Dressed in an old brown tunic, and well-darned leggings, he'd have passed for a workman were it not for the fur-lined coat slung over his shoulders and, of course, the fair hair.

'Signora.' He gave a perfunctory nod.

188

Eighteen years had taken their toll on me, but I couldn't miss my chance.

'Ambrogio, it's Clara.'

He looked blank. He'd been so much to me, yet I was nothing to him.

If not by my name, how else would he know me? 'The Salimbeni kitchen girl. We met on the day of Duccio's festa.' Remembering the colours of that day warmed me, despite the chill.

'Your father was murdered.' Ambrogio frowned – a look I remembered from our first meeting – 'and you witnessed my humiliation by the Contessa when I asked for a commission!'

Then his face changed to a sly grin. 'And you had to take refuge in our studio some years later. The old man in there must be the grandfather who left you behind.'

I stepped back to maintain a distance between us and, too late for politeness, I remembered my Siena manners and curtsied.

'No need for that,' he raised me to standing, then dropped my hand. 'I'm on my way to the refectory. I can't draw with that Bruno around. I'd ask you to join me, but the monks don't cater for women out of the pilgrim season.'

'Don't go! I need to tell you something.'

'What?' he snapped.

'After you left for Florence, I found myself with child.' No point in softening the blow if he was going to be so brusque.

The blood drained from his face. 'Ridiculous. How do you know it's mine?'

'Because there was no-one else.' How dare he accuse me of infidelity after all the women he'd been with?

'But it was years ago. What can you want from me now? I've a wife and children in Siena.' He put his hand to his forehead. 'Of course. Now I'm famous, you want money! Well, I'm sorry, your ploy won't work.'

'I won't accept a lentil, and neither will my husband.'

'Then what? And why wait 'til now to tell me?'

I tried to speak, but my rage turned to shivering – I hadn't expected him to be so hostile, and my woollen cloak wasn't up to this cold.

'Here, have my coat.' He thrust the fur round my shoulders and I breathed the once-familiar smell of Ambrogio, linseed spiced with cinnamon.

'Pietro gave me money for a dowry but refused to tell you. Once I married, I put you out of mind. But now you're here, you need to know you have a son, because I shall have to tell him before people start asking questions.'

'A son?' He leant against the wall and gazed at the hills slowly emerging from the morning mist. 'Simona has only given me daughters. When can I see him? I'll ride over tomorrow while the roads are still dry.'

'No, you must stay away. My husband deserves some respect for bringing up Gabriele as his own.'

'Gabriele? What a lovely name. Did you know Duccio used my likeness for the archangel when he painted the Annunciation?'

'Yes, that's why I chose the name, for my Gabriele

has fair hair too.'

'He must be that lad I saw in the workshop. Good looking – like his father!' Ambrogio laughed, sitting next to me, so close I could feel his warmth.

'Yes, and he's my pride and joy even though in having him, I had to give up all my hopes. Do you remember? You promised to take me into your world.'

'A young man will say anything to get under a girl's skirt!' Ambrogio laughed.

'How dare you make light of it. If it hadn't been for Pietro's money, I'd have been ruined. Did you ever consider the girls whose lives you destroyed?'

Ambrogio stared at me, thoughtful rather than contrite.

'I have an idea. Come into the chapel.'

I handed back his cloak and followed him.

Stefano was at the top of the ladder, calibrating the height of the room with the measuring stick. Bruno, stood a few rungs down, arms round his son's legs. 'No funny business out there, I hope.'

'The brother in the reliquary will assure you of our propriety. And if you wish to complain, do so to my guild.'

'Just a joke.' Bruno said.

The tiny chapel measured about four paces by six. Ambrogio leant against the left-hand wall and stared at the one opposite.

Niccolò issued instructions for the final measurements. 'We thought a platform you can move around would meet your needs. We'll lower it as you come to the walls.'

'Maybe two, so after I've done each lunette, my assistants can paint the sky around while I move on to the next.'

'Splashing paint on? Stefano can give you a hand with that,' Bruno said.

'Or he could hold the platform steady.' I winked at my cousin, guessing he'd hate painting even more than carpentry.

'If it's a craftsman you want, Gabriele has a better eye,' Stefano added.

'Bring him over, and I'll try you both out. My men in Siena are reluctant to freeze here in the middle of February, though come August they'll be begging me to work in the cool!'

'Hold it there, Signor L' Bruno guided Stefano down the top rungs. 'You don't take our best workers without compensating for our loss.'

Ambrogio caught my eye. 'I haven't decided whether I want either of them yet. When I've seen what they can do, we can talk terms.'

I was dumbstruck. Without even asking, Ambrogio had arranged to meet his son.

'That's us done,' Bruno said, and Niccolò nodded. 'Stefano, take that ladder back to the cart, there's a good lad. Brrr, we need warming on a day like this.'

'If you walk down to the refectory, I'm sure they'll provide you with some refreshment. I'll join you shortly. Niccolò, would you allow me one final word with your granddaughter? As you were concerned about her honour, Bruno, perhaps you'd stay to guard it?'

Give up the chance of a drink? Pigs might fly tail first. And I'd throttle Ambrogio before succumbing to his charms again.

'She'll be fine,' Bruno said, and strode out, arm around Niccolò's shoulders.

I assumed he wanted to discuss meeting Gabriele, but instead he steered me to the right-hand wall of the chapel.

'You've given me an idea for the Annunciation I'm going to paint. I'm going to use this new son of mine as the archangel. Remember how Pietro populated his paintings with family, or maybe you didn't get to know him that well. Afraid his hands are too stiff to wield a brush these days.' All the while he talked, he rolled chalk between his fingers and his eyes darted between the wall above and the slate in his hand.

The intensity of his gaze made me afraid what he'd do next.

'Tell me what it felt like to be unmarried and with child – when you first found out.'

'I've told you already.'

'Then tell me again.'

I raised my chin in defiance, as I was no longer prepared to bend to his whim.

Suddenly, he stepped forward and kissed me; fully, passionately, on the lips. But it wasn't the memory of our intimacy that came to mind, but the attempted rape by Blackbeard. Suddenly he pulled back and scratched lines on his slate with frightening fury.

How dare he kiss me. This toying with old feelings was too much. Wasn't it enough he'd made me endure

Orsola's insults and the neighbours' suspicions? Worst of all, bringing Gabriele into the world, had stopped all hope of returning to Siena. I sobbed as the weight of my feelings overwhelmed me. My knees turned to calf's foot jelly, and I slipped to the ground, my body wracked with well-overdue grief.

Still Ambrogio said nothing, reshaping lines, reaching over to move my chin, then moving it again until he was satisfied. I felt less in control of my body than when I was growing Gabriele.

At last I found some words. 'What were you thinking of, taking advantage of me – again.'

But Ambrogio remained in his own world. 'This is wonderful, Clara. You have shown me a completely new interpretation of the Annunciation. I promise your anguish won't have been in vain, for this fresco will make history.' He grinned as he raised me to my feet. Then at last remembering he might have done me a disservice, he put my hand to his lips. 'Forgive me.'

I left him, mind still on his conception for the right-hand wall, and walked down the narrow track to the main abbey. When I reached the refectory, I went straight to the cart and waited, still unable to believe his affrontery.

'Happy, now you've seen lover boy?' Brim-full of San Galgano wine, Bruno took the reins and whipped the horse into a canter.

No, I was livid he'd manipulated me again. Feelings of anger and shock swirled around my head, served up with a hefty portion of guilt that I'd betrayed Timoteo's trust in me.

Suddenly the cart lurched as we turned off the main road and into the woods.

'We're going to Giuseppe's; to order the wood,' Niccolò shouted to me. 'I'd like to choose it myself, and this will save me another journey. Who knows how long this fine weather will last.'

Under the trees, the air chilled further, a pale sun visible through the bare branches and I tried to compose myself.

While Bruno sang songs of the tavern to fend off the bitter chill, I thought of Ambrogio.

He was older of course - blond hair dulled with grey, his smooth face lined around the eyes, shallow gullies developing either side of his mouth. But his ability to evoke in me strong feelings remained unchanged. Desire, I couldn't deny it, but my real excitement came from being close to the process of creation, and the pictures I anticipated would soon be covering those walls.

'Here we are.' Bruno drew the cart into a clearing stacked high with wood.

As we jerked to a halt, I shuddered. I should have extracted a promise that he wouldn't take Gabriele from me.

But then, I already knew what promises from Ambrogio were worth.

Chapter 16

I was glad to get down and feigned interest in wood ordering to get in the warm. And visits to Giuseppe when I was young had always been a treat.

'Have you worked out what we need, Niccolò?' Stefano said as he tethered the horses.

'All up here.' He tapped the side of his head. As he passed the piles of maturing wood, he paused to run his hand over woods in different stages of drying out. Giuseppe came out to greet us.

'Niccolò!' Giuseppe gave his friend a hug. 'How long is it? Goodness knows when I last came to Monticiano.'

The ridge caught the wind at full blast, and I made for the cottage. Giuseppe's granddaughter, same age as Rosa, stopped in her chores. I'd not been here since having children but remembered it as a happy place. Like Niccolò's, it was full of the carved furniture you'd expect of a woodman. So why did it feel so much warmer here? The answer lay in the furniture, coloured by the juice of red and black berries gathered in the woods. I ran my fingers over shelves the same colour as Ambrogio's drawing ink.

'Giuseppe's gift to my grandmother when they married. Not that anyone will do the same for me.' The girl said as she washed the dishes. 'Sit by the fire, you look cold.'

What did she mean? Most young men would be glad of a share in Giuseppe's business.

'Come in, come in!' Giuseppe led the men to the table. 'Get us a drink, cara. This calls for a celebration.'

The girl retrieved a flagon from the corner and poured wine for the men.

Giuseppe raised a toast. 'Salute!'

'Salute!' They touched his beaker with theirs.

'Too many years, Giuseppe. These bones of ours don't get any younger.' Niccolò coughed.

'I presume you've come with the money.' Giuseppe said.

'You old skinflint!' Niccolò said. 'What money? Can't be much more than small change that should be lost in the rounding! But if you insist, take what you're owed out of that.' He threw his small change onto the table.

All bonhomie left Giuseppe's face. 'You mean you haven't come to pay?'

Bruno and Stefano took a suspicious interest in the quality of the woodgrain.

'Goodness, no! We need wood to make scaffolding for Ambrogio Lorenzetti. He's working on the chapel at Monte Siepe. Most people don't get to work for one artist in their lifetime and I've been employed by two.'

'I'm sorry, Niccolò.' Giuseppe slammed his drink on the table. 'Until you pay me what's owed – and it's a lot more than rounding, isn't it Bruno? – you're not getting a stick more, friendship or no.'

But the connection with Ambrogio was mine. The job was ours by rights. And, I realised, I wanted it for me and Gabriele, as much as for the family business.

'How much do we owe this good man, Bruno?' Niccolò said.

'Fifty, hundred florins? I don't know.' My uncle waved his hand in the air.

How could he? While we had scrimped on Timoteo's meagre wages, Bruno had been drinking away the profits. No wonder he was reluctant to pay Gabriele. And how long would it take him to get rid of Timoteo?

Bruno reached for the flagon but Giuseppe snatched it away.

'For the last year, nearly two, I've let you have your wood on credit – always believing that in time you'd pay me. But enough is enough, dear friend. I can't supply more until you pay me back. I have mouths to feed too.'

Without wood we'd lose the commission at San Galgano and, regardless of Ambrogio's kiss, we needed the work more than ever.

'I don't understand how this happened,' Niccolò looked to his son, 'but I'll get to the bottom of it. One way or another, you'll have your money, Giuseppe.'

'I knew our friendship would count for something.' The two old men hugged each other and went out to the yard.

I too was shaken, for we'd never live off my Casa Grande wages. And the last thing I wanted was for

Gabriele to feel unsettled.

'Giuseppe won't admit it, but your uncle has ruined us,' the girl whispered. 'What hopes have I of a good husband when the world finds out we're paupers.'

'I promise you, my grandfather knew nothing of this, but he'll sort it out.' Yet what could be done? Bruno ran everything, and Bruno was the problem. At least when I'd faced ruin, Pietro had provided me with a dowry.

I took one last look at the colourful kitchen then walked back to the cart.

'You go up front.' Bruno pushed me out of the way to climb in the back.

How much had he drunk in the refectory that he needed to sleep it off?

'The devil take you, Bruno,' Niccolò shouted once we were out of earshot. 'How could you humiliate me in front of my best friend? What's been going on?'

Stefano cleared his throat. 'Giuseppe isn't the only one we owe money to. No vintner will serve him until his slate's cleared.'

'I've a mind to kick you off the cart, Bruno,' Niccolò said, 'for I'm as angry as a wasp smoked out of its nest. We don't even know how much is owed.'

'Unless Orsola's kept note,' I said remembering the meticulous book-keeping at Palazzo Salimbeni. For once I was grateful Dorotea kept a tight rein on our purse strings.

'I'll go round the shops and make a tally,' Stefano suggested.

'Anyone else we owe?' Niccolò shouted to the back.

Bruno's response was a honking snore.

Light was fading by the time we reached the workshop. As we climbed down from the cart, Niccolò said, 'we'll discuss it further when we know where we stand.'

He climbed the steps to his home above the workshop, looking old beyond his years. While Bruno and Stefano went to stable the horse and cart, I paused. Did Gabriele really need to know about Ambrogio, after his despicable behaviour in the chapel. Maybe we'd keep it from Gabriele for a while longer. Around me workmen dragged their aching end-of-day limbs across the piazza while, beyond the gate, bells called monks to vespers. Even Macellino was making his way home and waved a joint of something wrapped in hessian.

No, I had to do what was best for my son. I braced myself and entered the workshop. Timoteo's face was guarded, and I gave him a nod. In that simple gesture, I conveyed that Ambrogio knew about Gabriele, and it was time to tell our son.

Gabriele looked up and smiled. Now I'd seen his natural father again, I could see how alike they were: not just the hair, but the shape of nose, the angle of their eyes.

'It's time to leave, Timoteo. Come home with us, Gabriele. 'We've something we need to talk to you about.'

Gabriele ran his hand over the wood he was working on, then, satisfied with its smoothness, put it to one side. 'I hope you're going to tell us about San

Galgano, Mamma? I still don't see why you went, not me.'

'That's why we need to talk.'

Tight-lipped and pale, Timoteo limped out, arm around Gabriele's shoulder. Outside the sky was blue and pink – the colours of Ambrogio's outfit at the festa. I linked arms with Gabriele. The sky turned deep red and demanded to be watched. 'Let's sit outside the Porta,' I said when we reached Incrociata.

'In this weather?' Gabriele hugged himself. As usual, he'd come without a coat.

'Just for a moment, to please me.' I steered the equally reluctant Timoteo through the gate and we sat on the low wall to the right. The fields beyond glowed gold. Above the hill opposite, red was already giving way to dark grey. Gabriele sat between us, and I watched both faces in the dying light. Timoteo looked as though a nail had pierced the sole of his shoe. I took a deep breath. 'Eighteen years ago, when I married your father, I was already with child.'

Gabriele blinked and pulled away.

He was ashamed of me – no more than I deserved.

Then he nudged Timoteo and smirked.

I put him right. 'No, it wasn't Timoteo, though he's always loved you as his own.'

'I don't understand. Are you telling me I'm another man's child?' Gabriele frowned.

He looked so lost, I'd have taken him in my arms if he'd let me. And Timoteo was too pained to look at either of us.

'Who is he? Has someone in town been keeping a

big secret?'

I had to fight myself to get the words out. 'He's not from here, and as you were unlikely to meet him, we thought you'd never need to know.'

Gabriele kicked at some stones. 'So, why tell me now?"

'Because he's working at San Galgano. I went there today to tell him about you.'

'He must be someone special to work for Ambrogio Lorenzetti.'

I spoke slowly and deliberately. 'He doesn't work for Ambrogio Lorenzetti – for he is Ambrogio Lorenzetti. I knew him in Siena before I married Timoteo.'

Gabriele stood up and took a few paces from us, looking out over the valley beyond. 'Are you really telling me I'm the son of a famous painter?'

'And a scoundrel,' Timoteo growled.

'Please, Timoteo,' Although after today's behaviour I was inclined to agree with my husband, I was determined our son should make up his own mind.

Gabriele took off his cap, ran fingers through his fair hair, then sat with us again. 'And what did he say when you told him? That he wants nothing to do with me?'

'Is that true?' Timoteo looked hopeful.

'Until now, he didn't know you existed; his brother, Pietro, saw to that. Now he knows, he wants to meet you.'

'I'll go tomorrow.' Gabriele was in danger of being blinded by his father's fame.

'No, you won't.' Timoteo's face was as black as the coal he'd once hewn.

'Bruno's wangled a job there for you and Stefano, but Ambrogio wants to meet you both first. You'll go when Bruno's ready.'

'And not before,' Timoteo added, though he knew nothing of the discussion.

'Let's go home.' Gabriele picked up his hat and we followed him back to the house.

'Hey Rosa!' he shouted on entering the kitchen. 'Now I know why I'm so much cleverer than you – because the famous Ambrogio Lorenzetti is my father!'

Rosa and Viola looked at their brother as if he'd gone mad.

'Gabriele!' I shouted. 'Couldn't you let me tell your sisters?'

'It's no longer a secret, so why should I keep it to myself?' Gabriele tore off a piece of bread. 'Now I understand why Bruno sneered when Ambrogio came to the workshop. I bet Stefano knew too. How could he claim to be a brother to me and say nothing?'

'I didn't know, Gabriele.' Viola put her head on his hand. 'I'd never keep anything from you.'

'Of course, you wouldn't, cara,' Gabriele roughed her hair.

Timoteo sank into his usual chair and put his head in his hands. Dorotea put her arm around his shoulders. I should have been the one to comfort him, but my emotions were already stretched to their limit.

'Did you know, Nonna?' Gabriele asked.

'Well yes, your mother was expecting you when she

married.'

'You've made a fool of me, the lot of you.' He swiped the bread onto the floor.

'Pick that up!' Dorotea said. 'I won't stand for such behaviour in my kitchen.'

'I'm sorry, Nonna.' He had tears in his eyes as he retrieved the bread. 'But you're not my Nonna, are you, because Babbo's not my Babbo.'

'I knew this would happen.' Timoteo, too, had tears.

'Timoteo will always be your Babbo, Gabriele. He's more your father than Ambrogio will ever be!'

'But he lied to me like everyone else. Keep your supper. I'm going to Nicolò's. At least there's no doubt he's my great grandfather.'

'Wait!' I tried to hang on to him.

'Go to the devil!' Gabriele said through tears.

I despaired, as he stormed out the door.

That night I had a fitful sleep, waking from nightmares of being smothered. No longer needed at the Casa Grande as the family had returned to Siena, I raced to Ugolina's, as soon as I'd finished my chores at home.

'Come in!' she wiped her hands on her apron and pulled me inside. 'I'm baking castagnaccio. Help yourself.' As her matronly girth evidenced, she could afford to use flour for sweetmeats, even without a special occasion. While she prodded the open fire to raise the heat, I sat at the large wooden table and pinched a raisin off the flat bread she'd just baked.

'What've you been up to? You look like you've not

slept a wink!' Ugolina pounded the next batch of dough.

'I don't know where to begin.'

'Tell Aunty Ugo!' She added chestnut flour to the dough until it reached the right consistency.

'Only if you promise to speak to anyone, especially not your mother.'

'God be my witness.' Ugolina crossed herself, leaving flour marks on her dress,

'That lazy uncle of mine has saddled us with a fortune in debt. He may even have ruined us.'

Ugolina peeled the sticky mixture off her fingers. 'I did wonder whether to mention the meat tab Orsola's built up.' She pressed out the dough with the heel of her hand and sprinkled it with raisins and spears of rosemary.

'I wish you had, though goodness knows what could we have done? Tackle him on anything and he slips into the long grass, like a lizard. It's so unfair. Gabriele and Timoteo are wonderful workers, yet our family will suffer too. But that's not why I needed to see you.' I rolled the charred raisin between my fingers, for I was struggling to explain what had happened – even to myself. 'I've just seen Ambrogio Lorenzetti. He's working at San Galgano.'

'Ooh, you saucy sausage!' Ugolina sat next to me on the bench. She was the only person outside the family who knew the source of my son's fair hair. 'Good thing it was somewhere sanctified or who knows what would have happened.' She winked as she tore off a piece of the cooled bread and stuffed it in her mouth. 'And is he still like a beast on heat?'

I slammed my palms on the table. 'Double swear you won't tell a living soul.'

Ugolina crossed herself twice. 'What did he say about Gabriele?'

'Seems is wife has failed to give him a son, so he was overjoyed.'

'And then? Did he rip off your dress and take you by the altar - his eyes smouldering with memories of your former passion?'

Perhaps Ugo was right. Only a few moments with my former lover and it was easy to imagine rekindling the excitement of those days with Ambrogio. It might even add some much needed spice to my marriage.

'The others went down to the refectory and left us alone in the chapel.'

'And...'

'He kissed me.'

'The rogue!' Ugolina cackled. 'And in a holy place, though I suppose he could be forgiven for a peck on the cheek for the mother of his child.'

'Nothing of the sort. Pressed me against the wall for a full, on-the-lips smacker. I was terrified he wanted more.'

'Madonna preserve us. And did he?' Ugolina stood and walked around the kitchen. 'He needs his balls cutting off. I'll do it, for Macellino's taught me to be handy with a knife!'

'No, just the kiss. Then he stood back and drew. But the way he took what he wanted without asking, reminded me of when Blackbeard tried to rape me. And I can't even get absolution because, with the whole of

Monticiano listening to my confession, it'll get back to Timoteo in no time.'

Ugolina stood with her arms outstretched. 'My poor love. Come to Aunty Ugo!'

I broke down, but sinking into her rolls of fat was as comforting as being cuddled by Cook.

'Apparently I gave him an idea for one of the frescos.'

'That's a good one!' Ugolina wiped her hands on her apron then took the unbaked dough to the open fire, tutting at every step.

'Timoteo will know something happened, and that'll make things worse between us.'

Ugolina wiped her forehead then put her arm around my shoulders. 'Take some advice from your old friend. Pull yourself together, Clara. And don't give up the decent man you've got in Timoteo, not unless you want to lose all your children.'

'He's bound to guess something's up.'

'Then when you're in bed, think of those passionate times with your artist. Timoteo's not to know what's going on in your head.'

I'd always suspected Ugolina disregarded church rules in her love life with Macellino.

'He'll wonder what's got into his wife of eighteen years!'

'As long as it's not the man with the paintbrush. And if you're even tempted, come round here and I'll throw a bucket of water over you! No! the pastry's burning.' Ugolina raced to the fire. 'Caught it! Here, take some for the family or I'll eat it all myself.'

'Thanks, Ugo. I knew you'd sort me out.' I gave her a hug.

'And about the workshop – tell them to start making something people want to buy. Those designs haven't changed since Niccolò was an apprentice.' Ugolina swept the crumbs onto her palm, then into her mouth.

'You're right. Something needs to change before Niccolò hands on his bradawl.' I said as I let myself out, wondering if that remark also applied to me.

Chapter 17

Talking to my friend hadn't solved the problems of the workshop but telling her of my encounter with Ambrogio had helped me see there was a vast difference between that kiss and Blackbeard's assault. And that old me, the one that had hoped to be an artist, was proud to be the source of inspiration, however much it had shocked.

Dorotea asked whether something I'd learnt from the Salimbeni might save the workshop. But half a lesson from the factotum hardly made me an expert in running a business. Nevertheless, as Timoteo and I trudged in silence to the family meeting, I was ready to play my part. If the workshop were no longer successful, there was no chance of Gabriele staying.

We needed a new direction, if only we could identify what it should be.

As we entered the kitchen – wood fire burning against the damp outside – Gabriele wouldn't even greet us.

'You all know why we're here.' At the end of the table, Niccolò looked like a corn doll pecked free of stuffing.

All eyes turned on Bruno, who slammed down his drink. 'Don't look at me. I'd no idea we owed so much.'

'Then you should have!' I said. Sienese merchants were famous for their method of keeping track of income and outgoings.

'Contrary Clara is back! We haven't heard her since you had the children,' Orsola sniffed.

'I count the money in all right.' Bruno scratched the palm of his left hand.

I nudged Stefano to speak up. We needed to know the extent of Bruno's debts.

He stared at the table. 'We owe the shops and ale houses almost as much as Giuseppe.'

My mild-mannered husband slammed his fist on the table. 'Your personal debts have nothing to do with us. We live within our means!'

'Families stick together in times of trouble.' To make plain what he was referring to, Niccolò put his hand on Gabriele's shoulder.

Timoteo shook his head. 'Even if we sold all our stock, wobbles and all…'

'And fair play, we have a lot of wobbles,' Bruno took another swig.

'I say we give up now.' Gabriele frowned, 'and I'll find work elsewhere.'

The wood crackled in the fire and I put my head in my hands to hide my tears. I'd survive losing the workshop, but not my son.

'It's my fault,' said Stefano, 'The only people who'd buy my work are blind hermits!'

'Then sell it to blind hermits!' Gabriele was bitter. Life with Ambrogio would be far more appealing than this.

Stefano cleared his throat. 'Not blind hermits, but – no, this is a stupid idea.'

'Go on,' I said, clutching at whatever this straw might be.

'Carbon burners and shepherds live in the middle of nowhere. They'd turn a blind eye to my mistakes if we sold cheap.'

'Bad time of year to be out in the hills,' Niccolò said.

The others nodded. But, as the only practical idea we'd come up with, I couldn't let it rest. 'If we sold every stick we have, would we raise enough to pay off Giuseppe?'

'If we tidied it up a bit first,' said Bruno.

'It would need more than me on the job. You'd help, wouldn't you?' Timoteo looked to Gabriele, who nodded.

I wanted to hug them both.

'Then the least I can do is go out and sell it. With the roads so bad, people won't come to town.' Stefano's sunny smile showed he knew he was making a useful contribution at last. 'If you'll forego Siena market, I'll stay on the road until I've emptied the cart.'

It didn't solve everything, but it was a start.

'And you'll have to ask lover-boy for an advance to pay for his wood!' Bruno looked at me before draining his beaker.

'If you call him that one more time, I swear I'll knock you senseless.' Timoteo thumped his clenched fist on the table.

'Steady!' Bruno held up his palms, 'or Gabriele can ask. I mean, now he's a journeyman, he can earn his pay.'

'I'll do it,' I said. It was too cruel to expect Gabriele to ask his father for money the first time they met.

'We'll both go,' said Gabriele, 'as long as you stop calling him names. He's Signor Lorenzetti from now on.'

Timoteo held his head in his hands.

'But if I'm putting myself out, so can you, Bruno.' Gabriele faced his uncle. How like Ambrogio, so sure of himself. 'Since I started working here, you've not been sober a day. We need someone in charge who does a proper day's work. If you can't, you should hand over to someone who can. Me, for instance.'

'You scheming hussy! Ever since you turned up from Siena,' Orsola pointed at me, 'you've tried to push us aside!'

'Drunk every day! Ridiculous.' Bruno slammed his fist on the table. 'And as for carpentry, I'm as good as the next man.'

'Only when you're sober,' said Niccolò. 'And your job, Orsola, is to make sure he is.'

I didn't envy her the task, for Bruno was as slippery as an eel when it came to finding a drink.

Niccolò continued. 'So by Easter we might have paid off Giuseppe and built the scaffolding. But with nothing to work with, we'll have nothing to sell.'

'Not that anyone wants to buy our stuff.' Gabriele muttered.

I added, 'Ugolina says it's too old fashioned.'

Niccolò looked hurt. 'It's traditional!

'That woman's nothing more than a gossip.' Orsola sniffed.

'I'm just a poor journeyman – yet to be paid, by the way – but I agree. We need something fresh and different,' Gabriele said.

'We should paint our furniture!' My words came from nowhere.

Niccolò and Timoteo looked at me in horror.

'Like Giuseppe's – but with real paint, not wood stains, just like the rich in Siena have in their palazzi.'

'We can ask Ambrogio for some paints!' For the first time since we'd broken the news to him, Gabriele smiled. Even Timoteo's frown eased as he contemplated the idea.

'All sorted! That calls for a celebration.' Bruno clipped Gabriele's head as he made his way towards the cantina where the wine was stored.

'Bring it up,' Orsola called after him, 'because it'll be your last for a while.'

When I woke the following morning, Timoteo had already left. Gabriele and I walked up to the stable where Bruno and the cart were waiting. We travelled in silence through the early morning mist. Along the way, green shoots had appeared in some of the hedgerows, though, of the trees, only the pines had leaves. Rains had softened the earth and, as we approached the abbey, a monk was instructing labourers from the surrounding villages to prepare the ground for planting. At the hermitage, Bruno tethered the horses, while Gabriele put a stone under each wheel. Then we entered the chapel. Bruno pushed through the canvas sheet separating off the workspace from the main chapel. I held Gabriele back, wanting to savour the last moment when he was mine alone. I looked up at the domed ceiling. What did the red and gold rings surrounding the apse remind me of? Before, I'd thought of a beehive, or ripples from a stone thrown in a pond? But today they only represented one thing, the different hair colours of the Lorenzetti brothers.

'At last, the scaffolding! I've been freezing my fingers off, sketching, when I should be up there, drawing the ceiling.' Ambrogio shouted. I hoped his annoyance wouldn't extend to Gabriele.

'Lots of rain we've had, er, Signor Lorenzetti. Lucky our wheels stayed on through all this mud.'

I had to admire how Bruno made out he was the one granting the favour.

'You're here now, so get it up as quickly as you can.'

'That's not why we came.' Bruno pulled back the curtain. I put my arm around Gabriele's waist and steered him towards Ambrogio, who was again dressed in the improbable combination of ink-stained tunic and fur-lined coat.

'This is Gabriele.' My mouth went dry; son, mother and father together the first time.

Gabriele pawed the ground, afraid he'd disappoint. Indeed, many fathers – including Vanni's – took little interest in their offspring. Ambrogio tilted his head from side to side, studying the width of his son's shoulders, the shape of his face, their relative heights. Gabriele, a smidgeon taller, looked to me for guidance. I indicated for him to take his hat off.

Slowly and deliberately Ambrogio removed his hat too, and they stood facing each other. I caught my breath for they were two versions of the same man: broad-shouldered, fair skin unblemished by sunlight, and hair, gold as cornfields waiting to be harvested.

'I admit, I was dubious but now I see you, there's no chance I can deny you're mine. You're more like me than my own brother.' He put his arms round Gabriele and hugged him.

I was grateful for his reaction, even if eighteen years too late.

'Excuse me, sir,' Bruno's politeness was excessive when on the scrounge. 'Given the inclement weather, might the refectory have a little something to warm me up.'

'You know where it is. '

Bruno disappeared like a rabbit down a hole.

'Are you interested in art, Gabriele?' Ambrogio asked.

Gabriele's head indicated neither yes nor no.

I helped him out. 'Art is only for churches up here

in the hills, and not often then. But Gabriele has an excellent eye. Though only a journeyman, his carpentry is worthy of a master.'

'Then allow me to introduce you to art in the making.' He pulled out the most detailed of his drawings. 'Anything you can tell me about the composition that's going there.'

Gabriele followed his gaze to the space above the altar then squinted at the drawing. 'The woman is reclining on the floor at the bottom of the painting, and all the other people go this way.' Gabriele held his forearm vertically. 'It's as though she's holding them up.'

'Bravo!' Ambrogio hugged the boy and kissed him on both cheeks, transforming Gabriele from sulky young man to top student. 'He has the makings of an artist, Clara!'

My cheeks burnt. Once upon a time, I'd been the one whose opinion he'd sought. And much as I loved my son, I resented him enjoying these conversations in my place.

'Now you've seen my plan, Gabriele, will you help me achieve it? If you're as good a carpenter as your mother says, you'll be able to hold the brush steady. If you have a head for heights, too, you can be one of my assistants. If not, you can help mix the paints.' Without Gabriele seeing, Ambrogio winked at me. At times he seemed to recall nothing of our time together, at others everything.

'And cast him aside when you've no further use for him,' as he did me, 'I won't have it.'

'Please yourself. I'll make do with Bruno's lad.'

'That would be so unfair, Mamma. You know he's useless.'

'And he's not available,' I said. 'Since I was last here, we've discovered the workshop is in financial difficulty. Stefano will be away, selling our faulty furniture, and before he goes, we need Gabriele to help make it good. Would you be able to pay us up front for the wood we need for the scaffolding?'

'Let me guess, something to do with Bruno's red nose.'

How could he have got to the truth so quickly? In his youth, he'd been far too interested in himself to notice what was happening around him.

'Let's make a deal, Clara. You agree to Gabriele working here, and I'll ask the abbot to give the workshop an advance.'

I looked at the piles of drawings, the blueprints for what would eventually appear on the walls. I should be here, helping him, not Gabriele. Colour meant more to me than it ever would to him. But my life was already determined. It would be churlish to deny him the chance of learning from Ambrogio while he was here, even if I was fearful of what would happen after that.

'Go, find your uncle, Gabriele. He must be part of this discussion.'

'Straight down the hill for the refectory,' Ambrogio led him to the door then watched him disappear down the track. Then he took my hands in his. This time I was prepared for his physical exuberance. 'I've fallen in love with him, Clara. He's bright, good-looking,

216

opinionated, just like me at that age! He already has a good eye, but I can improve it – if you'll let me.'

'You'll seduce him like you seduced me all those years ago.' I was angry and upset in equal measure. 'For you he's a novelty, but he's my life. I've taught him well, hoping if you ever met him, you'd be proud.'

'And I am.' He took one of my curls and tucked it behind my ear, standing so close I had to turn my face away. 'He wants to get to know me, so let him. What's the harm in that?'

'You'll get under his skin and then do what you like with him.'

Ambrogio pummelled the wall with his fist. 'You dangle him like bait, only to snatch him back. If that's what you wanted, why tell me about him and why bring him here?'

He had a point.

'Let him work with me for as long as the job lasts, then I swear on my girls' lives, I'll give him back to you.'

Did I believe him? Yet I nodded, and Ambrogio hugged me to seal the deal.

'What's this, what's this?' Bruno burst into the chapel, Gabriele a few steps behind.

'Clara's upset at the idea of not seeing Gabriele while he works here.' His deft choice of words suggested an innocent reason for comforting me.

'I can come?' Gabriele said.

'Yes, son!' Ambrogio put an arm round his shoulders.

'Not possible, Signor L – not 'til he's finished sorting

out our old stock.' Bruno wasn't so drunk he'd forgotten the workshop's problems.

'You can have him for a week. If he's not here in seven days' time, no advance payment. Understood? And if the scaffolding isn't delivered soon after, I'll go to a carpenter in Chiusdino, which is what I should have done from the start.'

Bruno opened and closed his mouth like a carp in the abbey's pond. And I was reminded of being bundled out of Pietro's studio.

'You'll have to live here, Gabriele, if we are to make best use of the light at this time of year. The monastery will pay for your board, and I'll reimburse the workshop whatever you currently pay him.'

'Hah!' Gabriele said, dryly.

'He's paid as a journeyman,' Bruno cut in quickly. 'And when Stefano joins you – he's away on another job – he'll have to be paid too. Same price as Gabriele.

'Agreed in principle,' Ambrogio said, 'but we'll discuss the rate when I've found out what they can do. Come with me, men. I'll ask the abbot now.'

I stayed behind and stared at the blank walls. Then I leafed through the sketches on the table. On one sheet he'd drawn the figure of the angel Gabriel announcing to the Virgin that she was to give birth to God's son. So far, the face was blank, but I pictured how it would now be filled in.

Chapter 18

In the days after Gabriele's departure, a cloud hung over our house. Rosa had no-one to swop sharp words with, Viola missed the horseplay with her brother, and, from the way he ignored me, Timoteo blamed me for the loss of our son. My thoughts were at the hermitage, wishing I too, could be learning from the artist now considered a master. But most of all, I feared for the web of charm he was weaving round my boy. I yearned to eavesdrop on their conversations, watch Gabriele's talent grow, smell the egg and linseed in the paints. But a visit was out of the question. One of the maids at the Casa Grande had fallen ill, and I had to help prepare for the overlord's Easter visit. And I knew that, absorbed in his new-found world, it was too much to expect a visit from my son.

Though supportive when we'd first discussed the idea of painted furniture, Timoteo now ridiculed it, seemingly to punish me for Gabriele's absence. Luckily Orsola's friends liked the idea, so she now claimed it as her own. All depended on Niccolò.

'Do you remember that chest you made for my mother as her dowry? Contessa Salimbeni loved your carving on the panels.'

'A labour of love which took me weeks.' My grandfather's eyes were moist at the memory. He took my hand but his was shaking. 'If only I could still make items like that.'

'People will love painted furniture just as much, Nonno. I could ask Ambrogio to borrow Gabriele for a few weeks to show what we can do.'

Niccolò wasn't convinced but agreed to a small trial. We had just enough wood to make a three-panelled chest.

Typical of Bruno's cheek, when he next went to the abbey to move the scaffolding, he asked Ambrogio to produce some designs for us. But as Lent progressed, neither Gabriele nor the designs had appeared. If they hadn't arrived by the Easter Monday pilgrimage to the abbey, I'd talk to him myself.

The Good Friday before, I was still waiting. Ugo and I linked arms to walk to the local market, though given our family finances, I was not there to buy. 'I do miss him, you know.'

'Can't understand why you ever let him out of your sight.'

'For once I was thinking of Timoteo, not Gabriele – though of course I miss him too. I hadn't realised how much I needed my husband's warm regard until it disappeared.'

'My poor love.' Ugo pulled me to her. It was like sinking into a feather mattress.

I squeezed her arm as we made our way down the main street. Then out of nowhere, I saw my cousin's face. 'Stefano! When did you get back?' He was sitting on the back of our empty cart, skin ruddy and hair down to his shoulders.

Never one to hold back, Ugolina rubbed his new beard. 'My, aren't you the wild man of the Maremma! I'll leave the two of you to catch up while I do my shopping.'

'Tell me how it went.' I jumped up next to him.

'Sold nearly everything, as you see.' A couple of stools were on the ground in front of his cart. 'Arrived back this morning and thought the horse could rest here as easily as in the stable. The last chair went just now.'

I lowered my voice. 'Did you make enough money?'

'Enough to pay Giuseppe.' Stefano grinned.

'Well done!' I slapped his knee. 'Don't let your mother get her hands on it.'

'Too late! I've given her some already.' Stefano looked sheepish.

'You didn't?' I hated to think of his expedition being in vain.

'Only enough for a capon to celebrate me coming home! The rest is here.' Stefano tapped his shirt. He hesitated, then pulled out his money pouch. 'You take it so I can't be tempted to give her more.'

'You deserve more than a capon for getting rid of that lot!' I stuffed the purse in my bodice. 'So how was it? I'd go mad cut off from the world like that.'

'At the start, they thought I was a bandit. Then I passed a forge and asked them to make me a bell. After that people came out when I rang, if only out of curiosity.' Stefano jangled his bell and a man stopped to look at the stools.

'You've enough there to buy them both,' Stefano said, as the man counted his coins. 'They're sturdy, and for that money you won't do better.'

The man tried them, handed over the coins and walked off with his purchases.

'To begin with, I sold things too cheaply. But most of them have money for creature comforts; they just can't get to market to buy them.'

'We'll make a merchant of you yet!'

'And I met someone.' Stefano blushed. 'Don't tell Mamma, will you?'

'Since when was Orsola my confidant?' and we both laughed.

'Her name's Lucia. I thank God for the snowstorm that forced me to beg shelter from her father, a carbon-maker, for she's the sweetest person ever.' Being in love made Stefano more good-looking than ever and I was happy for him. 'When my hands were blue with cold, the thought of her kept me going. I want to marry her, yet all I have to offer are my father's drinking debts.'

'We'll find a way,' I said, expressing more optimism than I felt, for I knew how hard it was to lose a love.

On Easter Monday, the townspeople gathered outside the monastery ready to walk off the previous day's excess. We'd enjoyed lamb with Ugolina and today Dorotea was providing the picnic: Torta di Pasquetta – a tart of spinach, ricotta and hard-boiled eggs.

'No Timoteo?' Ugolina linked arms while we waited for the monks to bring out the cross that would lead us through the woods.

I shook my head. 'Not while Ambrogio's there, but I can't wait to see what they've been up to – and I need to speak to Ambrogio.'

'Careful, girl.' Ugolina shook her head but added a wink.

Just when the crowd's impatience would turn to annoyance, the monks emerged. We joined the women behind the cross, while the men brought up the rear, and a lengthy column of Monticianese set off through the woods. The ground was covered with a mulch of oak leaves and, though the chestnuts were in leaf, the acacia were still bare. A man with a donkey – jangling pots, food and kindling – trundled past us on the track. Viola grabbed my hand, nervous of crossing the Merse river.

'Don't worry, cara, Macellino will help you,' I said.

Ugolina's husband stood knee-deep in the water, lending his steady arm to the cautious and infirm.

'Looking forward to seeing your brother?' I said once we were safely across.

'He's not interested in us anymore,' and she ran off to walk the rest of the way with her friends.

At the abbey, I followed the crowd into the nave, all the while searching for two fair heads. Light poured through the east window onto the stone altar, the abbey resounded with monks' voices, and I turned to see Gabriele slipping in at the back. Abbot Angelo held out his arms to welcome us and the mass began. Once it had ended we flooded onto the grass.

As I pushed through the crowd to find Gabriele, I bumped into Giuseppe.

'Buona Pasquetta, Clara.' He took my hand in his callused palm.

'I have the money we owe,' I whispered, and thrust the purse into his hand.

Tears were in his eyes as he stuffed it in his jerkin.

'Yoo-hoo, here we are.' Ugolina beckoned us to a patch Dorotea and Orsola had claimed. The cloth was laden with enough food to feed the five thousand.

'Join us, Giuseppe. My grandfather will be delighted to see you.'

We climbed over family groups sat round their picnic feasts.

Giuseppe groaned as he lowered himself to the ground. 'So, Niccolò, what have you been up to without any wood.'

'Just made a beautiful cassone with what we had left, though I can't grip the tools like I used to.' Niccolò raised his badly swollen knuckles. 'Bruno helped. He's a good carpenter when he's a clear head.'

'Don't need one today!' Bruno took a swig from Ugolina's flagon.

'Now you've paid up, you can have as much wood as you like. Though don't make me wait this long again.' Giuseppe offered round his baby broad beans, then podded some for himself.

'Why does he get paid and not the town shops!' Orsola glared.

'Don't worry, my little dumpling, we'll have money

coming in soon.' Wine had restored Bruno to his carefree self.

I held my tongue and looked around to see Gabriele swagger towards us, his gait more Siena than Monticiano.

'Here's the golden boy! Give Aunty Ugo a hug!'

He did so, then hugged or shook hands with everyone else until he got to me. I stood up and held him at arm's length. There was the shadow of a beard on his chin, and his best tunic was splattered with paint. Before I could stop myself, I blurted, 'Where have you been? It's been months.'

'I'm sorry, Mamma, but I'm having such a wonderful time, I can't miss a moment.'

Though I'd only been at the Lorenzetti studio a couple of weeks, I remembered that feeling.

'Mmm, Nonna's Torta di Pasquetta!' He threw himself on the grass and grabbed a slice, while Dorotea leant over and pinched his cheek.

Giuseppe said. 'Tell us, is he as good a painter as they say?'

'Very much so.' Gabriele said through a mouthful of pie. 'He's taught me to paint, what colours work together, how much plaster equals a day's work.'

'Hands off that last slice of torta.' Rosa slapped Gabriele's wrist, 'I promised we'd take some back to Babbo.'

'Will you show us what you've been doing?' I jumped to my feet, but Rosa and Dorotea were clearing away the food, Viola had run off with her friends and the others were too full to move.

'I'm sorry, Mamma, he says no-one's to see it until it's finished, not even you.'

Ugolina winked at the 'even you', and I blushed.

'But he's left some designs for those panels. I'll fetch them for you now.'

'I'll walk with you.' I followed him up the path to the hermitage. 'Is he in there working?'

'Went back to Siena to see his family – the other assistants too.'

I was disappointed, and ashamed how much I wanted to see him, to be included in the work of creation as I had in Pietro's studio.

'But he left me plenty to be getting on with. To be honest, I think he needed to get away after the row with the abbot about Eve.'

I remembered the scantily clad woman in his drawings for the altar painting. 'A strange choice to put before celibates.'

'The abbot was shocked, too. I thought Ambrogio would have to paint over it, but he had an answer. Explained it brought together old and new testaments through the two most powerful women in the bible. Eve creates original sin, which the Madonna comes to the world to forgive.'

I didn't quite follow.

'No, I didn't understand it either, and nor did the abbot: so Ambrogio's adding a cartouche – a box of words telling the monks what they should be thinking. That man is so clever.'

Yes, he was, and now he was using that intelligence to capture Gabriele's affections. 'But now we need you back with us for a few weeks to paint these designs.'

'I'm far too busy. He's given me all the backgrounds. I'm working on the story of San Galgano now, but there's a lot of wall to cover.'

'Stefano's back. Let him take your place.' A little help from Gabriele would go a long way, as well as raise my spirits.

'You know he'll be useless. Anyway, Ambrogio says you should do the painting.'

'Me? That's ridiculous. And what's more, your father won't have it. Please, Gabriele, spare us a few days to give us something to sell at Pentecost?'

'I can't, Mamma. I promised I'd have the background done by his return. Wait, while I get the sketches.' He went into the chapel.

I looked out beyond the picnicking crowds to the woods beyond. Gabriele was winding himself round his natural father like bindweed. If he didn't return to me soon, the son I'd thought closer than my breath, would be a sophisticated stranger.

'Here you are.' Gabriele handed over a scroll of papers. 'And he's left you a present.'

I struggled not to cry. These days I could expect no such kindness from Timoteo.

Gabriele pulled out from behind his back a small, hessian package. 'Colours. He said you should mix them with linseed oil rather than egg if you're working on wood.'

Clutching the bundle to my heart, I felt excited. Ambrogio was right about one thing. Without Gabriele, I was the workshop's best option for putting the painting idea into practice.

'Mamma, we're leaving!' Rosa appeared at the top of the path from the abbey.

'Thank Ambrogio for the designs and the paints. I'm so pleased for you, Gabriele, but don't forget your family. We need you too.' I held him closer and longer than he'd like.

'So much so, that Babbo won't even come and see me.' Gabriele pulled away. Timoteo hadn't even sent greetings.

'It's not about you, caro. He's jealous of Ambrogio, what he can offer you.'

Gabriele ran to his sister. 'Come Rosa, I'll race you to the bottom of the track.'

'Let's go together!' I laughed taking one of his arms while Rosa took the other.

We walked so fast, we reached the bottom, panting.

'Promise you'll come to the market at Pentecost and see what we've made. Then you can tell Ambrogio how we've used his paints.' We parted with a hug at the track to Monticiano.

I kept to myself on the walk back, the only way I could nurse my disappointment; of not having seen Ambrogio and that Gabriele wasn't coming back with us. More than ever, I needed some of that enthusiasm he'd infected Gabriele with; that spice of Siena I still missed so much.

As soon as we reached Monticiano, I went to the stable. If I was to do the painting, I needed a 'studio'. It could be in the workshop, but with Timoteo frowning on everything to do with Ambrogio, I'd be unable to work under his critical eye. Nor did I want to listen to Bruno's litany of ribald remarks. On his return Stefano had put the horse straight out to grass, and the cart was propped against a wall in the corner. Almost as big as Pietro's studio, it would make an adequate workspace, as long as I left the doors open for light.

Kneeling on the floor, I brought the bundle to my face. Smelling it reminded me of Duccio's studio. I untied the knot, excitedly studying each lump in turn: the green of terra verde, the autumnal hues of the umbers, a lump of blue azurite and, buried among them, a mortar, pestle and brushes. I'd sweep out the old hay, borrow a table from the workshop, and beg flax oil from Dorotea. With Pentecost fair only eight weeks away, I couldn't wait to begin.

Chapter 19

The weeks after Easter passed in a flurry. I used all available light before and after work at the Casa Grande, at my 'studio'. Bruno jeered at me calling it that, but it meant a lot to me. The family were unhappy at the time I spent away from them, but without Gabriele, who else would decorate the furniture?

I felt Ambrogio's encouragement in every

brushstroke. Even so, my first attempts were more like a child's. However, I was soon reproducing the designs to a standard he'd approve of and started trying out some of my own. I had plenty of opportunity now we had wood. We were making good progress, until Niccolò was summoned to the monastery to supervise moving the scaffolding for Ambrogio wanted to start the last wall. He'd learnt Conte Salimbeni was coming to inspect progress on Pentecost Sunday and his presence made me wonder why the family had chosen now to endow a chapel at one of the most popular pilgrimage sites in the region. Perhaps I could ask him, for Bruno had wangled an invitation for us all to attend the private viewing.

It was thirty years since I'd seen the man who'd ordered me out. But I thought only of the kindness he'd shown when my father died and wanted to thank him for it. Anything to get him to forgive my mother's sins and allow me to see again where I'd grown up. The hope urged me to complete as much as I could for the Pentecost Fair, and soon Pentecost Sunday was upon us.

Such a prestigious occasion warranted the cart. The girls wore clean dresses, and the men had shaved. Orsola was trussed up like a chicken, wearing an excess of ribbons bought from a peddler. Even Timoteo swallowed his scruples and was coming. Only Dorotea stayed at home, pleading a painful hip. I removed all stains from my everyday outfit and tucked a few margaritas – left over from decorating the girls' hair – into my curls.

The sun shone on our outing; acacia festooned with white blossom flanked the road. As we turned towards the abbey, I shuddered. What if the Conte threw me out again? It would be a cruel blow to miss celebrating Gabriele's efforts. Thanks to Orsola's fussing, we'd set off late, so instead of attending mass at the abbey, we went straight to the hermitage.

Rosa and Viola jumped off the cart, Timoteo helped Niccolò, while I gave Orsola a hand down. She bustled into the chapel and we followed. The frescoed area was shielded by a curtain, and we waited in the main chapel with the half-dozen painting assistants.

'Gabriele!' Viola ran to hug her brother, the special invitation having overcome her earlier resentment of his absence.

'My, aren't you the gallant,' Rosa said. 'Where did those clothes come from?'

'Ambrogio, of course.' Gabriele was dressed in a blue and yellow outfit that emphasised his fair hair. 'Funny you should be jealous, when you dress like a nun.'

Rosa dug him in the ribs, and their relationship was back to normal.

'Babbo, I'm so happy you came!' Gabriele's face shone as he hugged us both.

At the sound of voices outside, we all turned. First to enter was the abbot, his white habit light against the main chapel's stone walls. Of medium height, but with an oddly long body, he seemed too young to be head of one of the richest abbeys in Tuscany. He bowed in our direction and Orsola bobbed a double curtsy – this from a woman who'd told me such skills were useless in Monticiano. Behind him Ambrogio was dressed in pale green brocade, sleeves slashed with a rose pink that would look effeminate on anyone less manly. The assistants arranged themselves in a line, the most senior next to the door, the first to be introduced. Stefano was at the end of the line, his wry smile saying 'I know my place!'

At last, we heard the main party reach the porchway. 'I'm looking forward to seeing how you've decorated our chapel, Signor Lorenzetti. I understand it's almost complete.'

The voice was cold, demanding – but it wasn't the Conte's, and I was delighted to see they'd sent Vanni in his place. From his outfit, he'd returned to the city. Was it too much to hope that one day I, too, might go back?

Ambrogio presented his assistants, and Vanni said a few words to each of them. When it was Gabriele's turn, I prayed he'd make a good impression.

'Fair hair like you, Signor Lorenzetti. Following his father into the trade, I presume?' Vanni studied Gabriele's face.

True, they were two drops from the same bucket, but I gasped. Timoteo clenched his fists, and I stayed his arm.

Ambrogio moved to Niccolò. 'Gabriele's the grandson of my scaffolding supplier; a fine craftsman who also helped my brother, Pietro, when he did the stained glass in Monticiano's monastery.'

'But I run the workshop now.' Bruno spat in his palm and wiped it on his tunic before offering it to a frowning Vanni.

'And we are Gabriele's parents.' I pushed Timoteo forward to make sure he was acknowledged as Gabriele's father.

'Clara! I was hoping to see you, so you've saved me a visit to Monticiano.' Vanni took my rough hands in his and turned to his host.

'Father Abbot, this woman and I grew up together.

I reined in a quip about his fancy outfit, and said instead, 'so they've allowed you back in the city!'

'Unfortunately, not. On his way here, the Conte took ill at my monastery. He's young in mind, but not in body. I'm here in his place, in his clothes too!'

'Pleased to meet you, I'm sure.' Orsola's ribbons quivered as she thrust herself before Vanni, forgetting her decades of disparaging the Salimbeni. 'My son's the good-looking one.'

Was I imagining, or did Vanni wink at me as he took her hand?

Abbot Angelo pulled back the curtain to the side chapel. 'Time to show you the impressive work itself.'

I gasped to see the colours so bold, the impact uplifting. This wasn't Duccio reworked, or Pietro copied. Ambrogio had thrown away centuries of tradition to create something totally Ambrogio. How proud I was that Gabriele had shared in its creation.

'Push forward, Rosa,' Viola whispered. 'I can't see.'

'Push yourself.' Rosa paused to pray at the sword implanted in the stone in the centre of the main chapel.

'I hope this man understands art,' Gabriele whispered, 'for it's not just with Eve he's taken a risk.'

Remembering Vanni's reaction to our one art lesson, I felt uneasy.

We squashed into the archway between side and main chapel, craning our heads as Ambrogio directed our gaze to the ceiling. Gabriele exuded pride, for the largest part of the work – the background blue – was his. After suitable congratulations to the men who'd helped paint the four medallions in the sky, the party turned to the left-hand wall, now complete with the story of San Galgano. Then Vanni disapproved of the lusty Eve above the altar, giving half-hearted acceptance when the abbot showed how the words in the cartouche would put the monks' minds on the right path.

Finally, the abbot turned our attention to the Annunciation, the work in progress on the final wall. The archangel bringing the message to Mary that she was about to bear God's son was complete. With his bright golden hair, the messenger could only have been Gabriele. So like the Ambrogio I first met. Handsome and imposing, he knelt on a perfectly-perspectived square-tiled floor and handed the virgin a fertile green palm. No wonder a young girl, even one as virtuous as the Madonna, would find his request irresistible. I caught Ambrogio's eyes and smiled my thanks for acknowledging his son.

At the other end of the wall – Mary's answer to the call – was still being worked on. Instead of the usual, modest – almost simpering – girl holding a book, this Mary – as yet only depicted in red-ink – was distraught. Sagging under the weight of the burden being thrust upon her, she had sunk to the floor, and was holding on to the pillar at her side for support. I turned away in horror as I remembered the day of Ambrogio's kiss, here in the chapel, and the memory of Blackbeard it had resurrected.

I tried to compose myself, but I'd already been observed. Vanni was watching me, his face like thunder.

Ambrogio eyed his work as he spoke. 'Though still incomplete, I am confident the Salimbeni will be honoured by this radical interpretation, undoubtedly my best work to date.'

'Radical? Scandalous more like!' Vanni had his fists clenched.

'Since when do the Salimbeni know anything about art?' The senior assistant muttered, loud in the silence that followed Vanni's outburst.

The abbot raised his hand to silence further comment. 'It's a fine religious interpretation, Signor Salimbeni. Would you allow me to elaborate?'

With Vanni too angry for words, the abbot continued. 'This shows us Mary at the very moment she becomes divine; an ordinary girl from Nazareth chosen to bear God's son, as we too are chosen to be faithful Christians. A very proper message for my monks to contemplate. But, if unclear, I am sure Signor Lorenzetti would consider another cartouche.'

Vanni faced the abbot, fists still clenched. 'This is no virgin, Father Abbot, but an unmarried girl who's terrified to find herself with child. I know because she told me of her plight when this scoundrel got her with child. And to add further insult, he's painted himself as the Angel! If you don't believe me, ask her, for she's here today.'

'He's got it wrong, Timoteo,' I whispered, before he said something. 'Vanni never understood art.'

But Ambrogio was unable to contain his rage. 'How could you think I'd betray the trust placed in me; by the Salimbeni or the abbey. Worshippers will be inspired by the courage it took to be the mother of Christ. Far from diminishing her glory, it shows the courage it took to be the Queen of Heaven.'

'Fine words but they don't convince me.' Vanni was now shouting. 'How dare you use my family's money to celebrate your youthful exploits.'

The artists' assistants nudged each other. Ambrogio's past was no secret.

'Come now, Signor Salimbeni,' the abbot said, 'I am sure we can reach an understanding.'

'Remove that degrading picture, Abbot, or you'll get no more money from my family. And if you refuse, I shall make sure the Pope learns of this this blasphemy. And when he marshals his theological powers against you, your nice flood of pilgrims will reduce to a miserable trickle.'

I could no longer control myself. 'Vanni, you're going too far!'

He was right about the depiction capturing my degradation, but by Blackbeard not Ambrogio.

'Gentlemen, may I suggest some reflection over some refreshments. Our fare is famed among pilgrims.'

But Ambrogio hadn't finished. 'Father Abbot, we prayed together for God to guide our interpretation…'

236

Vanni interrupted. 'A shame you didn't do that eighteen years ago. Might have saved you ruining a girl's life. Now you misuse her again. Shame on you.'

Bruno smirked, Timoteo looked mortified, and the artists' assistants studied the flagstones.

Ambrogio faced Vanni square on. 'I have long repented of my sins and do my best to live an honest and righteous life. This is a fine work, and I'll not bow to the opinion of a family of murderers.'

If it hadn't been a chapel, I'd swear Vanni would have landed a punch.

Ambrogio continued, his eyes on fire. 'Father Abbot, the Salimbeni have made their position clear. Let me do likewise. I cannot work for someone with so little appreciation of what he has before him. I resign with immediate effect. As soon as I have cleared out my things you can forget the name of Lorenzetti.'

'Good decision,' Vanni's crowing was infuriating. 'Lead us to the refreshments, Father Abbot.'

Bruno pushed to get out and was the first down the track to the refectory.

This was Vanni at his hot-headed worst, and I rushed to speak to him. 'I thought you were my friend, so why shame me like that? and for what?'

'He thought he could get away with it, but this time he's met his match.'

'I hope you're satisfied, for you've denied the abbey a great work and lost my family their jobs.'

'A small price to pay for preventing your fall from grace being witnessed ever after.' Vanni tried to take my hand.

'Don't touch me. You've hurt me beyond measure.'

Vanni looked shocked until the abbot steered him towards the refectory.

I turned back to the chapel. Inside, Ambrogio was sitting at the top of the scaffolding, staring at his drawing. I climbed up and sat beside him.

'He was right; it was meant to be you, though nobody would have known.'

'Why, Ambrogio? Who am I to represent the holiest woman in Christendom?'

He ran his fingers over the drawing. 'I've never captured a moment of intensity so well. You made me think about how this moment was for Mary. A shock? And not only a blessing, but a huge responsibility with a tragic end.' Ambrogio took his eyes from the drawing and took my hand in his, compassion not passion. 'But that oaf was right about it being personal – just not in the way he said. It was my way of asking you to forgive me for having to bear this alone while I pursued my own selfish ends.'

'You didn't know,' I said.

'Even if I had we both know it would have changed nothing. Art was, and is, my life.' Ambrogio took my other hand, making me face him. 'And it was to give thanks for Gabriele. How he's captivated me. He's bright, alert, and ten times more curious than I was. At his age, I thought I knew everything, whereas he believes he has all to learn. He's a joy to teach, though you've educated him well. What a gift you bestowed on me in letting me share this time with him.'

'And now I'm taking him back.' I said before he

went further.

Ambrogio turned on the full charm of his hazel eyes. 'He won't thank you.'

I pulled my hands free. He'd not turn my world upside down again.

'Too early to say whether he'll be a great artist, but he's as good as many in my studio, so I'll be happy to give him an apprenticeship. I can offer him the chance to explore ideas at art's frontier. Will you deny him that for the sake of a few coloured chairs?'

How dare he? Those chairs were the closest I'd come to an artistic life. I needed to explain what taking Gabriele away would mean.

'Remember Pietro's stained glass at the monastery in Monticiano; how he captured the all-consuming grief of Mary witnessing the crucifixion? At the risk of being sacrilegious, that's how I'll feel if you take Gabriele from me. You can ridicule our coloured furniture, but if you take him, those colours will be all I have left. I beg you, don't wrong me again.'

Ambrogio hammered his fist against the wall, then sighed. 'Then I'll respect your wishes. Take the lads home with you. The other assistants can pack up here.'

I climbed down the scaffolding but before I left, I had to ask, 'You said the Salimbeni were a bunch of murderers; what have they done now?'

'Didn't you know? Last year, they persuaded the Tolomei nobles to come on a picnic and murdered all eighteen of them. Paying for these frescoes was their idea of atonement.'

Much as I hated the Tolomei, I was shocked at such

bloodshed. Did Vanni's arrogance derive from there no longer being any opposition to his family's power? Glad for once that my home was here in the hills, I was happy to see Timoteo waiting for me outside the refectory.

'It's all right. Gabriele's coming home with us.'

'That's the only good thing to come out of the day,' Timoteo smiled for the first time since Ambrogio turned up. I, too, looked forward to Gabriele coming home.

I took his hand. 'We should go. With the fair tomorrow, Bruno should stop drinking.'

Shortly after, Timoteo had prised them all out of the refectory and helped Niccolò into the cart's front seat with him. The rest of us piled into the back.

'Jump in too,' I said to the boys. 'Ambrogio says he no longer needs you.'

Stefano eagerly took the reins, relieved of further obligation to masquerade as an artist but Gabriele stood firm. 'I can't just leave. He's my father.'

'Don't leave it too late to walk back through the woods,' I said. 'We're so looking forward to having you back.'

'Better make sure we get paid for erecting all that scaffolding,' Niccolò said once we'd set off. 'Nothing goes off faster than a contract that's not being fulfilled.'

But Bruno's only response was loud snoring.

Chapter 20

y mid-afternoon we'd reached Monticiano, and I was so happy my son was coming back. But tomorrow was the fair, and we immediately directed our efforts to the final preparations for displaying our new wares. I was excited and nervous, for a lot hung on my idea being a success. Stefano examined the painted areas for gaps in the colouring – the light in my studio was not all it could have been. Orsola took a rag and removed all smudges, and Bruno slept off his lunch. Niccolò gave each item a final inspection, returning to Timoteo anything failing to meet his master craftsman's standards. As the customer-ready goods mounted, Niccolò forgot his earlier reservations and glowed with pride. I'd be doing the same but where was Gabriele?

'Should we ask Stefano to go look for him?' I asked Timoteo as we walked home.

'Leave him be. If he chooses to run off with that reprobate, he's out of our lives forever.' When angry, his limp was more pronounced.

I tossed through the night, one moment punching the pillow in rage at Vanni, another crying into it as I faced the horror of losing my son. I resolved to go to the abbey first thing in the morning for one last attempt to persuade him to stay. At last I fell asleep, only to wake too late. How would I survive if he left without a goodbye? As soon as the fair was over, Timoteo and I would go and shame him into coming home.

Unlike the regular market in the lower piazza, the Pentecost fair took place in the upper square, so we only had to move the goods outside to display them. The sun shone on our wares and the colours beckoned. As the trading started, the townsfolk wandered stalls piled with wicker baskets, olive wood utensils or woven wool. Happy babble filled the air. We attracted attention too, as husbands paused, examined tenon and mortice joints, but then, alas, walked on. Their wives – hair garlanded with spring flowers – ran their fingers over my painted embellishments.

'These are just examples,' a hungover Bruno said when he caught someone's eye. 'If you don't like these, we've plenty other designs, and any colours you want. Even match the sky's blue though that'd cost you more.'

Despite his way with customers, no-one was buying and still no Gabriele. I bit off a nail.

'Clara, I'm so impressed!' Ugolina ran her hand over a table edged in a flower pattern, her red hair aflame with poppies. 'I want it. I want everything!'

'Then buy. The first sale gets a good price.'

'You've sold nothing?' For once in her life, Ugolina lowered her voice.

'I guess no-one came out today planning to buy something as substantial as a piece of furniture.' I was so disappointed after all our hard work.

'Honestly, I'd die for this table, as long as I had time to enjoy it first!'

'Then tell that husband of yours to treat you!' I'd never heard of a poor butcher.

Ugolina leant into my ear. 'We can't have the whole of Monticiano saying we're rich.'

'If everyone thinks like that, it's the end of us.' I couldn't have been more despondent.

'Tell you what, I'll find Macellino and see what he says. That table of mine is a bit shabby and, now I've seen this one, I'm not sure I can live without it!'

'Let me walk with you. I've a headache fit to burst.'

'So?' Ugolina said when we were out of earshot of the men.

'Ambrogio's walked out on the job at the abbey. Gabriele was supposed to come home with us, but he's still there. I'm afraid he's not coming back.'

Ugolina raised her eyes heavenwards. 'Forgive me saying, but I told you so. Oh, there he is!'

'Gabriele? Where?' I searched for the fair hair.

'No, Macellino! Get back to your stall and I'll see if I can bring you a buyer.'

As Ugolina girth had increased, her walk had become more of a waddle. I watched her sway towards her husband and stroke his arm. Turning away, I searched the crowd in vain for bright clothes. The truth was, Ambrogio's was the only opinion of my work I wanted to hear.

When I got back to our stall, Giuseppe was installed on one of the chairs 'You stole my idea! I think I deserve a cut!' He winked.

'Our carpentry's better,' Niccolò said. The two men looked settled for the day.

'And Clara's painting,' Giuseppe smiled at me. 'Puts my efforts to shame.'

Then through the beige melee, colour approached: side by side, two golden heads glowing like sunflowers in bloom.

'I've brought him back.' Ambrogio pushed forward the sulking Gabriele.

'I was so worried.' I gave my son a hug, but he was a sack of roots in my arms.

'I'm sorry.' Gabriele's voice was thick with emotion, his eyes red.

'This looks good, I knew you could do it.' Ambrogio ran a hand over the table Ugolina fancied.

The sun had come out again.

'Nice designs too. I'm glad you came up with some of your own. How are sales going?' People turned to stare at his colourful garb.

'Absolutely nothing.' I reached out to Gabriele's hand for strength, but he pulled away to search out Stefano.

'Ladies and gentlemen, Ambrogio Lorenzetti, master painter, at your service!' He jumped onto a chair and everyone gathered round. 'Some of the designs on this wonderful furniture are mine. Others are the workshop's. I defy you to tell the difference! For a fraction of what you'd have to pay me for just one of those panels,' he pointed to the chest, 'you get three and the chest itself. Or how about a beautifully decorated table. Buy now, while you have the chance, for these items will only go up in value.'

'Me, me,' Ugolina waved her hand from the back of the crowd. 'I want that table.' Ambrogio worked his way out of the crowd that pushed forward, and soon all the carpenters were deep in discussions with interested buyers. I stepped back too, to find Ambrogio at my shoulder.

'Don't turn round,' he said, 'Go somewhere we can talk, and I'll follow.'

I left Gabriele, sitting, head in hands, on Orsola's steps then made my way to the Porta. Ambrogio joined soon after and we sat side by side on the wall.

'I told him he had to come back – though it took all my powers of persuasion. But if you want my honest opinion, he'll not stay. I've shown him a different life, and he wants it.'

In Gabriele's position, I'd want it too, but Ambrogio had given his word.

'So your promises are still worth nothing.'

'That was true then, but now I'm thinking as a father, what would be best for my son.'

'Your son? He was mine alone before you burst in on our life.'

'Hear me out. He's talented. He's found his world and he'll never forgive you if you take it away from him.'

'And my world was Siena, yet you took it away without a thought.'

'But I must have given you something in return. Your apprenticeship at Pietro's was all too short, but it was enough to give you the confidence to design that furniture.'

'Gabriele can design furniture too.'

'Saints preserve me, Clara. People would cut their hands off for a place in my studio. I can grow him as an artist, everything I had to fight Pietro to allow me. I thought you of all people would jump at this chance for your son.'

'I can't. He's my life.'

'Then don't blame me if he leaves anyway. He's seventeen and has a mind of his own.'

Cruel, but right. 'You needn't have been so nice to him!' I let the tears roll.

'You'd have been the first to complain if I'd treated him badly!' He put his arm around my shoulders. 'Remember I hardly knew my father – he died when I was still young – it's important to me that Gabriele knows his.'

'Timoteo's his father. Gabriele owes him everything.'

Ambrogio removed his arm. 'Don't ruin Gabriele's life for the sake of gratitude. I thought you, of all people, would understand the pull of art. Talk to your husband. The abbot has given me a letter of recommendation to the Duomo in Massa Marittima, and I shall set off there at noon tomorrow. Let Gabriele join me, and if he's unhappy, I'll return him to you on my way back to Siena. I couldn't give you a life in my studio, but I can give one to your – our – son. And if I read him right, he'll be with me tomorrow, with or without your blessing.'

246

I followed him slowly back to the piazza, deep in thought. This was a gentler, more confident Ambrogio than the one I'd first met, but I marvelled at his ability, yet again, to ruin my life. For I knew that keeping Gabriele in Monticiano would be selfish, and he would never forgive me for holding him back.

Timoteo's smile as he completed his sale turned to scowl when he saw us return.

Ambrogio gave me a wave, nodded to Gabriele and left. I sat on one of the unsold chairs, covered my eyes and contemplated two yellow stars falling from my heaven. The first time I'd held Gabriele in my arms, I'd loved him with an intensity I hadn't known existed. How could I bear life without him for, once gone, there was little chance he'd return.

I moved to join Gabriele on the step. Months earlier, I could have anticipated every emotion flittering across my son's face. Yet now he was almost a stranger.

'How can you reject what I'm being offered – me, a carpenter from Monticiano?'

My eyes welled up for I knew, far more than he'd ever appreciate.

'Soon I'll be doing medallions, and folds in cloaks. He says I might be good enough to do faces in time. If you knew anything about art, you'd understand.'

His words cut to the quick. Yet to part with him was to tear out my heart. Holding back my tears, I said, 'I'll speak to your father.'

I approached Timoteo as soon as the crowd had died down. 'Look at Gabriele.' He was staring over the rooftops towards Chiusdino. 'He came back, but he'll run away if we don't let him go.'

'I knew it, that man's poisoned his mind.'

'He's not choosing Ambrogio over you, but painting over carpentry, and to be honest, I would too, given the chance.' We walked down Half Street, through the Porta, and sat on the wall where I'd just sat with Ambrogio. 'He'll never forgive us if we make him stay.'

'I'll lock him up until that man's out of our territory.'

'Timoteo, you offered me a better future when I married you, and I'll always be grateful for that. Now we must do the same for Gabriele. Let him go with Ambrogio. Don't let your jealousy of the man – or your anger about what happened two decades ago – ruin our son's life.'

'But if Gabriele leaves, what'll happen to the workshop? Who will run it after Niccolò's gone?'

'We'll manage. And today's success was nothing to do with him. Viola and Rosa could have children, Stefano too. Any boy would be grateful to learn a trade like carpentry.'

'Except Gabriele.' Timoteo hung his head.

'If we let him go willingly, we can have a meal together tonight; say our proper goodbyes. If we don't, he'll slip away in the night, and we'll never see him again.' My voice jagged as I held back my tears.

Timoteo stared out towards Monte Quoio then squeezed my hand. 'You're right. I'll ask Mamma to prepare something special for supper.' He went straight home, leaving me to tell Gabriele.

'You've missed some good sales,' Bruno rubbed his

248

hands. 'Giuseppe's taken the chest as a dowry for his daughter. We let him have it in return for that last lot of wood. Ugolina bought a table and the overlord took the settle decorated in diamonds.'

'Not the one with the shields we thought he'd go for?' I put my arm around Viola who was wilting, like the bluebells in her hair. Rosa sat on a carved chair, a chain of daisies round her neck. Gabriele hovered, waiting for Timoteo's answer but I wasn't quite ready to seal my fate.

Stefano smiled. 'He said he might come back for it.'

'Prior Benedetto took a look too.' Orsola added, claiming ownership for my idea now it was successful.

'The next time someone dies and leaves money to the blessed Antonio Patrizi, we can expect an order,' Bruno chuckled.

'Did any of them pay up front? Who's got the money?' I said.

'Half for Bruno's debts, that's what we agreed.' Orsola tapped her bosom and continued shelling beans for supper.

'She's promised me wine tonight, eh, chicken?' Bruno plucked at Orsola's cheek.

The crowd drifted back to their homes. Bruno and Stefano stored what remained of the furniture. The sun was still warm in the piazza. Through open shutters came the clatter of utensils and the smell of meals being prepared. I put my arm around Gabriele's shoulders – one of my last chances to do so. 'Your father and I have decided, you can go with Ambrogio.'

'Oh Mamma.' He sobbed into my neck, and soon I,

too, was in tears.

'We'll have a meal together tonight, and you'll set off for San Galgano at first light. He'll wait for you until noon.'

'Babbo agreed?' Gabriele wiped his eyes.

'Like me, he only wants the best for you.' I forced myself to sound cheery.

'Rosa, I'll race you to the Porta and back!' He kicked his sister in the ankle and they ran through the streets as they'd done as children; Viola catching on late, and trailing behind.

That evening, in Dorotea's kitchen, was like better times. Ugolina had supplied us with meat, Orsola the beans she'd spent the afternoon shelling, and we all squashed into the tiny space to wish Gabriele well. That night, I lay with the girls, though I hardly slept, while Gabriele shared the bed with his father of seventeen years.

Gabriele woke before dawn, to be sure Ambrogio wouldn't set off without him. I rose with him, to enjoy every second of those final moments.

'Bye, stone face,' Gabriele kicked Rosa awake.

'I'll miss you too,' she said from under the covers, then dressed to see him off.

'You can't go! I'll stop you leaving.' Viola sat on his shoes.

'Don't be stupid, Viola,' and he pushed her to one side.

I felt my heart racing. Would I ever see him again? What if he forgot us, for the distractions of life with Ambrogio would be immense. If only there were something I could give him to remember us. Then I recalled my only comfort on leaving Siena and reached under the mattress for my bag of stones. 'Take these. My father gave me them just before he died. If you're ever lonely and miss us, get them out. This one can be Viola.' I picked out the smallest. 'The next biggest, Rosa.'

Gabriele poured them onto his palm. 'Then this black one can be Stefano; this rough one Bruno. And these two shiny ones are you and Babbo. Thank you, Mamma.' Gabriele looked teary as he tied the bag to his belt.

I forced my face into a smile as I stroked his hair. If I saw him again, he'd be too old for such mothering.

Timoteo gave him a tight hug.

'Here's some bits and pieces for your journey,' Dorotea handed him a bundle wrapped in muslin. 'I'd have baked you a pie, but you didn't give me much warning.'

'Thanks, Nonna,' he gave his grandmother a hug. 'I forgot to tell you Mamma, Ambrogio left you all his paints. I put them in the stable. The abbey's already paid for them and they'll be no use by the time they find another artist.'

We all walked Gabriele to the Porta; smiling and tearful waves as he took the path down to the fonte and up the other side of the valley. The bundle he carried was pitifully small to last the rest of his life. The birds' early morning chorus was in full throttle and the poppies opened their petals for the day ahead.

Gabriele disappeared and Rosa and Viola returned

251

home with Dorotea, but Timoteo and I remained sitting on the wall.

At last, I wiped my eyes on my sleeve. 'This painted furniture is going to be popular, and I can't go on fitting it around my work at the Casa Grande. I think I should train Rosa to take over.'

'My mother won't be happy; they work together as one.'

'I know, but Rosa's too old to stay at home not contributing, and it's time Viola helped more.'

'Too much change. You know I don't like it. But if that's what must happen, we'd better make a start,' Timoteo put his arm around my shoulder, and we hobbled to the workshop where he gave me a cursory farewell.

Could we mend the cracks in our relationship as easily as we had Stefano's chairs? I knew he'd never fully forgive me for persuading him to let Gabriele go, though his departure hurt me just as much. Rosa was close to her Nonna Dorotea, and Viola was her Babbo's girl. Without Gabriele, I had no special person. On reaching the stable, I curled up in a ball on the floor and howled. Still crying, I moved to the table, laying my head on Ambrogio's parcel. How could I live with the loneliness that engulfed me? I unloosed the rag containing the bases for making colours and reached for the yellow ochre – the only gold left in my life. Snapping off a lump, I added water. I squelched it through my fingers to mix a runny paste, then ran it through my hair. I barred the door and stripped off my clothes. Golden yellow – I smothered it over my arms, my legs, my breasts, my belly. As the paint caked on my skin, I curled onto the floor, hugging my knees until the sobs eased, and my breathing calmed.

This was all the gold I had left to comfort me. Pietro and Ambrogio painted their family and friends into their pictures to keep them company while they worked, but my designs contained no figures. However, they could include this colour, and henceforth always would. Slowly, methodically I used the rag to wipe myself clean of paint, pleased that a vestige remained embedded in my cuticles.

Part Four

Black

Monticiano, 1348

Chapter 21

Stand still.' I said as I helped Viola into the pink dress. A hint of cinnamon wafted towards me, and I closed my eyes, remembering Babbo tying that sash on the day of the festa – the last day of my childhood. Today Viola would be crossing a threshold too, no longer my baby, but Gregorio's wife. I'd spent nostalgic hours undoing the tucks Mamma had put in to make it fit me after she'd tired of wearing it; all the while ignoring Timoteo's carping that the gown was too grand for a Monticiano wedding. But now the furniture business was a success, we belonged to the town's elite, and I wanted to pass on to my daughter some of the joy I'd felt dancing in the Campo that day.

'Are you sure the colour suits me?' Viola pinched

her cheeks until they matched her dress.

'It's perfect.' I glowed with pride at the girl before me. Timoteo's features had been poured into Rosa and Gabriele followed Ambrogio, but Viola had taken her looks from me.

'Will Gregorio be impressed?' Viola did a twirl. Ugolina's son had won out against the competition, by forcing her to choose between her suitors.

'Sit down and let me do your hair. Good thing you've got my curls to hold the flowers!'

'I'm so happy, Mamma.' Viola sighed. 'This is the best day of my life!'

How unlike my wedding, where I'd been so sick, I'd needed Niccolò's strong arm to make it to the altar. Gratitude to Timoteo felt no substitute for a life with Ambrogio, and I'd little enthusiasm for what marriage promised.

'If only Rosa could be here, too. Why did she have to be a nun?' Viola picked up the glass and examined herself from all angles.

'She followed her heart, as you are following yours.' If only I'd been able to follow mine, I thought as I plaited each side of my daughter's curly locks, then tied them in the style the overlord's wife had worn that Easter. (No longer my mistress, I was now the closest she had to a friend in Monticiano.) 'Remember how lost she was after Nonna Dorotea died? If you miss her, ask Macellino to give Gregorio a few days off. You could visit her in Siena, Gabriele too.'

'Oh, he forgot us long ago.'

'Not entirely, for he gave a donation to secure

Rosa's place at Santa Maria della Scala, though Ambrogio's recommendation must also have helped.' For years I'd been angry and heartbroken that he'd stolen my son. But from Bruno's occasional encounters with Gabriele at Siena market, I knew he was living the life I'd have loved. 'But don't you forget me too!'

'Don't be silly. I'll see you every day and still do your housework.'

'Thank you!' I needed help at home now that I ran the business. But a daily visit wouldn't replace waking to see my daughter's black curls strewn over the pillow, or listening to the small grunts she made in her sleep. Yet I couldn't complain. Though the contentment at the heart of my marriage had fizzled out, Ambrogio had been right. Producing designs and painting them had saved my life, as well as being the cornerstone of our business success.

'What do you think?' I watched as Viola made a final inspection in the glass.

'Mamma, you have such a good eye.' She gave me a hug.

'May as well put the last of the cyclamen in my own hair.' I was wearing my best grey linen, trimmed with fine lace the overlord's wife had given me for the occasion.

'Ready?' Timoteo knocked on the bedroom door. Though his hair was thinning, it had kept its colour and he looked spruce after his shave. As he opened the door to claim his daughter for the last time, he gasped.

'What's the matter, Babbo?' Viola's hand flew to her hair as if there were an earwig crawling out of one of

256

the flowers.

'Only that you're more beautiful than a Contessa.' He took her arm.

Most of the guests had gone straight to the church, but what remained of our family was waiting in the street below.

'A corker you've got there, Timoteo!' Bruno propped up Orsola and her stiff legs, while she provided support for his wobbly ones.

Laura, now comfortably plump and motherly, had travelled from the next village for the occasion and fussed over her brood. Stefano, tanned and weather-beaten, smiled, emphasising the creases around his eyes.

'No need to ask how you are,' I took my favourite cousin's arm, and we followed my daughter up the street. 'The outdoor life suits you.'

'Best thing I did, however much it upset "her",' Stefano nodded towards his mother. 'And you've more than filled my place in the workshop. Babbo's too, in terms of running the business. He tells me you've just decorated a wardrobe for the monastery vestments.'

'Who'd have guessed Giuseppe would leave the church so much money? Sly old fox!' I'd learnt of the bequest when discussing the monastery's specification. 'If we'd known his mattress was stuffed with coins, we could have made him wait for payment when we were so hard pressed. Anyway, how are Lucia and the children? Can we tempt you back to town and an easier life?' Few would take on the life of a charcoal-burner out of choice. '

'We're as happy as nobles in their palazzi, as long as I do as she says!' Stefano laughed. We crossed the piazza to a packed church. Everyone in town was the butcher's customer and most had turned out to see his only son married.

'Wish me luck, Mamma.' Viola hesitated at the top of the steps, and I gave one final adjustment to the flowers in her hair.

Then Stefano led me through the congregation to the front. I smiled at the nervous Gregorio standing the other side of the aisle. Ugolina, next to him, waved. Then all eyes turned to the back, and the crowd gave a communal intake of breath at the sight of Viola. Timoteo made little of his limp as he walked his daughter down the aisle, Gregorio's face a mixture of pride and adoration. And as Timoteo took his place next to me, I had a lump in my throat. The mass, the vows, the throwing of petals as the couple left the church, and Viola was no longer ours. Would the business now be enough?

'May I escort the mother of the bride to the piazzetta?' The now-greying Macellino offered his arm. 'Looking as lovely as her daughter.'

'Stop it, Macellino. I'm not a customer you need to charm money out of!' Nonetheless I was flattered. I'd received no compliments from Timoteo for years.

'That means you and me, Timoteo!' Ugolina shoved her arm through his. With the other she adjusted the crimson sash tied around what passed for her waist.

The semicircle of the piazzetta glowed peach in the afternoon sun. Plaited branches and flowers were garlanded between the upper windows and each family had disgorged their tables and chairs into the yard between the houses and the main street. Pride of place was taken by the pig, roasting from early morning above a stack of white-hot embers.

Over the years, Orsola had maintained her vigil over Bruno's consumption, but today's wine was free and he was the first to sample it.

Through the afternoon, each of Ugolina's neighbours brought out a plate of delicacies and presented it to the bride and groom: pasta primavera, salad of artichokes, cake of pine nuts and much more. Gregorio and Viola sampled each dish then returned to their own private world of touching foreheads and whispering. Their joy rubbed off on the rest of us.

'Bruno's not going to be good for much tomorrow,' I whispered to Timoteo, as my uncle staggered out of the piazzetta clutching a flagon.

'That's nothing new,' Timoteo said.

'Then just as well the workshop has you.' I squeezed his hand.

'Now, everyone, you've got to find room for my milk pudding.' Ugolina paraded it with as much pride as Duccio's presenting his Maestà to the Siena Signori. 'The spices have come all the way from ... from outside Tuscany anyway!'

As the sun lowered behind the town walls, the food was cleared away, and tables returned to their homes. Women fetched shawls, men their pipes and tambours, and the music began. Youngsters copied their elders in the steps of dances handed down through generations.

The infirm looked on with pleasure, and in shady corners, new friendships formed under the stars. Then as Viola and Gregorio started yawning, the music became gentler, and people began to leave.

'Off you go, you two. We'll come and wake you if you're not up by noon!' Ugolina shooed the newlyweds into her house. The couple were to live with her – though our dowry was the promise of Dorotea's house after our days. 'We've done our bit, cara. It's over to them now.'

I linked arms with my best friend and we walked the few steps to our house. Macellino and Timoteo were waiting on the steps.

Ugolina giggled as she grabbed Timoteo's arm. 'Shall I share a bed with you, Timoteo, and we'll let Clara have that snoring husband of mine.'

'Or I'll have your snoring husband and you two can talk yourselves to sleep,' Timoteo retorted.

'Come on, caro.' Ugolina pushed Macellino up the stairs. 'Take me in your arms and remind me of when we first got married.'

In our bedroom, the visitors took Viola's bed. Timoteo turned away and was soon snoring, but I was kept awake by the sounds of my friend fulfilling her wishes.

'Mmm. What a good day that was!' Ugolina stretched, her grey-red curls splaying out of her flax cap. While the men still slept, we dressed and went to the kitchen.

'And a good night for someone.' I prodded the fat

around my friend's middle.

She winked. 'You wouldn't begrudge me a little dolce to finish off the celebrations, would you?'

I handed her a pail. 'Come on! Something tells me Viola won't be fetching water this morning.'

We paused under the arch of the Porta to breathe in the spring air. Across the valley, smoke snaked from the woodman's hut. The fruit trees in the orchard opposite were festooned in blossom. The grass was rich and green, watered by winter rain and drawn out of the ground by the spring sunshine.

'Didn't they look lovely?' Ugolina linked arms as we steadied each other down the steepest part of the slope to the fonte. 'Viola so beautiful and Gregorio so handsome – like two cooing doves. I'd have eaten them both if I hadn't already stuffed myself silly!'

'The only drawback is that now I'm related to this noisy woman with red hair!' I nudged my friend. 'As if I hadn't been punished enough having Maria as a mother!'

'Cheek like that and it'll be the end of our friendship!' Ugolina gave my arm a playful slap.

I laughed and we turned the corner. From now on the path to the fonte was straight, though the spring was obscured from view by the flattening of the path part way. We walked on down, listening to the birds outdoing each other in their search for a mate.

I sighed. 'How I envy them being in love.'

'What do you expect after thirty years? And you and Timoteo work so well together on that pretty furniture. My house is full of it!'

'Listening to you and Macellino last night made me realise how empty our marriage has become. Our life will be so much duller without Viola to leaven it.'

'Be happy for them and stop feeling sorry for yourself, you old nanny!'

At the half-way point, I paused to enjoy the early morning sun on my face, listening to the trickling of the spring below. Ugolina was right. However mundane my marriage, I had much to be thankful for.

'What's that? Looks a bit odd.' Ugolina pointed at the trough.

I ran towards the pool then dropped my pail. Bruno's knees were hooked over the low wall of the tank, but his top half was bobbing below the surface of the water, his face bloated. An empty wine flagon bounced in the spring water flowing into it. I covered my mouth to stop myself being sick. Behind me, Ugolina screamed.

His body moved. Could he still be alive?

'Help me get him out.' I tugged at his arm.

Ugolina turned away. 'I'm not touching him.'

I tried again to pull him out of the water, though nothing with skin that cold would still have life. As if to confirm, his bulging eyes gave no response and his body stayed glued underwater. I let go the arm and turned away. 'He must have passed out and fallen backwards into the water.' My voice was shaky, and I feared I'd faint.

'I knew he'd drunk plenty, but I never imagined this.' Ugolina sat on the edge of the trough, back to the body. 'Why didn't Orsola send Stefano to look for him?

I'd never let Macellino stay out all night.'

'Too late for that now.' I stared at the white ghostliness in the pool.

'You'll have to fetch the men. I'm too queasy to make it up that hill.'

I didn't feel much better myself, but one of us had to get help. 'Will you be all right on your own?'

'I won't look. But be quick because he's crying from purgatory, "get me a drink, my lips are parched".' Ugolina joked in her nervousness.

'Are you sure it won't be you in purgatory, making remarks like that.'

'Just trying to keep myself cheerful. But fetch Macellino before I die of fright.'

I set off up the hill as fast as my forty-seven years allowed, glad he'd been around to accompany Viola to church. I'd almost reached the Porta when the shutters above opened.

'Buongiorno, Mamma!' A radiant Viola appeared, her nakedness wrapped in a sheet.

I forced a smile, not daring to check whether the fonte was visible from the window. Then Gregorio nodded a brief greeting, put his arms around his new wife's shoulders, and steered her back into the room.

I climbed the steps to our house and threw open the shutters.

'What the ...' Timoteo raised himself onto his elbows.

'Does this mean the happy couple are up and I can go home?' Macellino rubbed his eyes and yawned.

I sat on the side of our bed.

'Something terrible's happened.' I covered my face, trying to shut out the dreadful image. 'Bruno's dead – drowned in the fonte.'

Macellino swore, and Timoteo frowned.

'Ugolina's down there on her own. You'd better go at once.'

'I will, or we'll have two corpses to bring up, not one.' Macellino said. 'She passes out at the sight of me strangling a chicken.'

I stood up, trying to blot out those bulging eyes. 'You must get him out of the water before the whole town comes to gawp. I'll break the news to Stefano.'

'Wait, I'll come with you. We've some boards in the workshop we can use to carry him back.' Timoteo pulled on his clothes then walked with me to the piazza. 'I used to hate him, the way he made fun of my limp. But since it's been just the two of us, I've got used to him. He was a very funny man.'

'And though he wasn't always sober, he never ran up drinking debts again.'

'Crusty old sot, though.' Timoteo said, and we laughed.

'I should stay with Orsola. Stefano can help you with the boards.' I hovered outside as Timoteo disappeared into the workshop, then crept up the steps to the kitchen. My cousin was asleep on the settle that was once Niccolò's bed. 'Stefano!'

'What are you doing? I thought the devil had come for me.'

'He has in a way.' I sunk onto one of Niccolò's chairs, glad of its firm support.

Stefano rubbed the black hairs on his chest. 'Then tell me. Nobody makes a social call this early.' Although the sun was up, the piazza outside was still quiet.

'You must have noticed how much your father was drinking at the wedding. For some reason he went down to the water tank where I think he passed out. Unfortunately, he fell into the water and drowned. He's dead, Stefano. I'm so sorry.'

He blinked and stared – his eyes unfocussed.

'Ugolina and I went to fetch water and found him.'

'Bastard!' Stefano punched a fist into his pillow. 'The flagon has been his only friend for years.'

'He was a huge character, with a great spirit.' I took my cousin's hand.

'And selfish, leaving Mamma like this. How am I going to tell her?' He looked so lost.

'I'll do it, if you like.'

'Would you?' Stefano pulled on his tunic and wiped his eyes. 'I'd like to see him before he's moved.'

'Timoteo's waiting for you downstairs.'

Stefano glugged some water, but at the doorway, broke down. 'He may be an old soak, but he was still my Babbo.'

I ran to him and pulled his head onto my shoulder. 'Larger than life, and we'll all miss him.'

He wiped his eyes on his sleeve and the saddest Stefano I'd ever seen left the house.

I stood in the empty kitchen, remembering my life when this had been my home. With Bruno gone, and her children left home, who would Orsola harass now?

I tapped on the bedroom door.

'What are you doing here?' Orsola sat up in bed, her hair matted.

I sat on the bed and repeated the news.

Orsola howled until her eyes were red and snot streamed from her nose. 'Niccolò's dead, Laura and Stefano gone, and now Bruno. Who's to look after me?'

'Too soon to think of such things.' I stroked the sunspots on my aunt's arm. After her cruelty to me as a young girl, I would never offer.

Bruno's funeral took place the following afternoon.

In the full black cloak of widowhood, Orsola followed the coffin from the workshop to the church. Macellino and Gregorio – now bound to the family by marriage – joined Timoteo, Stefano and two of Bruno's former drinking mates as pallbearers. The coffin was placed in the nave, a quieter presence than Bruno had ever been in life. At the end of the mass, the priest sprinkled it with holy water. Then the pallbearers hoisted it onto their shoulders, and we all walked the mile to the cemetery beyond the town walls. After he'd been safely put to rest, we gathered round Orsola's table.

'Forty years married. How can I live without him?' Tears dribbled down her cheeks. 'I've never been on my own.'

'I'd love to stay, Mamma, you know I would,' Laura, pale after the strain of the funeral, dandled her youngest on her knee. 'But I must get home.'

I remembered, too, how happy Laura had been to

come and live with us, her first step in escaping her mother's clutches.

'Don't worry, Mamma, after I've seen Laura home, I'll stay a few more days.' Stefano covered his mother's hand with his. 'But then I must get back to Lucia and the family. We'd be happy if you came to live with us.'

'In a hut in the middle of nowhere? No thank you!' Orsola folded her arms, confirming her lifetime of stubbornness.

Why should I step in when her own children wouldn't help? She had the stiffness of advancing years but was able to get around. Yet I had to offer something.

'I'll call in to see you every day. And Timoteo will be downstairs in the workshop. Anything you need, you only need stamp on the floor.'

Orsola nodded and wiped her eyes.

Timoteo cleared his throat. 'Or you and I could move in. Then Viola and Gregorio can have our house now.'

He looked so pleased with himself. But the look I gave him was as black as the carbon of his hair.

'That would be wonderful.' Stefano looked so relieved, I felt ashamed of my resentment. 'Then Laura and I can go back to our families knowing Mamma is being taken care of.'

'It's not a solution either of us would relish.' I glared at Orsola.

'You'd be prepared to sleep in the kitchen, wouldn't you, Mamma?' Stefano stroked his mother's hand; still in essence, her little boy, 'then you and Timoteo could have the bedroom to yourselves.'

'I'd still be in charge of the house, you know.' Even in her grief, Orsola was defiant. She put out her hand to Bruno's empty chair. 'It'll be quiet without him.'

'I'll miss his banter while he did his work.' Timoteo added.

'What about Siena?' Orsola said. 'Who will take the stuff to market now he's gone. We'd come to enjoy our little outings together, but I couldn't think of going without him.'

Who indeed? I smiled inside.

Bruno's death had given me the opportunity I'd been waiting for.

Chapter 22

The night before we left, I woke often, checking to see if the sky was lightening. I was longing to see the familiar places of my youth; the area round Palazzo Salimbeni, the Duomo and of course the Campo. All that dampened my excitement was the fear of an encounter with Blackbeard, for the memory of the stable never went away. I shook Timoteo awake before the first chink of grey appeared. How reluctant he was to stir, though our income could be halved if we missed the monthly

Siena market.

'Should I take a weapon?' Timoteo trembled in the gloom of our bedroom for I'd put off moving in with Orsola.

'You'll be safe. It's nobles and their servants, like my father, who get killed.' So many years on, yet his death still felt raw. 'But we must set off now, to be sure of getting there by nightfall.' I cut chunks of pecorino and bread for the journey and wrapped them in a square of rough cloth, filled a gourd with water and waited at the door.

At last, Timoteo appeared, and we walked in silence to the stable. Now it was just the two of us, I'd moved my painting things into the workshop. I held the two horses we now owned, while Timoteo harnessed them to the cart. As we trundled down the road in the dark, I wondered what had happened to the Salimbeni. Domenico would be dead of course, but what about the others? Frisky Francesco would surely have stopped lusting; Cook, if still alive, would be an old woman, as would the Contessa. And had Vanni returned to the city or was he still an exile like me?

But most of all, I wanted to see my son. Maybe I'd get the chance to see his work, better still to be in the studio with him. Or had he become the disgruntled young man Ambrogio had been at his age? Even if he had, he'd still bring sunshine to my life.

Through the day, we passed through towns and hamlets as foreign to me as Venice or Milan, my impatience increasing as Timoteo delayed us with several generous rests for the horses. Finally, we turned a corner and on the hill before us, I made out the black and white tower of the Duomo bathed in the blush red glow of evening. But around it, the towers of the nobles' palazzi had sprouted several storeys, so the skyline resembled the back of a porcupine. But I was unable to recognise my old home as none of them flew flags.

Timoteo shook the reins, cajoling the horses up the hill to the Fontebranda gate.

'Shall we go and see Gabriele while we're here?' I put my arm through his.

'Don't you go running off and leaving me, like you did Niccolò. Now where do we stay the night?'

'Niccolò slept under the cart. Follow that cheesemonger. They'll all be going to market.' In Monticiano, since I ran the business, I let Timoteo be master of our household, but here, I took charge.

We quickly declared our business and were allowed in. Past the dying district and into the narrow streets, a man ran across our path – hair matted and dirty, yet he clutched a garment of lovat green edged with black velvet, the cloak of a merchant. I guessed it was stolen, but when would he wear it? The council used to fine anyone breaking the sumptuary laws. Above us, a girl leant out a window flaunting her cleavage to a boy below. Our cart's wooden wheels rattled over the rough tiles; the sound, so unlike that produced by the earth tracks of Monticiano. But the gutters were filled with rubbish and a revolting number of dead rats. What had happened to the cleanliness the city was so proud of?

Timoteo slumped over the reins. After a life in Monticiano, the noises were too loud, the streets too

270

crowded, the smells too strong. I looked in vain for the bold colours of servants' liveries; that walked and bowed, chattered and laughed, that I hoped would bring me back to the self I'd been forced to abandon decades earlier. I may not be able to live in Siena, but I had the comfort of knowing I could come here every month.

The Campo was busy and enhanced. The Tower next to the Palazzo dei Signori was now complete, and in the centre was a fonte, so all could get the drink of water my mother had craved on the day of the festa. I remembered where Niccolò's stall used to be and we made for the far end. I helped manoeuvre the cart into position, while Timoteo wedged stones under the cartwheels – Monticiano ones he'd brought with him so he could trust them to do the job. He led the animals to the new fonte and, when they'd drunk their fill, tethered them to one of the rings attached to the buildings around the piazza. Timoteo wanted the protection of sleeping under the cart though I'd have preferred being under the stars.

Early the following morning, we woke to the racket of stallholders unpacking their wares. Timoteo instinctively clutched his purse.

'Not seen you here before.' The man to our left, skin tanned like the leather he was selling, set out reins, belts and buskins on a trestle table. 'Recognize that pretty furniture, though. Where's Bruno?'

'I'm afraid my uncle died. My husband and I will be coming from now on.'

'What killed him? Not this thing going around?'

'Drowned after drinking too much at my daughter's

271

wedding.' Timoteo shook his head.

'That's Bruno for you,' the man laughed, 'died as he lived. Let's hope that tongue of his can persuade Peter to open the pearly gates for him. He was no saint but he meant no harm.'

'Not unless you count leaving us to deal with this.' Timoteo said.

'You'll get used to it. If you need help, just ask.'

We lifted the furniture off the cart, putting at the centre a chest I'd decorated with yellow sunflowers. Around it we placed chairs with diamond-shaped holes cut out of the backs, and a solid chestnut table with no embellishment – Timoteo's favourite. On it we scattered kitchen implements made using left over pieces of wood. It was an impressive display, and I hoped we'd do well.

'Don't be shy,' I said, remembering my visits to market with Cook. 'Explain how well our things are made, and only mention the price when you're sure they're interested. A good one. Plenty of money in this city.'

'Think of a Monticiano price and double it?'

I'd not checked my book of receipts before I left but had some notion of what Bruno had charged. 'Try marking up by half and see what happens.'

Timoteo dealt with the few customers while I looked for anyone with fair hair. We were missing Bruno's patter for by mid-morning, we'd only sold a couple of platters.

'Market was much busier in my day.' I said to the weaver to our right. His blankets were of a quality unseen in Monticiano, but he, too, was struggling.

'Something nasty going around, so I guess that's keeping them away. Oy, oy! Here come the Tolomei. They'll have coins in their purses.'

The last colours I wanted to see were theirs. Three dark-blue-clad servants were taunting an old woman they pulled along by a rope tied around her waist.

I froze.

Blackbeard. And the person he held by the rope was Mamma.

I thought back to that young woman who had skipped off to join him thirty-seven years ago. Whatever her sins, she didn't deserve this.

'That's my mother they're dragging along. I've got to stop them,' I said.

'No!' Timoteo held me close as the group lurched towards our stall.

'Well, well, well! If it isn't the little plum – though you're as wrinkled as my old cucumber these days!' Blackbeard leant in so close, I could feel his breath on my cheek.

'Be polite when you speak to my wife.' Timoteo clenched his fists.

'Careful, Timoteo, they have daggers.' I clutched his arm. I couldn't lose anyone else to this despicable man.

'Where's that old soak who's usually here?' Blackbeard addressed Timoteo. 'We came to buy him a few drinks to take her back to that piss-poor place where she was born. '

He must have been cultivating Bruno's friendship all these years.

'He's dead. Not that it's any of your business,' I said.

'Can I interest you gentlemen in a new leather belt?' the tanner shouted.

'Stay out of this. It's family business.' Blackbeard shouted back. 'Then, little plum, you'll have to take her. I knew one way or another you'd be of use to me.'

I trembled, remembering our last encounter. But I wouldn't give in without a fight.

'You married her. She's your responsibility.' And how would I run the business if I had to look after someone in her state?

'You won't be able to prove that, for the priest is dead, and I can assure you no Tolomei witness will come forward.'

The sidekicks pinched Maria to make her jump and she tried to fight them off. Yet even when half-crazed, she had saved me from a fate worse than death. But I wouldn't take her on for nothing.

'I'll take her off your hands but only if you buy all the goods we brought.' Only good could come of severing all links with this despicable clan.

'Are you sure?' Timoteo looked pained that I'd not asked him first.

'Nice move, little plum. We never want to see her again, so let your husband name his sum.' Blackbeard jingled the coins in his purse.

Before he spoke, I demanded a ridiculous sum.

'Cheap at the price. I should have got rid of her years ago. Pile everything onto the cart and bring it to the palazzo.' Blackbeard pulled Mamma by the rope, leaving his henchmen to do the loading.

She hadn't even noticed I was there.

As the servants loaded the cart, it pained me to think of my beautiful work going to these ugly toads. With Mamma to look after, when would I find the time to paint again? And it would take Timoteo ages to replace our stock. But to free myself of my link to the Tolomei no price was too high.

Once all was packed up, the servant climbed onto the front seat with us and drove the cart back to their palazzo.

'I'm sorry, Timoteo. I just had to.'

He patted my knee. Then he turned to the servant, 'what's up with the old lady?'

'Lord knows, I don't.'

'Blackbeard tired of using her for punching practice?' I sneered.

'Yeah, he can be a bit rough, but he thought she liked it. Never complained.' The driver smiled. 'But now the nobles have gone to the country for the summer, and he wasn't happy being made to stay to keep an eye on her. Now we can leave too. Good for everyone, for she'll be better off without Blackbeard as her nurse!'

A second servant slapped the horse's flank to goad it up the hill.

'He should be ashamed of himself,' said Timoteo. 'I treat my horses better than he treats her.'

I was glad he understood. But how bad was she when not tied up like a wild animal? Would she require so much care I'd be a prisoner in my own home?

We reached the palazzo, and the servants made short work of unloading.

Shortly after, a weird wailing heralded my mother's return – less a song, more a one-sided conversation without words. Now she wasn't being toyed with, I could see her better. She clutched some sort of blanket. Her dress, though elaborate, was dirty and slipped off her sagging shoulder, and she dragged a foot. One side of her face was expressionless, the other filled with despair, and I searched in vain for vestiges of the woman my father had adored.

'Maria of Monticiano! Sour as month-old milk and head soft as fresh ricotta. You're welcome to her.' Blackbeard gave Timoteo the rope. 'That quilt is her latest favourite. She disappears and wanders the streets, then comes back with some booty.'

The patchwork of brocades must have come from a wealthy household.

'Where's the money?' I put my hand out.

Blackbeard leant towards me, his face so wrinkled, his hair so grey. His smile revealed a large gap in his teeth one side of his mouth. 'We both know this stuff is worth half what you asked, so fight me for the money!.'

I reached down, pulled out the dagger that had killed my father and put it to his throat. 'Take his purse, Timoteo.'

'That's the spirit, little plum,' Blackbeard whispered in my ear. 'If I still had it in me, I'd have brought you to your knees.'

'Let's get out of here.' Timoteo said, as one of the younger servants lifted Maria between us, on the front seat.

'A lifetime with the Tolomei and this quilt is all she has?' I removed the knife from Blackbeard's throat.

'There's a tunnel between her legs that most of the carriages in Siena have passed through.' Blackbeard reached over and put his hands on her crotch, squeezing until she howled. 'She can take that and good riddance.'

Maria tried to spit at him but the gobbet of phlegm ran down her chin.

Timoteo shook the reins, face as white as refined flour.

I threw Blackbeard's dagger onto the road, 'How did you like being bettered by someone half your size!'

'Farewell, little plum.' Blackbeard smiled and waved, as if I were a long-loved friend.

'Straight up the main road. It'll take us longer but it's less steep.' I found myself trembling, despite sensing some sort of justice had been done. We passed Palazzo Salimbeni – already closed for summer and turned my attention to my mother.

Without Blackbeard she was calmer. Hemmed in between us, there was no chance of her escaping, so I untied the rope around her waist. Despite the heat of the day, she shivered so I arranged the quilt over her knees. She rested her head in my lap as we joined the queue to leave.

How excited I'd been to come through the city gates the previous evening, But now I had no chance of returning. We had nothing left to sell and I had an old woman to nurse. I was further from returning to the city than ever.

'I've been letting them out all day.' The guard pointed to a carriage belonging to one of other noble families. 'They must know something about this illness we don't!'

Perhaps they did. The rich had contacts everywhere.

'Here,' the man plucked some sprigs from a rosemary bush at the side of the gate. 'Breathe that. It's protected me from whatever it is. '

'We should never have come.' Timoteo stared at the road.

We'd never seen eye to eye about Siena, but for once I agreed with him.

Before we reached the outskirts, my mother was asleep.

We took advantage of the moon to travel through the night. Meandering up the final hill to Monticiano in the early hours, I made out the outline of the monastery and, as we passed, heard the monks' chanting Lauds, the first rite of the day.

We stopped outside the workshop. Maria woke and looked around the moonlit square. Using her good side, she let herself down from the cart and, clutching the quilt, hobbled up the steps to Orsola's. Her good hand traced over Niccolò's carvings on the door, found the handle and let herself in. She must have lived here as a child.

I followed her into the bedroom, where Orsola was asleep. One half of Maria's face was smiling as she smoothed the covers on the children's bed. Before I could stop her, she curled up on the mattress.

'Come on! I'll help you get her home.' Timoteo called from the piazza.

I went out to speak to him. 'She seems to think this is home. You go, and I'll sleep in the kitchen. We can sort things out in the morning.'

I am in a nest, sitting on my eggs, when, a curly-feathered cuckoo, perches next to me. One by one, she knocks my eggs out of the nest. I try to trill for help but no sound comes. On the earth below are broken shells mixed with yellow slime. Then the cuckoo starts pushing me out of the nest too.

I woke, heart pounding.

Outside the kitchen window, birds sang their early morning chorus. Snores came from the next room, and I continued to doze.

'What's she doing here?' Orsola poked me awake.

What indeed. I told her about the Tolomei.

'She's sleeping as sound as if she'd never left. But you'd better wake her or she'll be there all day.' Orsola pulled herself a hunk of bread. My mother was more at home in this house than I'd ever been.

I opened the shutter, then sat on the bed. I remembered the woman whose beauty was the envy of all in the palazzo, the Contessa included. Now, her hair was no longer black, though it retained the distinctive curls I'd passed on to my girls. The face was lined on one side and sagged on the other as if a heavy weight were pulling it down. Half the mouth was shut tight, the other open and dribbling, and she hugged the quilt that was her Siena keepsake. She was my burden now.

'Mamma?' The word stuck in my throat, for what sort of mother had she been to me? Nonetheless, I tried to take her chapped hands in mine, but she snatched them away, her eyes venomous. She narrowed an eye and tried to spit at me but it only came out as more dribble.

'You never change!' I snapped.

'Shame on you, Clara! At her age, she deserves some respect.' Orsola pulled me away and stroked Maria's cheek. 'There, there. my pretty girl. Do you remember me – I'm your brother Bruno's wife? We played together as children. Come and have some food.' Orsola coaxed Maria – and the quilt – into the kitchen.

'We shouldn't impose on your hospitality, Orsola, not after all you've been through. Timoteo can help me get her home.' I tried to pull my mother to her feet but she refused to budge.

'She can stay for now,' Orsola said. 'I'll be glad of the company.'

'Ffff,' Maria said and pointed at the bread.

'You're hungry, Maria. Let me soften it with a drop of milk; Bruno's favourite when his stomach was bad.' Widowhood had mollified Orsola into the essence of kindness.

Maria hummed a song without tune or words, stopping when she saw me. Here was the woman who'd lost me everything: my father, the Salimbeni, and Siena again. Now she was poisoning my life in

Monticiano, too.

There was a knock on the door and Viola twirled into the kitchen. 'Babbo told me I've a new Nonna and I've come to say hello.'

'Best to leave it for now, cara. She's very confused.' Then I saw the telltale protruding lip that was my daughter's precursor to tears. 'Very well, but don't expect anything sensible. There's even more wrong with her head than when I last saw her.'

'I picked some flowers for you, Nonna. I'm Viola, your granddaughter.' She knelt at her grandmother's feet, bowing her head as if waiting to be blessed.

Maria dropped the quilt and put her hands on the mass of dark hair.

'Weedo, Weedo!' She lifted Viola's head with the palm of her hand, then pulled her granddaughter close to her, rocking her back and forth.

'She thinks you're like my father, Guido – your grandfather.' A lump came to my throat at the mention of his name. 'This is Viola. She got married last month.'

Maria lifted the quilt and gave it my daughter.

'I couldn't. It's far too grand for me. And you hardly know me.' Viola's smile radiated like the gold thread in the brocade patches.

But Maria stuffed the material into her arms.

'Oh, you're such a lovely Nonna.' Viola gave her grandmother a hug. 'You must promise to eat with us tomorrow, so you can meet Gregorio. He's the most wonderful husband in the whole world.'

I linked arms with Viola, but her talent for restoring everyone's good humour failed to restore mine.

Chapter 23

'How's the mother from hell?' Ugolina called to me across Monticiano's market.

'Orsola's looking after her – seems they were friends in childhood – so I slept sound at home.' Too little to relieve me from my new responsibilities as I was still struggling to take in what I'd done.

'Bet Timoteo's glad to have you back in his bed!'

'You think of only one thing, Ugolina.'

'I think of food too!' she laughed.

'That reminds me, I must stock up on flour with an extra mouth to feed.' I knew it was right to take my mother away from Blackbeard, but her presence gave me no joy. I'd have liked to spend time with the woman I'd spent the festa with, but she had long gone.

'I'm just glad to have a glimpse of you.' Ugolina linked my arm with hers as we inspected the stalls.

'Is Viola here?' She would cheer me up.

'At home, preparing the meal she promised your mother. Gregorio's got hold of some wild boar. Once that's stewing, she's going to beat the fleas out of that quilt for their bed.'

'That's Viola for you, wanting to delight everyone, even that old harpy.'

282

'Don't speak of your mother like that.' Orsola appeared behind me. 'She's not well, not well at all.'

'I'll leave you to it,' Ugolina said. 'That girl of ours won't be happy if I forget anything.'

Not well? She had so much wrong with her already. We walked up to the workshop and entering the bedroom, I was hit by the acrid smell of vomit. I unlatched the shutters to let in air, only to be knocked back by a barrage of heat from the noonday sun. My mother's hair, grey and dank, splayed over the pillow.

'She'll have to go. I can't look after her, not after losing Bruno.'

I closed my eyes. There was no escape. 'We'll take her back to ours.' I stamped on the floor, the signal for Timoteo to come up and help. While I waited, I fanned my mother's face with the edge of the sheet, marvelling at her capacity to mar the lives of those around her.

Timoteo appeared in the doorway and stared at my feverish mother. 'Do you think it's that new illness they talked of?'

'I shouldn't have brought her back.'

'What choice did you have? She's your mother.' Timoteo hooked one of Maria's arms around his shoulder, while I took the other. Her balance had gone, and she was more confused than ever. People stared as we dragged her down the street.

'You get back to work,' I said after we'd manoeuvred her onto what had been Viola's bed before her wedding. 'And sleep in the kitchen. No point in us both having sleepless nights.' I shut the door on my husband.

Ignoring the groans, I removed my mother's vomit-steeped clothes and bathed her flushed body. When I saw how much pain that caused, I decided against dressing her in a clean shift. Instead, I covered her with a sheet, fetched more water and bathed her brow. Not that she'd ever done this for me. My father had stroked my face with a damp cloth and I had a vague memory of once being cared for by Cook.

The light faded and the outside temperature cooled, but my mother remained on fire. She tossed her head – eyes unseeing and bloodshot. She winced at the slightest movement, and I searched for the source of her pain.

'Madonna preserve us!' I crossed myself. In her armpit was a swelling – black and menacing, infused with blood and the size of a hen's egg. Through all the childhood illnesses I'd nursed my three through, I'd never seen the like. My mother had brought with her a curse only the devil himself could devise.

When Timoteo returned home, he tapped on the door. 'How is she?'

'A high fever, and she has this dreadful black swelling. You were right,' I sobbed, 'only evil has come from our visit to Siena.'

I heard him crying too, as we leant on opposite sides of the door. 'Go to Ugolina's and make Viola promise not to come round. We don't want them catching anything, the poor things not married a month.'

I heard Timoteo go out and, when he returned, go straight to the kitchen.

I turned back to my mother; old, battered by

284

Blackbeard and seriously unwell. But she had saved me from rape, and I was determined to nurse her to the best of my ability. Through the interminable night, I listened to her groans. The next day she was delirious, her skin infused with red blemishes that turned black by evening. Her nose seeped blood. All the time, I fed her spoons of water and bathed her brow, but the disease was relentless. The following morning, she soiled the sheets, adding to the suffocating stench. If I'd wanted God to punish her for getting us thrown out of the palazzo , he couldn't have done a better job. Lack of sleep was affecting me too and despite the warmth outside, I felt a chill.

How much longer could her agony continue? Each intake of breath, a saw rasping across soft wood. The black bruises, now as large as my palm, covered her chest and arms, and oozed a fetid pus. As dawn approached, her breath became shallower, rattling gently in her throat. Finally her good arm dropped down by the side of the bed and all was quiet.

I sat and stared. She wasn't. She couldn't be.

I leant forward and put my ear next to the gaping mouth.

Nothing.

Those dark eyes stared, red and accusing and I squeezed down the lids. But the skin was still warm. I put my ear to her mouth but there was no movement against my cheek, not even the fluttering of a butterfly wing.

I crept outside and sat on the wall at the Porta. Three days earlier, I'd brought her back from Siena, hoping to enjoy with her one of her rare, good moments. But as ever, I'd been disappointed. Ministering to my mother had left me exhausted. I made my way back to our house with feet of lead and a creeping fear that her curse would extend beyond the grave.

Head hot and skin sticky, I lay on my bed. Someone hammered on the door, but my head was so confused, I was unable to put together the words to respond. I drifted in and out of a world inhabited by green lizards, like the ones that lived in our orto. Dreams chased each other through my mind. Whenever I moved my head, the room spun and I saw black. Under my arms were small lumps.

I am in Siena's Duomo, kneeling before the painting of the Maestà. 'Timoteo's been a good father to me,' I tell the Madonna. The words sound wrong. The Virgin Mother wraps her arms around me, and I prepare to be wafted to the heavens, but she drops me. I call after her as she flounces off.

Am I waking or dreaming? A bright bunch of flowers comes towards me, and with what little strength I possess, I try to hold them at arm's length.

'Don't push me away, Mamma. Nonna's gone, and I don't want to lose you too,' the lower lip quivered. She cools my brow and forces lukewarm broth through my lips until I drift back to purgatory. I am being visited by an angel come to take me back to Siena at last. The hair is dark and curly and in a flash of lucidity, I recognize my daughter.

'For the love of Macellino, get out!' I scream. The

words are wrong, but I don't know how.

'What sort of daughter do you take me for?' Viola comes closer, my attempt to push her away no match for the strength of youth. I accept the water sinners crave when cast into hellfire.

Time passes and my nightmares continue. Then someone like Bruno arrives, carrying a sack, like a thief.

'Macellino will be angry at you stealing his meat,' I tell him.

'He told me to take this old baggage off your hands,' a hoarse voice, not at all like my uncle's, says. Then, like the witch who gives presents to good children at Epiphany, he walks off with his sack and the room smells better.

Now someone is in the other bed. Is it Timoteo? Or Blackbeard waiting to take me to hell? The girl with the quivering lip gives us water and softened fruit. I welcome anything that moistens my dry mouth.

I sleep again, and when I wake all is quiet. There's a devil in the next bed, covered in black spots. I sleep some more. Then I'm awake, or am I? The stench is dreadful. Am I alive or have I woken in purgatory? I pinch myself and it hurts. This tells me nothing.

Light comes through a slat in the shutters, but I have no strength to open them. There's a ringing in my ears, and my flesh smells – a living person could have a wash, but I can't sit up, let alone find water and I'm parched.

What is that mess on the other bed? It looks like an animal – but who would let a wild creature into a house? I remember my husband's name and call it out. Leaning on an elbow, I raise my head, perspiring from the unaccustomed effort. I rest to slow my heartbeat then try again. The effort is almost too much and I long to return to my monster-ridden doze. But I must open a window, to shed light on what is going on.

The bones in my legs have softened like cooked spaghetti and can't take my weight. So I ease along the bed until I reach the shutters. I manage to lift the catch and fling them open before sinking back on the sheets. My vision turns black and I feel giddy. When the room stops revolving, I turn to face the other bed and scream.

The body is covered in black marks and has blown up like a pig's bladder. It's the demon from my dreams, and the source of the hellish smell. Yet that white-lipped, green-skinned creature is dressed in Timoteo's clothes. I gag in revulsion, then lie down, head spinning.

When I came to, it was still light, and I remembered: Timoteo was dead. I'd not felt so alone since I was banished from Siena. How I'd taken for granted his constant presence. Too late to acknowledge my feelings for him as love, for they'd always lacked the passion I'd enjoyed with Ambrogio. Sitting on the edge of my bed, I stared at his remains, and pieced together the fragments of my memories. My mother had brought the black spots, which had killed her, spared me, and had now claimed Timoteo.

'I'm sorry, so sorry.' So much I should have asked his forgiveness for; for pushing to go to Siena when I knew how reluctant he was to go; for inviting my

288

mother to Monticiano bringing with her the plague; for never loving him enough because my first love was elsewhere. Now it was too late and my tears flowed. 'Forgive me, Timoteo. You were too good for me.'

Through the night I cried myself into a doze, drifting in and out of sleep. With the coming of light, some of my strength returned and I pulled on a dress. With leaden steps, I went to the kitchen and drank my fill. Even there the stench was unbearable. Yet before I worked out how to remove the body, I had to break the news to Viola. I worked my way slowly down the steps and dragged my feet to piazzetta. I was so weak, the slightest breeze could have blown me over.

I knocked at my friend's door. The window above opened, and Ugolina's red curls appeared over the sill. 'I didn't expect to see you alive!'

'Seems I am, but I've been dead to the world for I don't know how long.'

'Stay away. Gregorio will never forgive you for taking his wife away.'

'Viola's gone?' I wailed for the radiant bride I'd watched walk down the aisle only a month earlier. 'My baby, my baby.'

'I'm sorry, I thought you knew. She died the night before last. The ugliest of deaths. And we're terrified we'll get it, too.' She started closing the window.

'Please, let me see her.' However damaged her body, I longed to stroke that innocent cheek again, touch the black curls I'd so recently prepared for the wedding.

Ugolina's voice softened a little. 'Already buried. The sexton wouldn't touch her and the priest refused to

289

bury her in the cemetery. So, one of Bruno's drinking mates collected her and we buried her in the woods - in that beautiful wedding dress. Next to your mother.'

'Timoteo's gone too. I came out of my fever to find his dead body.'

'I feared as much. We've not seen him for days. Macellino will get someone to take him away for you. But after that, we're strangers.' Ugolina closed the shutter. I stared, unable to believe our years of friendship were at an end.

I cried into my sleeve, bereft of comfort from my friend. Why had I with sins too many to number, been spared when Viola was a bundle of goodness. Even my mother had fallen for her charms. 'My little treasure, why did you have to be taken from us?' I struggled to my feet, and shuffled home.

'Our little one, she's gone, Timoteo.' I said, as I bathed his bloated remains, the only service I could perform for him now. 'Look after her in heaven.'

The light outside faded and I lit our last candle. While I waited for his body to be taken away, I watched the flames take my orisons to heaven until it burnt out and I was left in darkness.

For days, maybe weeks, I cried and slept, sustained by some kind soul – it could only have been Ugolina – who left food and water outside my door. When I'd regained enough strength, I tried another outing – at first light, to avoid the townspeople. At first I only made it to Incrociata, but within days I reached the piazza and entered the workshop.

Someone had been in and daubed the walls with the colours I'd prepared in another lifetime. The ores and ochres from which they'd been mixed were ground underfoot; useless, just like my life, now all the goodness had been squeezed out.

Bruno's tools were thrown all over the floor but most of Timoteo's were still laid out neatly on the other bench. I smiled remembering his satisfaction at becoming a master craftsman when his birthright was to be a labourer. I lifted the hammer – the handle worn thinner where he'd held it – then the plane, its wood steeped in sweat from his palm. Who would use them now?

Then like a bolt from the heavens, the consequences of Timoteo's death dawned on me. If he wasn't making furniture for me to decorate, I had no means to support myself, or Orsola. Had she even been spared? The stairs to her dwelling were almost too much, but by taking them slowly, I reached the door and let myself in.

'Who is it?' She called from the bedroom.

When I entered, she was sitting up in bed, with a cotton shawl around her shoulders.

'Wore me out, your mother did. How is she?'

'Dead, I'm afraid. A new disease she brought from the city. Timoteo and Viola too.'

Orsola looked frightened. 'Your mother was always creating havoc, but this time she's surpassed herself.'

'Is there anything you need?' I asked.

'I'll be in a very bad way when I have to rely on you for help.'

I closed the door after me and dragged myself to what had been our favourite family place outside the Porta.

At a time of year when everyone lived outdoors, the area was deserted. Windows above were closed and women went singly to the fonte to collect water. The river beckoned, tempting me to fill my pockets with stones and wade into the deep, for what had I to live for? A fractured friendship with Ugolina and an ungrateful aunt to mind until the end of her grumpy days? I'd already done my duty to my mother. It was time Stefano and Laura took responsibility for theirs.

Day by day, I grew in strength and so did my conviction to return to the city. At first I was driven by desperation to know whether Gabriele and Rosa had been spared. Then I realised that my heart had never left Siena and if I was to live again, truly live, to there I must return.

No sensible person would return to a disease-ridden city. But I cared little if death called again. As my strength improved, I determined to say goodbye to my half-life in Monticiano and return to the colours in my blood. I walked down to the fonte, happy to find myself alone. Cupping my hands under the flow, I drank some spring water, then put my head under the cool cascade. Checking I was still alone, I took off my dress and washed, naked, in the pure spring water, tingling with cold and with life.

Back at the house, I lit a fire in the kitchen grate. To it I added what remained of Timoteo's clothes. Once those were burning, I stoked the flames with anything

Gregorio wouldn't want; the bedding, our threadbare mats, my country clothes. I found our payment from the Tolomei, gave half to Orsola and put the rest in my purse with the Salimbeni ring. The embers glowed red and I watched my life in Monticiano turn to ash. My only regret was leaving Ugolina, who had stuck by me through so many troubles. The following morning, I tried one last time to speak to her. I feared the worst but was relieved when the shutter opened.

'I told you to stay away.' Ugolina shouted down.

'And I have, but I've come to thank you for leaving me food. I'm leaving for Siena.' As I said the words, I faced the enormity of my decision. The reality was I was now as much a stranger to the city as Timoteo. 'The house is Gregorio's, as promised at the wedding. I pray he's well.'

'Thank the Lord,' Ugolina crossed herself, 'though without Viola, he wishes he were dead.'

'I know how he feels,' I said, 'but I need to know if Rosa and Gabriele are alive. When Stefano or Laura next come, tell them Orsola's all theirs now.'

Ugolina nodded, 'I'll keep an eye on her until they do.'

'I'm keeping my distance, but pretend I've given you a big hug, for you've been the best friend a wayward girl like me could have wished for.'

Ugolina wiped tears from her eyes. 'When are you setting off?'

'Tomorrow, if I can manage it.' Now I'd spoken to Ugolina, nothing need hold me back. I turned to leave the piazzetta.

'I'll miss you, Clara,' she called after me and blew me a kiss.

Waking at first light next morning, I clasped the Salimbeni ring. Whatever doors I needed to open, this would be the key. I took one last look around my erstwhile home, tied the purse to my belt and left. A lump came in my throat when I saw on the doorstep Ugolina's last gift - food for my journey.

I harnessed one of the horses to the cart, remembering the many times I'd watched Niccolò and Stefano do the same. When all was tied fast, I climbed up front and shook the reins. Only when I reached the turn to San Galgano did I realise I'd not looked back.

Chapter 24

I crossed the plane of Feccia and climbed the hill to Frosini. At the top, the road turned back on itself and I saw the outskirts of Monticiano in the distance. Already tired, I stopped at the trough to let the horse drink and rested on my bench. I could still turn back.

Surely it was folly to leave my home of nearly forty years; never again to sit on the wall outside the Porta, or stand in the church recalling Viola's pledge to Gregorio? Could I really bid adieu to the sights and places that had filled the greater part of my life? I hugged myself as tears spilt once more. Yet none of them brought back the husband and child I'd lost, nor would they bring me closer to the children I still hoped to see. I wiped my eyes on my sleeve, took a bite of Ugolina's sweet bread – I'd miss her too – and drank from her gourd.

With a flick of the reins, I resumed my journey, and thought of Rosa; wondering how she'd changed in the three years since she'd left. Would working in the ospedale have made her sanctimonious? On whom did she now use the wit she'd once sharpened on Gabriele? And what about my beloved son, now the age Ambrogio was when he'd given me sanctuary from Blackbeard. Of the many skills Gabriele could have learnt from his father, I hoped seducing naïve country girls wasn't among them. And colours – how I longed to live again among the banners, liveries and paintings that defined the city. But soon, driving the cart took all my strength, and I fixed my eyes on the road. As I approached the outskirts, passers-by urged me to turn back, but I drove on, impervious to the risks.

At last I turned a corner, and gasped at the glorious proliferation of towers on the hilltop ahead. I willed myself to keep going the last mile, but first I had to convince the guard to let me in. A squat man in Siena's black and white blocked my path. 'No fools allowed in, and you must be one or you'd be going the other way.'

I said the first thing that came into my head. 'Let me through, I have to see the Salimbeni.'

'And how would a country bumpkin know them?'

The man breathed wine as he pulled me towards him. 'I know a moll when I see one. Give me a free one if you want to pass.'

'Let me go!' I tried to push him away but had the strength of a flea. 'I've lived in Palazzo Salimbeni for nine years. If you harm me, there'll be trouble.' I clutched my purse, knowing their ring was inside, but to show it would be to give it up. 'And my son works with the painter, Ambrogio Lorenzetti.' I flung out another famous name.

'Then you'll not be needing this.' He tried to prise my purse off my wrist.

I cared nothing for the money, but I was hanging on to the ring. Remembering my father's last moments, I lunged towards his ear. My bite lacked the strength to draw blood, but he drew back and I seized my chance.

'Giddy up!' I shouted at the horse, and it lurched forward, taking me inside the city. But the road was taken up with carriages full of frightened people trying to get out. None was minded to let me through, and if I turned round, I'd fall prey to the guard. A bunch of drunken marauders poured out of the nearby tavern, and staggered towards me, shouting, 'Take her in the back of her cart!' In my short time away, the city had descended into hell on earth. If only I'd turned back at Frosini.

'Protect me, please!' I grabbed the arm of a woman heading out with her husband and four children, each carrying a bundle too big for them. The marauders veered off to find another target.

'They think if they're going to die, they may as well

296

raise Cain first. Leave this hell while you can,' she said. Twelve large eyes stared at me from hollow faces. 'And allow us to share the cart with you.'

'My children are here and I have to see if they're alive. But take the cart.' I'd make better progress without it.

'God bless you and preserve you from the Black Death.' The woman bundled her children into the back before I could change my mind.

Is that what they called it. The name couldn't be more apt.

As evening bells rang out, I hurried towards the Campo. Yet without the cart as my bed, where would I stay?

My only hope was that the ospedale would take me in. I staggered through the human filth and decaying vermin, pervaded by the stench of rotting flesh I remembered from my delirium. Hoping there'd be more room to walk in the side streets, I turned from the queue of exiting carriages into a labyrinth of alleys where I was instantly lost. I was about to ask a monk for directions until I realised he was thrusting into a man facing the wall in front of him. In plain daylight! Such sins made mine with Ambrogio look paltry.

Stymied by the bending roads, I lost all sense of direction. Propped in corners, women hugged flagons, piss trickling between their splayed legs. Church bells were drowned out by the drums and chants of young men, stripped to the waist and scourging themselves with ropes spiked with nails. From the bulges under their robes, this was more about sexual gratification than penitence. Then I looked up and caught a glimpse of the Duomo's tower and, with my last ounce of strength, found my way to the hospital opposite and knocked at the main door.

No reply.

I burst into tears. It had cost me my all to reach the city. Before, my enemy had been the Tolomei, but now perils lurked at every turn. 'Help me, Babbo?' I pleaded in a voice that came from childhood.

I dragged myself across the piazza and entered the cathedral. Duccio's Madonna had helped me before and could do so again. I staggered from pillar to pillar towards the main altar. But before I could reach it, my legs turned to jelly. I veered into a side-chapel and all went black.

When I came to, a white robed monk was kneeling beside me, cradling my head in his arm. 'Here, take some water.' After what I'd just seen of the sexual habits of holy men, I scrambled out of his grasp.

'You fainted, and I'm offering you refreshment.' He held out a wooden cup.

I sat up and drank. As I did, my eyes strayed to the painting above the chapel's altar. Room beyond room receded towards a point on the horizon, so unlike the normal convention of sizing according to religious importance.

The monk followed my gaze. 'Ambrogio Lorenzetti. One of our greatest. It was my pleasure to commission this.'

His work now alongside Duccio's! How I longed to run my hands over the brushwork; for some might be

Gabriele's. 'Do you know where he lives? My son is one of his assistants, and I've come from Monticiano to find him.'

'Then our paths might have crossed! I'm Abbot Angelo, and when I'm not responsible for public spending, like the works here, I'm abbot of San Galgano.'

I frowned. 'I remember you well, for you deprived me of my son when you dismissed Ambrogio for his Annunciation at the hermitage.'

'As I recall, he dismissed himself – after a row with the Salimbeni. It caused me much sadness too.'

'This plague has already taken my Monticiano family, so I fear for my son. Have you news of his studio?'

Acknowledging the dead souls, Angelo made the sign of a cross. 'I was speaking to Lorenzetti only yesterday. I want him to paint something to inspire hope in these dreadful times. But he's too busy governing the city, so I dare say you'll find him at the Palazzo dei Signori.' The abbot helped me to my feet.

'A City Councillor?' My disgruntled paint-mixer had been elected to the highest office in the state! But I had nowhere to spend the night. 'May I beg a further favour. I'd hoped to stay at the ospedale, where my daughter is a sister, but can get no reply. Is there anywhere else you could suggest?'

'Follow me.' The abbot led me out of the cathedral to the far left of Santa Maria della Scala's enormous frontage.

I put my mouth to the grill, explained my situation

and was let in. A woman with a white hair-covering and dark dress led me along corridors and up wide stone stairs, until we reached a dormitory with many empty beds.

'Sister Rosa's.' The woman nodded to one which had been slept in.

'Then she's alive!' I cried with relief. 'When will she be back?'

'When God spares her from her duties. You can sleep here.' The sister tapped the empty bed next to Rosa's and left.

I opened the window, too high to see the piazza, and listened to the end of day sounds – wooden wheels on cobbles as merchants removed their wares. I lay down and spoke to the wooden cross on the wall. 'Thank you for bringing me safely to Siena, and for saving my daughter.' Back in the city of the Madonna, I fell into a long, deep sleep.

The following day I woke to someone stroking my cheek with the softness of a paintbrush. I opened my eyes and saw my daughter's smiling face, now framed by the white head covering the sisters wore. They lived as nuns, even though they didn't take Holy Orders.

'Rosa, carissima.' I sat up and wrapped her in my arms.

My dear daughter burst into tears. I'd have expected them from Viola, but Rosa had always been the strong one.

'I was sure you'd be dead.' She wiped her eyes on her sleeve. 'At the start we were flooded with victims but nothing we did was of help. We lost so many of our patients; the destitute and foundlings too, and many of the sisters. I got it too but by some miracle was spared. We lost so many, the rector closed the halls. No more pilgrims or sick. Said we'd do more good with our prayers. So now we go out and help the dying.'

I took her hand, but where to begin? 'The pestilence came to Monticiano too. I'm afraid it took your Babbo, and then Viola. And before that, Bruno got so drunk at the wedding, he drowned in the fonte.'

Rosa sobbed. 'God rest their souls.'

I put my arms around her shoulder. 'My mother, the curse she always was, brought the Plague with her when she came to live with us.'

'What sort of God lets good people die, while the devil roams the streets?'

'Poor love.' I unwound her wimple revealing her short and spiky hair and ran my fingers through it. 'You're all I have in the world now – you and Gabriele – that's if he's been spared. Have you news of him?'

'We used to meet at the church of San Francesco before we were plunged into this chaos. If he's alive, he'll be there next Saturday. And I'll find you a habit to wear while you're here. It's small protection, but all I can offer.'

'He'll never recognize me in this.' I wound her wimple round my head. 'I've not seen him in ten years.'

'You've not aged that much, Mamma!'

'I thought he was ashamed of me.'

'Grateful more like, for without Ambrogio, he'd never have had the chance to paint. The brothers did some murals here, in the men's chapel. I'll show you them after we've had something to eat.'

After breaking our fast in the refectory, Rosa led me out into the piazza then to a chapel in the centre of the vast building. The façade was covered in one of those brilliant masses of colour I loved the city for, this one depicting the life of the Virgin. Rosa directed me to the inscription. "Pietro Lorenzetti and his brother Ambrogio painted this. 1335". 'Gabriele worked on it too, though it was long before my time.'

I imagined Ambrogio and Pietro drawing the figures, completing the faces. The bulk of the painting – the backgrounds, the folds in the materials, the tiled floorwork – would have been down to their assistants, among them Gabriele. How I envied my son, for my only opportunity to work with colour, painting our furniture in Monticiano, was now behind me.

'The journey's worn you out.' Rosa led me back to the dormitory. 'The Sopra Donne – she's in charge of the women's side – will let you stay if you attend at least one service a day and help with our work. I go out to comfort the dying. Why don't you come with me when you feel up to it. For now, rest, and regain your strength.' Rosa disappeared to her duties.

In the days before Saturday, my hoped for meeting with Gabriele, I helped in the kitchen and attended as many offices as I felt up to. Now that little fresh food came in from the ospedale's rich resources in the country, we lived on bread and dried beans.

When Saturday came, I woke early and Rosa helped me dress.

'I'll come, too, and show you the way.'

I needed a guide, for my former time in the city revolved around Palazzo Salimbeni. And I wanted her company. The heat was brutal as we made our way through the streets skirting the Campo. Drunken sots felt free to leer in our faces and place hands on our buttocks. But when one grabbed between my legs, I'd had enough. 'Fry in hell, you rotting rat.'

Even in these dissolute times, the man reeled at such language coming from a nun.

Then I stopped. We were outside the door to Palazzo Tolomei's stables and, though the whole palazzo was locked up, my heart pounded.

'If I'd not taken my mother from Blackbeard, Babbo and Viola would still be alive. But I had to save her from him – the man's pure evil.'

'God will forgive your trespasses, but only if you forgive those who trespass against you.'

I knew the words of the Lord's Prayer but this was the first time I considered the harshness of its demands. Since sinning with Ambrogio, I'd never been a good Christian.

We turned down the road before Palazzo Salimbeni. After my row with Vanni at the hermitage, I had no wish to see him, even if he had returned to the city.

As we approached San Francesco monastery, I held my breath. Then, as we entered the church, I searched in vain for the once familiar fair hair among the hatless men.

Finding Rosa alive should have been enough, but I wanted both.

'Since the pestilence, they leave the door to the

cloisters open, and he's often out there,' she whispered. We slipped out the side door into a delightful garden in the centre of which was the monastery's well. Sitting in the shade, his back to the wall, Gabriele was more than alive, he was handsome and healthy; a more solid version of the boy who'd left Monticiano ten years earlier. We glided towards him in our dark habits – stark contrast to his colourful clothes – and Rosa tapped his ankle with her foot. 'Look who I've brought to see you.'

He shaded his eyes from the summer light. 'Mamma! You're here, and alive!' He stood up and put his arms around me. I felt his chin resting on the top of my head and knew how right I'd been to come.

'How I've missed you, carissimo.' I hugged him back.

'But what are you doing here? And dressed as a nun?' His voice was deeper than I remembered, but his smile was as radiant.

'Can I leave her with you, Gab? I need to make some visits. Show her back to the ospedale, will you?'

'Bossy as ever, Rosa!' he said.

My daughter disappeared, and we sat on the low wall surrounding the garden. 'What news of Monticiano? Tell me about the wedding? Bruno told me Viola was marrying Gregorio. He was only a boy when I left.'

'Bad news, Gabriele, such bad news. Babbo ...' I hesitated '... do you still think of him as that?'

'I've always called Ambrogio by his name. Timoteo will always be my Babbo.'

'I'm so sorry – he died of the plague. Viola too – only a month after the wedding. She was so happy that day. I wish you could have been there.'

Gabriele fell on my lap and wept.

'I know, I know.' I rocked him in my arms. 'Bruno too, but he died of drink.'

'I always meant to come back and now it's too late.' Gabriele moaned.

I ran my hand through his fair locks. 'But you have your memories, Gabriele; sitting around the table in Dorotea's kitchen; you and Rosa battling it out with words and poor Viola too young to keep up!'

'Then along came Ambrogio.' Gabriele got up and pulled me to my feet. 'Some people don't have one good father. But I've had two.'

I was glad Ambrogio had looked after him. 'Have you worked with him all this time? Rosa told me you worked on the ospedale chapel.'

Gabriele nodded. 'I couldn't let anyone take my place. He's become the most famous artist in Tuscany.'

'More famous than his brother?'

'Very much so. He's more adventurous. Whatever he's interested in – astronomy, the weather – he incorporates in his paintings. Shall I show you what he did here?'

He led me to a darkened room, the wall of which was an abundance of crimson, yellow and many shades of green. I examined the frescos in detail. 'That storm surrounding the martyrs – I can almost feel the rain!'

'How I cursed him for making me paint all those raindrops!' He reminded me of Ambrogio at that age, annoyed at not being allowed free rein.

'I'm so proud of you, Gabriele, being a part of all this.' Part of me wished he regretted leaving home, but I knew that. in his place, I'd have done the same.

'Beats painted furniture, doesn't it!' he said.

I bit my lip, for that had been my salvation. But he was right. Nobody was going look at one of my tables and turn to God.

'Now let me walk you back, for he'll be waiting to give me his latest instructions.'

At mention of the artist, I longed to see him too. 'What are you working on now?'

'To be honest, most of my time's spent helping him with council business. Without him, the fabric of the city would collapse. You must have seen the chaos?'

'Not too busy to meet up again, I hope,' I said when we reached the ospedale.

'Of course not.' Gabriele enveloped me in a hug. 'Meet me in the Campo next Saturday and I'll show you our work at Sant' Agostino.'

'Surely I won't be allowed into another monastery?'

'In times like these, everyone's breaking rules.'

Over the next week, I searched out what remained of the colours of the city and worshipped art in the Duomo. When Saturday came, I picked my way through the debris littering the Campo. Surrounded by beggars, the Fonte Gaia looked anything but a Fountain of Joy. A drunk, next to it, had passed out. Shops had been ransacked leaving overturned counters and ripped-down signs. Surrounded by such lawlessness, I moved closer to the Palazzo dei Signori, praying Gabriele would arrive soon. A man came out of the main door and turned towards me. Despite grey hair, slightly hunched shoulders and a stockiness that made him look less tall, I recognized Ambrogio. The boy I'd touched toes with at the festa was now one of the most powerful men in the city.

'Clara!' The warmth of his smile, creased his eyes, quarter moons delineated his mouth and I remembered why I'd fallen for him decades earlier. 'He warned me you were masquerading as a nun! You must be mad to come to the city in such terrible times.'

'I've lost everyone apart from Gabriele and Rosa. I had to see them.'

'He told me about your husband and daughter, your mother too. I'm so sorry. I've lost several colleagues, Pietro too.' He looked around the Campo. 'I'm trying to persuade the Signori to tile here; nine segments of stone radiating from the palazzo to represent each of the Nove. What do you think?'

'How clever! And I noticed the bell tower's finished.'

'They've named the bell after Duccio! He filled the studio with his pompous pronouncements. Now the whole city will have to listen to him! We'll walk up to Sant' Agostino to meet Gabriele. I had to send him to deal with a dead dog in the aqueduct that brings water to the city. Can't have the water killing us on top of everything else.'

He led me up the road towards where Pietro had lived, to a tree-covered piazza outside Sant' Agostino.

307

We leant on the balustrade, looking out over the extensive plain to the North.

'Gabriele was so happy to see you again. Blame me for him not coming to visit. I'm a hard taskmaster. Learnt that from Duccio!'

'You've given him a great life, Ambrogio, for which I'm grateful. But now I'm here, I want more of him.' If I was to build a new life in the city, Gabriele had to be part of it, especially if he was painting.

'Meet him whenever and wherever you like – except at my house. My wife thinks of him as her own, and Gabriele winds her round his little finger!'

My eyes burnt at the thought of another woman taking my place.

'Ah, here comes your escort!' Ambrogio turned towards Gabriele, who was running towards us.

'Come quick! It's Mamma.' He tugged at Ambrogio's arm. 'I went home to change and found her in a fever.'

He'd been happy to tell me he only had one Babbo. How dare he have two Mammas! Yet what if she were going down with the disease? I feared for my son – and his father.

Ambrogio closed those hazel eyes, Gabriele took his arm and they hurried up the road where Pietro had lived, too preoccupied for farewells. This was their life's drama. On top of that I felt guilty, for in some dark corner of my heart, I hoped the woman they were rushing to see would die, leaving me as Gabriele's only mother.

But the disease had already massacred my

Monticiano family. I couldn't stand by and see it take Gabriele too. I ran to find Rosa. With her experience of working with those afflicted, surely she could help prevent the worst.

Chapter 25

We have to save Gabriele.' I said, as soon as I found Rosa. She was making bread with an older sister and I was reminded of her life with Dorotea.

'Is he sick?' Rosa's already pale face blanched.

'If we don't get to him soon, he will be.' I told her about Ambrogio's wife.

'We should leave at once!' she said, and her sister cook nodded approval. We hurried down the stairs.

When we reached the piazza I told her, 'We may not be welcome. Ambrogio told me to stay away from the house.'

'She won't know you're there, far less who you are. But we should make Gabriele leave the city. The doctors at the ospedale say that's the best option.'

As we faced the Duomo, I said, 'Let's ask the Madonna to look after him.'

We ran up the steps to kneel before the Maestà and made hasty pleas to Siena's protectress. After making the sign of the cross, we ran out and bumped into two men coming up the steps, one in Salimbeni livery. He looked like Francesco, though was too young to have been around when I'd lived in the palazzo.

'Clara?' The older man addressed me.

His hair was greying at the temples but despite the now-lined complexion I recognised my childhood playmate. However, I was still sore with him for losing me my son.

'All the nobles have gone to the country, so I've taken my chance to come back. But you, a nun! I'd never have expected you to take Holy Orders.'

'The habit's for her protection,' Rosa said. 'I'm the fool who's committed to tending the sick in this God-forsaken city.'

This idle chat was keeping us from Gabriele. 'Excuse us. We have news the pestilence has reached Lorenzetti's house and I'm concerned for my son.'

'Don't go to a house of death, Clara.' He held my arm, 'especially not his.'

How dare he stop me. He might have forgotten his outburst at San Galgano, but I couldn't. 'The Salimbeni have no hold over me since they threw me out.'

'Then come back! Come and see me, though, without the servants, it's more monastic than you'd remember.'

I turned away, put my arm through Rosa's and together we hurried the short walk to Castelvecchio. Along the way, some drunken men pushed past, clutching rich garments stained with blood.

Rosa said. 'They go round graves, tearing clothes off dead bodies.'

A gruesome task, I thought as I remembered Timoteo's ulcerated corpse.

As we approached the Abbey of Sant'Agostino, we saw a toothless man piling bodies onto a cart. Breathing into the fabric of my habit to mask the stench, I asked him where Ambrogio lived and he directed us. A fine house, with many external embellishments, it was only a short distance from Pietro's.

Ambrogio opened the door, his eyes moist.

I felt for him. 'How is she?'

'Gone!' He left the door ajar and sank into a chair. 'My daughters are bereft, Gabriele too.'

I felt for his loss but there was no time to lose. I knelt before him. 'I beg you, take the rest of your family to the country. It's your best chance.'

'I'm a Consigliere. I can't leave. Who else will sort things out?'

'Then let Gabriele take your girls.'

'They've just lost their mother. I can't deprive them of their father too.'

'Then send my son away, I beg you. I've asked so little of you. Surely you can grant me this.'

Ambrogio held his head and closed his eyes, then nodded assent.

'Thank you.' I put my hand on his knee as he let out more tears.

While Rosa ran up the stairs to fetch her brother, I looked around at the house I'd once pictured myself sharing. Niccolò would have approved of his well-made furniture. Colourful tapestries hung on the walls and a wooden staircase led to the first floor. Down it came Gabriele who stood, hovering at the bottom. He'd been crying and I ran to comfort him.

Ambrogio got up and put his arms around us both. 'I miss her too, son. But Clara and I agree, you must leave the city at once. Go to Pietro's place in the country.'

'But what if you get sick?' My poor boy looked so worried.

'I'll take care of them.' Rosa said.

'And I'll help her,' I added, before Ambrogio could change his mind.

Gabriele was about to object again.

Ambrogio fumbled in his purse and gave Gabriele some money. 'Go. And that's an order.'

'The Madonna will take care of you,' Rosa said from the stairs.

He gave us one last hug and left.

But as I watched him walk down the street, I feared, not for the first time, I'd never see him again.

'I came down to ask if I can arrange for someone to take away your wife's body?' Rosa said. The church had long since given up funerals, and the ospedale had dug up the cellar to bury their dead. 'It's not good for the children to see her in that state.'

'Very well.' More tears trickled down Ambrogio's face.

I held him as the body was removed, then sat with him, listening as he poured out his grief while Rosa looked after the children upstairs. Later that evening, she appeared ashen-faced, and for the next three days, we held small hands and prayed as, one by one, the girls succumbed to nose bleeds and black buboes – deep, bloody bruises spreading from groin to torso and beyond. I filled bowls with water and cooled brows with a cloth bearing signs of old paint, yet their fevers raged on. Working with Rosa was a comfort, though we both struggled to keep Ambrogio out of the sick room as the disease took its course. By the end of the week, three small corpses had joined the mountain of bodies in the city pits.

'I've done my duty here,' Rosa said, as the cart trundled away. 'Time I returned to the ospedale.'

I should have gone too, but as I watched Ambrogio slumped in his chair, I knew I had to stay. The city needed him, not to keep the basic services running, but for his art. If anyone could communicate the horrors of the last few weeks and give them meaning, it was Ambrogio. I told Rosa, 'I have to make him see he has reason to live.'

'Then promise me you'll rest, for you've not slept since we arrived.' Rosa gave me a fulsome hug. In these black times, every meeting could be the last.

Remembering how right the purging of our house had felt after Timoteo's death, I went up to the kitchen and started a fire. I bundled up the children's clothes and burnt them, their straw mattress too. I'd have done the same with his wife's but that seemed too presumptuous. I wasn't here to take her place – decades too late for that.

When, at dusk, I returned to the living area, Ambrogio was still staring into space, blind to the wisps of smoke permeating from upstairs.

'Try and sleep,' I led him to his bedchamber, 'and I will do the same.' I let myself into Gabriele's room and fell into a deep sleep.

Waking with the light, I wondered if we both might ease back into the world through the love of painting we shared. Once I heard him stirring, I went to him. 'Would you feel up to showing me your work in the Palazzo dei Signori. Gabriele said I should see it. We could go there now.'

'I can't bear to look at it. My enemies say I brought on this plague in my depiction of Bad Government, though I was commenting on the mercenaries and the chaos they leave in their wake. See for yourself and tell me what you think. You'll see I included in Good Government that dance we had in the Campo the day of the festa!'

He remembered the day too! But I wanted to involve him, not leave him.

'What if all this is down to me, Clara! That's why I've worked so hard for the city, to make amends, but it's not been enough. And now I've been punished. If only God had taken me and not my girls.' His body convulsed with sobs.

I held his head against my belly and rocked him like a child.

At last he exhausted the tears, he lay back on the pillow and gave a great sigh. 'I think I need a wash, could you get me some water.'

314

I was pleased to hear this change of tone and fetched a pitcher. He attempted to clean his face but gave up after a few wipes.

'Allow me to help you?' I said and dipped the flannel in the water. I brushed it across his face wiping away tearstains, traces of his wife's blood and vestiges of paint. Then his neck and shoulders, his skin as silky as I remembered. It seemed that with each wipe of the flannel he was coming back to life.

'Thank you. You've given me the strength to do the rest,' he said.

Shortly after he emerged from his room dressed in a clean tunic.

I prepared him some light food which we ate together, but I needed more to draw him into the land of the living.

'Would you show me what you're working on.' I said before he sank back into his dark thoughts.

He led me to the studio at the top of the house. Facing the doorway was a part-painted wooden panel – two or three times the size of the book cover he'd worked on with his brother. A traditional Crucifixion – Christ in the centre and the Madonna, below, both completed, the Magdalena next to her in outline only.

'Gabriele,' Ambrogio pointed to the dying Christ, then to the grieving mother. 'And this was my wife.'

He started crying again and slumped into a chair, his back to the painting. But I refused to let him give up.

'Turn and face it, Ambrogio. You should paint your grief. For the Madonna and Magdalena, the Crucifixion was all about loss.'

He held his head in his hands and I waited. Then he raised his head, groaning as he pushed himself out of the chair. He found an old paint rag to blow his nose, then studied the panel.

It was a narrow piece of wood, and the outline of a second figure stood at the base of the cross.

'Only if I can paint you as the Magdalena.'

'Didn't I suffer enough from being Mary, the fallen woman, at San Galgano.'

'Please, Clara! I did you a disservice, and I'm sorry. But wouldn't you like to be here for eternity, alongside your son?'

'Very well.' His wife was with Gabriele already. It was only right I, too, claimed my place. Again, he'd charmed me into submission. 'Make me human, though. I'm no epitome of virtue.'

'I can only paint you as I see you.' Ambrogio removed his tunic and replaced it with the paint-stained one hanging over the back of a chair. He stood back and studied the panel. But when he looked at the paint table, his shoulders sagged. 'Where's Gabriele to mix the colours?'

'I can do it. After ten years of painting furniture, I'm an expert!'

'Then mix me green and pink for the skin.'

I thinned the yellow ochre with oil and added a few grains of the previously-ground azurite and mixed them into a thin paste.

While I was doing that, Ambrogio studied the panel – then me. The outline of the Magdalena had been drawn earlier, but he used the red ink to adjust his drawing. When he was ready, he changed brushes, took the green paint I'd mixed and began on the face.

'I look like a corpse!' I said.

'Don't you remember? An undercoat of green makes the skin tone more realistic.'

'I do.' Ever since he'd told me that trick, I'd loved the idea of everyone having secret colours bursting to get out. 'If I had colours under my skin, they would be the red and gold I was surrounded by at the palazzo. And yours?'

'A rainbow, like this.' He indicated his spattered tunic.

How perfectly Ambrogio, I thought, as I handed him the pink paint. As the day's temperature rose, and his skin glistened with sweat, I watched as he lost himself in the work. Only when the light began to fade did he put down his brush.

'Thank you for suggesting this. It's moved some of my pain onto the wood. Pietro always used his family in his works, and now I know why it took so much out of him. I'm so tired I can hardly stand. Have a look before the light fades and tell me what you think.'

He stood behind me as I stared at the Magdalena. As well as deeply sad, she was angry and determined. Yet, he'd managed to convey, not only her feelings, but that death was not an end, but a beginning. I was about to try and put this into words when Ambrogio put his arms around me and rested his chin on my head; the closeness of two people who had together created, not just a son, but a work of significance. Then he collapsed on the ground with a thud.

His forehead was burning and blood dripped from his nose. He stared at the smear on his hand then at me. 'This morning it's what I wished for, but now you've convinced me to live for my work.'

'And so you shall!' I said, praying he'd be one of the lucky few.

'I wouldn't put money on an old crock like me.' He took my hand.

'Given all you've done for the city, the Madonna is sure to look after you.'

'I know it's too much to ask, but will you stay? I don't want to die alone.' He stroked the back of my hand with his thumb.

He'd no need to ask. I'd stay in the studio forever if I could.

'Forgive me, Clara. I was a rogue.' By now he was sweating profusely.

'If you need forgiveness, you have it.' His belief in my talent had sustained me more than he'd ever know.

He tried to say more but what he mumbled was incoherent.

I ran to Gabriele's room and picked up the pillow I'd rested on all night. Underneath was a well-used leather pouch and, inside, my stones. He'd kept them! As I dragged the mattress and pillow up to the studio, I felt Babbo smiling on me from the heavens. I made a makeshift bed on the floor and helped Ambrogio onto it. I cooled his brow to stop him sinking into delirium, for I could still save him. Hoping the painting would help him cling to life, I propped him up with pillows. As I did so, he winced. A ghastly bubo in his armpit was ready to burst and I was frightened for him. Mine had never been this big.

'You finish,' he pointed at the panel.

'Then help me. Tell me what to do.' Anything to stop him slipping into oblivion.

'Cloaks. Deep blue – both. Equal.' Ambrogio wiped his brow with his arm. 'Shadows.' He waved his hands, to show me where I should paint the folds.

I followed his instructions as best I could, asking him frequent questions to keep him engaged.

'You – my best apprentice.' Now his words were muddled.

Yet we worked by candlelight until he was too feverish to see the panel. When I put down the brushes, I hoped I'd completed all that needed his guidance.

'Falling,' Ambrogio slurred. He slept for a bit then woke with a start. 'My will!'

I searched the workshop for something that could be written on, but the only surface was the wood of the panel, and I wasn't going to give him that.

'Everything – to – you.' The struggle to get out the words was immense.

'No, Ambrogio. I want nothing beyond Gabriele's safe return, and you can't give me that.'

'Then to ...'

I charged a brush with paint while Ambrogio reached for the sheepskin rug thrown over a chair. Writing quickly but with frequent pauses, Ambrogio gave all his worldly goods to the people who ran the ospedale. His eyes closed. The paintbrush dropped.

319

Resting my head on his damp chest, I lay with him on the mattress through the night, his arm, heavy, in the crook of my waist. How many nights in Monticiano had I dreamt of one more night with my lover? But as day approached, his breath become shallower. Several times I put my cheek next to his mouth, willing him to keep going. Then, after one slow exhalation, he fell silent.

'No!' I screamed.

Those hazel eyes, now deeply shot with blood, stared into emptiness and I pressed the lids closed. I ran my hand through the fair hair, darkened with sweat. I leant over and kissed his forehead. Then I lay beside him and wept, for with him had died my dreams.

When the sun poured through the cracks in the shutters, I rose, and with the last of the water, washed away the blood, the sweat, the shit. I searched through the matrimonial chest for his brightest garments and dressed him in them. I left his hair loose and tucked behind his ears, like the young Ambrogio I'd first met. Then I opened the shutters onto the street and waited for the man with the cart who took away the dead.

'More business?' He shouted up.

I let him in and showed him the body.

'Shame. He was one of the best – did so much for this city. The devil must be in charge, for he takes the good ones and lets people like me survive.'

'Can you stop his clothes being stolen?' I paid him generously.

'They'll stay on him to the pit, and I'll bury him deep enough for the dogs not to find him. After that, it's anyone's guess.'

I watched the cart trundle away, the vibrant colours of Ambrogio's clothes resplendent against the grey of the street.

Chapter 26

Outside the day was warm, but I shivered. Was I coming down with another dose? My loved ones were dying as fast as the street rats. How long would it take before Gabriele and Rosa were taken too?

After he took my son, I thought Ambrogio had disappeared from my life. But now I knew he'd always been with me; each time I picked up a brush; in every golden-headed sunflower I painted, as I looked out on the Monticiano hills and saw more than brown. Ever since our first meeting, I'd seen the world through his eyes. Blinded by my tears, I reeled through the streets, not caring the direction.

On every great building in the city – Sant'Agostino, San Francesco, Duomo; Santa Maria della Scala and the Palazzo dei Signori – he'd made his mark. And who would get a dead dog removed from the aqueduct now? I felt bereft and longed to go home, if only I had one.

'Why did he have to die?' I leant against the wall of the Salimbeni orto. But for whom was I grieving? Ambrogio, Timoteo or even Babbo? Perhaps all three.

The place reeked. No time to take the bodies far, the orto was being used as a burial pit. I looked over the wall and thought I saw Ambrogio's bright clothes, his fair hair, but when I wiped my eyes, the image was gone.

At Palazzo Tolomei, the stable doors were open and I shouted to the stable boy, 'tell Blackbeard his wife's dead,'

'Then they'll meet in hell! The plague took him soon after she left.'

Justice at last!

I walked on, so tired I could hardly stand. My head spun and there was a loud ringing in my ears. My knees buckled under me. I slid down the wall and the world turned to black.

I came to, to find the young servant with Vanni at the Duomo slapping my face.

'You're back with us, sister. Would you allow me to move you into the shade.' Without waiting for a reply, he carried me into the Salimbeni entrance hall, sitting me in Domenico's favourite chair. Then he disappeared.

My head buzzed with the voices that had once filled the hall, so I failed to hear footsteps approach.

'Fancy a game of jacks?'

As if the last forty years had never happened, I recognised the voice and smiled.

'Fetch her some water,' Vanni said.

The servant disappeared and returned with a mug. It was the first time I'd drunk from pewter since leaving Siena and the metallic taste revived me.

'Better?' Vanni knelt beside me.

I nodded, though I felt far from strong.

'You look exhausted. Tell me what happened.' The servant melted into the shadows and haltingly, between tears, I told Vanni what I should have told him on the steps of the Duomo; of surviving the plague and losing my family. The only thing I had the sense not to speak of was Ambrogio's death.

'You need rest, so stay here. Use my mother's old room and take the pick of her clothes. Alas, she has no more need of them. I'll arrange a bath for you too.'

I'd not had a proper bath since leaving the palazzo, when Mamma dunked me in the Contessa's water before throwing it out.

'All I ask in return is that you dine with me. I've no-one for company and I'd welcome yours,' he said, showing me to the room I'd last glimpsed when Ambrogio had his audience with the Contessa. I stood in the middle, taking in the pots of unguents and fragrances my mother loved so much. On the washstand, were the smelling salts thrust under my mother's nose at Babbo's graveside. I took a sniff and felt more alert.

When a female servant arrived with warm water for the bath, I stared at the steaming pool and my reflection in it: I looked like a spectre.

'If you please, ma'am, I'll help remove your clothes.'

She unwound my wimple and removed my habit. 'You'd best get in while the water's warm. I'll fetch some more to top it up.'

I put my hand in the bath and swirled the water. Then I peeled off my undershift and eased myself in. The water put its arms around me, and the sweat, the pus, the blood – every vestige of the last few days – washed away. If only grief dissolved as easily. I dunked my head under the water, then rested my head on the bath's rim to catch up with my racing thoughts.

As soon as the water began to cool, the maid held out the towel. I wrapped myself in its softness, wondering if it had come from Constantinople, one of the Salimbeni's sources of fabrics.

'The master asks you to choose a dress.'

I remembered the Contessa's gold brocade at Duccio's festa. 'Something plain, but bright, to bring me back to life.'

The maid opened the chest – not unlike the one I'd hidden in at the Tolomei – and pulled out a red shift in the same style as the one I'd taken to Monticiano, that Viola had worn at her wedding. Then I sat in front of the glass while she made plaits to take my hair away from my face, though errant strands, riddled with grey, insisted on springing free.

I'd expected to eat in the kitchen, but the maid led me to the banqueting hall. There I found Vanni, dressed in a simple tunic, though the belt round his waist was made by a fine craftsman.

'Are we allowed?'

'I'm in charge for now, so why not! There's little

enough to celebrate these days.' The male servant pulled out a chair for me. Vanni poured me wine and offered me bread. I'd not taken mass since Monticiano but this felt as absolving.

The meal was simple and, aware how close I was to crying, I steered the conversation away from myself. Vanni took the hint and talked of generalities; the outrages on the streets, the various remedies being touted, our own good fortune at having survived.

'Is Cook still around?' The meal lacked her touch.

'Worked into her dotage, bossing everyone about until her heart gave out.'

'I'd have loved to see her again. When I was here, I was a bit afraid of her, but she was kinder than my mother.'

'She had a soft spot for you; very upset when you left.'

The more we talked the more at home I felt surrounded by these once-familiar walls. And yet Rosa was expecting me at the ospedale.

'It's been a lovely evening, Vanni, and I thank you for rescuing me, but I should be going.'

'At least let me show you round first. The place hasn't changed much.'

I was tired and longed for sleep. However, being cradled in the familiarity of my old home, put off the sadness I'd face alone in the ospedale. I followed Vanni as he pointed out familiar spots from childhood; where we'd had our lessons together, the bedroom I'd shared with my parents and the kitchen where I'd spent most of my waking time. Despite everything I was glad I'd returned to the city.

'What happened to Francesco?' I said, as we passed the dark corner that had been his favourite haunt.

'One of the first to die of the pestilence. Do you remember that time when we hid under the bench on the roof? Shall we go there now and enjoy the air?' Without the constant movement of an army of servants, the atmosphere inside was stale.

'These are steeper than I remember,' I panted as we climbed the narrow stairs. 'Remember how we used to run up them!'

'All the way from the front door – I always beat you.' Vanni winked.

'Only because you were the one who said start. You never gave me a chance.' A warm red sunset glowed on the horizon, and I leant on the battlements to recover my breath.

Vanni nodded towards Palazzo Tolomei. 'When the Nove clamped down on fighting in the streets, our families took to fighting with the height of our towers. I think we've ended up with a couple of inches on them!' Vanni's rare smile was compellingly attractive.

'I expect they say the same!' I laughed.

We leant on the balustrade and I felt the warmth of his body next to mine.

'Spot a shooting star for me, Vanni.' My voice nearly broke as I remembered all those I'd lost.

'It may take a while to find one. Wait. I've an idea.'

He disappeared and returned with a servant carrying a mattress, which he laid on the warm stones and covered with a sheet.

'We're too old to crane our necks for hours,' Vanni said. 'Now we can stare at the sky for as long as we want.' We lay side by side and looked up at the heavens.

'I used to look at the stars in Monticiano, but they were never the same. Before he died, Babbo promised me something special when I reached ten jacks.'

'You were always better at them than I was.'

'I succeeded the night of the funeral and looked up to see one shooting star after another. I was sure Babbo was clapping me from heaven!'

'Then we must definitely find you one,' Vanni's soft voice wrapped my bruised soul in its gentleness and I pulled his arm around my shoulder for warmth. He'd always felt closer when it was just us.

'There!' He put his head next to mine to get the same viewpoint. 'Just beyond Orion's belt. And there's another. Can you see them?' He pointed.

'Oh yes! He's still looking after me. I shouldn't need him at my age, but I was so young when he died.' I gave in to more sobbing. Vanni smoothed my hair and kissed me gently on the forehead.

I curled into a ball and nuzzled my head into his neck. His arm was around me, his caresses gentle, his kisses soft. He was the strength I needed. Drawing myself closer, I melted into his all-protective body, as if I were coming home.

Waking with the light, I found Vanni beside me, and studied him in slumber. Sleep had eased away the frown lines, transforming him from authoritative Salimbeni to the good-looking man beside me. His hands were smooth, apart from the small callous on his middle finger from holding a stylus at the monastery. His body was as spare as it had been in our youth and I yearned to run my hands over it again.

I felt so safe in his arms, yet the night before should not have happened. I stared into the gradually lightening sky. How I'd despised my mother for throwing herself at Francesco after my father's death. Yet here I was, doing the same with Vanni after Ambrogio's death. With him all the colour in my life had crumbled away, like fresco painted on dry plaster. Only now did I understand the emptiness she must have felt.

As dawn rose over the rooftops, a small bird chorus – quiet by Monticiano standards – greeted the light. Vanni woke, reached out his hand and drew me to him like a lodestone and kissed me. My body wanted more, but that didn't make it right.

I pulled away. 'I'm so sorry. I promise it won't happen again. I've behaved as badly as my mother after Guido died!'

'I don't see the similarity.' He put an arm around me.

And then it gushed out of me, like water from a spring: the final hours leading to Ambrogio's death. Vanni moved onto his back and stared at the heavens. Telling him made it all feel more real, more final, and not part of some waking nightmare.

'I see.' Vanni frowned, then turned to face me. 'Then this time it is I who have taken advantage of your vulnerability. I thought ...'

328

'Thought what?'

I'd never conceived of Vanni as anything other than a friend, but here, with my shoulder snuggled under his armpit, I wondered if my life had fallen into place.

'Doesn't matter.' He raised my lips to his, and kissed me again, long, warm and loving.

Yet the distance between our positions in society could only mean one thing. As with Ambrogio, I was the fallen woman, the Magdalena.

'Vanni, I'm not one of those nuns on the street, lifting her habit for every passing man!'

'That artist may have seen you like that, but I don't.' He studied my face with the intensity of an artist, then smoothed the furrow between my brow with his thumb. 'You've been through so much. Why don't you rest here until you're ready to come back to the world. If you need to be on your own, use the Contessa's room.'

'I'd feel an imposter among that grandeur.' Yet the spirits of my dead were everywhere and I needed to let them go. Being cradled in the calm of the palazzo might be the best place to do that 'I'd like to sleep here, under the stars.'

For the next few days, I slept solo on the roof as I mourned my losses. During the day, I sat and slept and wandered the empty rooms, while Vanni worked. Over meals together, he listened to my ramblings, gently leading me back to normality. He was a true friend, but Ambrogio still came between us. I broached the subject again over dinner.

'You blame Ambrogio for seducing me, but I was as

329

guilty – desperate to get back to Siena. And married to him, I'd have the chance to be an artist – even if only behind closed doors.'

'Damn his eyes! Can't you see? He dangled that promise to seduce you!' Vanni stood up and paced the banqueting room.

'And you need to understand! That day of the festa he opened my eyes to colour, and how to work with it. When you, the Salimbeni threw me out, I thought it was the colours of the city that I was missing, but Ambrogio showed me that it was working with colour I most missed. Without his encouragement, I'd never have painted furniture, which became the basis of our business success and, I might say, the means of my survival after he'd taken away Gabriele.'

'He's always going to come between us, isn't he?' Vanni kicked a chair.

'Have you ever thought, Vanni, even a Salimbeni can sometimes be wrong?'

Vanni paced round the table then sat opposite, fists clenched, knuckles white. 'Very well. I admit I was jealous.'

'Is that as close as a Salimbeni comes to apologising?'

'I want to do more than that.' He paused to clear his throat. 'Under normal circumstances, I should have made a politically useful marriage by now, but no prospective bride worth their salt allowance would accept a banished monk! For me, our night on the roof was more than an accident, it was the culmination of a long-held wish. I want to marry you.'

'Marry!' It broke all the laws designed to keep people in their place. 'Don't be stupid. You accuse me of throwing my life away on Ambrogio, yet you propose throwing yours away on me. Your family will never allow it.'

'What if they did?'

'I'm fond of you, Vanni, but ...' Fondness was a word I associated with Timoteo. And my head was still swirling with my last days with Ambrogio.

'How can you refuse me when you have nothing!' Vanni kicked a chair across the room.

'I thought you were offering me a choice, not an ultimatum. I may own nothing, but I do still have my self-respect. Now, if you'll excuse me, I must find Rosa.'

'But Clara, the Salimbeni are your family!' He sounded desperate.

'Not for the last forty years, they haven't been. I thank you for your kindness, but it's best we don't see each other again. Rosa will return this dress in the morning.'

I ran down the stairs and Vanni followed me. As I reached the entrance hall, I remembered Ambrogio's will and turned pale. I must have left it in the piazza when I fainted.

'We kept it safe for you.' Vanni picked up the sheepskin from Domenico's chair and placed it in my arms. 'It's getting dark. My servant will escort you to the ospedale.'

I walked so fast the young man had difficulty keeping up.

331

Chapter 27

Though late when I reached the ospedale, I went straight to the woman in charge, the Sopra Donne. The will was too precious to lose a second time. As I walked into her room, she raised a critical eyebrow. 'Come to ask forgiveness for your indiscretions?' Against the grey of the room, my costly dress screamed paramour.

'I've brought you Ambrogio Lorenzetti's will. He's left everything to the Order.' I handed her the parchment.

She closed her eyes. 'God rest his soul. We owe him so much already.'

'I nursed him to the end.' I wiped away my tears, though not the memory of those final hours. 'These are the keys to his house in Castelvecchio. I don't know what else he possesses.' I kept quiet about the panel.

'Someone will have to search for his papers, someone who doesn't mind being where the plague has been. Could that be you?'

I shuddered at the idea of returning, but a stranger rummaging through his belongings would be worse. 'Of course, Sopra Donne.'

'Go first thing tomorrow. We don't want the place

332

ransacked once they know he's dead.'

I hadn't thought of that and prayed nobody had taken the painting.

'And wear a habit while you remain under our roof.'

While you remain? Was she about to throw me out? I'd just rejected Vanni's offer and the ospedale was my only alternative. Worried for my future, I made my way to the dormitory and threw myself on my bed.

Rosa got up from her prayers. 'And where the devil have you been?'

Her language shocked me awake and I sat up.

'You knew I'd be worried. I heard Ambrogio was dead and looked for you everywhere.'

'I er...' I couldn't explain my actions to myself, let alone her. I shook my head, unable to meet her eyes. 'I couldn't take it in. I've known Ambrogio for ever. Wandered the streets. Fainted outside Palazzo Salimbeni.'

'Give you this fancy silk, did they.' She grabbed a fistful of the red material. 'Too busy enjoying Salimbeni luxuries to think about your daughter?'

She must be talking of my mother, not me.

'I'm so sorry, Rosa.' I put my arms around her and sobbed, ashamed I'd abandoned her for a mattress on the palazzo roof.

We undressed in the dark. Then instead of getting in my own bed, I slipped alongside my daughter, wrapping myself around her back. As I did so Rosa's body convulsed as she broke into tears. 'I'm here now.' I stroked the tufts of her hair until she calmed, and we both sank into sleep.

I woke late, delighted to find my dear daughter had left me a clean habit at the bottom of my bed.

Vanni would have to wait for the dress, for I had work to do.

I made my way across town noticing how empty the streets were now the disease had taken its great toll. Two dead dogs lay in the road at the end of Ambrogio's street. When I reached his house, I was relieved to find the shutters fast and door still locked. I let myself in and climbed to the studio. Light poured on the panel. Gabriele and I immortalised. If only Ambrogio had lived long enough to complete it. Yet I'd studied Pietro's stained-glass in Monticiano for so many hours – imagining how my life might have been – I knew what was required. I removed my habit and put on Ambrogio's paint-spattered tunic. It smelt of him still. How I'd miss him, his words of encouragement echoing in my brain every time I picked up a brush. I couldn't provide him with a headstone to his grave, but this would be my memorial to him. Wiping my eyes, I started mixing.

By midday, I'd completed the hill of Golgotha using a mix of colours. Then I went to town on the dark clouds overhead; blues and greys, but with splashes of everything else too. Red for my anger at him dying, green for my envy of his wife sharing his life with him, yellow for the gruesome pus that seeped out in his final hours, orange for Pietro who denied me the opportunity to live, here, in this studio, purple for the bruise I'd have in my heart mourning all that he'd given me, and all that I'd lost. On and on I went, mixing more colours, adding streaks, until at last I stood back to assess. It was done.

I changed back into my habit and went in search of Ambrogio's papers.

Starting in the matrimonial bedroom, I fingered the linen sheets, so superior to those on my marriage bed. The room also contained a chest for clothes. Opening it released the smell of cinnamon I remembered from my Salimbeni days but it contained only clothes. Under the bed, I found what I was looking for; a large box containing bundles of scrolls. I tried to read them but the Latin I'd learnt with Vanni was too rusty. Yet I couldn't hand them over before finding who had commissioned the panel and there was only one person I could ask for help.

'Would you tell Signor Vanni, Clara would be grateful for his assistance.' So many emotions I'd felt in this entrance hall, but never such awkwardness. I suspected he was making me wait, but at last I was ushered into the factotum's office where Vanni was hunched over an abacus.

He raised an eyebrow then stood to welcome me.

'I thought you wanted nothing more to do with me.' Though business-like, he failed to disguise how much I'd upset him. Returning to Siena seemed to have transformed me into my mother, or the thoughtless girl who had left, aged nine.

'Needs must.' I felt ashamed to have hurt him, as it was a comfort to see him again. I put down the bundle of scrolls. 'Ambrogio's papers. In Latin. He's left everything to the ospedale. But before I hand over the panel he worked on before he died – I worked on it too – I'd like to know who commissioned it.'

'You've changed your mind about returning the Contessa's dress?'

'I'm sorry, I forgot. I was so absorbed in sorting out Ambrogio's affairs.'

'Keep it, return it, I don't care.' How angry he still was.

I picked up the scrolls. 'I'm sorry, I shouldn't have asked.'

'Leave them.' He stayed my arm. 'I could do with distraction now I dine alone. Come back tomorrow evening. I'll have an answer.'

He indicated a bench where I dumped the scrolls.

'And does this visit mean you've forgiven me for our night on the roof?'

He sounded so wistful I could almost have fallen into his arms again.

'You seem to think I'm so desperate I'll do exactly what you want,' I said. 'You forget that for the last forty years, I've had my own life. And for the last ten, I ran the family business. Please don't assume you can bid me, as if I were still your kitchen maid.'

'Not a mistake I'll repeat, I assure you. Until tomorrow.' He hands returned to the abacus as I made for the door.

Once outside, I burst into tears. Why was I treating him so badly? Now Ambrogio had gone, he was my only friend in the city. But given his hatred of art, could we ever be close again?

When I returned to the palazzo the following evening, the scrolls were set out in three neat piles.

'I've put you to a lot of trouble.' And on behalf of a man he hated.

'He had a lot of money going through his hands over the years, even made use of merchant-bankers like us. These are contracts for property he's bought and sold over the years.' He pointed to the smallest set of scrolls. 'All he owns now is the house in Castelvecchio. He sold his country estate last year, or I dare say he'd be there now, and alive.'

I suddenly thought of my precious son at Pietro's and prayed he was safe.

'Did he tell you that he'd purchased a house in Gabriele's name with the proceeds? You're lucky he did, for though your son's the only surviving progeny, as a bastard, he has no claim on the estate.'

I couldn't speak for my gratitude. Ambrogio had had the foresight to look after our son.

Vanni turned to the middle pile. 'These relate to some financial investments – they must be liquidated. It'll take effort, but I'd be happy to do that for the ospedale.'

'I'm sure the Sopra Donne will be grateful.'

'And the final pile covers his painting commissions.' Vanni picked one at random. 'For example, this covers the Maestà at Massa Marittima.'

'Gabriele's first assignment.' I wondered how it had turned out. 'But what about his latest – it was a

Crucifixion?'

'You won't like this, for I certainly don't.' The furrows on Vanni's brow deepened. 'Commissioned by the Tolomei for their chapel.'

'Absolutely not! Their filthy eyes gazing on something so personal?'

'I couldn't agree more.' He took the parchment and ripped it in two. 'If you've still got the keys we'll go and steal it as final reparation for your father's death.'

And for Blackbeard's treatment of my mother – and me.

'Once they hear of Ambrogio's death, they'll be looking for it. I could keep it here, where they'll never find it, and you could come see it whenever you liked.'

This was the Vanni I loved. As much as the Vanni with whom I'd spent a night on the roof.

The maid, who'd helped me with my bath, came in with a fresh jug of water.

Vanni said. 'Would you fetch us some hooded cloaks?'

She returned with the two my mother and I had worn at my father's funeral. 'I'm sorry, I could only find these.'

Vanni looked dubious.

'Come on, nobody will suspect it's you dressed as a woman!'

I took off my wimple and wound the band round his head and chin to cover his beard. Then, with our heads covered by the hoods and hands tucked into the arms, we made our way to Castelvecchio. I unlocked the door, the house again as I'd left it.

338

'Where's the panel,' Vanni looked around. I led him to the studio and we stood in front of it. 'You know I know little about art but look what he's done with that sky.'

'What do you mean?' Had I been over-zealous in my use of the palette?

'All those colours. That dark blue must signify death, that red for the blood spilt. But look at this golden yellow – I'd say he's wanting to tell us there's a new dawn after the resurrection.'

'Well actually, Vanni, that's my work. I painted the sky after he died.'

Vanni looked from me to the painting. 'Though I'm no expert, it's people like me who commission these things, and I'd say such painting would earn you membership of the Artists' Guild. As you've never been taught, it must be a gift.'

'Ambrogio called my first attempt at painting "bold and different"!'

'As apt for the woman as the painting,' Vanni said. 'Come, let's wrap this up. The sooner it's safe in the palazzo, the better.'

All that was left from my burning spree were some paint-spattered rags, but they were enough to cover the panel, which Vanni hid under his cloak.

As we were about to leave, Vanni paused. 'Take his materials too. I'll keep them for you.'

I wrapped the pigments into a bundle, tied together the brushes and carried both under my cloak. By the time we reached the palazzo, it was getting dark. As soon as we shut the doors behind us, Vanni ripped off the wimple and roared. 'That's the best fun I've had for years – one in the eye for the Tolomei!'

We put our treasures on Domenico's chair, removed our cloaks and danced around the entrance hall.

'Where will you hang it?' I asked when we'd finished laughing.

'The obvious place would be in our church – or the banqueting hall - but either place would risk people talking about it to the Tolomei. I'll hide it in my room for now. Will you stay to eat? I'm hungry after our adventure.'

'Thanks, but no. Rosa will be worrying, and I should use the last of the light to take the scrolls back. I can't thank you enough, Vanni. The painting's safety means so much.'

He walked me to the door and, with arms full of parchment, I turned to see his joyous face. It was a face I could have spent the rest of my life with if Ambrogio didn't come between us.

Over the next couple of weeks, we worked together on transferring Ambrogio's assets to the ospedale. In the afternoons, I returned to Castelvecchio and cleared the house ready for whatever use its new owners chose to put it. By the time it was emptied, my heart was lighter too.

In the old Salimbeni orto, the trenches were now so shallow, bodies were dug up daily by scavenging dogs. However, it seemed to me the piles on the body cart were less high, and that it passed though less often.

As September approached, the heat dropped and it

gradually dawned that the pestilence had receded. The population of Siena had halved, and several trades, like notaries, were almost extinct. The government had also lost its best men, like Ambrogio. Those who'd fled the city began to return. Two girls from north of the city came to join the ospedale and there was discussion of the men's and women's halls being re-opened to patients and pilgrims.

The Sopra Donne called me to her room. 'I'm impressed how you've dealt with the Lorenzetti estate and would like you to stay; to share the responsibility of running the women's section.'

A return to normality would mean the restoration of strict segregation, and I'd no longer be allowed to study Ambrogio's murals in the men's chapel. But Santa Maria della Scala's riches were so great – even richer after the legacies they'd received from those dying over the summer – I'd never want for bed and board. More than that, I'd be with Rosa. However, living in seclusion wasn't how I'd ever imagined my life,

'I know I'd not be required to take Holy Orders, but I assume the rules would be much the same as if I had – obedience, daily offices, habits, wimples?'

'That's right, but for someone with your capabilities, I'd forgive a lot.'

I wasn't called to this life, like Rosa. But what choice did a woman have?

'Mother Superior, you've been generous to let me stay this long, and forgiven me much. But before I make such a commitment, I'd like to take advice.' I indicated the heavens above, but the counsel I needed

341

was temporal.

But instead of going straight there, I walked to the gate where I'd left for Monticiano.

'Want me to let you out, sister?' the guard said.

'No thank you.' I stared at the massive wooden gate and high walls built to keep a Florentine army at bay. Monticiano was already so distant; a period in limbo from which I was finally free. When Ambrogio had left me with child, I'd opted for security with Timoteo. If I accepted the Sopra Donne's offer, I'd be safe again. But was that what I wanted?

I retraced my steps along the via Francigena to Palazzo Salimbeni.

'What's happened?' Vanni smiled from his seat in the factotum's office. 'Someone challenging my work?'

I shook my head and slumped into the chair facing him. 'The Sopra Donne wants me to stay at the ospedale. I wouldn't have to take holy orders, but I'd be expected to live like a nun.'

'Isn't it normal for God to have something to do with such commitments?' Vanni raised an eyebrow. 'Or are you choosing Rosa over Gabriele?'

It was true. If Gabriele was dead, I'd be happy to shun the world.

Though I said nothing, Vanni read my thoughts. 'I know you're worried about Gabriele. Why don't we find out how he is. Where did you say he'd gone?'

'Pietro's country estate.'

'Give me the day to find out where that is, and I'll take you there in the morning.'

I could hardly believe Vanni was going to help me

342

find Ambrogio's son.

Sitting side-saddle in front of Vanni reminded me of riding back to Monticiano with Ambrogio And it was impossible to have his arm around my waist without feeling some echo of our night on the roof. I relished the cooler September air, thankful that the pestilence hadn't killed off the seasons. Yet I was terrified of the news our journey's end might bring.

Pietro's 'estate' was no more than a cottage set on a hillside. All was quiet as we approached.

Vanni helped me dismount.

'Would you go?' Sick with worry, I watched Vanni walk to the cottage. He knocked on the door and disappeared inside. I turned away and, hearing footsteps approach, I braced myself for the worst.

'Mamma!'

My golden boy had survived and I held him in my arms.

But I had to tell him Ambrogio was dead.

'I should be dead too,' he said, covering his head with his arms, 'for my life is nothing without him.'

The tears ran down Gabriele's face as I described Ambrogio's final days. 'You must carry on his legacy. He'll be up there admiring your work, even if you can't see him.'

'And he must have loved you,' Vanni added. 'For not long before he died he bought you a house. I went to inspect it and it's ready to be lived in. Come back with us and I'll give you the deeds.'

'I'm sorry. I need time to take this all in.' That was

my Gabriele, dancing to nobody's tune but his own.

Vanni said, 'Then we should be on our way. Come see me when you return.'

I set off back to Siena with a lighter heart. 'I do appreciate what you've done, Vanni, today and all the handling of Ambrogio's affairs. It can't have been easy.'

'It was worth it to spend time with you. What are your thoughts about the ospedale?' he asked as he lifted me onto the horse's back.

'I suppose it's my best option.' As soon as I said it, I knew how much I'd miss working with Vanni.

We rode on in silence until we came within sight of the city's towers. 'Can we stop and enjoy the view. This could be my last chance to see it.'

Vanni tethered the horses to a tree and we side by side on the grass, looking over the valley to the city we could once again call home.

'I've been thinking ...' we both spoke at once and laughed.

'You first,' said Vanni.

'No, you.'

'That time at San Galgano – my father hadn't been taken ill. He just couldn't be bothered to make the journey.'

'You were angry and took your annoyance out on Ambrogio?'

'Yes, and I'm sorry, especially for the impact it had on you and your family.'

How much had it cost Vanni, a Salimbeni to the core, to say this?

'Thank you.' Now I had to be honest too. 'And you

were right about Ambrogio, in part at least. His reasons for showing me how to mix colours were far from honourable. I can see that now, especially in comparison to how you've treated me over the last weeks; with more respect than Ambrogio ever did.'

He took my hand in his.

'But he opened up in me a love of colour which is now so much a part of me, I'm not sure I can give it up.'

'What if you don't have to?'

I searched his eyes for scheming, but saw only love, and longed to be in his arms again.

Eyes still locked on mine, Vanni continued. 'When I asked you to marry me, I was being hasty and insensitive. But over the last few weeks, I've come to believe we are far more than friends.'

I could feel my insides catch alight, like tinder catching a spark.

'For me happiness means you, Clara. And if part of your happiness is being able to paint, I'll make sure the Conte allows you. He owes me that, for I've paid dearly for defending family honour. Now is our chance. I think we've both earnt it.'

Vanni, my best friend, my lover – my husband? I pushed his shoulders to the ground, rolled on top of him and kissed him.

'I'll take that as a yes,' he said breaking for air.

The horse neighed, reminding us we still had ground to cover.

'We should get married at once,' Vanni said. 'Better to present my brother with a fait accompli than ask his permission. Though once he learns about stealing the Tolomei panel, he'll love you for life.'

For the rest of our ride back to the city, we caught each other's eyes, smiling, unable to believe our luck in finding true love so late in our lives.

'By the way,' I said, as Vanni walked me back to the ospedale. 'I can save you the expense of a ring. Do you remember giving me one before I left?'

'Of course,' he said. 'It's done what I intended. It brought you back.'

We were married in the Salimbeni church, with Rosa, Gabriele and the Sopra Donne, our only witnesses. After a modest celebratory meal at the palazzo, the guests left. Vanni took my arm and walked me up the main staircase. When we reached my old bedroom, he kissed my neck. 'This is where I sleep now.'

I could have found myself around that room blindfold and I crossed the room to open the shutters. Outside was a crisp, clear, late summer day. My grandfather's chest was still there, but our old bed had been replaced by a better. Above it hung the panel.

I removed the pouch that hung around my neck, laid the stones along the window ledge and turned to my new husband.

THE END

Acknowledgements

A great pleasure of this endeavour has been the many art books I consulted.

Most referred to was *Ambrogio Lorenzetti, Il Buon Governo*, edited by Enrico Castelnuovo, which offered close-ups of Ambrogio's work and of contemporary life in Siena.

Also invaluable in describing the rapidly changing medieval city was *Siena, Florence and Padua, Art, Society and Religion 1280-1400*, volumes I and II, edited by Diana Norman.

I'm grateful to the Wellcome Library for granting me access to research the Black Death; even more so, to my former colleague and leading expert on infectious diseases and public health, Professor George Griffin CBE, who talked me through the plague's physical manifestations.

Many people have supported me on this long labour, and I'm grateful to you all.

Special thanks go to Susan Lee Kerr and Jacqui Lofthouse – one could not wish for more empowering guides on a writing journey – and to my lifelong friend and art historian, Valerie Holman, for long phone calls swapping notes on our different writing lives.

Thank you to writers Lindsay Staniforth, Wilma Ferguson, Ruth Hunter and Diane Chandler for their perceptive comments on the full draft. They and fellow writers Peggy Hannington, Cath Hurley, Joy Isaacs, Jana Ferguson, Janice Rainsbury and Barry Walsh listened and commented on later versions and encouraged me to publish.

Most of all thank you, dear family, for your love and support and for giving me so much, just by being.

As an early reader of this book, please review it on Amazon, Goodreads and major bookshops' websites. It helps debut authors be found by new readers.

Keep up to date with Judith May Evans' news and new titles on:

Instagram: @JMayEvansAuthor
Facebook: @JudithMayEvans